His Surrogate OMEGA

AN OMEGAVERSE BOOK

Kelex

A TWISTED E PUBLISHING BOOK

His Surrogate Omega
An Omegaverse Book
Copyright © 2018 by Kelex

Cover design by K Designs
All cover art and logo copyright © 2018, Twisted E-Publishing, LLC

ALL RIGHTS RESERVED: This literary work may not be reproduced or transmitted in any form or by any means, including electronic or photographic reproduction, in whole or in part, without express written permission.

All characters and events in this book are fictitious. Any resemblance to actual persons living or dead is strictly coincidental.

ISBN: 9781791894924

Omega Gray Tomlinson is positive he'll remain unmated for the rest of his life. By his mid-thirties, he remains unclaimed and without prospects, and lives confined to the Omega Quadrant, where he's sure he'll end up dying alone.

When his older brother, Silver, and Silver's alpha die in a tragic accident, Gray's nephews come to live in his little sequestered world. Without an alpha, he knows he has little means to help support the boys. The only choice he can stomach is to offer his services as a surrogate.

The minute Gray meets Jamie, the infertile omega who so desperately wants a child, he senses a bond like none he's ever felt before. It's brotherly love at first sight, and Gray decides Jamie is the one, agreeing to carry his and his alpha, Rohan's, child.

But when circumstances change, Gray is faced with new challenges, a new love interest, and a battle for the very life that grew inside him. And maybe there's an alpha out there for him after all...

Dedication

I want to dedicate this book to *Rachel Emily*… for reading it, giving me feedback, and letting me bounce ideas off her in a low moment where I was completely sure this book was a total pile of shit.

Author's Note

This book has been a long time coming…

The idea sparked over a year and a half ago. I wrote half of the book and realized something wasn't right—so it sat on the back burner for months before I came back to it. I ripped it apart… glued it back together in places… changed main characters… and then added a whole bunch of new words.

Then I worried because this book is SO MUCH DIFFERENT than the ones I normally write and I feared some of my readers wouldn't get it.

Six years ago, I started out writing short, kinky fantasies. It was all fluff and fun and wasn't meant to be too deep.

But you can only write fluff so long before you need more.

This book is more.

Not only is it the longest book of my career thus far but it was the hardest, most angst-filled, tearjerker I have ever written.

(Side note – you might want to grab a box of Kleenex, just in case. I had my first ugly-cry while writing, so consider yourself warned.)

This is an omegaverse story, occurring in an alternative universe very similar to our own world in many ways, with one major difference.

There is only one gender—male—and those males are separated into three classes—alpha, beta, and omega.

This story involves non-shifter male pregnancy. Only alpha and omegas can reproduce. Each omega and alpha have their own fated mate, the one male who he is forever bound to. Instinct and fate pull the pair together, their scents triggering an intense, animalistic reaction in both.

While they have fated mates, omegas can usually conceive with any *alpha male, so those unmated and in reproductive age are kept isolated, away from regular society.*

For those who are mated, they are freed from those shackles, especially if they are with child. Nothing is more precious or protected than a pregnant omega. But pregnancy brings its own dangers. Birth does not come easily for many omegas—some even struggle to conceive at all.

In extreme cases of infertility, a surrogate can be brought in, if the couple can find a capable omega who has no alpha and is willing to help the pair have the child they want.

A good surrogate is hard to find, especially due to the omega-child bond that will threaten to tear the surrogate apart.

Most surrogates are desperate… for one reason or another… and will endure the pain and hope it doesn't destroy them.

His Surrogate Omega

Chapter One

An end in the beginning...

Gray ushered the boys from the long black limousine, handing over umbrellas before they exited into the near torrential downpour. Once out, he rose to his full height and opened his own umbrella before trailing behind the three young men through the maze of headstones. Still, water seemed to creep in and roll down his back somehow. A shiver raced down his spine—along with a droplet of cold water. The scent of open earth, death, and the cold, wet ground filled his nose. On he trudged. Just a few more hours and he could collapse.

Planning the dual funerals, all while moving the boys into the house, had been a mind-numbing exercise in multi-tasking—a skill he'd always assumed he lacked. Together he'd sat with what was left of his family, making the hard decisions he had no desire to make.

Their walk ended, and they turned to face the two black shiny coffins side by side as the rain splatted against their metal exteriors, his mind a swirl of emotion.

Fortunately, there was a small tent over where they'd been asked to sit. Gray closed his umbrella and sat in the lone row left for family. A few others crowded under the awning and stood behind them, silent as the graves around them.

Gray stared at the caskets, his mind as numb as it had ever been over the last week.

Far back in his mind, he thought he recalled his grandparents' funerals. It happened so long ago, it was hard for him to be sure if the glimpses in his mind were accurate. With a bit more clarity he could see his father and papa's funerals, one not long after the other—as so often happened with long-bonded alpha and omega mates.

Memories of people murmuring their condolences as he stood there trying to act strong, barely hearing the empty words that fell from their lips, came to mind. Today, there would be more of those and again, he had to act strong…

When he was anything but.

Especially as he hadn't planned to bury his own brother and his brother's mate. Or have to hold on to the pieces left behind.

Gray glanced down the row at Avery, the eldest of the three boys.

At nearly twenty, Avery was more man than boy, particularly now. His nephew was already pursuing custody of ten-year-old Auggie and thirteen-year-old Lake, which had left Gray again feeling like the outsider in his own family, but how could he protest? The boy was whip smart, like his papa and father. Avery was responsible. Trustworthy.

Unlike me.

Gray was the air-headed artist of the family. The one no one *ever* saw as responsible. But then, he hadn't done much to prove otherwise in his lifetime.

Yet here he was, feeling more responsible than he'd ever felt in his life. It made his throat tighten. He clawed at the black pants he wore, his knuckles growing white as he dug into his thighs, trying to feel… anything.

Avery can't raise the boys on his own... Nor would I make him try. I can be responsible.

I can.

And I will.

His stare moved back to the caskets, imaging Silver lying in the dark confines.

For him... I'll do whatever I can. For Silver.

Gray's heart thundered in his chest... the panic coming in waves. He heard the preacher begin the service but couldn't listen to one word. His own mind was too chaotic.

What came next for them?

Four omegas under one roof, with no income, no alpha to protect them...

How in the hell were they going to make it without an alpha?

Gray turned back to those shining onyx coffins, his throat so tight he could barely breathe. And in that moment, it hit him like a ton of bricks. Logically, he'd known it, but he'd focused on the necessities. Helping Avery plan the funeral. The logistics of moving the boys. Making sure the day-to-day bullshit of life happened when all he wanted to do was slide under the covers and not come back up for a week or three.

If he focused on those things, then he didn't have to think about the obvious.

Silver was gone.

His beautiful brother was simply... *gone.*

The one person he could always turn to and tell anything. His best friend. His confidant. His lifeline to the outside world.

Gone.

Gray's vision blurred, eyes stinging, as he stared at those two long boxes, willing his mind to not see Silver and Gilead as he had on those cold metal slabs in the morgue when he'd had to identify the bodies days before. He had seen… yet not seen. His mind wouldn't allow him to.

But now…

Now that the planning was over and the funeral was nearly done…

There was little else he could think of but those bodies, cold and pale and broken. Gray wanted to cry and scream and blame the gods above for stealing the one person he could count on in their world. But he had a reason to stay strong…

Three reasons…

Gray's stare washed over his nephews. All three omegas. All three strong and somehow holding it together as they stood in the rain watching as their father and papa were committed to the earth, their final resting place.

Resting? As if they sleep. If only they would wake up and end this madness.

He hadn't expected the boys to hold it together so well, but then his brother had always been stronger than he. Silver had imparted that strength to his boys. Gray felt as if he was falling apart inside and here they stood, their chins up, their red-rimmed eyes dry. *They* made him want to hold it together, more so because he feared he was the weak link in the chain and would bring them all crashing down along with him.

Gray turned back to look at the coffins while the reverend spoke eloquently about loss, as if those words meant anything to any of them in those moments.

I must be the one asleep. Dreaming. A nightmare that won't end.

The rain began to lessen as the funeral progressed. The clouds slowly parted. Eventually, Gray could see the reflection of the sky along the surface of the shining metal, the world almost appearing upside down.

But then again… it *was*.

The ceremony ended, and there was a blur of people… and then the same big, black car to escort them back to the small cottage they all now called home. Later, at the small gathering of mourners in that cottage, Gray watched the people eating the food, drinking the drinks, and offering their condolences to the boys. Apparently, he was invisible—just that unmated omega brother of Silver's who barely existed.

A part of Gray welcomed that silence yet he railed against it, too. Always the outsider, imprisoned in the O Quad most of his life.

"What will you do now?" someone asked Avery when Gray was within earshot, clearing a left behind plate.

Curious, Gray paused, wondering what his nephew would say.

"I'd already been living here with my uncle for the last couple of years. Now Auggie and Lake have come here, too." There was no explanation needed as to why Avery had been living with Gray. At seventeen, Avery had finally gone into his first heat. He'd immediately been packed up and sent to the Omega Quadrant for his own protection.

Where Gray had lived most of his life in the old family cottage. Unmated and alone… forgotten.

"Well, hopefully you'll find your alpha soon and he can take care of all three of you," the beta said, a soft smile on his face.

Gray saw the blank expression overtake Avery. The boy didn't know what to say to the man. Anger roiled within Gray... all the emotions he'd been stuffing down deep came out in in a flash of anger that surprised even him. He marched up to them both, pinning the beta with a glare—a stranger he'd never even met—and dumped all that anger on the man.

"How dare you?"

The beta frowned before looking around a bit.

"Do you imagine Avery sitting here, mourning his parents and thinking *if only my alpha would come save us*? We are *more* than wombs with legs, you know?"

Everyone in attendance turned to look at the three of them, silenced.

The beta looked stunned, searching between Avery and Gray's faces. "I only meant... that he and his brothers... could have some... *security*. I meant no disrespect. That *is* the way of things..."

"It *was* disrespectful," Gray said. "*Regardless* of what you meant."

"Why? Because you never found your alpha and now we're stuck here with you?" his nephew, Lake, asked before storming upstairs.

Gray gasped inwardly at the strike of the words, feeling the stares of everyone in the room. Heat filled his face, and he looked down at the floor, wishing a hole would open up and swallow him. *Why did I bother opening my mouth?*

"We're not stuck *anywhere*," Avery said, his voice loud and clear before turning to his uncle. He lifted a hand to take Gray's. "We're family... and I wouldn't want to be anywhere else but here. I'm grateful we have him to lean on in our time of need."

Gray felt the sting of tears as he held his nephew's stare, thankful. *Thank you*, he mouthed.

His nephew smiled softly and squeezed his hand. Avery was so very much like Silver. Kind and considerate—even if he could be singularly focused and obstinate at times. Outwardly, he looked more like Gilead. Powerful and tall, Avery could easily pass for a beta if not for the thick, long braid of dark hair sliding down his back.

Gray smiled, pushing back the tears, before giving Avery a quick hug. Needing to avoid the stares around him, he headed up to check on Lake. He was more than ready for the house to be quiet again... but then, it hadn't been quiet since the three had come to live with him.

Loud music cranked on just as Gray neared the boy's door, and he sighed. He knocked but was, of course, ignored. Resting his forehead against the wood, he felt the vibrations of the bass against his face and closed his eyes. Gray stood a few moments trying to decide if he pushed or let the boy go, for now.

The biting comments from the teenager had grown more and more harsh—but then, he'd just lost his parents. How much was Gray supposed to let the boy get away with? He wasn't a parent and very much doubted he ever would be, so he had no clue how to answer that question or the millions of others that would pop up in the days and months to come. He supposed it all depended on how much longer could he deal with being the boy's punching bag.

Hearing a noise coming from Auggie's room, Gray moved away from Lake's door. He soon found the ten-year-old curled up on his bed, crying. Gray slid in behind him and wrapped his arms about the slight child. Auggie turned and buried his face into Gray's chest and sobbed. He struggled to hold back his own flow of tears as he felt those tiny sobs wracking them both. Slowly, the crying faded some, and Auggie grew silent.

"You smell like papa," Auggie whispered quietly.

Gray smiled slightly, but then wondered if that caused the boy more pain than good. "I do?"

"Uh-huh," Auggie said.

He bit the inside of his cheek, thinking of all the things this boy had now lost. There were so many words tumbling within his mind... sentiments that weren't true. *It'll be okay... no, it won't.* What in the world did he tell this child?

"I wish I knew the words to say to make you feel better," Gray whispered, swallowing back a sob of his own.

"It's okay," Auggie whispered, his voice sounding raw from his tears. "I don't feel much like talking. The hugs are better."

Tears stung Gray's eyes. "I'm glad they're better."

Silence filled in around them. To call it comfortable wasn't exactly true. They were just there, side by side in that moment of time, both of them aching and raw. Gray wasn't sure how much time had passed when he realized Auggie slept.

He stared up at the ceiling, his mind unwilling to let him appreciate the quiet he'd longed for. The last conversation he had with his brother replayed in his mind.

"You'll find someone... eventually," Silver had said. "I've never given up hope. Actually, I was reading a story about a second chance ball they've started to hold in Alexandria once a year. Older omegas who never found a mate attend, as well as older alphas. You'd be a perfect fit. Perhaps we could escort you up there and... you know... maybe there's someone for you."

"No," Gray had said. "I'm a lost cause, Silver. I don't have a mate... and the sooner I accept that, the better."

Silence had hung on the other side of the line before Silver had spoken. "I know you're jaded, and I understand why. I know you see the mating of an alpha and an omega as some biological contract, but it's so much more. Gilead..." Gray had almost been able to see the wistful smile on Silver's face as he'd talked about his alpha. *"Gilead makes me feel safe. Loved. Protected. He values me and my ideas... he's a true partner. He's given me three beautiful boys. A family. That's all I want for you. A legacy of your own with a partner who loves you."*

Gray had known Silver was one of the lucky ones. Many omegas were happy in their relationships, but only a small few had an alpha as perfect as Gilead.

As perfect as Gilead *had been.*

They'd paid a staggering price for that happiness and perfection... and their boys would continue paying for it. Now, Gray was convinced even more that an alpha was more trouble than it was worth. One way or another, he and Avery would figure a way out of this...

Sadly, he was fairly sure he knew how. Gray slowly slipped from Auggie's bed before covering the boy with a light blanket and wandering down to check on Avery and their guests.

By the time he came back downstairs, many of the mourners had departed and others were gearing up to leave. He was thankful for it. The shame he felt from Lake's words still haunted him. Avery stood at the door, shaking hands and murmuring his 'goodbyes' and 'thanks for coming'. Not ready to face anyone, Gray moved to the kitchen and began to clean up the dozens of trays and containers of food that had been sent or brought.

They wouldn't need to cook for a month, from the looks of things. Not that any of them had much of an appetite anymore.

When Avery stepped into the kitchen, Gray lifted his stare to the boy. "Are they gone?"

Avery nodded silently before moving to the island to help clean up.

"I can do this. Why don't you go upstairs and get some rest? You look exhausted," Gray said.

"And you don't?" Avery asked. He continued his cleaning.

Gray walked over and tried to still Avery's hands.

"Don't," Avery mumbled, pulling his hands away.

"Avery," he murmured softly.

His nephew kept moving, covering dishes and pulling out used spoons.

"Avery."

The boy paused. "If I stop, I'll—"

The tears came. They spilled over his handsome cheeks as he gasped. Avery was in pain, and he'd held it in for too long.

Gray stepped closer and grabbed Avery before the boy dropped to his knees. The spoons he'd held clamored on the floor tiles, the sound of them sharp in the quiet of the house. Gray slowly lowered them both down. His back against the island, he held on tight, letting the young man mourn his parents.

Eventually, the sobs faded away.

"What are we going to do?" Avery asked, lifting his tear-stained face to Gray's.

He wished he had answers for Avery.

He wasn't sure what would happen to them—four unmated omegas in a world where they were nothing. They were all confined to the Omega Quadrant now and would have to hope they could make it work.

"We'll find a way through this," Gray answered, trying to convince both of them his words were true.

Avery nodded before leaning his head against Gray. He held his nephew close, a gentle hand sweeping up and down the boy's back.

Suddenly, Avery chuckled.

"What's so funny?" Gray asked.

"Wombs with legs." He sat up and looked at his uncle.

Gray laughed as well. "Well, that *is* how most see us. We're helpless and incapable of managing much else, in their minds. Poor, helpless omegas." Gray leaned his head back against the island. The fact of the matter was they *couldn't* be much else, thanks to the rules of their society. Without an alpha, an omega of child-bearing age was stuck in the Omega Quadrant—where there wasn't much opportunity. Until Avery was freed by his alpha, there was little he could do.

Avery grew quiet a moment. "I want to be more than that," he said. "That beta you railed against—that wasn't the first time I'd heard someone say the same exact sentiment today. Over and over again—*I bet you can't wait to find your alpha.* As if I had no other alternative. I was so angry, but I bit my tongue all day. Nearly bit it off a time or two."

Gray didn't want to tell Avery there were no chances he'd be much more. Not now, when the boy looked so crestfallen. "I'm sorry I made a scene."

Avery shook his head. "Don't be sorry. You said the things I'd been wanting to scream all day."

Gray smiled at his nephew. "Lake didn't approve."

"Lake was being an asshole. Which he's been since… since the—" Avery paused, apparently unable to say *accident. Crash. The terrible, horrible day the world flipped upside down.*

"He's hurting, and he wants everyone else around him to know how much he's hurt by making them feel like hell," Gray said, trying to look unaffected. He wasn't. "I can forgive the outburst. *This time.*"

"You're a better man than I."

"Then perhaps it's good I seem to be the focus of his angst, hmm?" Avery sighed before rising to his feet. He offered Gray a hand up. "Let's get this finished."

They were silent as they completed their clean-up. It took nearly an hour before they'd filled the dishwasher and washed everything. When it was done, Avery headed upstairs after giving Gray another quick hug.

Alone for the first time in what felt like forever, Gray stood there in their clean little kitchen, everything in order.

Everything was in place, just as it always was.

Tears stung his eyes, knowing everything in their world was *not* in order.

Nowhere close.

Gray went out to his studio—an old converted garage out in back of the house—seeking solace in the paints and scents of his creative space. Bringing brush to canvas, he wanted to bleed through the oils and put his pain there. Anywhere but inside his chest where he couldn't breathe from the weight of it.

No matter what he did, his hand wouldn't listen. Everything went wrong, the colors not right. The depth of the stroke unbecoming. Perspectives skewed. Finally, he threw his brush and palette across the space and screamed in frustration.

And then he dropped onto the battered, paint-splattered stool and cried all the tears he'd held on to, not wanting the boys to see his pain.

Gray was not strong, but he'd tried to be.
And failed.

Chapter Two

Two weeks later...

Gray awoke, the soft sun shimmering in through the gauzy curtains of his bedroom. The breezy sway of the grand oak just outside allowed the shadows from the broad leaves to dance across the wall. A movement caught his eye. He lifted his head to see Silver sitting in the oversized chair across the room.

"Sleeping late this morning? The day's a-wasting."

Gray sat full upright, the air sucked from his lungs. And just like that, his brother was gone and the terrible realization that he would never come back gnawed through him. Fighting back tears, he scrubbed his hands over his face, begging that *this* was the dream—the nightmare—that he needed to awaken from.

Still in a haze that had wrapped around him for nearly two weeks, he forced himself to get up. A little part of him almost wanted to slip back under the covers and go back to a place where Silver and Gilead were still alive. After washing his face and taking care of his needs, he headed down to the kitchen to put on a kettle and saw Avery hard at work over the island.

"What'cha working on?"

Avery lifted his stare from his work. "Our financial situation."

Gray eyed the boy, knowing his nephew was all about budgets and plans and savings—all the things that were completely counterpoint to the creative being he was. He'd never balanced a checkbook, and when Avery had come to live with him at seventeen the boy had taken over all things to do with money and paying bills.

Which had been a blessing. Gray hadn't been able to do any of it well.

From the look on Avery's face, *this* wasn't a blessing.

More like another nightmare.

"How bad is it?"

Avery's face screwed up, so apparently, it wasn't good.

"After the cost of the funeral and all that entailed, the hospital bills, etcetera… and if we sell the old family home… added to what was left of the life insurance policies, papa's and father's savings accounts… we might be able to make it four to five years—*if* we live frugally."

"Well, that's a good thing," Gray said. "Right? Five years. That's enough time for you to make the rounds at the Alpha Balls. Find your alpha, and then you and the boys will be fine."

Avery lifted his head and glared at Gray. "Did you *really* just say that? What happened to not being *wombs with legs*?"

Gray eyed his nephew. "I don't like our situation any better than you do—and it makes me just as angry to think it—but what that beta said? He said it at the *worst* possible moment, but unfortunately, it was true. The only way to save you and the boys is for you to be mated."

"And what if my alpha doesn't come?"

Gray grew quiet a moment. He was unmated and nearly thirty-five. Omegas were typically mated by the time they were twenty-five, at the very latest. Most were much, much earlier. Avery's age. His nephew could meet his alpha in a matter of months... and then he might end up all alone again.

Until Lake went into heat and was sent to live back in the Quad.

That'll be a joy.

Gray let Avery's last question roll over him again. He then steeled himself. "What if your alpha doesn't come? Or rather... you mean... if you end up like me?"

"That's *not* what I said."

"But it's what you were thinking," Gray replied.

Avery didn't speak for a moment, the crease at his brows making it apparent he was searching for the right words. "Maybe I *was* thinking it. But come on, Gray... what *do* we do if I don't find an alpha?"

"We find jobs," Gray said, knowing full well that wasn't going to happen without a miracle or two. Or twenty.

Avery rolled his eyes. "In the O Quad? So, would you like stripper or... stripper? I hear they make all kinds of cash in the beta clubs, especially one as pretty as you."

"There *are* other jobs."

"Yeah, and they all have a line wrapped around the corner with a million other omegas just like us who desperately need the work. We've been lucky not having to worry. Until now."

The steam kettle screamed out its warning, and Gray turned to pour himself a cup. When he spun to face Avery again, he spoke the thought that had been circling in his mind for days. "I *could* become a surrogate."

Avery's face twisted with disgust. "No."

"Why not? The pay's good, *great* if you find the right mated pair. I come from a good family. My papa and brother both had more than one live birth. I'd likely be in demand."

Avery shook his head. "And what of *your* alpha? If you carry another alpha's child, yours could deny the claim. And he'd have the law on his side."

"What alpha?" Gray said. "You're living in a fairytale if you think I have an alpha out there."

"You stopped going to the Alpha Balls. Perhaps if you went back?"

Gray sighed, Silver's words whispering through his mind. "To the shame of my parents, I quit attending. After *eight years*. Four times a year. I had over thirty chances to find my alpha... and he *wasn't* there. I have no alpha. And as an unmated omega, I have nothing. I can *be* nothing. I *am* just a womb with legs and no alpha to fill it. I can go be a stripper and lose all shreds of self-respect—or I become a surrogate. Only one of those is something I can live with."

"And what about the child-bond?"

Gray grew quiet. The bond between papa and child was strong. Severing that attachment and handing the child over would destroy him. He'd seen what became of the omegas sentenced to forced surrogacy. They were empty shells of the men they'd once been.

"What choice do I have?" Gray asked quietly.

"I have a plan."

Gray narrowed his stare. "What?"

"If I can pull this off... we won't have to worry so much about money," Avery said.

Gray eyed his nephew, worry filling him.

"What do you know about scent blockers?" Avery asked, lifting a brow.

"Scent blockers? There isn't such a thing."

"There are. And I've found someone with a connection."

Gray glared at his nephew. *No, no, no... he's not thinking what I think he's thinking...* "Whatever you're considering... it would be illegal."

"But... if an omega was to find a supply of scent blockers... he could be protected from alphas. He could go to college. Get a degree... get a job... and support his family."

Gray sat there silently, panic settling in. "No. Absolutely not." He shook his head. "No. You *can't* do this."

"I *can*. I know I can pull it off. I'm tall for an omega. I'm smart. I've got a good head on my shoulders. I can do this." He smiled. "I can be a beta."

Gray felt his stomach knot. If Avery was caught... he'd be one of those omegas in the forced surrogacy program—broken and empty when he was finally freed years and babies later. "I forbid you."

Avery eyed Gray. "*Forbid me?* You have no right to forbid me from doing *anything*, uncle. I'm an adult."

"Okay... what about the boys?"

"I'm doing this for them!"

"You've just gained temporary custody and are awaiting full legal rights. How are you going to pull that off while pretending to be a beta?"

"I can manage it. With your help."

"What you plan is *illegal*." Gray pointed toward the second floor. "What happens to those boys if you end up sent away? *Forced surrogacy*. Because that's what's going to happen when you're caught. Not *if*. *When*. *When* you're caught, Avery."

Avery wouldn't look him in the eye. "They'll still have you if something bad happens to me. Which won't happen. I know I can manage all this."

Gray fought back the lump forming in his throat. "I need you as much as you need me, Avery. Please, reconsider this. You can't go through with it."

"I have to." Avery turned to leave.

"Please, Avery. *Don't* do this." Gray spoke to Avery's retreating back, sensing his nephew's mind was made up.

Alone again, he reached for his cup but saw Lake's tablet lying on the kitchen island—making him reach for that instead. Swiping his fingers over the screen, he searched for a browser. Once he opened it, he typed in his search.

Surrogacy solicitors.

A few listings came up before he saw an ad for one of the centers he knew catered to the wealthiest of clients—or so he'd heard. The only way he was going to get Avery out of this mess would be to come up with the money they needed to survive himself. Once he'd had a moment to breathe, he lifted the phone from the receiver on the wall and dialed the number.

"Hello? I'd like to make an appointment."

A warm male voice answered him. "Yes, I can take care of that for you. Are you looking for a surrogate?"

"No. I wish to become one."

Chapter Three

A few days later...

"Where in the hell have you been?" Gray asked Avery as his nephew rested against the door, winded. Gray had been pacing for hours. Avery had ignored his calls and texts and sent Gray into a total panic. It was nearly midnight and well past curfew for an omega. His mind had gone to the worst places.

A handsome omega, out alone at night—there had been stories of males being scooped up and sold on the black market. Breeding houses where alphas had their way with omegas in heat.

Avery lifted his stare to meet his uncle's. Gray saw the glint of something in Avery's eyes and sensed his nephew had been up to no good.

"I took the long way home... so I could test this."

Gray let out a slow breath as he looked at the ID in his nephew's hand. Bile rose up in his throat. "Please tell me that isn't what I think it is."

Avery drew down his hoodie, and Gray gasped. Gray crossed the foyer and ran a hand through his nephew's shorn locks. Gone was the long, silky hair Avery had been growing since his birth. Gray's knees grew weak as he stared at the ID. *Abraham Norcross.* "My gods. *What* have you done?"

"You knew it would have to happen."

Gray lifted his stare to his nephew. "I told you this plan of yours is insane. You're going to be caught." Tears lined Gray's eyes as he looked at Avery's hair. "I told you I was going to meet with the solicitor about the surrogacy option. That you didn't have to go through with this. Why couldn't you listen?"

"I won't have you carrying others' children just for us. We aren't legally your responsibility."

"We're *family*, Avery. Family takes care of one another. No matter what."

"What if your alpha's out there?" Avery asked. "I won't let you throw away your future for us."

"But you'll risk your own?" Gray sighed, leaning up against the closet door across from him. "We've been through all this. I have no skills. I don't have a head for numbers like you do. I *do* have a womb. I could make a fine surrogate and support the family. *Legally*."

"I love you for being willing to make that sacrifice, but I just can't let you do that," Avery said. "My brothers are *my* responsibility."

"*Our* responsibility," Gray said. "One I don't take lightly. I know I've never been the responsible type… but we're a family… and we take care of one another."

Heavy footfalls on the stairs above announced those younger brothers were storming down.

"Ave!" Auggie said as he made it to the bottom and wrapped his arms around Avery's waist. The ten-year-old lifted his head… and then his eyes and mouth grew wide.

"Why aren't you two in bed?" Gray cried.

Ignoring Gray, Lake took one last slow step. "What the *fuck* have you done?"

"Language!" Gray snapped.

"Whatever," Lake snapped back, his normal broody self. He turned back to face Avery. "You look like shit."

"Watch your mouth," Avery cried.

"Why did you cut your hair?" Auggie asked, frowning. He reached back to pull his own braid around over his shoulder. "I don't have to cut mine, do I?"

Gray realized he was absently pulling at his own long braid without noticing. He released the length and stood up straighter.

"No," Avery answered. "I need you both to go sit in the family room. We have to have a discussion."

"Pass," Lake said before spinning to head back upstairs.

"*Lake Anthony Stephens*, get your ass downstairs and in the family room, or by the gods, I *will* make you," Avery blasted.

Gray tried to hide his grin. They'd both likely been too lenient on Lake the last weeks, but given the situation, they'd done their best. Lake looked over his shoulder and glared. Gray could see the boy weighing his options from the look on his face. It could start World War V or Lake would sulk.

Finally, Lake turned and angrily marched down.

Sulking, it is. Thank the gods.

"This better be quick," Lake said in passing.

Auggie followed Lake.

Once they were out of earshot, Gray quietly asked, "Are you really going to tell them?"

"Not about what I did. But they need to know about the money situation. They need to know the truth of that."

"Make it fast. Just because you were out all night doesn't mean they need to be up at all hours."

"It's Friday night," Avery said, shrugging. "They can stay up."

Yeah and they'll be zombies in the morning. Gray sighed before following Avery into the living room. His nephew pulled out an envelope from his hoodie and slipped the new ID inside before gripping the lot of it between his hands.

"As you know, Papa and Father left us a little bit of money... and both this house and the family house," he began. "I've crunched the numbers, and if we sell the family house, an—"

"Sell our house?" Lake demanded, frowning. "No!"

"We can't live there anymore, Lake. And we need the money."

"*Auggie and I* can live there," Lake spat.

"Yes, neither of you have had your first heat yet, so technically you *could* remain in the Family Quad for a few more years... but under whose supervision? We have no other family members. It's Gray and me... and as we're both forced to live in the O Quad, this is now our home. *Period.*"

Avery paused, eyeing Gray before turning his gaze back to the boys.

"*If* we sell the family house, and with what's left over from the life insurance policies... and the little bit our parents had in savings... we should have enough to live—*frugally*—for a few years. But after that... I don't know what we'll do." He took a deep breath.

"What has that got to do with your hair?" Lake asked, an eyebrow rising.

Gray eyed the boy. The kid was too smart for his own good.

"I sold it," Avery answered.

"Sold it?" Auggie asked. "You can sell hair?"

"There are omegas who have lost their hair… through old age or sickness… and they want to hide that loss. Wigmakers will pay for strong, long hair," Gray answered, trying to strengthen Avery's account. He sensed there was more to the story with that cutting, though. A story he planned to get once the boys were gone.

Auggie slid a hand down the braid lying over his shoulder. "I'll sell mine, too."

"You don't need to do that," Avery said, reaching out and drawing his baby brother into his arms. Avery settled Auggie beside him on the loveseat and gave him another squeeze. "One shorn head is enough in this house. But I love that you're willing to contribute. There are other ways you can do that without giving up your hair."

"How?" Auggie asked.

"No more music downloads… no more game downloads… no movies… no more new clothes… no more dinners out… no more *anything*," Lake muttered. "It might as well be prison."

"*Stop* being a spoiled brat," Gray said to Lake.

"Stop telling me what to do," Lake spat in response.

Gray turned to his middle nephew, his hands clenched. "I've had about enough of your mouth."

Lake turned to argue, but Avery intervened. "Stop this!"

The teenager clenched his jaw, glaring at Gray.

Avery continued his speech. "Not *none*... we'll just have to hold off on new things for special occasions. We'll have to consider second-hand shops for clothing and items we need. And you both could help around the house... if we can find ways to save here, we might have a little more to spend on things that aren't necessities."

"Maybe you'll find a rich alpha," Auggie said, smiling up to Avery. That smile faded. "But will he want you with short hair?"

"If I find my alpha, I'm sure he'll accept me, short hair and all. It's not like it won't grow back, Auggie," Avery answered, though Gray wasn't completely sure what an alpha would think of his nephew's new style. "But we can't rest on the hope I'll find an alpha to support us. We need to take strides to do what we can now." He looked at Lake and then to Auggie. "I'm going to get a job to help out. I need the two of you to listen to your uncle when I'm gone... do your homework without argument... and help with chores."

"What kind of job?" Lake asked, his eyes narrowing.

"I don't know yet," Avery murmured.

"He's going to pretend to be a beta so he can go work on the other side of the wall," Lake said. "That's why he cut his hair off."

Auggie spun to face him. "You are?"

Avery sighed and met Gray's stare.

Damn him. Lake was too close for comfort. There was no way Avery was going to be able to hide four years of college and a job in the Beta Quadrant from his brothers, particularly Lake.

"No," Avery said, lying through his teeth. "I'm *not* doing that. I told you I *sold* my hair."

Lake was silent, his narrowed gaze telling everyone that he wasn't completely convinced.

"He couldn't get away with passing as a beta. If he crossed paths with an alpha, he'd be scented in an instant," Gray added, trying to help Avery's lies. It had been all of five minutes and he was spouting them left and right. *I won't be able to keep up.*

"I hope you get a fun job. Father always came home grumpy. I don't think he liked his job," Auggie said.

Avery leaned over and smiled at his baby brother. "I hope so, too."

"It's not easy to find a job as an omega," Lake said, narrowing his eyes.

Avery gazed at the teen, a challenge in his stare. "I'll make do."

Lake rolled his eyes. "Whatever." He rose from the couch and headed for the stairs.

"You understand what's expected of you, right?" Avery called down the hall.

"Yes!" Lake cried angrily before footsteps stomped up the stairs.

"Can I go play video games with him?" Auggie asked.

"You should be in bed," Gray murmured.

"Is he actually letting you play?" Avery asked, ignoring Gray's comment.

Auggie shrugged. "Not really. But I like watching."

"Tell him I said he had to let you play, too."

Auggie grinned before racing away. "Avery said you had to let me play!" he screamed up the stairs.

Avery chuckled before turning to Gray.

"He should be in bed."

"It's Friday night!"

Gray shook his head. "I thought *I* was the lackadaisical one?"

"I don't know what's happened to my laid-back uncle, but I want him back."

Gray tilted his head and stared at Avery. Maybe he was trying too hard—but he wanted to do right by the boys. "I was reading something about schedules being important for children, especially ones his age. Staying up a little is fine, but it's midnight. And he's ten, not twenty."

"He'll be okay. The summer's almost here."

Gray shook his head, knowing Auggie's bedtime was the least of his concerns now. "You're letting them get away with too much."

"I'm sorry if I don't have the energy to be a disciplinarian right now," Avery spat. "Especially when they have so little to be happy about at the moment. If staying up past his bedtime on the weekend puts a smile on his face, so be it."

Gray nodded and leaned back against the couch. He stared at Avery's hair, still shocked at the sight of it. "How are you going to hide four years of college and a part-time job as a beta from them?"

"I don't want that strain on them," Avery said. "A secret wears on people. They're boys… let them be children as long as they can. They've already had enough stripped away."

"And what about you?" Gray asked. "You've had the same things stripped away. I'm the grown-up here. *I* should be the one making concessions for you."

Avery eyed him. They'd already had this same argument more than once, but Gray could see how well his nephew listened to him.

"I'm not a child. I'm nearly twenty. And I've been running this house for almost three years as it is. I can do this."

Gray eyed his nephew. "Technically, this *is* your house. You're legally an adult. I can't force you to do anything."

"You're right. You can't."

The house had belonged to Gray and Silver's papa. It had gone to Silver upon their parents' deaths, and Gray had been *allowed* to live there, as he had nowhere else to go. Silver and Gilead had supported him, when they didn't have to. He'd been fortunate to have a brother who cared so much about him. Then once Avery had gone into heat at seventeen, he could no longer live in the Family Quad, and Gray had been given new purpose, as guardian to his young charge.

But Avery had proven he was better at caring for himself than Gray had ever been of himself.

Now they had a houseful and Avery was making it clear he was in charge.

Gray felt unneeded.

Unwanted.

That's all he'd felt for the last twenty years. Lake's words from the funeral rang in his ears.

"Do you... do you wish me to leave?" Gray asked.

Avery frowned, his eyes widening. "Do you... do you *want* to go?" Before Gray could answer, Avery leapt to his feet. "I know suddenly having three boys in your house is a lot of change."

"*Your* house."

Avery paused at the correction. He turned and looked at Gray.

"It's now your house. Not mine. I've been a leech on your family for many years. I don't contribute anything. You three would be in better shape financially if it wasn't for all your parents gave me over the years."

Avery walked closer and placed his hands on Gray's shoulders. "Listen to me and listen well. You belong here, with your family. *Period.* I can't do this without you. I want you to stay. I need you."

Gray held Avery's stare a moment before looking away. "Okay."

Avery took a step back. "Who's going to watch the boys while I attend classes and work?"

Of course. He was to be a glorified babysitter. "College isn't free. How do you plan on paying for that?" Gray asked.

"Loans… grants… a part-time job… whatever I can do," Avery answered.

Gray shook his head. "So you'll go into debt in an attempt to pay for *everything*?"

"I'll do what I have to," Avery said. He rose, stretching. "I'm tired, and my neck is itching like crazy. I'm going to grab a shower and go to bed."

"You don't want some dinner?"

"Not hungry." Avery smiled before pulling a bag from his hoodie and heading for the kitchen.

"What's that?"

His nephew turned and showed him the vials and syringes inside. "I might need your help with the injections."

The illegal drugs inside that bag would supposedly hide Avery's scent—and keep the alphas away. Gray hoped like hell they worked as they claimed because alphas were free to be in all quads except the omega one. "And truly make me your accomplice?"

Avery's face fell.

Gray sighed. "You know I'll help."

Avery turned to hide the vials and syringes inside a container within the refrigerator. "We'll have to think of something to hide these from the boys."

"Mark the container vegetables. They'll avoid it like the plague."

Avery chuckled as he closed the fridge. "Night, uncle."

"Goodnight."

After cleaning a few dishes in the sink, Gray snuck over to the refrigerator and opened it up. He opened the container and looked at the series of vials inside. Lifting one, he released a sigh, knowing how much danger Avery could be in.

Omegas were born to reproduce. It was their sole purpose. At least, in the minds of those in charge. Most of whom were alphas. Omegas had few rights, and those they had only appeared once they were claimed by their alpha.

Those without an alpha lived in a limbo in the Omega Quadrant, using *Heat Repress* to survive the violence of an omega's heat. It kept an omega from climbing the walls and begging to be bred when the time came.

Only, it wasn't meant to be used for decades without end.

Like Gray had been using it.

He replaced the vial and covered it again before he shut off all the lights downstairs and wandered up.

He paused at Lake's bedroom door and watched his nephews playing their video game a moment. They were oblivious to his watchful stare.

Lake instructed Auggie in the game, a softer side to the teenager slipping out. Gray smiled, thankful to be reminded Lake wasn't all anger and vitriol.

Maybe there's hope for him yet.

"Time for bed."

They both eyed him, Lake's more a glare. After sending the boys to separate bathrooms, he wandered down the hall and slipped into his own sanctuary. He pulled out a book and read as he listened to the water streaming. Once they were both in bed and he'd taken his own shower, he slipped in between clean sheets and struggled to find sleep.

Worry for Avery.

Worry for them all.

And nervousness for the meeting he had in the morning.

Chapter Four

Obstinate...

Gray walked into the solicitor's office, his heart thundering in his chest. The elegant waiting room was well equipped. Soothing music played softly in the background. Everything within was made to calm. He was anything but calm. Pausing before the registration desk, he waited for the man behind it to notice he was there. The butterflies intensified, and he considered turning around and leaving before he got in too deep.

Before he could act, the young beta lifted his stare and offered Gray a lovely smile. "May I help you?"

Breathe in. Breathe out. "I have an appointment with Mr. Atkinson at one."

"Lovely. Your name?"

"Gray Tomlinson," he murmured lowly as he nervously drummed his fingers on the dark wooden counter.

The beta checked the computer before lifting his gaze once more with a smile. "If you'll have a seat, Mr. Tomlinson, I'll let Mr. Atkinson know you've arrived."

"Thank you." Gray nodded, returning the soft smile he'd received, before he wandered over to one of the seats lining one wall. The chairs were ornately carved wood and leather, speaking of a wealth the firm had. Gray felt a bit out of place as he looked down at his quirky clothing. He was more comfortable in baggy pants and paint-splattered shirts than suits, ties, and men who sat in rich leather chairs, but he'd made an effort to wear something a little nicer and hopefully not covered in paint.

There was one other omega waiting there, an older man in a suit who more fit the profile of a client. He wondered for a moment if this was the male he was there to meet. Gray tried to catch the omega's eye, but the man was too engrossed in the book he was reading.

Tapping his fingers on the arm of the chair, Gray breathed a deep sigh and tried to calm himself. This had been his decision… it was the right thing to do, regardless of what Avery had said. He needed to help out in any way he could… and it was really the best decision. He could still be home to watch the boys and contribute to Avery's college fees. All he had to do was carry a babe.

It couldn't be all that hard. Omegas did it every day.

Most of them lived to tell the tale.

"Mr. Tomlinson?"

Gray looked up at a handsome, smiling beta. "Yes."

"I'm Tensen Atkinson," the man said, offering a hand. "So nice to finally meet you."

They'd talked on the phone a few times since making his appointment, so he felt as if he already knew the man. Gray had sensed compassion in the man's tone when he'd relayed his story and why he wanted to become a surrogate. The smile on the solicitor's face, along with the twinkle in his lovely green eyes, put Gray even more at ease. Smile creases wrinkled at the corner of his eyes—suggesting he smiled often. He looked kind, and in that moment, Gray needed kindness. He'd have to guess that

Tensen was a good five or so years older than him, but it was hard to be sure. "You can call me Gray."

"Gray, feel free to call me Tensen. You can follow me into the office. Jamie's already here, excitedly awaiting your arrival."

Gray withdrew his hand, frowning. "Am I late?" He knew arriving anywhere on time wasn't his specialty, but he'd made an effort to be punctual. He lifted his watch to peek.

"Oh, no, you're right on time. Jamie and I had a working lunch so we could discuss a few legalities before you arrived."

Gray nodded. "Oh." Had they been discussing him? Had they judged his qualities, or lack thereof, over a table in some posh restaurant he couldn't begin to afford?

What am I doing?

He came to a stop, pausing long enough to get an odd look from Tensen.

What if... What if there is an alpha for me?

"Everything alright?"

Don't be stupid. This is the only way. Gray nodded, reassuring himself. He headed through the door when Tensen urged him forward and then paused to await the man. Once the inner door closed, Tensen placed a gentle hand to Gray's back and coaxed him to continue. "Excited?"

"I suppose you could call it that," Gray murmured.

Tensen chuckled. "Nervous, then?"

"Very."

"I think Jamie will help put you at ease," Tensen said before luring him toward a closed door. He opened it and led Gray inside.

A small omega rose to his feet, a wide smile on his pale face.

His *very* pale face.

Gray's stare took in the other man. The knit cap over his head. The pale skin. The sunken eyes... he was obviously ill.

Incredibly ill.

"Gray Tomlinson, meet Jaymes Parker."

"Hello. You can call me Jamie," the omega said, seeming nervous. "Jaymes is way too stuffy." He stepped forward and offered Gray a hand.

Gray took it and forced a smile. His stare swept over the delicate features of the man's face. Before whatever was ravaging him, he'd likely been lovely. "Hello, Jamie."

"Have a seat, gentlemen... this is just an introductory meeting, there are no definites right now. We're just getting to know one another and seeing how you each feel about the situation to decide if you'd like to move forward."

Gray took a seat beside the chair Jamie settled in.

"How was the trip over?" Jamie asked, leaning in a little closer to Gray.

"Good. Easy. I don't live too far from here." His stare lingered on Jamie's. The man looked so exhausted... yet there was a life behind those eyes that spoke of a battle valiantly waged. A twinkle there hinted Jamie wasn't done yet.

"That's good. At least we've got a nice, warm day. It's been so cold lately," Jamie said before he coughed slightly.

Gray eyed him, concerned. "Are you okay?"

Jamie grinned. "I am." He paused, the smile fading some. "I'm sure you're concerned with my appearance... and let me put your mind at ease some. *Yes*, I have cancer. *Yes*, I'm in treatment, and that treatment is nearly over. The chemo does more damage than anything else and has left me weak. My doctors feel I have a *very* good chance at remission once treatment is complete. I plan to beat this disease."

Gray smiled feebly, his mind reeling.

Jamie went on speaking, but Gray's mind stuck on one point.

"But... what if?" he interrupted. Gray paused, hating himself for questioning the omega's conviction and sounding like a bastard, but it was a reasonable question. "I hate to be that forward... we've only just met, but given the circumstances of our meeting... what happens... if...?" Gray paused, unable to say the words out loud. *What if you don't make it?* "You want me to carry a child for you... a child who..." Gray couldn't bear to finish the sentence.

"But he *will* have a papa," Jamie said firmly, assuming Gray's missing words correctly. "I *will* beat this."

"Attitude is everything," Tensen said. "I myself had concerns. I've had multiple conversations with Jamie's alpha as well as his oncologist. The doctor did indeed have favorable things to say about the treatment and prognosis. Had it not been for that, I wouldn't have agreed to help Jamie and his alpha begin their search for a surrogate."

Gray nodded, feeling a little more at ease, but only fractionally.

"And as I said before, this is just an introduction. We're not rushing into anything. Jamie's last round of chemo happens soon, and we'll have a better idea how his health is faring in the coming weeks."

"I didn't realize there would be such an extensive wait before we entered into an agreement." Gray wanted to be able to help Avery with tuition. His nephew had sent off several applications in the past days... so it was just a matter of an acceptance.

"There's no rush," Tensen said. "As I said, we need to make sure it's a good fit between all three of you." He paused. "If this goes well, we can have a special meeting with Jamie's alpha approved. And then move on from there."

"Of course." Gray turned to Jamie. "*If* it reaches that point."

Jamie's smile faded some. "I know you have concerns, and I understand them. This isn't my first meeting with a potential surrogate. I know I should've likely waited until my treatment was over, but this disease... well, it reminded me that none of us can expect tomorrow. Cancer or no. We have to live in the now. It could take months, if not years, to get to the point of holding a child in my arms, so I won't wait another moment."

"But taking on all this strain when you're in treatment? Isn't that stressful on you?" Gray asked.

"No," Jamie said with a wide smile. "It gives me something to look forward to. And in making such a grand plan, it has a sense of... continuity. I'm planning for my future, a future I *will* be here to see." Jamie smiled. "And in some ways, this plan has been ongoing for many years before now. I've tried myself so, so many times. Miscarriage after miscarriage... and then the cancer. They took my womb, it was filled with tumors." Jamie paused, tears shining in his eyes. "I've wanted this for so long... to give my alpha the son he deserves."

"Any alpha worth his salt wouldn't put you through that stress," Gray said. He'd seen good alphas. His father had been wonderful to his papa. Gilead had treated Silver like gold. He knew what to expect in his own, had he found one to cherish him. If Jamie's alpha was pressuring for a family, perhaps this wasn't the right couple.

Jamie smiled. "I love Rohan and want to provide the family he expected when we mated. He says it doesn't matter... that he loves me and doesn't care if we have a child. But it *does* matter. It matters *to me*. I want to know there's something of that wonderful man to live on. I want to see his child... *our* child... grow up and be like his father. This world needs more men like him."

Gray could see the desperation in Jamie's eyes... and he understood it. Somewhat. He felt something akin to it now. A desperation to ensure the next generation lived on. For him, that was his brother's children...

Also, he'd been brought up like any other omega. They'd been raised to be breeders, and the expectation to deliver was huge. Those who were unable to provide children for their alphas were looked down upon by society as a whole.

Just as those who were left unclaimed were looked down upon.

Jamie had the alpha Gray didn't. Gray had the womb Jamie didn't.

Added into the equation was that biology was beginning to take its toll on Gray. Their species was hardwired to mate and breed. Omegas went through heats, and alphas were drawn to them like moths to the flame. Gray's body, after years of unfulfilled heats, was beginning to drive him mad. *Heat Repress* was only meant to be used a handful of years, until an omega had found their alpha and started a family. And then used in between children, until the childbearing years were over.

Nearly twenty years after his first heat, and *Heat Repress* was starting to fail him. If he didn't have a child soon…

He might end up climbing the wall into the Alpha Quad and begging to be bred.

Gray reached over and took Jamie's hand in his. The omega's hand was cool to the touch when he squeezed it. He wanted to change the subject. Talk of better things than breeding and dying. *Anything* was better. "Where did you grow up?"

Jamie looked up from their bound hands and smiled softly at Gray. "The Berkshire neighborhood."

"Oh really? Do you know Riley Haversham?"

"I went to school with his younger brother, Sydney."

"Ah, so you must be a few years younger than me." Gray hadn't been sure. The ravaging of Jamie's disease had made it harder to guess. "Riley and I went to art classes together at the Basin Community Center when I was younger."

"Do you paint?"

"A little," Gray answered. "Mostly sketches."

"You any good?" Jamie asked with a grin.

Gray shrugged. "Not really. It's just something to occupy my time."

"I saw some of your work when researching you," Tensen murmured. "It was beautiful. You have an amazing talent."

Gray felt his face flame a bit. He wasn't aware any of his work was accessible to the public. "Where?"

Tensen shrugged, evading the question.

"I'd love to see some of it someday," Jamie said, giving Gray's hand a squeeze.

"Maybe," Gray answered.

They spent the rest of the hour talking about their shared likes, dislikes, and by the end of the meeting, Gray felt a bit of a bond forming with Jamie. He liked the man very much…

But there was still a dark cloud lingering above them.

"Well, I believe this was a good start," Tensen said with a smile. "Perhaps we can schedule a meeting soon with Rohan?"

"My alpha," Jamie added with a soft smile. "I think you'll love him."

Gray nodded. What would it hurt to get the introduction out of the way? He still wasn't completely settled on being Jamie's surrogate considering the health issues, but he was willing to continue the conversation. If Jamie's alpha rubbed him the wrong way, then it would be easier to know that sooner than later. Before he grew any closer to Jamie. "Sure."

The smile that blossomed across Jamie's pale face was lovely.

"Great. I'll get everything arranged with the government and get a border conference room reserved," Tensen said. "It'll likely take a month or so before we get a date."

Because Gray was an unclaimed omega, he wasn't allowed outside the Omega Quad. Rohan, being an alpha, wasn't allowed in. Hoops had to be jumped through in order to make a meeting like that happen, so Gray knew it would likely be a few weeks before he'd meet the alpha.

"Perhaps you could come for tea one afternoon if you're feeling up to it?" Gray asked Jamie.

Jamie nodded excitedly. "I would love to. I have an appointment the week after next—on Thursday afternoon—and the office isn't far from here. I could stop in after, if that works?"

"It's a date," Gray answered.

Jamie took Gray's hand and squeezed it. "Thank you."

"I haven't made any decisions yet," Gray murmured.

"I understand… but you didn't give a decisive no, either. I've heard a lot of no's in the past weeks…" He paused, a shine to his eyes that was only eclipsed by the warmth of his smile that came after. "I appreciate your willingness to keep an open mind more than you could ever know."

Gray gave Jamie's hand another squeeze. "I'll see you next week."

"Next week…"

"I'll give Jamie your information," Tensen said. "If that's okay?"

Gray nodded as he pulled his bag across his body. "Perfect. I really need to get home to the boys. They'll be getting home from school soon."

After a couple of quick goodbyes, Gray headed out of the solicitor's office feeling a lot less nervous, but with much to think about. His nephew hadn't wanted him to become a surrogate, and he understood why. The bond between omega and child was strong, and to sever that, handing a child that had grown within his womb to another—it could be devastating.

But his nephews were all he had left.

But Jamie? Jamie's own life was uncertain, and if Gray did this, he could be putting a child into the same situation his nephews were in now. He was still reeling from the loss. Silver and Gilead had been so young. The accident had come as such a shock to them all. One day, they were all one big happy family. The next their hearts had been ripped out; a family shattered.

Neither Silver nor Gilead had expected to pass so soon. They'd saved some for the nest egg down the road, but youth is the ultimate foil. Silver had only been forty-two. His alpha was only a few years older. They hadn't truly prepared anything for the day they'd ultimately die—leaving a ten, thirteen, and nineteen-year-old behind.

And neither Gilead nor Silver and Gray's parents still lived. All had been older when the alpha and omega had been born and had passed on due to failing health and old age in the years leading up.

They'd all gone to too many funerals over the years.

And he didn't want to be involved in another. Already the thought of Jamie passing made him uncomfortable. Jamie's health was a major concern, but he also felt compelled by how desperate the omega was to bring new life into his fading one.

What if he conceived and Jamie never made it long enough to witness that babe come into the world? Was he to hand over an infant to a grieving alpha, knowing that man was likely breaking inside? Should he condemn a child to live in a world with a papa lost and a father shattered?

The omega-alpha bond was strong. If one passed, the other was left devastated. It was just the way of things. And there were some cases, usually with older couples, where if one passed, the other was not much longer for the world. The pairing was a matched set, fated by the gods. They were bound in life and in death.

Jamie was young... a few years younger than himself. That youth could bring him more strength to truly fight the battle and survive. Over the weeks, they'd hopefully know one way or the other.

He knew he had more questions than answers.

And there was plenty of time to make a decision once he had more facts.

His gut told him he wanted to give Jamie what the omega wanted.

Let's wait until after I meet Rohan. Then I can make a decision if I'll continue to consider becoming their surrogate.

Gray stepped onto a passing trolley moments later and headed toward home.

Chapter Five

The coming heat…

"You take your dose yet?" Gray asked Avery as he swept into the kitchen to set a kettle on the fire the following morning.

"Not yet," Avery said.

Gray reached for his bottle of *Heat Repress* he kept in the cabinet. Searching the name, he took his down and then handed his nephew the other bottle. Popping a pill, Avery washed it down with a sip from Gray's cup. It was a special herbal blend made to help combat the body's need for sex. It didn't help much, but it did take a little of the edge off.

"One down, eleven to go," Gray said after taking his.

They had to start their course of *Heat Repress* the day before their monthly heat to ensure it was active. Three pills a day for four days—the day before and the three days of their heat. Omega heats cycled around the full moon, which occasionally came twice a month. Fortunately, this month was not one of those, yet they were both in for a long few days. *Heat Repress* dulled their instinct but didn't take it away completely.

"You want some broth?" Gray asked.

"I'm not very hungry," Avery said, leaning back against the counter.

He finished preparing his broth and tea before casting a look over his shoulder. The coming heat would take a lot out of them both. *Me, especially*. "You really should put a little bit of *something* on your stomach." He met Avery's stare and saw a smile played at his nephew's lips. "What's got you smiling so much this morning?"

"Papa had a dressing robe like that," Avery answered. "It just made me think of him."

Gray looked down at it. The long, flowing dressing gown was made of silk and absolutely beautiful. He hadn't worn it often, in fear of ruining it. "Silver got this for me on some holiday he and your father went on... I believe he did say he got one for himself, too." His uncle twirled the fabric around him some, his unbound hair flying about his shoulders "I've rarely worn it... but when I saw it in my closet..." He gave a smile, his gaze appearing to look at something faraway. "I suppose I just wanted to feel closer to him today."

"Why today?"

Gray shrugged. "Why *not* today?" His mind was on life and death and his mind had, of course, gone to his brother. He missed their quiet talks over tea in the sunroom each week. *Boy could I use him right now.*

Avery grew quiet. "Anything you want to talk about?"

Gray met his stare. There was so much he wanted to discuss, but he knew what Avery thought of surrogacy and he wasn't in the mood to argue, not with the coming heat. They both would have their hands full over the next days, and the last thing he wanted to do was quarrel now. "No. Is there something on *your* mind?"

"No," Avery murmured, looking unsure.

Auggie wandered into the kitchen and climbed onto one of the island's stools. "What's for breakfast?"

Avery grabbed a box of cereal and placed it before the boy. "Make your own day."

"Awwww," Auggie complained. "No eggs and bacon and toast?"

Just the thought of food made Gray's stomach flip over. "What's today?"

"Satur-morn," Auggie said earnestly.

"What *about* today?" Avery asked, pressing the boy.

Auggie looked bemused. Gray didn't know how much either of his young nephews knew about heats... he'd been fairly clueless himself until they actually came on and he'd then experienced them for himself. He knew the schools had started to explain more during breeding education classes—something Gray hadn't had when he'd been in school.

Luckily, Silver had handled Avery's first heat and helped the boy through it. Now he and Avery would have to be the ones there for Lake and Auggie one day. That thought made him cringe.

And it made him sad for the boys not to have their papa for that life-changing moment.

"They go into heat tomorrow, idiot," Lake said as he strolled in and headed for the cabinets where the bowls were kept. "So we're on our own for the next few days."

"Oh," Auggie said, his face growing a beet red as he looked away.

Gray felt the very same sentiment. He was in no mood for educating any of them on the ins and outs of mating rituals, even at the most basic levels.

"Not true," Avery answered. "You're not on your own. Gray and I made sure there are a few casseroles in the fridge for you guys for your dinners... and there's plenty of deli meat and cans of soup for lunches. If you get hungry, you can get something started if we're not right here. You're old enough to help, Lake."

Lake took two bowls down and placed them on the island, rolling his eyes as he passed. "As if I don't do enough around here."

"Just what is it you do besides play video games?" Avery asked.

"More than you know!"

"You want to eat? You can help make the food," Gray grated. "You're *thirteen*, not three. Start acting like it."

Lake glowered at him.

"I can make a sandwich," Auggie said, playing peacemaker. "I'll make lunch today, Lake."

Lake grabbed the milk from the fridge as Auggie poured his own cereal. "And have your dirty, grubby hands all over my food? No thanks."

"I'm fairly sure your little brother knows to wash his hands before making food," Gray replied.

"I do now," Auggie said with a smile before taking the milk from Lake.

"We really need to get them more involved with cooking around here, so they don't burn the house down," Gray said. "You know... *after* the next few days are over."

Avery nodded, watching as Lake poured milk onto the cereal he'd poured before heading out with his bowl. "You can't even spend a few minutes in the morning with us?"

The only answer they got was to hear Lake's feet stomping up the stairs.

Avery sighed, shaking his head.

"He'll calm down. In time," Gray murmured softly. Lake was lashing out at everything and everyone, but more often he and Avery.

More often *him*. Gray was an outsider to Lake—that weird uncle they came to visit every so often. The middle boy had always been distant with him for some reason, and Gray had always wondered why.

"I'm not so sure you're right," Avery said before lifting his cup to his lips.

"What's it like?" Auggie said after munching a few bites of his cereal.

"What's what like?" Avery asked absentmindedly.

"Heat."

Avery's stare went to Gray's. It appeared neither of them was ready for this conversation with the boys.

"Haven't you discussed it some in school?" Gray asked, hopeful.

"They just say that we go into heat around sixteen or seventeen… and then it comes on the full moon for a few days… and that alphas make us pregnant then, but I'm not exactly sure how." Auggie stuffed another spoonful into his mouth as he watched for Avery's explanation.

What the hell do I say? How much is too much at his age? Damn you, Silver! He turned to look at his nephew, searching for answers.

Avery looked away, apparently unwilling to help.

"All that talk of them being *your* responsibility?" Gray snapped. "I see what happens when the tough questions come."

"Oh no, you were quite adamant that you wanted to help," Avery said with a wide grin. "So help."

Gray sighed and looked over at Auggie. "What you've learned is correct. You'll be ready to know more when you're older. Just know that we feel... *sick*... for a few days. We... rest... upstairs through those days."

"We rest *a whole lot*," Avery mumbled before Gray shot him a glare.

"Is that why you don't eat much? Because you're sick?" Auggie asked before stuffing another spoonful in.

"Yeah," Avery answered. "Pretty much."

"Do you feel hot?" Auggie answered. "Is that why they call it heat?"

Avery lifted the cup to his lips, avoiding the question.

"In a manner of speaking," Gray answered.

"I don't think I want to go into heat," Auggie announced. "I don't want to feel sick every new moon."

Gray chuckled. "I wish it were that easy."

Auggie didn't ask any more questions, which Gray was thankful for. He went back to sipping his tea and focusing on calming his mind and body.

After breakfast was over and Auggie was reading a book as he lounged across the living room couch, Avery tidied up the kitchen while Gray finished his broth and tea. He would need whatever strength the broth could give him over the next days.

"You were up earlier—why don't you go take a nap? I'll keep an eye on the boys for a bit and you can spend some time this afternoon with them," Gray said from his perch on the island.

"Good idea," Avery said before tossing the dishtowel to the counter and marching upstairs.

He lay across the chaise in the sunroom and closed his eyes, hoping for a bit of peace... until Lake's loud music shook the entire house. Sighing, he rubbed his temples, not in a mood to argue with the boy.

Gray's heats were coming on stronger and stronger as the years passed and soon... soon he feared he'd be lost to them. At seventeen, that first heat had been traumatic. One day Gray had been a boy, and by the next, considered a man. He'd been ripped from the only home he'd known and put into safekeeping. Now capable of bearing life... of being a papa... he'd been hidden away. Like many omegas, his first had hit him early—days before the full moon. It had lasted a good seven days and *Heat Repress* had barely touched the need swamping him.

Now, it was reaching a point where it again barely assuaged the need.

By the time Avery finally returned hours later, sweat beaded Gray's forehead and the back of his neck. It was a full day before his heat would truly take effect, and his body was already roaring with the desire to mate. Avery eyed him when he slipped into the sunroom.

"Are you not well?"

Gray closed his eyes. "I'm not, Avery."

His nephew sat at the end of the lounge, near Gray's feet. "What is it?"

He shook his head. There was no way he'd discuss this with his nephew.

"Uncle? We're all each other has. If you're not well, tell me," Avery said.

"You wouldn't understand," Gray murmured.

"Try me."

"Eighteen years of *Heat Repress*."

Avery frowned. "What do you mean?"

"Eventually… the medicine grows less and less effective. It wasn't created to keep an omega from his heats this long. For males like you… who await their alpha for a few years… and for claimed omegas between babes—not for an omega who's been on them for nearly two decades without pause. My body is fighting the medicine."

Avery said nothing for a moment. "How bad will it get?"

"I don't know. It's not like most omegas are very open about their heats. It's simply not discussed."

"Will it stop working? The *Heat Repress*?"

"Possibly. I've spoken to a doctor about it, and even he was unsure what the outcome would be." Gray eyed his nephew. "Hopefully it won't come to that point, but…"

He let his words trail off. He knew there was a possibility he'd go mad with the need and beg to be bred. If he became a surrogate, a pregnancy would give his body time off the medication and perhaps it would start working again after the babe was born. But he couldn't bring that up with Avery.

Not now.

"Why don't you go rest?" Avery glanced at his phone. "It's late enough now that I can keep an eye on the boys until they go to bed."

"That's too long," Gray said.

"I've got this," Avery stated. "If I'm to start living as a beta, I'll have to learn to be stronger. I won't get to take off four days while I go into heat. I need to learn to suffer in silence."

Gray shook his head. He couldn't imagine going through a heat in public. It sounded like torture. "Another good reason why you *shouldn't* do this."

"I've found an herbal supplement online that supposedly helps take the edge off of heats a little more. Maybe it'll work for us both." Avery smiled. "I found it a few moments ago in a search—I'll pick some up as soon as this heat is over to be ready for the next."

Gray shook his head, still concerned.

"I'll be fine."

"So you say," Gray said before forcing himself upstairs and into his bedroom. As soon as his door was closed, he let the dressing gown slide from his shoulders. Hours of ignoring the heat pulsing through him had nearly driven him mad. Gray stretched his head and neck before stretching the rest of his body. Looking down, his cock was thick and hard, the tip oozing. He grasped it by the root and stroked the throbbing shaft, trying to release some of the pent-up need.

Again and again.

But no matter how many times he drove himself to completion, it wasn't enough. He drifted off, still writhing in the sheets. Always knowing nothing would ever quench the lust he felt.

By the next morning, the heat had arrived full on. He awoke to unchecked lust before swallowing the waiting pill he'd left on his nightstand. It took nearly an hour for the pill to truly take effect—and in that time he used the dildo he'd also left beside the pill, knowing he'd have to slake some of the desire. His slick ran freely, so he needed no lubrication. His passage was slippery, and the dildo slid in with ease.

Gray drove the dildo deep, rubbing the head of it against the opening to his womb. The dildo wouldn't be enough to open it—his body knew fake from the real thing—but the pressure there helped push him toward the edge. As he'd done a million times before, he imagined what it would feel like for an alpha to open him fully and knot inside his ass, filing his womb with seed and breeding him.

It wouldn't leave him feeling as empty afterwards as the silicone version did. Not that he'd ever get the chance. Once he'd come twice, he lay breathless on the bed, his cries of pleasure all screamed into his pillow. The pill had finally started to kick in, it felt, and he didn't feel the same intense urge to masturbate again.

Not yet.

It would come, he knew, as the pill began to run its course and before he could take another. Omegas couldn't take more than three pills each day, as the medicine could have side effects in too great a dosage, taken too often. Or so they'd been told. Horror stories of the pills no longer working after a couple of years of misdosing and those omegas going into irregular, severe heats were enough to scare anyone with a womb.

Perhaps that's all it was—scare tactics—but Gray wasn't going to attempt to find out. He worried enough about when the medicines might stop working for him and what might happen then.

Once he felt up to it, Gray rose from his bed, showered, and slipped on the dressing gown once more. There was no point putting on too much as he'd likely be back in bed several times through the day, trying to command his body through the insanity of lust. After assuring the boys were awake and alive, had eaten some breakfast, and were okay, he returned to his room to battle the lust within.

For three days he battled that roaring need alone, taking care of his needs in an attempt to quell the lust ravaging his body and mind—and trying to maintain some semblance of stability for his nephews by checking in to assure they were alive and well. When the sun rose on the fourth day and his body was exhausted, but sated, Gray stared up at the ceiling, hating the vicious cycle he was stuck within and wishing it could all be over.

The shackles of his lust bound him in so many ways.

Chapter Six

In a boardroom in the Alpha Quadrant...

Rohan Parker, Esquire, sat at the end of the table, to the left of his boss and father-in-law, Warden Jaymes, listening to the man across from them drone on. He glanced at his cell phone under the table and saw the time. He was going to be late.

Jotting a note on a scrap of paper, he then slid it over to Warden.

Jamie's appointment?

Warden scrawled across the paper and slid it back.

I need you here. It won't be much longer.

Rohan seethed quietly. His father-in-law knew full well he preferred sitting at his omega's side at Jamie's appointments at the chemo clinic. Rohan wouldn't allow his mate to sit alone as they forced poison into the omega's veins. After he fished out his phone, he typed a message to his brother-in-law, Wilder, who had somehow miraculously gotten out of the meeting.

I'm stuck. Jamie needs someone with him at chemo. Can you go?

He only half listened to the meeting as he willed a response to flash on the screen. Holding his breath as he saw a bubble form as Wilder typed, he stared at the screen, willing a yes.

Got it. I'm on my way in two seconds.
Thanks. I appreciate it. He needs someone there.

Rohan laid his phone on the desk beside his notes, thankful his omega wouldn't be alone. He could always trust in Wilder to be there for Jamie. The rest of the family? Not so much. As an omega, he didn't seem to rate as highly in the family hierarchy—especially now that he was barren.

Barren.

He hated that word with a passion. Rohan had seen it scrawled over countless medical documents—and now—surrogacy applications. How the love he felt for his omega could be considered void of life was beyond him. They didn't need to have children. Jamie was more than enough to make him deliriously happy for the rest of his life.

Or the rest of Jamie's, at least.

The thought of losing his mate...

It was enough to make him stop breathing.

"Rohan?"

Rohan lifted his stare and felt all eyes on him. He turned to Warden, offering a bemused smile and nothing else. "Sorry, I, *ah*..."

Warden lifted a brow. "Do you think you'll have time to comb through the contracts for the bid this afternoon or not?"

Rohan sighed. He planned to leave and take care of his omega. "I can take them with me when I go."

"No," Warden said, shaking his head. "I need you to stay."

Rohan clenched his jaw and nodded. "Of course." He wouldn't argue with the man in front of their staff and a client. Warden wrapped up the meeting, and everyone exited—all but Rohan and Warden.

Once they were alone, he had his say.

"I'll take the contracts home and review them there. I *won't* be staying this afternoon," Rohan said.

"This is a multi-billion-*reno* project. I need to know it's right before I sign."

"And I have an omega—your son—who's getting chemo right now. You know how sick he gets afterward."

"I pay you enough to get nurses for him. To tend to him afterwards. You're more than a nursemaid, Rohan."

"You really think I'm going to let some stranger hold him when he's sick? Is anyone else going to care for him like I would?"

"You're an alpha. We don't tend to a sickly omega. It's not who we are," Warden said. "We're the providers. If we don't provide for our omegas, *that's* when we fail them."

"We're also their *protectors*," Rohan blasted. "And I *will* show my omega the love and care he deserves, whether you like it or not."

Warden glared over the rim of his glasses.

"I can review the contracts as Jamie sleeps. I've never failed you before, and I don't plan on it now." Rohan sighed. "If it was your omega in Jamie's shoes… you wouldn't be at Wynter's side?"

Warden sat back in the big chair at the head of the table and sighed. "If I didn't keep Wynter in the lifestyle he was accustomed to, he would have my head."

Rohan felt the anger swelling through him. "I realize you and Wynter don't have the same kind of relationship I do with my omega… but I love your son more than anyone in this world."

"Are you trying to say I don't love my omega?"

"No. That's not what I said. But Jamie comes first in my life. *Period.* And if that means I need to resign so I can go and stand by his side in the moment he needs me most, then I'll submit my resignation here and now."

Warden eyed him a moment. "You're weak for your omega, Rohan."

"I am. And I find no shame in that." *And I pity you for not being weak for yours.*

Warden sighed. "You will have this contract reviewed—every line triple checked and confirmation that not one loophole exists—and on my desk by nine tomorrow morning."

Rohan released the breath he'd been holding. "If not earlier."

Warden eyed him again. "One of these days, this weakness of yours is going to get you into trouble. Trouble you can't get out of. It might tear you both apart."

"Won't happen," Rohan said, sliding the copies of the contracts over the surface of the table and adding it on top of his notepad. "We love each other too much for that to *ever* happen."

"Mark my words, boy. It will."

* * * *

At the chemo clinic…

"What're you doing here?" Jamie asked as he lifted his stare and smiled. He rested in one of the recliners in the clinic, getting his weekly dose of poison into his veins.

"I missed a chance to catch up at dinner last week," Wilder said with a grin. He took a seat in the empty chair beside the recliner typically reserved for family. "And Rohan called me. He said he was stuck in a meeting with father and couldn't make today's treatment—so I thought I could come spend a few minutes with you if you don't mind."

Jamie rested his hand on Wilder's and smiled. Rohan hated leaving him alone during chemo and had been at his side for nearly every one. He'd likely asked Wilder to be there so Jamie wasn't alone. A smile came to his lips, thinking how wonderful his alpha was. "I would never mind seeing more of your handsome, smiling face. Especially when it's not at the circus papa calls dinner."

"Well, you have to put part of the blame on our wayward brother for that," Wilder said. "I'm not sure who's the better ringmaster—papa or Vaughn."

"I'd once say papa, but it is definitely Vaughn these days," Jamie said with a smile. He loved his family, but they could be a handful when all together.

Wilder was more like their quiet, staid father and was the apple of Jamie's eye. A few years younger than Jamie, Wilder had been a sweet boy who'd followed him around as a babe. Jamie had helped papa care for both his brothers, but Wilder had been the first, and therefore, a little more special to him. It had been just the two of them for a few years before Vaughn had arrived, kicking and screaming.

Both Wilder and Vaughn were alphas, leaving him as the sole omega child. While Vaughn and he had grown apart some over the years, he and Wilder had always remained close, no matter if they were of two different classes.

"So, any news about these chemo visits? Or more to the point—when they're to end?" Wilder said, taking Jamie's hand in his big, strong grasp.

"This is the last one. Hopefully there won't be another round."

Wilder lifted Jamie's hand to his lips and pressed a soft kiss to the knuckles. "I'm glad to hear it."

"My doctor is very optimistic. The last two rounds of tests were *promising*, from what I'm told."

"That's wonderful news. I knew you had enough fight in you to conquer this dragon," Wilder murmured. "Any day now and that precious R-word will get flung about. I won't jinx it by saying it too early."

"There's no jinxing *anything*," Jamie said. "Remission. Remission, remission, remission. I'm going to will it into existence."

Wilder laughed, his wide, open smile good for Jamie's heart.

"So what news do you bring from the Alpha Quadrant? Has our father finally given you one of the big offices yet?"

"Not quite yet," Wilder said. "Although, father did just announce my promotion a few days ago."

"Congratulations!" Jamie cried, pulling his hand away so he could lean over to hug his brother. "Is papa planning a party?"

"You know he is," Wilder said with a sigh.

Jamie chuckled under his breath. "You don't sound thrilled."

"I'm not," Wilder admitted.

"It's *good* to celebrate your accomplishment."

"Accomplishment? You mean nepotism."

"Stop," Jamie said, patting Wilder's hand. "You work harder than father does anymore. I've barely seen you these last couple of years—you're always at the office. Father crows on about your efforts and hard work… and so does papa. Not that you're ever around to hear their praise."

"There are others in the office who work just as hard as I do and haven't flown up the totem pole. I sometimes feel like a pretender."

"Yes, perhaps you have had opportunities others haven't… but take note of those men who work just as hard as you do and once you're in a position of power, you lift those men up with you. If you do that and continue to work as hard as you have—no one will *ever* see you as a pretender. They'll see you for the strong leader you are."

Wilder smiled. "I don't know where I would be without you some days, big brother."

Jamie eyed Wilder. "I long ago stopped being the *big* brother, alpha. I'm just the older and wiser one now."

Wilder smiled, his eyes bright… but the smile faded a little. "I need you to be here to tell me whenever I'm being an idiot. For the rest of my life."

"I plan on being here a long, long time."

"Good," Wilder said. "I'm rather selfish in that way. I won't let you go."

Jamie tried not to notice Wilder glancing away and dabbing at his eye. He hated the worry in his brother's eyes when they looked his way. He hated what he was putting everyone through, especially Rohan and Wilder.

"I have some good news of my own."

Wilder lifted his stare, a soft smile on his face. "What's that?"

"After some discussions, Rohan has agreed to us seeking out a surrogate. We have a prospect willing to meet Rohan. I met him and didn't scare him off."

His brother was quiet.

"Please don't tell me you also don't approve of this. I've heard enough from papa."

"Rohan told me a little about it. It's not that I don't approve of you and Rohan involving a surrogate. I believe you should, if you both wish to have a child. But do you really think this is something you want to tackle? I mean right now… your focus should be on your own health. Maybe after you're better would be time to think about that family."

"I *need* this," Jamie whispered. "A baby, Wild. A brand-new life. An innocent babe at the start of a new adventure. Our new adventure *together.*"

Wilder's stare washed over his face. "I understand that… I just don't want you to sacrifice *your* needs for this. Rohan's worried, too."

"I know. He's spoken about his fears with me."

"Then why now? Why not a few months from now, once you get some strength back and good news from your doctors?"

Jamie smiled softly at his brother. "Because tomorrow's never promised to us, Wild. If not cancer, it could be a trolley accident, or a fall, or any number of accidents. I don't want to wait. I want to live today, not tomorrow." Jamie sighed. "And it could take months to find the right surrogate… and more months to finally get pregnant. And then the pregnancy itself… it will likely be a few years before we actually become parents."

Wilder held his gaze for a few seconds. "Okay. You're obviously set on this. If it's truly what you want, then you have my support."

Jamie placed his hand on Wilder's. "Thank you." He leaned his head back on the recliner and smiled at his brother. "Any idea what's on the menu for this party of yours? I've been craving some of papa's pâté for weeks now."

"I'll have to make sure it's on the menu, then," Wilder said with a tilt of his head.

"I wonder why papa hasn't called me to invite us already? He's probably still upset with me about the surrogate."

"He's likely just worried about you."

Jamie shook his head. "I fear papa is more worried about what others will say. As it is, I'm *barren*—which has apparently just about ruined the family."

"Fuck other people," Wilder said. "I don't care what they think. And I hate that word. Never say it again in my presence."

Jamie smiled. "But it's true."

Wilder glared down at him. "Promise me."

Jamie sighed. "Fine. I promise." He paused. "Still doesn't make it less true."

"When I think of something barren, I think of something cold, unfeeling, and empty. You have more love in your pinky than most people have in their whole bodies. You're not barren. Nowhere close." Wilder squeezed his hand and smiled. "You're *alive*. That's the important part." Again, Jamie saw the same worry filling Wilder's eyes, and he had to look away from it. He had to focus on healing himself and needed those around him to be as sure as he was that he would survive.

"Remission, Wild. Remission. It's only a breath away."

Chapter Seven

An hour later...

Rohan walked through the nearly empty clinic and found Jamie napping in the oversized recliner. Wilder held his brother's hand and stared at the IV drip. The look on Wild's face—the love the alpha had for his brother—it made Rohan freeze in place.

Early on in their relationship, Rohan had almost been jealous of the friendship Wild and Jamie had. Over the years, he'd eventually realized they had latched on to one another as a means of self-protection. Of course, he was sure the pair didn't see it that way. They loved their parents, even when it bit them in the ass.

How Wilder and Jamie had turned out as they were considering they were being raised by two of the most self-centered people he'd ever met, he didn't know. Knowing Wilder would one day run Jaymes & Associates was one of the only reasons he stayed on and didn't go off in search of other work.

Hopefully I can last that long.

Wilder eventually seemed to notice his presence. He turned and smiled as he saw Rohan leaning against the divider that separated the rows of chairs. Wilder turned back, pressed a gentle kiss to Jamie's hand and then placed that hand on the arm of the chair before he rose.

"I believe this is your seat," Wilder said lowly.

"Thanks for coming to be with him," Rohan whispered before slipping out of his suit jacket and laying it across the back of the chair Wilder had just vacated. "Any issues?"

"He hasn't gotten sick," Wilder whispered. "At least, not that I could tell."

Jamie roused slightly, his eyelashes fluttering some. His eyes opened slowly. A smile spread across his face as he looked up and saw both Rohan and Wilder standing there. "Hey there."

Rohan lowered his head to press his lips to his omega's. "Hey yourself."

"I'm going to get back to work now that Rohan's here," Wilder said. "If that's okay with you?"

Jamie grinned. "And if it's not?"

Wilder chuckled.

"I'm stingy. I need more time. You must come for supper soon," Jamie said.

"Just not tonight," Rohan said to Wilder. "He'll need rest after this."

"This weekend?" Jamie asked as excitedly. As excited as he could likely muster considering the circumstances.

Wilder hedged for a moment. "I'm working through the weekend. We've got a huge deal in the works."

"You have to eat sometime," Jamie cried.

"I do. But I don't want you going to any trouble to cook for me," Wilder said. "I know… Saturday night. I'll bring over pizza from DeNardo's. I can stop by as I'm leaving the AQ. I'll even get you one with sausage and pineapple, even though it's a crime against nature."

"My favorite," Jamie said with a smile. "I love it."

Wilder's smile faded some. "Will that be okay on your stomach?"

"Hopefully, the aftereffects should be gone by Saturday," Jamie said. "No worries. I'll be ready for DeNardo's."

Wilder leaned over and gave Jamie a kiss to the forehead. "Then it's a date."

Once Wilder had left them, one of their favorite nurses, Hale, came over to check the IV. "Looking good. Shouldn't be much longer now."

Hale left them alone, and Rohan searched the space. "Not many here today."

Jamie gave a wry smile that slowly faded. "I heard that Khalen died a few days ago. And Jeres just the week before."

"*And* Jeres?" Rohan asked, frowning. Khalen had been older and struggled with treatment. He hadn't looked well the last few times, so the news was less of a surprise. Jeres wasn't much older than Jamie and had suffered the same cancer—and had fought with a valiant effort. All signs had pointed to Jeres' recovery and remission.

Just as Jamie was thought to.

Rohan swallowed back the fear that swelled within.

"I won't be like him," Jamie said, placing a hand on Rohan's. "I've already beaten it. I know I have."

Rohan brought his omega's hand to his lips and held on for a moment before lowering it. "I know you have, too."

"Although, it's hard to think of what happens if I don't."

"Don't talk like that," Rohan said, squeezing his lover's hand. "You're going to make it."

Jamie smiled, but he could see the happiness didn't quite make it into his omega's eyes. "You're right. I'm going to make it."

Rohan returned the smile, willing strength to the man who held his heart.

"I have to. For the baby we'll have soon."

Rohan exhaled, the smile fading. "Perhaps we should wait."

"I thought you said you were on board?"

Rohan looked away, unable to look at Jamie's disappointment. He had said he was on board—against his better judgment. His omega wasn't ready for the stresses of a child. Nor was he. But he couldn't say no to Jamie.

Never could.

And he honestly hadn't thought a surrogate would agree considering Jamie's obvious health issues. He assumed they had time… that Jamie would be on a wild goose chase until he was in better health, and they were better prepared.

It had sounded easier than telling his omega no.

Now there was a meeting. He would have to come face to face with another omega who might carry his child.

An omega… who wasn't Jamie.

"I know what I said…. But your health should be our only priority now. You need to be stronger before we make such a huge, life-changing choice."

"I'm so tired of hearing people say that to me," Jamie grumbled. "If this disease has taught me anything, it's that we *can't* waste a single moment of time."

"Being with me is wasting time?"

Sorrow spread across the lines of Jamie's face. He placed a hand to Rohan's cheek and sighed. "You, my love, are *not* a waste of my time. Quite the opposite. If it wasn't for you at my side, I don't think I would've made it this far. *You're* the reason I fight. Because I want to be with you for as long as I can."

Rohan clenched his jaw, feeling emotion slamming into him. He'd stood strong for so long, trying to be everything Jamie needed in an alpha. The months had worn him down... enough that he felt the slight sting of tears at the backs of his eyes.

Throughout everything, he'd yet to shed a tear.

At least, not in front of Jamie.

He needed to remain strong. The battle wasn't over yet. "That's all I want, too." He turned his face and kissed Jamie's palm.

Jamie held his stare. "You, my husband... you are a gift to me and to this world. And I want to see your legacy continue. I want you to have sons who're just like you. Kind. Considerate. Loving. *Brave*."

"I'm happy and fulfilled... you're all I need, Jamie. All I will *ever* need." Rohan saw the worry in Jamie's eyes and knew he had to add a caveat. "But if this is what you truly want... if you *must* have this child, how can I tell you no?"

Jamie's father's words whispered through his mind.

Was this the moment?

He hoped like hell it wasn't.

Jamie's smile was brilliant, and it nearly broke his heart to see it. It had been so long since he had. Hope had given it to him... hope for a future they hadn't been sure was possible. "With any luck, Tensen will get us that meeting with Gray soon."

Gray. Even his name made Rohan tense in apprehension. What omega would be willing to discuss having a child considering how sick Jamie clearly was? Was this male so desperate for money he was willing to overlook the illness?

Or was he just toying with Jamie and stringing them both along? Rohan had heard horror stories about surrogates changing their minds time after time. He wouldn't allow anyone to break his omega's heart.

For that, Rohan might turn lethal. "I'm happy your first meeting went so well, although, you didn't tell me all that much."

"I'm trying not to get too optimistic." Jamie smiled. "I don't want to get too involved only to have him decide he's not for us." His omega's smile grew. "But he's perfect. Absolutely *perfect*."

"Oh?"

"He's beautiful. His eyes are this stunning blue-gray. His hair is long and beautiful," Jamie said before absentmindedly touching his beanie. He slid it off his bald head and ran a palm over the top. "About the color mine was before it all fell out."

"I kind of like short hair," Rohan said with a grin, glancing at the few sprigs trying to hold on. Those had changed color, lightening to almost white... and the doctors said it might remain that way as it grew back after chemo.

"You loved my hair. You told me so often."

"I loved it because it was connected to *you*," Rohan said. "Dark, light, thin, thick... it doesn't matter to me."

Jamie glanced down at the hat in his hands, a wry smile on his lips. "One day soon, I'll look more like the omega you mated."

"You look like the omega I mated now," Rohan said. "Every single day." He leaned closer and pressed a gentle kiss to Jamie's lips.

"How did I get so lucky to have you?" his omega asked.

Rohan smiled, knowing he was the lucky one. Hopefully he'd be even luckier and hold on to the man he loved with every bit of his heart. "You must've had some good karma," he joked.

"I could use some good karma right now."

"So, tell me more about this omega friend of yours."

Jamie smiled again, the excitement returning to his features. "He's an artist according to Tensen. Apparently a pretty good one. I'm having tea with Gray next week, so hopefully I can take a peek at some of his work. He knows someone I went to school with, they were in an art program together…"

Rohan barely heard the words coming from his omega's lips. All he could focus on was the smile. The thought of this child gave Jamie something to look forward to. A goal. A future. He still had his doubts, but there was no way he'd interfere with anything that could make his mate this happy.

They would make a baby together.

And live happily ever after…

If his luck kept rolling in the right direction.

Chapter Eight

A few days later...

Gray poured tea into Jamie's cup, noting a little of the man's color seemed to have returned. Not that he knew what Jamie looked like prior to his cancer. "You look as if you feel better today."

"I do. It's been a good couple of weeks," Jamie said before adding a light spoonful of sugar to his tea and stirring.

"So how was it good?" Gray asked, curious what made the man tick. What made him smile... what kind of papa he'd be.

If he had the chance.

"Well... I did have chemo this week, which isn't great. But it was my last one, hopefully forever, so this one didn't seem to hit me quite as hard as others. And I'm grateful." Jamie lifted his cup to his lips and took a small sip. He smiled, his eyes widening. "Oh, this is good."

"It's a new blend from the little shop on Main. It's supposed to help bolster the immune system, or so they say. After I sampled it, I had to buy some." Gray pulled a small bag of leaves from his pocket and sat it beside Jamie's cup. "I got you a little to take home, too."

Jamie reached out and squeezed Gray's hand. "How kind of you. Thank you."

Gray smiled and patted Jamie's hand with his free one. "Don't mention it."

He went back to fixing his tea, watching Jamie from the corners of his eyes. "You never finished telling me about your good week."

A smile spread on Jamie's face. "I got to see my brother Wilder, not once, but twice. He visited me while I was having my treatment. Rohan's usually there, but he was tied up at work and sent Wilder in his place."

"That was nice of him," Gray said.

"Rohan's very protective of me." Jamie's smile faded some.

"You act as if that's a bad thing?"

Jamie shook his head slightly. "It's not." He paused before sighing. "He's not completely sold on the idea of a surrogate. He's worried about me... that protective instinct is flaring."

Gray paused, his cup halfway to his lips. "Is he refusing to meet?"

"No...no, nothing like that. He's just worried—as everyone is—about my health and moving forward. I seem to be the only one who sees that the end of this disease is upon us. You'll all see it soon, though. Mark my words." Jamie took another sip. "Mmm... lovely. This really is good tea." He settled his cup down and smiled. "As far as the rest of my week. Wilder brought over DeNardo's sausage and pineapple pizza on Saturday night and spent a couple of hours regaling us with what's been going on at work. He and Rohan are co-workers—and great friends—which is a joy for me. Wilder is my favorite brother... but don't tell my youngest brother Vaughn that." Jamie grinned. "Do you have any siblings?"

"A brother," Gray answered, trying not to let the pain hit him too hard. He took another sip before he answered and lowered the cup to the table. "Silver. He passed a little over a month ago."

A frown creased Jamie's face. "Oh, no... I had no idea. I'm so sorry." He took Gray's hands in his. "How?"

"A car accident. He and his alpha were coming back from a long weekend on the coast. A truck driver who'd been up for almost a full day... he fell asleep. And we lost them..." Gray felt the sting come to his eyes.

"I heard you say something about the boys... Tensen was rather tight-lipped about them. Your brothers' children, I assume?"

Gray nodded. "Silver and Gilead left behind a ten, a thirteen, and a nineteen-year-old."

"All left in your care," Jamie said, *tsking*.

"Technically, left in Avery's care. The oldest. As he's of-age—he decided he wanted to become their guardian. He received temporary custody, and the family solicitor said it'll easily become permanent. He's very responsible, and now... now he's been forced into being even more responsible."

"But you still feel accountable? Is that why you chose to become a surrogate? To help them financially?"

Gray smiled wanly. "I'm still not sure I want to become a surrogate, to be honest. But I don't know how else to make sure we stay afloat."

Jamie was silent a moment. "The boys? Are they alpha or omega?"

"Omegas. All of them," Gray said.

"The eldest... he's close to mating age. Do you have him signed up for the next round of balls?"

Gray nodded, lying. He was beginning to hate being a party to Avery's lie. "Yes. Of course. But as I well know... he might not have an alpha to rely on."

Jamie frowned. "You truly believe you don't have one?"

Gray shrugged. "I'm thirty-five and unmatched. Most omegas have found their alpha by the time they're not much older than Avery. I'm... I'm not stupid enough to think there's a chance."

"I've heard of omegas finding their alphas later in life. It's not impossible."

"A chance in a million." Gray smiled. Silver's words whispered through his mind. *I've never given up hope.* "I'd much rather focus on how I can survive on my own than wish for something that might never be."

Jamie squeezed his hand. "If you do this... and he *is* out there... he might refuse you. Are you willing to give that chance up?"

"There's no one out there, Jamie. *No one.*"

Jamie didn't say anything. He only squeezed Gray's hand again. "Part of me wants to argue with you and tell you there's a chance. Another part of me wants to give in and allow you to make up your mind... you're an adult, and that's your right. But giving in so quickly makes me sound selfish—you giving up on your alpha is good for me."

"I didn't think that."

"I hoped you didn't... but know that I'm not selfish. I want you to really think long and hard about what you're potentially giving up if you agree to help us. I want a child. Desperately. But not one forsaking your chance at a future."

Gray held Jamie's earnest stare. "Thank you for that. I appreciate the sentiment—but on the sudden appearance of my alpha, I hold no illusions."

Jamie held his stare a moment. "Okay," Jamie said before taking another sip from his tea. He looked over Gray's shoulder at one of the paintings on the wall. "Is this one of yours?"

Gray smiled. The painting was one of his favorites among his work. "It is."

"That's beautiful! You must show me more."

Taking their tea, they strolled through the house. Gray showed off a few of the pieces he had on the walls… and then they made their way to his studio, where he displayed a few of his more recent paintings.

"My word, Gray. Tensen wasn't kidding. You really are quite talented," Jamie said, lifting one of the canvases before him. "Absolutely breathtaking."

Gray wasn't used to sharing his work—or receiving much praise for it. His face was burning. "Thank you."

"Is it for sale?"

"Sale?" Gray asked, confused. He'd never imagined selling his work. It was only a hobby. Something to occupy his long hours alone.

Jamie smiled. "I'd like to buy it."

"Buy it? You can *have* it."

Jamie shook his head. "Absolutely not. Talent such as this needs to be nurtured and applauded. I won't take one thing, but I *will* buy this piece." Jamie glanced down at it. "Say two hundred? Does that sound fair?"

Two hundred *renos* for one painting? "That… it's too much, Jamie."

"Not hardly. Why don't we make it three?"

Gray sighed. "You don't have to butter me up. I promise it won't affect my decision one way or another."

Jamie looked stunned. He stood up a bit straighter and lifted his chin. "I would *never* try to buy you, Gray." He chuckled slightly, relaxing. "Well, I suppose we *are* technically paying you if you agree. But that's for a service… I wouldn't attempt to buy your decision." He looked back to the painting. "It's absolutely stunning, and the fact you can't see that breaks my heart. You're so talented."

Gray watched as Jamie stared at his work. "You really think so?"

"Yes! I'm jealous of your talent," Jamie said. He tilted his head. "Is this the koi pond from *Mill Street Park* in the Family Quadrant?"

"What I remember of it," Gray said, staring across the surface, longing to relive those days. "I haven't been in nearly twenty years. I loved sitting there and feeding the fish when I was younger." A smile played over Gray's lips as the memories assaulted him. The warmth of the sun. The laughter as he raced through the park with his brother. He could almost hear the sounds in his mind—and how he longed to have the freedom to return there once again.

He swallowed back the sadness that suddenly slammed into him, harder than he could ever recall. Maybe it was because the omega standing beside him did have the freedom he lacked. Gray slanted a gaze at Jamie as the man began to speak and knew he had no right to hold on to any kind of jealousy. Not with the battle he'd just waged.

"Wilder and I used to sit on that little bridge and feed the fish on Sunday mornings," Jamie said, laying a reverent hand over the painting, a soft smile on his face. He lifted his gaze to Gray's. "It's a wonder we never ran into one another over the years. I loved this spot. So serene..." He turned back and looked at the painting once more. "I *need* some serenity in my life right now."

"I really wish you'd take it," Gray murmured. "I don't need your money."

"You have three boys to help support... and new paint supplies to purchase... so you can continue making these brilliant works of art." Jamie paused and looked down, cocking his head to the side. He took a step and then paused to glance at Gray, his eyes wide with joy. "Oh my... does that one go with this? It looks like the rose garden on the other side of the park."

"It does... and it is," Gray said with a smile. The fact Jamie could recognize those places was good for his heart. His memory had served him well, it seemed.

"I'd love them both if you can part with them. Do we have a deal?" Jamie placed a hand before Gray.

"I have a feeling I won't win this fight."

Jamie's grin only grew stronger, with a hint of something wicked within. "When I want something, I *don't* lose."

Gray chuckled before he shook Jamie's hand. "Deal."

Jamie set the painting down against the easel and rubbed his hands together. "Show me more. I might need another."

* * * *

Rohan came home to see three large paintings sitting in the foyer, propped against the wall. He lowered his briefcase and lifted the one at the front, his gaze drawn by the swirling play of color. Whoever it was, they were *very* talented. He tried to pick out the name scrawled at the bottom of the piece.

Gray?

Rohan frowned as a scent came off the canvas… one that had him growling and clutching the edge of the inner wooden frame.

"Isn't it stunning?" Jamie said as he strolled into the foyer.

"It is. Who's the artist?" Asking as if he couldn't guess.

"Our potential surrogate, Gray."

Rohan tried to hide the wince at having his suspicions confirmed. He lowered the first and looked at the others—all lovely in their own right. "And how much did you pay him for his work?"

"He didn't want me to pay, but I insisted," Jamie said before turning and heading back toward the kitchen.

"Of course he didn't," Rohan drawled as he followed his omega. "But he took your money, didn't he?"

Jamie was silent as he pulled a container of sparkling water from the refrigerator and poured himself a glass. And then poured another before handing it to Rohan. "I had to convince him. He was willing to hand them over for free. I wouldn't hear of it, not someone this talented. Gray needs to know how skilled he is."

Rohan took the glass. Before he took a drink, he added, "You shouldn't have done that, Jamie."

"And why not?"

"Why does a surrogate choose to carry another's child?" Rohan asked, setting the glass on the counter. "Because they need money. You barely know this omega. Be careful."

"If you'd met him already, you would understand. He's…" Jamie smiled. "Well, I've absolutely fallen in love with him."

Rohan paused, his hackles rising. "Fallen in love?"

Jamie smiled. "Not in the way I love you." He grinned. "No one will ever replace you in my heart. You know that."

"So this love of yours is brotherly?"

"I suppose you could call it that. And shouldn't I feel affection for someone who might carry our child? He'll be the true papa to our babe. The fact we already have a connection is wonderful."

"*If* he agrees… don't get ahead of yourself." Rohan leaned a hip against the counter. "And once any babe is born, he won't have any rights to it. He'll be ours. Gray will no longer be in the picture."

Jamie gave him an odd look. "I know, I know. I just sense something special about him. I feel it, Rohan. This is the one. This is the omega for us."

Rohan watched as Jamie twirled in the kitchen and added some spices to the pot simmering on the stove. "You seem in good spirits today."

"I am. I even feel *famished*. How about that? I can't recall the last time I didn't have to force myself to eat something."

"You had no problems eating a couple of slices of pizza this weekend."

"I didn't want to alarm Wilder," Jamie said. "But I really didn't feel like eating much that night. I made myself eat them since he'd gone through so much trouble."

Rohan sidled over to his omega and gripped Jamie's hips from behind. He left a peck on his mate's neck and then looked over his shoulder. "Beef stew? You *must* be feeling good." It did him well to see Jamie in such high spirits.

"I don't know how much I'll actually eat, but I'm going to try."

Rohan kissed the side of Jamie's cheek and inhaled his mate's scent. Closing his eyes, he felt his body respond. He inadvertently rubbed his thickening shaft against his omega's ass.

Jamie stiffened and pulled away.

"I didn't mean to…" Rohan sighed, backing up a step. Of course seeing Jamie so full of excitement and energy had gotten to him. It had been months since they'd been intimate. Not once had Rohan pressed sex during Jamie's illness—and he hadn't been pressing just then either. It had simply been a reaction to being close to the man he loved. A man who was slowly coming back to him, it seemed. "I wasn't trying to suggest anything. I was just caught up in the moment and excited to see you so well."

"I can't," Jamie mumbled over one shoulder.

"You don't have to."

They were silent a few moments before Jamie turned to Rohan. "What if my desire for you never comes back?"

Rohan couldn't breathe for a moment. The thought of never being intimate with the man he loved was enough to bring him to his knees. His instinct to breed didn't end just because his omega wasn't able—it wouldn't fade for some time. He'd squashed that innate need time and time again, refusing to let it come to the surface. "I've never once made demands on you. And I don't plan to now."

"Now. But what about six months from now? Or a year? Two?"

Rohan was silent a moment. "We'll cross that bridge when we get to it."

Jamie stepped closer, wrapping his arms around Rohan's waist. "You know I love you, right?"

Rohan drew his omega closer, pressing a kiss to Jamie's forehead. "I do. And I love you even more."

Jamie nuzzled closer.

Rohan told himself this would be enough.

Jamie would *always* be enough.

No matter what.

Chapter Nine

A couple of weeks later...

"Where are you?" Gray mumbled as he searched through the small recipe box, looking for one he knew was within. As soon as he found it, he slid it from the box and scanned the ingredients...

And realized they were in Silver's perfect penmanship.

Gray ran his hands over the surface, recalling in that moment when his brother had brought him a copy of their grandpapa's old family recipe after he'd hounded Silver for it. It had been when he'd been younger... and assumed he'd one day have an alpha to take care of. He'd wanted to practice the recipe and perfect it—as the way to an alpha's heart was supposedly through his stomach.

Gray chuckled mirthlessly.

How stupid and simple he'd been back then, when he'd thought there was a future for him to come. He stared at the recipe card for long minutes, wishing he had Silver with them again... so perhaps he'd feel a little less lonely.

An unexpected knock came to the door. Gray washed and dried his hands before he walked through the cottage—and he forced away the sadness trying to once again take over.

He found Jamie on his doorstep, nearly bouncing with excited energy.

"I hope you don't mind me stopping in unannounced," Jamie said, a glow of happiness to his eyes and face. "But I *had* to see you."

"Of course I don't mind," Gray said. He backed away from the entrance. "Come in."

Jamie swept through, bringing his nervous energy with him. He paused in the foyer and spun to face Gray.

"What has you so excited?"

A brilliant smile came to his face. "We did it."

"We? Did what?"

Jamie smile widened even more. "I'm in remission!"

Gray leapt forward, drawing Jamie into a fierce hug. "I'm so, so happy for you."

"Thank you," Jamie murmured, squeezing him back tightly before pulling away. He wiped a happy tear from the corner of his eye. "After Rohan and Wilder... I just *had* to come tell you. I know my health... I know it's weighed on you and this decision to come."

Gray grinned. "Are you only here for a moment... or did you want to come in and sit a few minutes?"

Jamie took a deep inhale and let out a breath. "I don't have long... but I'd love to sit and talk a moment."

Gray led Jamie into the breakfast nook before putting on a kettle while Jamie regaled him with more news from the doctors.

"I hope I'm not interrupting anything?" Jamie asked, fiddling with a saltshaker on the table.

"Not at all. I was just prepping for dinner, but it can wait a few minutes," Gray answered before grabbing two mugs from the cabinet and moving them to the table. He placed bags in each. "I have some time before the boys get back from the summer program."

"How are they enjoying it?" Jamie asked.

"I think they'd both rather be sitting at home, playing video games and eating junk food all summer... but after everything, I think it's best they keep busy."

Jamie nodded, his smile faltering some. "How are *you* doing?"

Gray paused a moment, feeling another swell of sadness come over him. "To be honest? A little lonely. I miss my brother more and more each day."

"I assume you two were close?"

"He was my best friend." Gray paused as the kettle whistled. He rose and crossed the kitchen, taking it from the burner. As he returned to the table, he finished, "He was my confidant... the person I could tell anything to."

Silence fell between them as Gray poured the water over the tea bags.

"I know we've only just met... but if I can ever lend an ear, I would be happy to."

Gray smiled. There was something safe and comfortable about Jamie. He almost felt compelled to share his secrets with the man. But the decision that faced him... he needed to keep some separation between them until he made up his mind. He set the kettle back on the stove before walking back to the table and taking his seat. "I appreciate that. But you're here to share good news. Not be caught up in my melancholy."

Jamie tugged the tea bag lightly, his nervous energy unable to be fully contained. He lifted his stare. "If I can be honest?"

Gray nodded.

"I feel this kinship to you. I can't explain it… but I feel like we've known each other forever. And even… even if you decided you didn't want to be our surrogate… for whatever reason… I think I would be sad to lose your friendship." Jamie lifted his stare and met Gray's. "I haven't felt this comfortable around someone… well… since I met my alpha."

Gray grinned slightly, a tiny glimmer of jealousy flaring deep down. He wished he'd had his own alpha to make him feel like that… but that wasn't his future. And he, too, felt the odd kinship Jamie had mentioned. "I wouldn't want to lose your friendship, either."

There were too few older omegas in the Quad. They came and went… leaving him behind to meet the new batch of omegas consigned to live there until their alphas whisked them away, too. After a while, making new friends felt almost too difficult. They would only leave him there alone at some point—so he'd just given up.

When Avery had come to live there, it had been his first friend in ages… but there was still only so much he could share with his nephew. And with Avery looking for work and applying to colleges… he had little time left over anyway.

"So tell me… what's been on your mind?" Jamie asked.

Gray stared down at his cup… knowing he should keep everything to himself… "This decision…

it weighs on me. Though now, I suppose your news today helps some."

"I can't even begin to imagine the thoughts running through your mind," Jamie said. "I'm asking the world of you... when all you can think of is providing for your family."

"There's more to it... than that."

Jamie cocked his head to the side.

"*Heat Repress*... it has begun to fail me."

A frown crossed Jamie's face. "I didn't know that was possible."

He took a sip from his cup. "My reasons for this aren't fully motivated by my nephews. I'm hoping nearly a year off the drug will reset my body and allow me to return to it once the babe is born."

"Couldn't you just go off it for a month or two?"

"I can barely get by with the drug now. I'd lose my mind without it."

Jamie frowned. "You do have someone... who helps you... a beta?"

Gray shook his head. "What do you mean?"

"I just assumed you had a lover... or someone who helped you through your heats," Jamie said, his eyes widening. "I mean... you said you didn't think you had an alpha out there... so I guess..." Jamie's frown deepened. "No one? So you're a..."

"A virgin. Yes."

Jamie looked stunned.

"Well, technically," Gray added, his face growing hot. "I've helped myself."

"Understandably!" Jamie leaned forward. "Perhaps that's your answer. A beta to help soothe you during your heats. I mean, I know they don't have the power to impregnate... but the real thing versus some toy should help take a bit of the edge off."

"I suppose," Gray answered. "But then surrogacy helps me provide for my nephews… so it seems the better choice. For now. After? Who knows…"

"You've saved yourself for a long time," Jamie said. "Now you'll lose it to someone other than your alpha." He sighed. "That can't be easy."

Gray opened his mouth to argue and realized there was some truth to that.

"For someone so sure he has no alpha, I would've thought you'd let go of that a long time ago," Jamie added after a moment of silence.

Had there been a glimmer of hope he'd held on to for all these years? "I guess… I don't know… we have so many ideals shoved into our heads starting at a young age. I suppose the thought of offering myself up to someone not my alpha just hadn't even come to mind."

Jamie took a sip from his cup, looking over the rim at Gray. There was something in that look that made Gray feel as if the man could see through him.

"I understand. It's just like this fervent need I feel to give my alpha a child—in any way possible." Jamie lowered his cup, the fine porcelain clinking delicately together. "No matter how many times he tells me he doesn't need a child, I know he can't mean it. We were all raised with the expectation."

"And you still persist."

Jamie nodded. "I do. For good reason."

Gray had already heard Jamie's tales of Rohan and how amazing he thought his alpha was. Soon, Gray would get the chance to see how well Jamie had described the alpha and if the picture inside his mind was anything close to the real thing.

Jamie took another sip before his eyes went wide. "Oh, I forgot to tell you about the dinner party my papa put on recently. My brother, Wilder, was just promoted at work—and they had this huge celebration. Of course, my papa demanded full dress. You should've seen my alpha and my brothers in their tuxes—so handsome. Why they're unattached at this point, I do *not* understand."

"*Neither* are mated?" Gray asked.

"No... and I don't think Wild is interested in mating at all. At least right now. He's *so* focused on his career..."

Avery suddenly rushed into the kitchen, carrying a letter, and Jamie's words faded in his ears. There was a mixture of panic and excitement in his nephew's eyes.

"What's wrong?" Gray asked, his chest tightening.

"Nothing," Avery murmured.

Gray sensed Avery pushing the envelope closer to him, as if he wanted someone else to open it.

Jamie looked between them and obviously sensed Avery's hesitance. He rose from his seat. "I'll get out of your hair and let you share your news."

"I can wait," Avery said, eyeing Jamie. "I didn't mean to rush you off. Stay, enjoy your tea."

Gray had only just introduced the two—and he sensed whatever Avery had to share might have something to do with illegal activities. Had Avery already been caught? Panic truly slammed into him then and there.

Thankfully, Jamie lifted a bag from the back of the chair. "No, no... you didn't rush me off. My alpha is likely waiting for me to return with news of my own." A smile crossed his face as he stepped closer to Gray and offered a hug.

Gray wrapped Jamie in a tight embrace. "Congratulations again."

"Thank you," Jamie said before he kissed Gray's cheek.

Accompanying Jamie to the door, Gray waved the man off before closing the door and spinning to see an anxious Avery waiting for him.

"What have you gotten yourself into now?"

Avery handed over the envelope.

Gray looked it over, his eyes growing wider. *The College of Waltyn & Marris.*

The prestigious college was Avery's first choice—not that there were many to choose from in the city. He knew Avery didn't intend to go far from the boys. They were lucky to have one of the oldest and best colleges in their province a trolley ride away.

"You haven't even opened it."

"I can't. I need you to do it for me."

Gray eyed him. "You sure? I don't want to steal your moment."

Avery lifted both his hands and waved Gray on. "Yes, I'm sure! *Open* it!"

After a second's hesitation, Gray sliced open the top edge and pulled out a thick sheet of paper. He scanned the letter silently, trying to keep a blank look on his face.

What if Avery *hadn't* been accepted? He almost wished his nephew wouldn't be. A stack of no's would potentially keep him alive.

Unfortunately, that wasn't the case. Horror filled him as he lifted his face to Avery.

Avery snatched the letter from his hands and read the first couple of lines aloud. The same few lines that had crushed Gray.

"Congratulations, Abraham Norcross! You've been selected as one of our incoming freshman class members for the school year 3713-14." Avery lifted his stare to his uncle. "Jerk," he said, grinning at Gray.

Lowering his head, Avery continued to read aloud. "We recommend you schedule a visit with one of our counselors soon to enroll in your first semester of classes. Orientation will commence on the fifth of Augustin, and another packet will arrive soon with more details."

"Congratulations," Gray said, forcing the word from his lips. "Although I'm scared as hell for you right now."

"I'm scared, too."

For four years Avery would have to hide who he was, in close confines, and that was before he made it out to the Alpha Quadrant's business district to use the degree he'd seek. Sure, there were companies all over their province, but the money was in the business district. Knowing Avery, he'd want to make as much as he could.

The boy had seemed to see himself as bulletproof lately.

Hearing that he, too, was scared helped Gray a little. Avery would need to be careful... not too self-assured.

"Hopefully I can keep up with the classes."

That wasn't the doubt Avery needed to have. Being caught, sure. His intelligence? Not hardly. "The transcript only faked your name, not your grades and test scores. You *earned* that spot, just like everyone else who applied," Gray said, giving him a hug. "You're bright. Always have been. You're going to do well, I know it."

Avery squeezed his uncle tight. "Thank you for reminding me. I needed to hear it."

Gray stepped back and looked up at Avery. "You've always had a head for numbers, just like Silver." Gray's eyes suddenly shined with tears. "If only he was here now, to see this."

"I doubt papa would be happy I was pretending to be a beta and going to college."

Gray lifted his chin. "I think the conservative side of him would hate it... but the part of him that was proud of his sons would've sent him through the moon that you'd gotten that spot."

Avery smiled at his uncle, his eyes shining with unshed tears. "Thank you."

"A little part of me is excited you'll have a chance to prove omegas can be more than husbands and fathers. I think Silver would've enjoyed that, too."

Gray patted the side of his cheek before wiping away a stray tear. He headed for the kitchen, scooping up the two cups on the table in the nook on his way. "Want a cup of tea? I think I need another myself. It's been an eventful day."

"Sure," Avery said. He trailed his uncle into the large kitchen and slid into one of the chairs behind the island. "Why's it been so eventful?"

Gray smiled softly as he filled the tea kettle at the island's sink. "Lots of good news today."

"You're not going to share?"

Gray place the kettle on the stove before turning back to lean against the island facing Avery. "Jamie just learned he's in remission."

Avery smiled. "That's wonderful news. I could tell he wasn't well… and you've been so reticent to share anything about him. Is it cancer?"

"*Was* cancer. He's now been given the thumbs up from his oncologist and has the rest of his life before him."

"I wish you'd told me sooner. I would've loved to congratulate him myself before he left."

Gray smiled absentmindedly as he gathered another large mug from the cup tree for Avery.

"Who is he? To you?" Avery asked.

Gray was silent as he placed a tea bag into each cup. He finally lifted his stare to Avery. "I'm in discussions to carry Jamie and his alpha's babe."

Avery frowned. "You can't."

"I can. And I will—if the meeting with his alpha goes smoothly next week. I plan to contribute to this family one way or another, Avery. I have no skills… no job. You'll need me here to watch the boys after school while you're off getting a college education. This way, I can help you pay for that education *and* take care of the boys."

"And the child-bond?"

"Jamie and Rohan might agree to let me visit the boy on occasion. To be a small part of his life. An uncle, they can call me."

"Is that wise? It could potentially make the severed bond worse."

Gray shrugged. "Only time will tell."

Silence fell between them… and was soon shattered by the screaming of the tea kettle. Gray walked over and lifted it from the flames before pouring their cups. One was slid before Avery, and the sound of spoons clinking porcelain was the only sound in the room.

"I know you think I'm irresponsible and this is a bad idea... but I've spent weeks getting to know Jamie. I've given surrogacy a lot of thought. I'm thirty-five, without an alpha, and my body *craves* a child. You of anyone understands the primal need to breed within us. Imagine what you feel now... eighteen years later without being sated. I've been on *Heat Repress* for over half my life. It might calm the instinct, but it *never* fades completely."

Avery was silent.

"Jamie lost his womb to cancer. All his life, he—like all omegas—has been told he was born to give his alpha a child. That his whole life would revolve around pregnancy and giving birth to a family. Now that's been ripped away from him."

"And what about *your* needs? Your wants? If you have this child, your own alpha could refuse you."

"*What* alpha? I feel like a broken record, repeating the same answer over and over again. Nobody listens. *Enough*. Let it go."

Avery released a sigh.

"You're refusing to sit back and let fate rule your life. So am I. It's my body... and my decision. I can help our family, help you and the boys, *and* help Jamie and Rohan with this one single act. And perhaps it will help me, too. Once I have a son, my biological need to reproduce will hopefully calm some. My heats are getting unbearable, Avery. The *Heat Repress*... it's not working as well as it once did. It wasn't meant for an omega to spend so long taking it without a pregnancy breaking up the use. I can't go off of it... so what else am I to do?"

After a moment of thought, Avery nodded. "You're right. It *is* your body... and I have no right to tell you what to do. It's apparent you've put a lot of thought into this. I might not agree, but I *can* support your right to make this decision. I'll stand behind you and help any way I can... if you go through with it."

Gray sighed. "Thank you for that."

"I just worry about the impact this will have on you and your future. That was my only cause for concern. I love you, Uncle Gray... and I only want what's best for you."

"I understand that. But this *is* what's best for all of us."

Avery didn't look convinced, but the boy had no right to make decisions for Gray—especially when he was being supportive of his nephew's own drastic decisions. "I hope so."

But his drastic decisions had been to eliminate Gray's need to do something like this...

If he failed there, how else might he fail?

Chapter Ten

In a border conference room…

"I'm glad you made it through okay," Tensen said with a smile as he opened the conference door for Gray a couple of weeks later. "Come in, come in."

Gray stepped into the room, just as nervous and excited as he was when he'd met Jamie for the first time. Once through the door, he'd expected a big board table and chairs circling it like he'd seen in movies. Instead, this was a small room of chairs and settees in a semi-circle and felt a bit homier than business like.

It helped put him a little at ease.

His gaze fell on Jamie's bright smile. "You're here!"

Jamie rushed over and spun Gray to face the man he was there to meet.

As soon as he set sight on Rohan, the air rushed from his lungs. The man was stunning… perfectly made in every way. Big and muscled as any alpha, he wore an expensive-looking tailored suit that showed wide shoulders and a narrow waist. The alpha's scent hit Gray… and he paused to inhale a little of it. Lust washed over him, his body rocked by need. He'd just gone through his heat the week before, so he didn't understand the sensations running through him.

Some of Gray's cream slickened his ass. Mortification filled him. There was also no missing the sudden clench to Rohan's jaw.

The alpha *had* to scent him...

Dark eyes met his before that stare swept completely over him. Gray saw lust there in that gaze and had to remind himself it was all an instinctual reaction. An alpha scenting an available omega—that's all it was.

And in that moment, he wished he'd injected some of Avery's scent blocker. He hadn't even thought about it... but then, why would he? He had little experience with alphas. His father, and a few friends who'd come over every so often when he was young—but once he'd gone into heat that first time, he'd been sequestered away. Even though Rohan had an omega all his own, it wouldn't completely subdue the animal instinct within Rohan. Jamie and Tensen couldn't scent him... only the alpha in the room would know.

Gray couldn't look away from the alpha's dark, fierce stare. His body shook with need...

And the desire to bow down then and there to be taken. He snagged his gaze away, shame filling him.

Jamie babbled on, seemingly oblivious to what was happening. "I couldn't wait for you two to meet... it feels like such a long time coming. So, without further ado—Rohan, this is Gray. Gray, my alpha, Rohan."

He lifted his stare to Rohan's once more. The alpha's gaze was locked on him. Gray felt his skin tingling... butterflies spinning in his gut...

All for a man he couldn't have...

A man he might carry a child for.

Gray clenched his own jaw thinking of his womb filled with Rohan's child. His womb clenched, too. *My gods... if only I could have him fill me the old-fashioned way.*

As soon as the thought whispered through his mind, he felt terrible. More shame mounted on the heaps already overwhelming him. He couldn't stand there wanting another omega's alpha. Especially when that omega had become so special to him.

Rohan rose to his full height, towering over them both, and put a large hand out before Gray. He was almost afraid to take it, fearful of what his body might do from even an innocent touch. After he saw an odd, fearful look cross Jamie's face, he took Rohan's hand with his and shook. It was a shock to his system, that simple handshake.

Electricity arced up his arm, and fire spread across his body. He looked down, unwilling to meet the man's eyes, not as lust slammed into him. "Very nice to meet you."

"Likewise," Rohan murmured.

The rumbling growl to Rohan's voice made him slick with more of his juices. He closed his eyes and yanked his hand away, ashamed. When he reopened them, Jamie wore an odder expression—staring between the two of them.

He belongs to Jamie.
He belongs to Jamie.
Stop wanting what you can't have.

The instinct didn't care about claims on another. The instinct simply *wanted*. The years and years of neglect had left his body ravished by desire, and now his failure to find an alpha of his own was coming back to haunt him in the worst possible way.

"Why don't we all take a seat and get comfortable," Tensen interjected, his normal jovial self.

Comfortable? Not hardly.

Jamie sat down beside Gray and across from his alpha. Gray did everything in his power to not look at the big, powerful man before him. Which, of course, soon grew impossible. His stare was drawn to the man like a magnet.

"I've told Rohan so much about you over the last few weeks. On the way here, he said it felt as if he already knew you," Jamie prattled on.

Gray smiled, struggling to think of what to say. Over their tea confessionals, Jamie had already shared much about Rohan, too. Gray sensed the two were very much in love. *He loves Jamie. Jamie loves him. Stop being such an asshole.* "I also... feel like I know a lot... about you," he mumbled, his mouth feeling as if it were full of rocks.

"Are you okay?" Jamie asked, frowning. "Is something upsetting you?"

Gray looked anywhere but forward. "I'm... I'm fine."

"You have to recall that Gray likely hasn't been in the presence of an alpha in a good many years," Tensen said softly.

Gray lifted his stare to the solicitor and saw the soft smile there. He was thankful someone seemed to understand, but to what extent, Gray wasn't sure. Tensen was the lifeline in the room, and he desperately wanted to reach out and hold on for dear life.

Save me.

"Oh, I hadn't even considered that," Jamie said, putting a hand on Gray's. "I'm sorry I didn't realize. How could I be so thoughtless?"

"I can leave, if you wish it," Rohan murmured.

The fine hairs on the back of Gray's neck rose, and he had to close his eyes against the wave of lust that washed through him. He felt his juices slipping from him, his womb clenching. The full moon was three weeks away, yet he felt as if he was in heat then and there.

"Just… don't talk," Gray spat in Rohan's direction.

"Well, how are you supposed to get to know him if he doesn't talk?" Jamie asked.

"Can you and Rohan step outside a moment?" Tensen suddenly asked Jamie.

Jamie frowned and turned to Rohan—confusion on his face—but he nodded. He rubbed Gray's arm lovingly before rising to his feet and trailing behind his alpha. Rohan eyed him a moment, eyes bright with lust before he, too, left the room.

Once the door was closed, Tensen opened two of the windows and let a breeze wash into the room. The air was warm, but it was as effective as a bucket of ice water. Tensen walked closer and sat down on the coffee table in front of Gray. He handed him a piece of hard candy. "Suck on this."

Gray frowned up at the man.

"I think you're having a case of contact heat. I didn't expect it in someone your age—it's typically much older unclaimed omegas who I've seen experience it. I'm trying to air the room some to clear his scent… the candy will supposedly help mask it a little, as well. Or so I'm told."

Gray took the small peppermint, unwrapped it, and popped it in his mouth. "Was it that obvious?"

"Not to Jamie, I'm sure. I'm assuming Rohan likely scented you," Tensen said. "But if he has he's holding onto his control magnificently." Tensen lifted a hand, as if he would brush back a few strands of Gray's hair—but he stopped and pulled his hand away. "But then, after seeing the two of them together previously and researching his background, I wouldn't expect any less from Rohan."

Knowing Rohan was likely battling the same demons—and apparently winning—only made him feel worse.

Silence fell around them for a moment as Gray tried to get ahold of himself. The peppermint seemed to be helping some. He wasn't sure if it was the power of suggestion or that it truly worked. Either way, he appreciated Tensen's keen power of observation and his kindness.

"Thank you… if it wasn't for you…"

Tensen smiled. "Don't mention it. It's why I'm here."

"Please don't tell Jamie how I reacted. I already feel enough shame that Rohan likely knows."

Tensen smiled softly. "I would never embarrass you like that. I've done dozens of these surrogate contracts, and I've learned a thing or two over the years. It would never do well for him to know."

"His alpha might tell him."

"I have a sensation that Rohan won't. I'm sure he's as uncomfortable as you are."

Gray sighed. "How in the world am I going to be able to help them if I can barely be in his presence?"

Tensen stretched his arms out and placed them on his knees. "Well, it might be difficult, at first. But once you're pregnant, there's little chance of it continuing."

But then what after that? Gray had hoped to see the child occasionally. Although, it would likely be Jamie bringing the boy to the Omega Quadrant, as Gray couldn't leave. He'd probably see little to nothing of Rohan over the coming months.

That allowed him to relax a little more.

"If you're not comfortable and want to end the meeting, I can ask them to go. I'm a strong believer in *all* parties feeling safe and secure with what's taking place. I won't force a potential surrogate into an untenable situation."

Gray smiled at Tensen. "You're *their* attorney."

"Legally, I represent the babe that might come from this contract. It's set up that way so I'm not to favor either side. I'm capable of putting an end to discussions if I feel there's an issue that one or both parties aren't confronting or fully truthful about. Like Jamie's illness… I had major qualms about looking for a surrogate for them because of it. I did my due diligence because I wanted to ensure that he would be around to be a papa to the babe that came. And that a surrogate wouldn't be left in the lurch if the worst was to come. I still haven't given my full blessing to this agreement—although the recent news of remission is a good omen."

"Has that ever happened before? Has a someone died while a surrogate was pregnant?"

"I'd be lying if I said no. Accidents happen at the most unexpected of times, as you well know."

Gray met Tensen's stare. If the solicitor had done his research, as he claimed, he would know of the accident that had claimed his brother's life.

Tensen gave a soft smile. "Does it happen often? No. Although—there are some solicitors who turn a blind eye to certain issues and approve a contract they shouldn't. Because of that, there have been a few instances that could've been avoided. The fact that Jamie and Rohan didn't turn to one of those less savory solicitors? That showed me they might be honest folks not tempted to take the easier route—which led me to my decision to keep an open mind about his illness."

"And now that he's in remission, it proves you were right to keep that open mind... and makes me think I need to power through and finish this meeting. For Jamie. He's already gone through hell and back."

Tensen smiled. "You ready? Or would you like another moment or two?"

"Give me another minute, please," Gray said. He rose and walked over to one of the open windows and took a deep breath.

"Good idea," Tensen said. He slid one of the chairs closer to the window before turning the small settee around to face it. "Stay by the window there. The breeze will help keep you calm."

He grabbed Tensen's arm. "I can't thank you enough. I never would've expected you to go to such lengths for an omega."

Tensen laid a warm hand over Gray's. "You are no less than anyone else. And should never be treated as such." The solicitor's stare met his, and he saw a depth of kindness Gray couldn't recall seeing in anyone but his own family.

The solicitor lifted his hand and this time, it didn't stop. He brushed a strand of hair from Gray's cheek and tucked it behind one ear. The graze of his fingers... while unexpected, wasn't unappreciated. He met Tensen's gaze and sensed more than just kindness there.

Perhaps it was just the residual lust from meeting Rohan... but he was sure he saw a hint of attraction coming from Tensen. Gray looked away, feeling awkward. The beta was brokering a deal where he might end up pregnant with another man's baby.

If only they were different people... meeting in any other way.

Betas remained with their own, marrying and living together in the Beta Quadrant. They were typically childness, unless they adopted, which seemed to happen more and more often in more recent years.

"Please, that was forward of me and I apologize." Tensen patted Gray's hand before pulling his away. "Just say the word when and if you're ready to proceed."

Gray took a seat and drew in a deep breath. "I'm ready."

Tensen nodded and headed to the door to ask that Jamie and Rohan return. Once inside, Jamie looked concerned. "Are you alright?"

"Yes," Gray said, avoiding Rohan's heated stare. "I just... needed a moment."

A hint of the alpha's scent came across the room, but Gray turned his head toward the window.

"Have you decided not to move forward?" Jamie asked, his voice and nature hesitant. He took short, brief steps, as if he was afraid to get any closer—fearful Gray would send them away.

"No. Quite the opposite. I *want* to do this."

A beautiful smile spread across Jamie's face. He walked nearer and then leaned down to hug Gray. "You don't know how happy I am to hear that. I was so worried…"

"Thank you," Rohan murmured, seeming to keep his distance. For which Gray was appreciative.

"Wonderful," Tensen added, but the smile seemed to have faded from his normally cheerful face. "I'll get started on the paperwork and have you back soon to sign the agreement."

"There's one thing I wanted to discuss first," Jamie said, turning to look at everyone there. "I don't want this child made in a lab. I want it created through natural process."

"What?" both Gray and Rohan asked in the same moment.

Jamie looked away. "I *am* within my rights to choose the method."

"Technically, he is… the law states the alpha's omega can choose the method of conception," Tensen interrupted, looking a bit confused before he turned. "But Jamie, that law was put in writing because most omegas prefer their surrogate have the babe implanted through artificial insemination. Not the other way around."

Gray had already done the research into the process. From what he'd seen, artificial insemination wasn't reliable. It didn't take in many cases, yet he'd still assumed that was the way it would happen between them. How could Jamie want the opposite?

Before medical advances had made artificial insemination possible, all surrogates were impregnated during a heat. While he was aware that a small percentage of surrogates still agreed to it, he *couldn't* do it naturally. Not after the reaction he'd just had to Rohan. He wouldn't bed another omega's alpha, especially not after how close he'd already become to Jamie.

It was insane to even imagine it.

"I don't want my child to be made in a cold, sterile laboratory. I've been stuck in too many of those myself as of late, and I don't want that to be the way this life is created."

Rohan spoke up as Gray sat there stunned. "You wish for me to lie with another omega? I can't. *I won't.* I made a vow to you upon our claiming, and I don't intend to break it. Not even for this."

Jamie turned to eye his alpha. "Please, Rohan… I don't ask much from you. I *want* this child."

"I've agreed to the child, even though I fear what stress it might put on you… I just can't agree to this manner." Rohan argued. "Please don't ask me this. I beg you."

Gray's flash of lust for Rohan now came back to haunt him. He'd told himself he'd have next to no contact with the alpha and here Jamie was suggesting they bed one another?

He'd been all prepared for a surgical approach. Gray would be put under for the three days of his heat while Rohan's seed would be implanted within, hoping for the best. What Jamie suggested wouldn't be so simple. He'd have to be awake through his heat. Rohan would have to accommodate him for three days of sex in the attempt to make a babe. And what if it didn't work the first heat? How many heats would it take?

Yet wasn't it what he'd wished for upon first entering and spying Rohan.

He'd asked for this.

Be careful what you wish for…

Gray struggled to speak. "I don't know that I can agree…"

Jamie walked over and knelt at Gray's feet. "I spent hours in chemo… sitting in a chair, hooked up to a machine shooting poison into my veins. Hours… week after week… watching the other omegas around me withering away and fearing I was, too. In and out of the hospital… surgeries… I don't want this new life to begin someplace like that. *It can't.*"

Gray stared into the man's face. Over the weeks, their long conversations… he felt like they'd known each other forever. There was a bond of friendship that had forged so quickly… but this was too much to ask.

"There *is* data that proves natural insemination is three times more likely to work than artificial," Tensen murmured. "Considering the fee for each artificial insemination… it could get costly. With the hormone injections and various procedures—it could wear on you all. I know of surrogates who try for years to become pregnant via that route with no luck."

"Years!" Jamie cried. "Or we could make arrangements for you to be brought to our home for your next heat. Rohan could tend to you. And the chances of you becoming pregnant the natural way are so much higher." Jamie paused, smiling. "A babe made naturally, the way the gods intended."

Gray lifted his stare, but he could barely look at Rohan. From the vibe in the room, he knew the alpha didn't like the idea any better than he did.

He shook his head. "It's not right."

"Please," Jamie pleaded. "You were ready to say yes… just *please*, think it over. It would be better for all of us this way." Jamie lowered his voice. He whispered, "*All those years of Heat Repress… Let me help you.*"

Shock rolled over Gray at the last comments. He met the omega's stare, his mouth falling open.

"No… you can't," Gray said, feeling numb.

And feeling sick that he sensed a rising lust at the thought of bedding Rohan and taking care of those needs. He'd never been with an alpha. Never had one to tend to him during a heat. His curiosity alone urged him to say yes.

But how could he lay with Jamie's alpha and make a child? A child he would hand over to the pair of them and potentially never see again—no matter if he got their promises for him to see the boy. Legally, he'd have no right, regardless if it was in the contract, and they would be free to keep him away.

He rose to his feet. "I need to go."

"Promise me you'll consider my request," Jamie asked, placing his hand on Gray's shoulder. "I don't want to wait years for a child. Do you?"

Gray shook his head silently before escaping the room. He rushed down the hall and took the corner before rushing into the bathroom. After splashing his face, he lifted his stare to the mirror.

How could he do this?

The bathroom door opened suddenly… and Rohan entered. Their eyes met in the mirror before

Gray looked down. He shook his hands to get more of the water off before heading for the door and passing the alpha.

Rohan reached out to stop him. "I didn't ask him to do this... I had no idea."

Another surge of heat spread through Gray, his asshole coated with cream. "I didn't think you did," Gray said without looking at the man.

Rohan dropped his hold. "I *love* my omega. With every piece of me. The thought of lying with another? Kills me... yet disappointing him and not doing something he desperately wants?" Rohan sighed. "I can't win, either way. You... on the other hand... you're not beholden to him. You haven't signed an agreement... no contract. If you were to say no... it would put an end to this madness."

Rohan didn't want him. Why would he? He loved his own omega—yet the sound in the alpha's voice tore at him. And made him feel even more lonely and unwanted than he'd felt before the meeting. "Are you prepared for me to break his heart and not give him the child he wants so desperately?"

From the corner of Gray's stare, he could see Rohan's jaw clench. "I've told him I don't need a child... I've told him that he's enough. He won't listen." The alpha released a sigh. "We just got through one hell and now this?" The alpha shook his head. "If you say no to his demand... he'll give in. He wants this child. He'll accept your terms, I know it."

"It's only been a few weeks since I met Jamie, I know, but he and I..." Gray paused, tears coming to his eyes. "He's special... your omega. Even in the face of tragedy and illness, he has a light... a fire inside him that you just can't look away from. I barely know him, but at the same time, I feel like I've always known him."

Gray could hear the smile in Rohan's response. "He *is* special. You should've seen him before the cancer. A wild, free spirit..." Rohan sighed. "Hopefully he'll soon be back to his old self. So we can get back to being *us* again. The *us* before we had to think about death and dying."

He lifted his stare to finally meet Rohan's. It was obvious the alpha was deeply in love. "He wants new life to hold close. He's told me as much. New life to breathe fresh air into his that was touched by death. I can understand this last request... after all he's been through. His life has hung in the balance, in the hands of doctors. He doesn't want this new life to be touched by that, too. I don't know that I can take that hope away from him. Not without guilt eating me alive."

Lies... that's not the only reason... I'm a selfish bastard...

Would a few nights in Rohan's arms give him a glimpse into what it would feel like to be loved by an alpha? This could be his only chance to feel two bodies connecting... to be bound and filled by an alpha. Confined in such a small place, the alpha's heady scent was doing things to his body again.

Lust like none he'd sensed before rocked him.

Rohan eyed him. "It sounds as if we're both stuck between a rock and a hard place." He growled lowly and looked away. "I'll see if I can convince him to change his mind. Otherwise... I don't know that I can do what he asks."

"You'd be able to refuse your omega?"

Rohan drew in a shaky breath. "I'll have to."

Gray struggled to concentrate. The heat sensation intensified. His ass was leaking his cream, ready for the alpha to take him. Instinct screamed inside for him to kneel down and show his ass, ready to take the man's seed.

Rohan's jaw tensed. He took two steps closer and stopped inches from Gray. He inhaled deeply before a groan rose from his chest. "Go. *Now*. Before I lose control."

The rumbled sound made Gray close his eyes for a brief second, the need to submit high. Instinct had him ready to kneel on the floor and offer his body up for the alpha's use. Gray fought it tooth and nail, unwilling to embarrass himself any further. He nodded before quickly heading to the door. He walked out, feeling as if he was in a daze. Gray made his way down the omega side of the building and showed the guard his ID at the entrance. Once outside, the warm summer sun shone down upon him.

In a couple of weeks, the seasons would begin their change.

College would start soon, and Avery would be away for long hours. The boys would start back to school a couple of weeks later.

And he would have little to no purpose other than cleaning and cooking, spending his days alone. Sketching… painting… idling away the time with no real commitment. Not that being a surrogate would change that much. The babe that could grow within wouldn't be there for him to hold. To love.

But there would be purposefulness to his days. He would be creating a life for two males who loved one another.

Gray walked down the street and caught an oncoming trolley before sitting inside the near vacant car, the quadrant whipping past him in a blur. He felt his world flipping upside down.

One thought commanded his attention.

Could he withstand Rohan's touch and not be forever consumed by it?

Chapter Eleven

Gone too far...

As soon as the door closed behind Rohan, he saw the drop of Jamie's shoulders. The ride home had been stress-filled, but silent. He sensed the argument to come and didn't want the entire world to see his anger.

And he *was* angry.

Angry enough that he wanted to punch a fist through a wall. He glanced down at his white knuckles as he tried to rein in the emotion. The more he willed himself to calm, the worse he felt. This wasn't how he wanted to spend his day... not when they'd been blessed with so many of them thanks to that single word.

Remission.

They'd been handed a miracle.

"Go ahead. I know you want to yell," Jamie said, his back still turned.

Rohan opened his mouth to do just that—and couldn't. There was no way he could vocalize how he felt in that moment.

Jamie slowly turned to face him. "I'm asking too much."

Rohan was silent a few seconds, trying to force his rage down. "If you know that, then why did you bother?"

But it was more than rage...

He felt as if Jamie was pushing him away. And he'd feared losing his mate for so many months only to still fear it now.

"I can't be the omega you need me to be. I did this for you."

"Did it for me? Are you insane?" Rohan could hear the bite of anger in his cry. He paused, drawing in some air to his burning lungs. "I don't want anyone else but you."

"You have needs, like any other alpha. Your biology drives you to mate. Drives you to reproduce. I know the long months without me to care for your needs has taken a toll."

Rohan took a step closer, only to watch as Jamie tensed. "I've never placed demands on you. I take care of my own needs just fine. I don't need some other omega to try to take your place."

"Why not? He's taking my place in another way. We're using his womb."

"That's different! I *don't* have to lie with him to get him pregnant. This isn't necessary."

"Oh, but I think it is. We could go years without a child, waiting for artificial insemination to work. I don't want to wait. I don't want to face disappointment after disappointment. Do you remember when we were trying to get pregnant? Facing another heat, knowing the last one failed? I can't keep going through that over and over again."

"And what if I can't get him pregnant? What if I keep at it over and over again, touching another omega when I've vowed to only be with you?" Rohan saw the ache in Jamie's expression, and hoped he was getting his point across. "You're asking me to break my vows. You're asking me to give in to my basest needs to give you a child—a child I've told you we don't need."

The hurt in Jamie's eyes was almost too much for Rohan to bear. He looked away, gasping for air in his lungs. How could the man who claimed to love him try to force his hand this way?

"I'm doing this for you… for me… and for Gray."

"For Gray?" Rohan asked, his head whipping up.

"You're not an omega. You don't understand the needs we have. He's never had an alpha. Never had a man. Years of heats have taken a toll on him. The *Heat Repress* is barely working anymore."

"Did he ask you for this?" Rohan roared.

"No!" Jamie shook his head. "He had no idea I'd demand this, but I could see the longing in his eyes when I talked to him in that conference room." Jamie tilted his head slightly. "And I saw how hard you had to work to hold back."

Rohan looked away, shame filling him. "Instinct. Nothing more."

"You wanted him. It was clear as day. And he wanted you."

"*Instinct.*"

"Regardless of what it was, it was there. Fire. Need. You connected."

"Any alpha would connect with an omega in heat."

Jamie paused. "In heat?"

Rohan sighed, closing his eyes. *Me and my big fucking mouth.*

"He went into heat?" Jamie demanded.

"It was a contact heat. If what you're saying about his long-suffered abstinence is true, it was likely brought on simply by being in the room with me." Rohan lifted a hand to stop whatever was about to come from Jamie's mouth. "Not *me*... an alpha. Any alpha probably would've sent him into that."

"But the fact he did with you is a good sign. There was a connection. I sensed it."

"Oh?" Rohan had felt it, too, but the hell if he was going to admit that to his omega. He had room in his heart for one man. One man only. An attraction to an omega in heat was simple biology. There was no connection other than he had a dick that could fill a womb.

"You need the intimacy I can't give you right now. He needs someone to break the cycle of *Heat Repress*. And I need this baby. We all get what we need. I don't see why you both can't see how perfect this is," Jamie said.

"Perfect? A perfect nightmare, perhaps," Rohan said before scrubbing his hands over his face. He could still scent Gray somehow... the need the omega had had rocked him to his core. How many months had it been since Jamie had gone into heat? Before the diagnosis, his heats had gone out of whack—it had been the first sign something was wrong. A year and a half, maybe? Longer? He wasn't quite sure.

"You're an alpha in his prime... and I saw how hard you worked to fight that instinct," Jamie murmured. "You need to mate, Rohan. You need him just as much as he needs you."

Rohan eyed Jamie, hating their situation. "I made vows to you. In sickness and in health..."

Jamie sauntered closer and cupped Rohan's cheeks. He looked up into Rohan's stare, his eyes shining. "Why are you fighting this hard? Do you feel shame for what you felt for Gray?"

Rohan was silent. He wouldn't answer that question.

"I don't want you to feel ashamed of any attraction you feel for him. He will be our surrogate, in more ways than one."

"You planned this all along. Didn't you?" Rohan asked.

Jamie shook his head. "No. I didn't. But there was something that reached out and told me this was right. That Gray is special."

Rohan chuckled mirthlessly.

"Why's that funny?" Jamie asked, pulling Rohan's cheeks to force his stare.

"He said the same thing about you."

Jamie frowned. "When?"

"In the bathroom. After our meeting."

Jamie lowered his hands and rubbed them on Rohan's chest. He closed his eyes… it was the closest thing to intimacy he'd had in months. Leaning his head, he claimed his mate's lips…

He was gentle at first, relearning the feel of Jamie's mouth against his. A few slow chaste kisses sparked within him, and he felt the blaze of need roaring to life.

Rohan deepened the kiss, moving closer and pressing Jamie against the foyer wall.

Only to be denied as Jamie pushed him away.

Rohan pressed his palm up against the wall as he shattered inside. "Do you not love me? Is that what this is? Because if that's the case, we shouldn't be bringing a child into this relationship. Not now."

"I do!" Jamie cried. "I do… I love you. I…" He paused, a tear sliding down his cheek. He pressed a chaste kiss to the side of Rohan's face. "You are the first person I want to see every morning when I wake up… and before I go to sleep every night. I want to share my life with you…" Jamie let out a sob. "I have failed you over and over again. You deserve more than me."

"You are my heart," Rohan said, his eyes stinging with unshed tears.

"I can't give you a child. And now I can't even give you the intimacy you deserve."

"Can't? Or won't?"

Jamie was silent a moment. "You have always been a considerate lover. You have treated me with respect and compassion—more so than I ever expected. You are kind… loving… and," He paused, smiling. "You're perfect. And now I am not."

"Who wants perfection? I surely don't. I've never said I did."

"You need Gray. He needs you…" Jamie whispered. "Please, Rohan. Do this for me. Give me the baby I want… and take what you need in the meantime."

"You don't know what you're asking of me."

"I do," Jamie said, brushing a few strands of hair from Rohan's forehead. "I know it won't be easy… but I'm doing this for us both."

"And if Gray refuses?"

Jamie shook his head. "He won't. I know he won't. And neither will you. Once you think this over and realize I'm right… you'll see this is the only way."

Rohan looked down into Jamie's face and knew there was no point arguing anymore. He wasn't going to get through to his omega. His mate's mind was set. He wanted what he wanted, period.

And there was something inside that told him Jamie was right. He would give in.

He was too weak in his love for his omega.

One of these days, this weakness of yours is going to get you into trouble. Trouble you can't get out of. It might tear you both apart.

Warden's words came back to haunt him.

He just hoped that last part didn't prove true.

And hoped Gray could be strong enough for all three of them… strong enough to say no.

Chapter Twelve

Paint therapy...

Gray stroked the brush across the surface of the canvas, letting his hand go where it willed. It had been weeks since he'd painted last, though he had gotten in a few doodles and sketches in between. Since his brother's death and the boys coming to live with them, his free time had been cut short.

But he needed this, with his mind in utter chaos.

Now that there was a little rhythm to the madness, he hoped to carve out more time to work. He dabbed at the oil paints on his palette before lifting to take another couple of short strokes. Letting his mind go blank, he focused on the image coming to life before him. An hour later, he realized what his subconscious had brought to life upon the canvas.

It was Rohan.

He lowered his brush as it became clear. Even now, he was preoccupied with the man. The night before, Rohan had invaded his dreams, touching his body and filling him. Gray had awoken to a wet spot on the bed and his cock in hand. Embarrassed to be lusting after another omega's alpha, he'd quickly cleaned up, changed his sheets, and tried to get some sleep.

Sleep hadn't come, so he'd used a new tactic. He'd gotten up early, fed the boys, and wandered out here into the old shed-turned-art studio and hoped to find solace in some creative expression.

Another failure.

He tossed the brush down before laying the palette onto a nearby table. Gray set about to clean up, leaving the unfinished painting on the easel. As he turned to leave, he looked at the painting—at Rohan staring back at him.

There had been such soul and heat in that gaze, but it hadn't truly been for Gray.

Instinct. That's all it was.

Nature, nothing more, and for him to think a few nights in the man's bed would give him any true insight, he was crazy.

Yet it preoccupied his mind.

Jamie wanted this. Nearly demanded it.

Gray had needs of his own, needs Jamie seemed to understand. He'd offered his alpha up to Gray on a silver platter.

As Gray locked up the shed and crossed the soft, green grass of the backyard in his bare feet, he felt his phone ringing. Lifting it after fishing it from his pocket, he saw it was Tensen.

Gray hit the Accept button before bringing the phone to his ear. "Hello?"

"It's Tensen Atkinson. How are you?" he asked.

"I've been better," Gray admitted before slipping into the kitchen's back door. The cool air from the air conditioning washed over him, cooling his heated body. "Can you hold a second?"

"Sure."

Gray put the phone to his chest and yelled upstairs to let the boys know he was back inside. Once they both replied to him from their rooms, he lifted the phone back to his ear. "Sorry, I'm back."

"That was a bit of a bombshell Jamie laid down. I just wanted to check in and remind you that ultimately, this is your decision. You don't need to agree to Jamie's terms if they're too much for you to accept—unless you wanted to."

Gray stood there, the phone to his ear and unsure what to say.

"Gray?"

"What would you do in my shoes?" Gray asked the attorney.

"I can't tell you what I would do. This is your decision to make."

"Technically... *legally*... you can't answer me. But as a friend... what would you do?" He knew Tensen wasn't exactly a friend. This was, at heart, a business arrangement. Tensen was the intermediary, nothing more.

But Tensen had shown a compassion Gray had never expected. He sensed he could trust the man.

"I would never be able to truly understand what you go through as an omega, so I can't make a decision based on that lack of knowledge alone."

Gray leaned back on the counter. "You're not helping me, Tensen."

"What does your gut tell you to do?"

"My gut tells me this might be my one and only chance to be with an alpha. To know what the experience is like."

It was Tensen's turn to be quiet.

"What if you have an alpha out there, waiting for you?" the attorney finally asked. "Artificial insemination lessens the risk of your alpha refusing you—if you're still untouched by another alpha."

"Everyone around me is so sure I have an alpha, waiting in the wings. If he hasn't shown up by now, it's not going to happen. I'm to be alone. I've accepted it. I wish everyone else would give up beating me up about it."

"There have been stories of late meetings. I've heard of omegas in their forties finally finding their alphas. It happens."

"And for that *one* late bloomer, how many others *don't* find their alpha? I haven't. Jamie has... He's lost a primitive part of who he is... and I can help them with this child."

Tensen sighed. "It sounds as if you might have your mind made up, then."

Gray didn't answer at first. Maybe he *had* made up his mind. The shame was almost too much for him to bear... but he wanted this gift Jamie was offering, no matter how terrible it was. "Tell them I'll do it."

"Are you sure you don't need more time?" Tensen said.

Gray wasn't going to second-guess his decision. "No. Call them and tell them I've agreed."

Tensen sighed. "If you're positive, I can have the documents made up and sent over for you to review and sign within a couple of days."

"Good. I look forward to looking them over," Gray mumbled before ending the call. He stumbled over to the sink and washed the remnants of the paint from his hands. After he'd scrubbed them, he filled his palms with water and washed his face.

Turning off the tap, he stared outside, not looking at anything in particular.

But it felt as if his entire world had suddenly tilted on its axis. He held on to the edge of the counter, praying he didn't topple over.

Not long after, he heard the front door open. Avery came in, an excited smile on his face.

"I take it enrollment went well?" Gray asked, turning and still clutching the counter behind him.

Avery nodded. "I have a job, as well."

"Wonderful! Where?"

"The campus mailroom."

Gray paused. "So you won't be leaving the Beta Quadrant. That's good news."

"Ultimately, the AQ business district is where the money is. I'll need to get a job there once I graduate, so I'll go there eventually."

Gray sighed, fearing he'd been worried for all the right reasons. "There are plenty of jobs in the Beta Quadrant. You don't need to put yourself into danger."

"Jobs in the AQ pay *very* well. If I want to ensure I can support this family, I need to be able to go where the money is."

"But… what if the blockers aren't strong enough? What if your alpha… or *any alpha*… scents you?"

"My advisor was an alpha. Sure, he was a bit older and likely mated, but he didn't seem to notice anything at all."

Gray was still worried for his nephew. "It's one thing to confront a lone, older alpha versus stepping into the alpha world. There are a hundred thousand alphas in that quadrant. A hundred thousand chances for you to be hurt."

"We're talking about years from now," Avery reminded him. "No point in arguing. I've got four years of school ahead of me before I step foot in the AQ."

Gray shook his head. "No, Avery. You're not going there. I have to put my foot down."

"As I've said before, you can't control me. No more than I can control you. We've both done what we think is right for this family. You ignored my concerns, so don't judge me for ignoring yours."

Gray sighed. "How my brother had a son so obstinate, I'll never know."

Avery walked closer and gave Gray a squeeze to the shoulder. "I'll be okay. I know I will. Everything is falling into place."

Gray wasn't so sure. "I hope you're right."

"I love you," Avery said to Gray. "I love that you're worried for me. I know how much you care about me and the boys. And I appreciate it."

"Even as you ignore it."

Avery smiled. "Even as I ignore it."

He patted the side of his nephew's face. "I love you, too, brat."

Avery grinned before heading upstairs to change into something cooler, leaving Gray to consider the decision he'd just agreed to. He grabbed a cool drink and headed outside to the backyard.

After setting his glass on the patio's table, he sat down on the old tree swing that had been there for years. Pushing off the large root below, he swung through the warm air, the great blue sky above him.

Wind rushed through his hair as the momentum picked up.

He felt like he was flying.

It was the closest to freedom he'd ever felt.

Chapter Thirteen

In the same conference room as before...

Gray leaned over the document, the words blurring together. He'd already read over the copies Tensen had couriered over a few days before. Hours had passed as he'd read through the legal mumbo-jumbo, trying to figure everything out.

Everything had appeared in order.

Now, they were all together in the same meeting room they'd met in the last time. Tensen had set the room up so the table where he sat was close to the open window. Unfortunately, the heat of summer was upon them, and there wasn't much of a breeze. Rohan's scent seemed even stronger today, and Gray teetered on the edge of need.

Sucking on the peppermint he'd brought along, he refocused on the document. Why he was hesitating to sign his name at the bottom, he wasn't sure. He'd already agreed to their terms. But once he wrote his name across the last page, he'd be forever bound to his decision.

Last chance.
I can't do this. I can't be with him like this.
What was I thinking?

Gray drew in a deep breath—which was an absolutely terrible idea. Rohan's alpha scent surrounded him, making the need mount with each passing second. His instinct nearly drove him off the edge, willing him to offer up his body then and there.

Across the table.

Both of them naked.

Rohan shoving his big, hard cock deep into Gray's womb.

A moan nearly rolled off his lips.

Sweat began to bead along the base of his neck. The primitive desire had turned him feral, it seemed. No longer caring what happened next.

He turned to Jamie, trying to will himself to refuse. But when he saw the desperate smile on Jamie's lips, he knew he couldn't back out now.

Sign it and be done.

"Second thoughts?" Jamie asked quietly.

Gray lifted his stare to Jamie and tried to ignore Rohan at the omega's side. "Are you…" He paused, sighing. "Are you sure this is truly what *you* want?"

Jamie smiled, looking supremely confident. "Absolutely."

Gray eyed the omega… They'd shared so much over the last weeks… "You want me to lie with your alpha… and make a child together."

Jamie nodded. "Yes."

Gray lowered the pen for a moment and took Jamie's hands in his. "I know we haven't known each other for very long, but I already consider you a friend."

Jamie smiled and squeezed Gray's hands. "And I, you."

"Will you be able to forgive me after it happens?"

Jamie frowned. "Forgive you? What would I have to forgive you for? I've asked you to do this… It's what I want."

"Getting what we ask for can have dire consequences… sometimes," Gray said. "And while I think you would recover from losing my friendship, I worry what this might do to you and Rohan."

Jamie lifted his gaze away from Gray for a moment and eyed his alpha. He took Rohan's hand and brought it to his lips. "He knows why I'm doing this," Jamie said, holding Rohan's gaze. He turned to look at Gray. "And I think you do, too."

Gray eyed Jamie a moment before looking up into Rohan's eyes.

He realized then… they all knew why they were here.

Need.

Their needs were all different yet linked by this one act.

Gray lifted the pen and initialed a few spots before flipping the page. Tensen pointed to another spot where he initialed. Moving to the last page, he signed his name with a flourish, holding his breath as he did it.

Tensen took the set of papers. "I'll have copies made and delivered to both parties by tomorrow. Arrangements will be made to collect Gray and bring him to your home the morning of his heat. We have a service we use for cases such as this, and I will have everything scheduled. Gray—you will need to forego your normal *Heat Repress* doses the day before and during the three days you will spend with Rohan. Bring a bag with a change of clothing and any toiletries you will need before you return home. A car will be on call, ready to take you as soon as you are ready to return home."

Gray lifted his stare to Tensen. The solicitor was all business now. He avoided Gray's stare and continued his comments. "You will need to assure there are no other alphas on your property during those three days. Jamie, you can remain, if you choose, but I recommend you make arrangements to leave for those days and spend the time with family or friends. If you choose to leave, as with any heat mating, ensure there is ready food for the alpha and water for them both before you leave."

Tensen paused and looked between them. "Jamie—are there any particulars you wanted to add? Any limits you need to make them aware of?"

"No," Jamie murmured quietly.

"Then the last thing required is the initial payment to the surrogate," Tensen said stiffly.

Gray looked away, hating the feeling he was being paid for. He listened as Rohan laid a checkbook on the table and stroked off a check. Rohan ripped it from the book, the tearing sound loud in Gray's ears. Instead of sliding it over, Rohan rose to his feet and walked to stand beside Gray. He lifted his stare, meeting Rohan's. The alpha offered the scrap of paper... a small fortune. Gray stared at it, not wanting to take it.

But this was the reason he'd chosen to do this... was it not?

Another wave of need rolled over him. A mew of desire came from his lips, and he felt shamed by it. He met Rohan's gaze again before lifting a shaking hand to pluck the check from the man's hands.

In that one moment, he felt cheapened.

They're renting my body. I've become little more than a prostitute.

Tears burned in his eyes as he rose to his feet. Barely looking at either of them, he gave them a quick thanks before tucking the check into his bag and trying to leave.

"Gray? Do you mind staying another moment?" Tensen asked. He turned to Rohan and Jamie. "You both can go. I'll send over the packet for you to review soon."

Gray watched as they both hesitantly left the room. He could tell Jamie wanted to talk... and that Rohan wanted something that required no talking at all. Finally, the door closed behind them and left him alone with the solicitor.

"Are you alright?" Tensen asked.

He wasn't. Nowhere near alright. Plastering a smile on his face, he eyed Tensen. "I'm great."

Tensen took a step closer.

Too close.

The beta collected Gray's face in his hands and shook his head. "No. You're not."

Gray swallowed back the emotion he felt. But that emotion was for what he'd just done... not for Tensen—which was a travesty. He sensed Tensen's concern...

"I'll be alright. I just need to go home, take a warm bath, relax..."

"I had no idea Jamie would want this," Tensen said. "I don't know that I would've introduced you two if I had."

"Why not?" Gray asked, confused.

Tensen reached out and rubbed the back of his hand against Gray's cheek. Immediately afterward, he took a step back and ran a hand through his salt and pepper hair. An odd smile crossed the beta's lips. "The thought of Rohan touching you—" Tensen paused, shaking his head. "If only things could be different in our world."

"They're not. This is the way of things," Gray murmured.

Tensen's face hardened. "Yes. It is." He lifted his stare to Gray's.

Gray was almost taken aback by the need he saw in the solicitor's expression.

"I'll take you home," Tensen said, collecting papers. "Just give me a moment."

"No," Gray whispered, shaking his head. He didn't want to give Tensen any reason to think there could be more between them. It was impossible. "I'd rather walk."

"Are you sure?" Tensen asked.

Gray nodded before squeezing the solicitor's shoulder. "Thank you for caring so much. But I'll be fine. I swear it."

Tensen's hand came across to cover and squeeze Gray's. Gray felt the warmth of the man leeching into him, hating the lines drawn between them.

And then that hand was gone—and he felt even emptier.

Gray left the conference room, even more shaken and wondering if his world would ever right itself again.

* * * *

Gray walked into the kitchen after departing his studio, wiping his paint-splattered hands on a spare cloth. Before he could do much more than get some water, Avery came bounding in. Excitement was etched over his face.

"Where are the boys?" Avery asked, near to bouncing.

"I'm not completely sure. I just walked back into the house. I assume you had a good time." Avery had had orientation that day. The first day of college was nearly upon them.

"Orientation was *amazing!*"

"Shhhh...." Gray hissed looking around. He glanced through the lower floor before angling his head toward the stairs. "You boys okay up there?"

He got two mumbled calls and was thankful the boys weren't close by.

"You know full well you can't extract Lake from his Z-box," Avery said. "And Auggie is never far away from Lake."

"But you need to be careful, regardless," Gray told him.

"I know, I know. I'm just excited." Avery was full of boundless energy. "I need to go change into something cooler. I think we need to go out to celebrate tonight."

"Celebrate?"

"It was a very good day, and the boys have been stuck in the house all summer."

"Not true. They go to the summer program a couple of days a week."

"But we don't have the money to go on summer vacations like we used to as a family. Papa always had us going somewhere—art museums and mini-golf and out for adventures. I know they're bored. We need to go have some fun tonight."

"We can't leave the quad," Gray reminded him. "Well, at least—I can't. And most of that stuff is in the Family Quadrant."

"We have a bowling alley," Avery said. "It's cheap, and it's fun. How about that?"

"And how much you want to bet Lake and Auggie end up in the arcade and never step out of it until we leave?"

Avery groaned. "Can we just do something and get out of this house as a family?"

Gray smiled. "Yeah. We can do that."

Avery grinned. "Good. I'm going to change and get the boys ready."

"Wait… before you go," his uncle said.

Avery turned back.

Gray slid a piece of paper from his pocket and pushed it across the island. "That should hopefully help cover your first semester's tuition at your fancy college."

Avery walked closer and picked up the paper.

Rohan's check.

"I can't take that," Avery said, shaking his head.

"You will. I'm doing this for you, Avery. I'm signing it over to you. Cash it and use it toward tuition, books, whatever it is you need. I know you've already taken some out of savings, but you can repay it now. I'll be getting another one once I conceive, and another once I give birth, which should come in time for your next few semesters or close enough."

"I can't tell you surrogacy is a bad idea in one moment and then use the money you earn from it in another. I *won't* be that person."

"Then I'll deposit it into the family account and it'll be yours one way or another," Gray said defiantly. "You might disagree with me, but I won't let you refuse this. Don't make me beg you to let me help my brother's children."

Avery eyed him. From the look on his face, Gray knew he was considering his response. "Thank you for the gift. You're amazing, Uncle Gray. And I love you for what you're trying to do for us."

"It's no gift. I expect payback."

"Oh?"

Gray walked closer and placed his hands on Avery's shoulders. "Good grades. A degree. And once your alpha claims you, you let me remain in this house until my dying day. Fair enough?"

"And what about your alpha?"

Gray tilted his head. "I need to focus on what's real. I need to secure a future for myself, too. You guys will one day go off, mated, and leave me here alone. I need to prepare for that."

He'd be completely alone one day... completely. It was suddenly too hard to breathe.

Avery offered his uncle a hand. Gray leaned across the island and shook it.

"Deal," Avery murmured.

Gray grinned.

Hours later, they arrived at the bowling alley and fed the boys. The youngest members of their tribe wandered to the arcade, leaving Gray and Avery alone. As expected. Gray looked over at Lake, watching as he argued with Auggie before one of the arcade games.

"We really need to do something about his attitude," Avery said.

"He just lost his fathers. He's lashing out in pain," Gray said, lifting his borrowed ball from the return. "I wasn't much older than him when my papa passed, and I made my father's life hell."

"I wished I'd had a chance to meet them," Avery said.

Gray smiled softly. "Me, too." He rolled a spectacular gutter bowl immediately after. Just like the one before it.

"Why did I suggest this game?" Avery asked, rising to take his own turn. "We both suck at it."

"Because you can fail and still have fun playing," Gray said with a smirk. "So, what comes next for you, college wise?"

"I still need to go in and purchase my books and download the syllabi for the classes."

"You haven't even started and you already sound smarter," Gray said with a chuckle.

"Hardly," Avery answered before getting himself lined up to the pins. He rolled the ball and split it right down the middle.

"Hey, at least you got some pins," Gray said with a grin once Avery turned around.

His next attempt cleaned up one half.

"We only have a couple of weeks to prepare. We need to get ready. The boys will be starting school not long after you do. You'll all need supplies."

Auggie rushed over, a wide smile on his face. "I need more coins!"

Avery reached into his pocket and handed his baby brother another couple of *renos* worth. "Lake playing nice?"

"No. But a kid from the summer program is here. We're playing a game together."

Gray brushed Auggie's hair. "Good. I'm glad you have someone to play with."

Auggie ran back toward the arcade, all youth and excitement. His gaze fell on Lake, hard at work killing aliens or shooting bad guys—whatever he was playing. He looked back to Avery and knew these were his reasons for helping Jamie and Rohan.

These boys. They were the only thing he truly had left.

"By the way… next heat, we'll have some help for the boys," Gray said suddenly. "I won't be there… and the solicitor is going to make plans for help at home."

Avery turned to his uncle. It took him a moment to realize what Gray was saying.

"The insemination? Already?"

There was no way he was telling Avery the whole of it. He couldn't tell his nephew just how craven and horrible he was. "The contract has been signed. You saw the check. It's a go." Gray looked straight ahead. "A beta babysitter is coming for all four days to take the stress off you. I won't be there… and if it doesn't take… it might be more than one cycle that I miss."

"A good sitter is almost impossible to find."

"Jamie and Rohan are going to supply someone. They're aware I have my nephews at home and offered."

"That was kind, but technically, they are my responsibility, not yours, so they don't have to do that."

Gray turned in the plastic bowling seat and faced Avery. "I really wish you'd stop saying that. I think I've proven how far I will go to ensure we're all okay."

Avery frowned.

"I know, by law, you took legal responsibility. But that doesn't mean I'm not responsible for them, just as much as you are."

"I didn't mean it like that—"

"Regardless what you mean, it makes me feel as if I'm a burden, getting in the way."

Avery paused. "I'm sorry. I didn't mean to discount what you bring to our family. I couldn't do this without you, Uncle Gray."

Gray lifted his chin. "Thank you." He looked over at Avery. "Jamie's aware of the legalities. That you are their guardian, but he also knows I help you when we're both dealing with our heat."

"Wait... you told him I was an omega?"

Gray paused, his mouth dropping open. "I suppose... I did. We discussed our families, and it just came out."

"Damnit. What if he sees me outside the quadrant? He's a mated omega... he has the freedom to leave here. I could run into him out in the world."

"I doubt your paths will ever cross. The city is huge and from what little we've talked, Jamie rarely leaves the Family Quadrant—other than to come see me or the surrogacy solicitor." Gray moved closer. "And even if he did see you, I know he wouldn't say anything. He's kind... and generous. Look what he's doing to help me take care of the family."

"Jamie does seem to be a very thoughtful man, what little I know of him."

Gray smiled. "He is. He'll make a wonderful papa."

"I'm glad to hear it. For your sake and mine."

Gray sat up a bit straighter. "I should invite him to dinner one night... so you guys can meet him, really get to know him a little. Perhaps you'd have fewer misgivings about what I was doing if you had that chance."

"Maybe," Avery said.

"I'll call him tomorrow. See what I can set up."

Avery sat down beside his uncle and put an arm around the man's shoulders. "If you'd told me a few months ago where we'd be right now, I'd have called you a liar."

Gray chuckled. "Me, too." He smiled at his nephew. "We're going to be okay."

"From your lips to the gods' ears."

Chapter Fourteen

Family matters…

Jamie sat beside his alpha at the family table as the servants moved about the outskirts of the dining room.

"Are you going to attend the ball slated for next Friday evening?" Jamie's papa asked his brother Wilder, making small talk as dinner was served.

His papa looked as elegant as always. An omega band of diamonds graced one middle finger, along with another band for each decade he was with his alpha. The trio could blind someone when they caught the light. That, along with his designer *Áo dài*—a long Asian inspired silk tunic over soft trousers—with gemstone clasp and the extensive up-do twisted stylishly, his papa was the epitome of how a rich, claimed mate was expected to present himself.

Wynter Jaymes always showed that perfect face to the world.

"I hadn't planned on it," Wilder admitted.

Papa gasped. "You haven't been to a ball in ages. How are you supposed to find your omega?"

"*I don't.*"

Jamie chuckled and met his brother's gaze.

Wilder seemed to notice the look of horror on their papa's face and quickly added a caveat. "At least not just now. I've got a lot to learn in the coming weeks thanks to that promotion. Father entrusted me, and I want to do the job well."

"Of course you're going to do it well," their father said from the other end of the table.

Jamie glanced down the table. His father's hair was nearly black opposed to his papa's blond, except for the thin layer of white over each ear. Warden Jaymes cut through his last bit of roast before looking up. He pointed the stabbed meat at Wilder. "I wouldn't have promoted you if I didn't think you had it in you. You've proven yourself time and time again." Father turned to look at Rohan. "Hasn't he?"

As the head of Jaymes & Associates Legal Department, Rohan was privy to much that went on inside the building. "From what I've seen and heard, he's a *very* hard worker."

Father popped the fork into his mouth and grinned as he chewed.

"He pays you to say things like that," Vaughn said to Rohan. "So you're biased."

Rohan forced a smile, glancing at Jamie from the corner of his eye. "I've always spoke my mind—even if it isn't what your father wants to hear."

"You'd get farther if you kissed his ass," Jamie's youngest brother said with a grin.

"Stop it, Vaughn," Jamie insisted before taking another bite.

"I have no doubts I can do the job," Wilder said. "I just want time to devote to learning my new responsibilities before I worry about searching for an omega. That's all I meant."

"Excuses, excuses," their papa said. "Last time, you had too much work preparing for the promotion. The time before that, you were feeling under the weather. The time before that? I think I've forgotten the lies you told me."

"*Wynter*, he still has time," father said.

"He's over thirty and unmated," his papa argued. "Don't you want to see another generation of Jaymeses on the way?"

Jamie tensed. His papa knew they were seeking a surrogate—that the next generation would be coming sooner than later, if he had his say.

Wilder sighed. "*I'm* not ready to see that. At least not from me." His brother turned and offered him a wink.

Papa shot him a wounded look.

"If you keep pressuring him, Wilder's never going to go," his father said before popping a last piece of meat in his mouth before a servant cleared his plate.

Wilder rolled his eyes and looked to Vaughn, smiling. "I'm sure my little brother is ready to hit a ball. He hasn't been in forever, either."

Vaughn met Wilder's stare and narrowed his eyes, shooting venom across the table. Jamie stared between the two, trying not to smile.

"Do you know how it would look for Vaughn to mate before *you*? To have children before you even found your omega?" Papa asked. He threw up his hands in aggravation. "I don't even want to imagine it."

"Oh, gee, papa…" Vaughn said, tilting his head to the left. "Once again put my brother first. Please."

"You know I don't mean it like that, Vaughn. It's just… your brother should've been mated by now. People will talk if he doesn't find his match soon… and they'd talk even more if you found one first."

"Let them talk," Wilder said. "I really don't care. If Vaughn wants an omega in his life, let him go seek one out. What does it matter who comes first?"

"For the record, I don't," Vaughn added. "I'm quite happy with my life the way it is, not that anyone cares."

"I wasn't much older than Wilder was when I met you," his father said across the table. "And we worked out just fine. It'll come when it comes."

"I don't want to be a grandfather at seventy," papa spat at Wilder. "I want to be a grandfather when I'm still young enough to dote on your pups. I haven't held a babe in too long."

"You're nowhere close to seventy," Wilder said. "You only turned fifty a few years ago."

"I'm not a day over forty-nine," his papa sighed. "Thank you."

"If you have kids, I'll fade into nothing," Vaughn said. "E-vap-or-ate. I won't exist anymore."

"Oh, stop being so dramatic," papa said to Vaughn. "You're so needy."

Vaughn sighed. "Takes a drama queen to know a drama queen, papa."

"If anyone cares," Jamie interrupted, placing his fork and knife down. "But the next generation is coming sooner than later, I hope."

Papa sat back, his head whipping to Jamie. "What?"

"We've contracted with an omega surrogate," Jamie announced, pride filling him. He turned and slipped his fingers in through Rohan's, and basked in his alpha's smile. He turned back to the silent table and looked around at their shocked faces.

"I'd told you all what we planned to do. Why it's such a surprise, I don't know."

"I knew you were searching… and had met a prospect… but not that you were this close to an agreement," Wilder murmured.

Wilder had been privy to that piece of news. The rest of the family hadn't. They knew Jamie and Rohan had been discussing a surrogate—not that they'd found one. The looks on their faces spoke volumes, particularly papa's.

And papa was, of course, the next to speak up. "Are you sure you're ready for this… so soon after your recovery?"

"It takes ten months for a baby to grow. And it might take a few months before we're pregnant. I'm already feeling stronger, and more so every single day. By the time the baby comes, I'll be ready."

"*We're* pregnant?" papa asked. "*You* won't be pregnant. Someone else will. Meaning… it won't be a Jaymes."

Silence filled the table again, and Jamie felt his stomach flip.

"You all could show a little more support for Jamie," Rohan spat.

Jamie rose from the table and tossed his napkin down. He fled the room, hot tears flowing down his cheeks. Rohan was fast on his heels and slammed the front door behind them as they left. He climbed into the passenger seat of their car and waited for Rohan to round the rear and slide behind the wheel.

Neither spoke until they were a few miles away.

"I won't have them speaking to you like that again," Rohan growled. "If they can't support you, they're banned from our home."

Jamie nodded, wiping away the wetness from his cheeks. He'd stopped crying. The initial shock of their reaction had hit him hard—but now that he'd had a few minutes—he knew they were the ones standing to lose. A new life would come, with all the joy and happiness a babe can bring. If they weren't there to see it—that was their own fault.

"Agreed," he said.

Rohan grew silent. They drove along a few more miles before he sensed his alpha sneaking glances at him.

"My parents have never treated me well," Jamie admitted. "I'm accustomed to this."

"I expected more from Wilder," Rohan said. "The rest? Not so much."

"I think Wilder was surprised, is all." Jamie glanced out of the window, his mind churning. "I don't know... maybe I hoped I'd finally make my family happy with this."

"Please tell me you don't want this child to make your papa happy."

"No... but it would've been icing on a big, beautiful cake," Jamie answered before sliding the fingers of one hand through Rohan's. He leaned over the console and rested his head on Rohan's strong shoulder. "You're all I need, baby. All I've ever needed."

"And soon we might be three," Rohan said, but there was a tenseness to his words.

Jamie squeezed his alpha's hand and smiled. "Yes, we just might. And it'll be worth all the chaos to get that babe in our arms. To be a family... to be better than the one I have now."

Rohan pressed a kiss to the top of his head as they roared down the back-country road, eating the miles and putting more distance between him and the ugliness of his papa.

* * * *

A couple of hours later...

"I tried calling Jamie, but it went straight to voicemail."

Rohan leaned back in the oversized chair and rested his head on the back. "He's in bed. He was tired after what you all put him through tonight. Can you blame him?"

"I should've spoken up before you left," Wilder said on the other end of the line. "Hearing that it's apparently a done deal was a bit of a shock."

"I was there signing the papers, and it's still a shock to me," Rohan admitted as he stared up at the ceiling, wondering how they'd gotten where they were.

"It took a moment for my brain to catch up. I'm sorry. Let Jamie know I gave papa a piece of my mind after you both left. What he said was uncalled for. Any baby you two have will be a part of this family."

Rohan winced. "I don't even know that I want to be a part of your family."

Wilder sighed. "Papa can be a handful. I know. But once there is a baby—I think his tune will change."

"I hope you're right. For Jamie's sake."

Silence fell on the other end for a moment. "I know Jamie's excited... but what about you? Your family?"

"My papa is excited," Rohan said. "On whatever tropical island he's currently sailing around with my step-father." The rich, powerful oil tycoon, Marcullis

Oberton, had swept into his widowed papa's life and quickly sent Rohan off to boarding school. College and marriage had soon come after, and he'd built a life of his own between the moments his papa strolled in for a day or two here and there for a visit.

Now, his family was Jamie.

"And you?" Wilder asked. "How are you feeling?"

"My feelings don't really matter. I just want to keep your brother happy." *Any way possible.*

My gods… what am I doing?

He closed his eyes and pinched the bridge of his nose. How could he be unfaithful to the one great thing he had in his life? Even if it was what Jamie had demanded…

Wilder was silent again. "You shouldn't be doing it for just him. It should be for you both."

"It is… it is," Rohan answered, not completely sure anymore.

"Okay," Wilder said. "If you guys need anything, just ask. I'll be there. Just give me a second to recover after you drop some news next time."

"Will do," Rohan said before he ended the call. He rose and climbed the winding foyer stairs toward the bedroom he shared with his omega.

After lowering his cell to the nightstand and disrobing, he slid in between the sheets. Rohan drew his sleeping mate closer and inhaled the man's scent. Need slammed into him, but he shoved it aside and simply lay, holding his mate.

Until Jamie pushed him away in sleep.

Rohan lay there for hours, lost and alone.

Loved yet unwanted.

Chapter Fifteen

Gray's heat...

The contracts were agreed upon, signed, and submitted. The government had approved the surrogacy request, and now Gray sat in the back of a very expensive car being taken via chauffeur to Jamie and Rohan's home in the Family Quarter. He rested back against the soft, leather seat, watching the scenery pass.

It had been years since he'd been outside the Omega Quadrant. Long, long ago, he'd lived in the FQ with Silver and his parents. Immediately after his first heat, he'd been sequestered—imprisoned, really—because of a simple classification at birth.

Omega.

A womb with legs.

He'd found a way to deal with it. He'd immersed himself in art and books and everything he *could* do while stuck inside his part of the city. Over the years, he'd lost friends. They'd been claimed and mated—forgetting about him still stuck in the prison they'd escaped from.

He leaned his forehead on the warm glass, the need spiraling. As suggested by Tensen, he'd not taken a *Heat Repress* pill that morning. He felt his body flooding with heat, his ass slick and ready to be taken.

It wasn't much different than it was with the pills now. By the time the car pulled up before their home, he feared he'd be a puddle of need, begging and crying for Rohan before he could make it through the door.

When the car finally arrived, pulling into a semi-circular drive before a grand home, Gray could feel his body trembling in anticipation. He tried to focus on the exterior of the home, but all he could think about was the ache pounding within.

The beta driver opened the door for him and offered a hand. Gray took it, not sure his legs would be strong enough to get him inside. "I'm to escort you in through the door—to make sure no other touches you except Mr. Parker."

Gray nodded, slightly thankful he'd have the beta to hold on to. His legs felt like rubber, and he expected them to buckle at any second. How he managed to make it to the door, he wasn't sure. Jamie whipped the front door open before they barely reached it—excitement on his face.

"Come in, come in," Jamie said, taking one of his arms.

"Are there any alphas in the house besides Mr. Parker?" the driver asked.

"No. No others."

The driver nodded. "I'll fetch Mr. Tomlinson's bag."

"Have a seat," Jamie said. As soon as he settled into a chair near the door, Jamie asked, "Can I get you a drink?"

"Water," Gray said before licking his too dry lips. His voice had sounded as raw as he felt.

Jamie wandered off. The driver came to the door and lowered the bag to the floor—beside another one. He pulled a card from his jacket pocket and showed it to Gray before tucking it into a pocket in Gray's bag. "Call me when you're ready to return home. No leaving the property otherwise, *understand?*"

"Yes," Gray answered as Jamie returned with a glass of sparkling water.

"If Mr. Tomlinson needs to leave this house, I'm to be called. You have my number, and now so does he," the driver said. "There's an emergency number, also, which you both have. If you can't reach me, they can send another beta to escort him home."

"Understood," Jamie said.

"No other alphas are allowed in the house until Mr. Tomlinson has left," the man added. "Just a reminder."

"We're all very aware of the rules, and we will follow them all to the letter," Jamie snapped, a little of his outward excitement slipping to show other emotions at play.

The driver looked between them before heading out and closing the door behind him. Jamie handed the water over, and Gray guzzled half of it in one drink.

"Nervous?" Jamie asked.

"I suppose I am a little," he fibbed. *A lot. It was a lot. A whole fucking lot.* His hand shook as he placed the glass of water on the table beside the chair. "Are you *truly* sure this is the way you want to do this? We still have time for you to change your mind."

Jamie smiled. "I'm quite happy with my choice." He walked closer and brushed hand over Gray's cheek. "You deserve to know how it feels to be claimed."

Gray frowned. "He's yours."

"I'm willing to share him… you're sacrificing your body for me. I don't take that lightly."

Gray closed his eyes, not truly understanding Jamie's logic. He was being paid for his services as a surrogate. He didn't need anything more than that.

Yet he wanted to know how it felt.

Desperately.

"Whose bag is that?"

"Mine," Jamie said. "I'm going to stay at my brother's apartment for a few days."

Jamie didn't want to listen to what was about to transpire, even if he'd asked for it.

An animal mating. Three days of rough sex that would hopefully create a life.

Just the thought of it made Gray moan. His back arched, his slick flowing thickly. Gray began to pant, the instinct quickly taking over.

"Let me help you upstairs," Jamie murmured, offering an arm.

Gray took it and felt the world spinning around him. It had been eighteen years since his first full heat, a distant memory. He sensed himself moving up the stairs, but he was drunk on lust. The world blurred.

A scent washed over him as they seemed to have reached the top of the stairs. *Alpha.* He groaned, his body crumbling to the floor. Gray went to his hands and knees, his ass pushed high. He needed to be filled. A growl sounded from a slight distance, and the rumble of it slammed into him. He mewled in return, bucking his hips up.

Writhing on the floor, he had no idea exactly where he was. He was so lost to the need, the world around him faded away. A cry tore from his lips as he felt a big, strong alpha male slide against him.

"Please," he cried. "Fuck me. Please…please."

His pants were slipped down, and he felt the head of a cock pressed against his ass. Gray pushed back on it, needing to be filled like he needed his next breath. A moan tore from his lungs and mingled with a deep cry from the alpha. Inch by inch he was filled, strong arms wrapping around him from behind.

Gray closed his eyes, focusing on the feeling of the head of the thick, long cock sliding inside him. Full... he'd never felt so full. And then the torrent came... the rutting thrusts of that huge cock filling him over and over again. He quivered all over, moans pouring from him with every drive. The slow, slick slide of that shaft fucking him took his breath away, leaving him gasping. Pre-cum drizzled from his cock.

He felt the pressure against his womb. It was already beginning to open to the alpha's claim. The instinct slammed into him—the desire to be filled with child.

"Give me your baby," he cried, tears stinging the backs of his eyes. "Fill me, my alpha."

The words sounded foreign to his ears. He knew it was the innate need talking, not him. He was a slave to his nature, and it had taken over.

A hand slid through his braid and pulled his head back—edging on pain. Warm breath washed over his ear. "You want my baby, omega?"

"Yessss," he hissed. The rich, deep voice washed over him, ramping up his desire.

"I wanna fill you full," Rohan murmured, his voice rich and deep. "I wanna put my baby inside you. My sweet omega."

Gray knew Rohan's words were instinct, as well. That the alpha's need to create life was the only thing driving him, but Gray couldn't help but wish those words were truly for him in that moment.

He had no right to them.

They were Jamie's, but that thought was buried under decades of unleashed need.

Rohan's body quickly drove him to the edge. The first orgasm slammed into Gray, his back arching as those strong arms held him tight. Another came on its heels when his womb opened to accept the thick head of Rohan's cock, his body barely able to withstand the force of it. When he felt the alpha stiffen behind him with a growl, he felt the knot at the base of the shaft thicken, locking them together.

A blast of heat filled his womb as the man's fingers dug into his hips. A roar sounded behind him before a set of teeth sank into his flesh, almost breaking the skin. They both slowed, the knotting bond forged. Now biology took over, shooting thick load after thick load into his womb.

He was rolled to the side, the alpha behind him.

They would be locked together until the knot faded.

As the post-sex haze drifted, he realized he wasn't even completely sure it was Rohan who'd mated him. Strong hands ran over his body, massaging and relaxing him. It was another instinct in the alpha. The more relaxed the omega was, the better his chances of being bred. The gentle caresses nearly made him moan in pleasure. He was so very needful of the little intimacies, as much as he was for the big ones.

Gray looked around and saw they hadn't even made it to a bedroom. They lay on the soft carpet in a hallway just outside several doors. A railing was a few inches away, showing a view down into the living area he'd barely seen.

He heard the front door softly close down below and winced, realizing Jamie had likely played witness to that scene, at least in part. He'd definitely heard a lot of pleading and begging—and grunting.

"Fuck," Rohan whispered behind him, apparently realizing Jamie's presence, too.

Gray lay there, not knowing what to say... what to feel...

When the alpha was finally able to withdraw—the knot having fading—Rohan rose from behind Gray and then lifted him. The alpha was big and powerful. He looked down at Gray, his eyes red rimmed and swollen.

Jamie had focused on what he wanted. Gray had focused on what he needed.

Gray hadn't bothered to truly think about Rohan's needs.

An alpha, he would be expected to be strong and do what was necessary to care for his omega. They were strong. They could endure. They didn't get emotional, yet emotion was etched into every line on Rohan's face.

"I'm so sorry," Gray murmured, looking up into the alpha's handsome face.

"No point in being sorry," Rohan muttered, carrying Gray into one of the bedrooms. "What's done is done. It's too late to stop this now."

The alpha didn't look at him. Rohan's jaw was tense, his expression weary.

He lowered Gray into the middle of the big bed and began to remove some of the clothing tangled about him. Once Gray was nude, Rohan stood back and looked him over.

"Pull your hair free," Rohan said, his voice deep and low.

"It'll get in the way," Gray said, running a hand over the thick braid.

"Pull. Your. Hair. Free," Rohan repeated, his tone brooking no argument.

Gray paused a moment, unsure. Finally, he pulled the tie at the end off and began to undo the braid. His long, dark hair spread out around him in a cascade. Rohan stepped forward and collected a handful, rubbing it in his hands. He lifted one hand to his face and drew in a deep breath… before a low sensual moan come from his lips.

"It's beautiful. *You're* beautiful."

Gray didn't know what to say.

And Rohan looked stunned the words had come from his mouth. An awkward silence fell between them, and he watched a myriad of emotions coursing across Rohan's handsome face. Finally he lifted his stare to Gray's and held it.

"But no matter how beautiful, how tempting, or how much the instinct drives me to tend to you these next few days—I am *forever* Jamie's. Do you understand that?"

An alpha would instinctively feel the need to soothe him after their wild couplings with words of affection. A relaxed omega was more susceptible to impregnation. There would be nothing more to it than their DNA and nature. Gray nodded that he understood, even knowing it would be difficult not to succumb.

Rohan stood frozen, as if he had more to say. After a moment, he pushed his pants the rest of the way from his hips and they dropped to the floor. Gray's gaze immediately went to the still hard shaft hanging thickly between the man's thighs. Rohan was huge, much larger than any of the toys Gray had used over the years. Thankfully, he'd been so slick, so needy, he hadn't sensed any pain upon entry. Perhaps he'd been too far gone to feel anything but desire.

Just thinking about Rohan having been inside him sent a rumble of need through him. His back arched, his head falling back. A cry tore from his lips, and Rohan was upon him seconds later, fistfuls of his hair tangled in the alpha's grip.

Rohan found his lips, capturing his mouth in a hungry kiss. Their mouths warred with one another, seeking that which they shouldn't want. He was spun to his belly, strong hands then moving to his hips. That big, thick cock speared him again. The sex was rough, animalistic, and all Gray needed. He body thrummed with the satisfaction in having an alpha tend to his need.

They fucked over and over again through the night. After, they would sneak in an hour or two of sleep between, but then their bodies would once again collide, drawn together by the mating instinct.

By the next day, some fatigue had started to set in. The quick, rapid fucking of the first day shifted into something slower... more sensual. Gray held Rohan's gaze and begged himself not to fall for the man driving deep within him.

It was just sex, not love, but he was so starved for either Gray struggled to see the line between them. He'd never had a lover, never had anyone care for him as Rohan did. Just as Jamie had said, Rohan was kind. Even in his alpha's aggressiveness, he didn't cross the line. He took, but he gave, as well. And when it was over, the alpha laid gentle kisses and massaged him.

Again, instinct.

Gray kept reminding himself of that fact over and over again.

It wasn't for him. Not one bit.

But the illusion… it was hard not to become entangled within it. Each sultry look… a deep, whiskey-roughened moan… a caress of a stubbled cheek or a calloused hand against him… and he fell deeper under the spell.

During those three days, he begged for more.

He pleaded in the deep of the night, wanting his womb to be filled. Wanting to be loved. Starving for the attention. Even as he had his fill, it wasn't enough, not after all the long years he'd spent alone. He both cursed and loved Jamie for this gift, one he never should've taken. Guilt and loathing mixed with the crescendo of lust and desire that threatened to consume him whole.

By the fourth morning, he awoke, his body so sore he could barely move. Rohan's heavy arm and leg weighed him down. His mouth was dry as the desert, and he pushed the alpha off him enough to reach for a few inches of water left in a glass by the bed. He drained it and was still dehydrated.

Sliding out from under Rohan's body, he tried to stand, only to fall to his knees and nearly lose the glass.

"Here, let me help you."

Gray lifted his stare to see a red-eyed Jamie. Their stares met for the briefest of seconds, but he quickly looked away. Heat filled his face, his stomach doing somersaults within. The glass was taken from his hand and moments later, returned full. Gray drained the glass, too thirsty to think about what Jamie was seeing in that moment.

After he'd emptied the glass, he lifted his stare to Jamie and felt hot tears slipping down his face.

"Don't," Jamie whispered. "Or you're going to make me cry."

From the look of Jamie, he'd already been crying. "I'm so sorry," Gray whimpered.

Jamie cradled Gray's face in one hand. "You've done nothing wrong. *Nothing*. Neither of you have… only what I asked."

Then why do I feel so terrible?

Rohan was suddenly at his side, lifting him. The alpha carried Gray to the bathroom and laid him into the oversized bath. Jamie started the tub, filling it with warm water.

"There are towels in the closet," Rohan said before turning to Jamie. "Let's give him some privacy."

"In a moment," Jamie said, not looking at Rohan.

Rohan stood there, staring at his omega, taciturn. Finally, he spoke in a low, roughened voice barely above a whisper that scratched against Gray's tattered edges. "I need you, Jamie."

I need you.

The ache in those words… Gray felt them soul deep.

Jamie looked up at his alpha, but only for a fleeting second. He was almost dismissive... but after the things he'd seen, Gray wasn't sure he could fault the man. "In a moment."

Gray lifted his gaze to Rohan and could see a little bit of brokenness in the alpha's eyes. He wanted to go to Rohan... console the man... but he had no right to it.

Rohan met his gaze for an instant... and then was gone.

Gray worried about Jamie's state of mind after seeing what had transpired. He had no right to speak on their relationship, but he didn't want a rift to form between them. As the water filled the tub, Jamie soaked a washcloth in the warm water and began to run it over Gray's back and shoulders. Gray searched for the right words.

"It's not his fault. Isn't that what you said?"

Jamie's hand went still.

"He's hurting, too."

Jamie's head bowed. "I asked this of him. I have no right to feel anger. He only did as I asked."

"Please... don't push him away. I wouldn't be able to bear the thought."

"Don't worry. We'll be fine. I just need a moment to get my head straight." Jamie paused, his eyes tearing up. "What you've done for us..."

Gray lifted a hand to stop him. "It's a service I'm providing. A business transaction," Gray said, knowing the words were a lie. It was what he was telling himself at that moment, trying to numb himself to the heartache he felt for what he'd done.

He'd fallen under the alpha's spell and had to disengage quickly or he'd be lost.

"You know full well it's more than that," Jamie said softly. "Look at me."

Gray couldn't at first. After Jamie coaxed him with a finger to his chin, he turned.

"I love you," Jamie whispered. "We're partners in this adventure, you and me. You're an extension of me—my surrogate—our womb swollen and filled with my alpha's seed. A baby will grow within us, *our* baby." Jamie rested a hand on Gray's abdomen. "I love you more than you can ever know."

Gray rested his forehead on Jamie's, tears streaming down his face. "You're also partners with Rohan—more so than me."

"I am. And I love him, too. I just didn't think this would hurt as much as it does."

Gray lifted his stare. "I feared it would. I don't want you hurt."

Jamie smiled wryly. "I know. Neither of you wanted that and begged me not to demand this."

Gray leaned forward and cupped Jamie's cheek. He leaned forward and pressed a kiss to the omega's lips. For a brief moment, Jamie kissed him back but then pulled away and placed a chaste kiss on his forehead.

Jamie continued to soothe him, washing him with the warm water until he felt a little saner and relaxed.

"Through the other door is another bedroom. I put your bag in there with your change of clothing. Your dirty things are on the bed, folded. Don't rush. You take all the time you need. If you want to lie in that bed and take a nap, by all means, stay. Your phone is charging in there on a plug, so you can call the driver whenever you're ready."

"Thank you," Gray whispered.

Jamie smiled. "I also put out some cheese and crackers on a table beside the bed. I know you're likely hungry. Let me know if you need more than that."

He hadn't eaten in days… he should feel famished, but the thought of food made him feel sick. "That's more than enough. I can get something more substantial once I'm home."

Jamie smiled softly. "I'm going to see to my alpha. And make sure he knows how much I love him, too."

Gray nodded and smiled.

Jamie rose to his full height. "Oh, I've also left an extra brush for you. Your hair is *full* of knots. It's going to take some help to get that all clear again."

Gray sighed, pulling a few handfuls over his shoulder to inspect. "*Great.*" But he remembered Rohan's hands twisting into his hair and dragging him closer for drugging kisses. He almost sighed… his lids drooping closed.

He was soon left to himself, and he almost hated feeling alone after the last few days. Gray was grateful that Jamie seemed to instinctively know he needed to be cared for in those moments after their days locked together.

It couldn't have been Rohan to do it.

There needed to be an uncoupling… a wall between them now.

Once the water began to grow cool, he climbed out. The bottom of his hair had swept into the water and grew soaked. Knowing he should've washed it, he sat at the small vanity and began to absently brush through the knots. Midway through, he eventually gave up and put his hair in a loose braid for the moment to wait until Avery could help him—after he went home and bathed again, washing the long strands.

And washing this place from his memory.

He walked into the other bedroom, away from the one he'd shared with Rohan. A large comfortable looking bed dominated the room and called to him. Days and nights of little sleep had pushed him to the edges of exhaustion. Instead he pulled on his loose-fitting clothing, his body sore in places he wasn't sure he knew he'd had. Everything ached, but he didn't want to remain there another moment, no matter how much he craved some rest. Grabbing his phone, he called the driver—who fortunately wasn't too far. Maybe he'd anticipated that he'd be needed now that the heat was over.

Gray wondered how many omegas the beta transported each month, dropping off fresh wombs door to door. He cringed at his terrible joke and lay across the bed, waiting to step out of the surreal world there and back to his reality of home. Luckily, he didn't wait for the car long and left the house silently. He climbed into the back and finally released a breath once the car pulled away.

He needed home.

He needed his family and to be reminded he wasn't this horrible person he felt like he'd become.

* * * *

Driving his fingers through his still damp hair to push it from his face, Rohan stared out through the bedroom window, not truly seeing any of the scenery.

He'd spent a fortune on their home, trying to give his omega someplace almost as impressive as the home the man had been raised in. He'd spent another fortune landscaping it and transforming it into a peaceful oasis where they could raise a family together, far from the troubles of the city. Tall trees dotted the outskirts, giving them a feeling of being out in the middle of nowhere.

Nothing he looked at made him feel tranquil.

A storm raged within him. A storm that threatened to break him completely.

He then saw his own reflection in the glass and cringed. Rohan didn't want to look at himself after what he'd done.

No matter if his omega had begged—he should've been strong enough to say no.

I'm weak. Too weak.

Either way he'd chosen, he would've failed. It was a no-win situation.

Only adding to his shame was the fact he'd found pleasure in the act.

Gray had welcomed him with open arms, looking up with longing. The man had never known a lover, and it had showed in some ways, but the need had been constant… and that need had propelled them on through their days together.

"Do you think it went well?"

Rohan cast a quick glance over one shoulder at his omega before turning back. "I can't know if it happened already."

"But it was a good match, I assume?"

There were occasions when an alpha and omega did not fit—their desire did not match. That hadn't been the case with Gray. They almost matched too well. "It was fine."

He heard the creaking over the wooden slats in the floor as Jamie took a few steps closer. Tensing, Rohan waited to see how close his omega would come to him.

"You did well… I'm pleased."

He slowly turned and captured Jamie's stare. "You're… pleased. I'm *so* glad for that," he spat snidely. The anger circling within made it hard not to snap.

"Do you hate me now? After I forced this on you?"

Some of Rohan's anger evaporated with those questions… even more so from the look of self-loathing on Jamie's face. "How could I ever hate you?"

Jamie just barely smiled, but it faded quickly.

"But you turning your back to me afterward?" Rohan paused, trying to hide the breaking of his voice. "That will take me a moment to forgive. I needed you… I needed to know we were okay."

What was he talking about? They hadn't been okay in months. Okay wasn't even anywhere in their general vicinity.

Jamie took a few more steps closer. "Seeing you two… in that bed… together. It hurt more than I imagined it would."

Rohan didn't say anything. A little part of him was glad Jamie hurt. It meant the omega still cared enough to feel jealous. After a few seconds, he took a few steps himself, closing the gap between them. "I did as you asked me to do… now I have a request of my own."

Jamie lifted his chin and fully faced Rohan. "And what's that?"

Rohan took a few more steps and stopped when he was barely inches from Jamie. He reached out and cupped his omega's chin. "Not now... not tonight... but sometime soon... help me forget what I just did. Let me love you again... in our bed. Let me have my husband back completely."

Jamie frowned before stepping back, away from Rohan's touch.

Something broke within him as he saw the disgust in Jamie's face.

"*I can't*. I can't be with you, Rohan."

"Could you at least sleep in my arms? Let me hold you close... kiss you. Hold you. That's all I really want. I promise I won't ask for more..."

Jamie shook his head.

A sob rushed up Rohan's throat. He bit it back before speaking again. "What did I do to make you hate the thought of my touch?"

Tears welled in Jamie's eyes. "You did *nothing*. Absolutely nothing. You are an incredible man. A kind and gentle lover. I'm just... *changed*."

Rohan couldn't breathe. He stood there, staring. Silent.

Shattered.

"I love you. I know it's hard to imagine that I do when I don't want to be with you in that way..." Jamie dropped his head in his hands and released a sob. "I just need more time."

Rohan wanted nothing more than to go to his omega... pull the man close. Hug him. Give comfort.

But he knew he'd be pushed away and it would only be another cut of the knife to his heart.

They'd been a loving couple. Having Jamie in his arms soothed his soul. Now, his omega could barely stand him being inches away. It wasn't just about the sex—though he missed that immensely—it was the loss of intimacy that had grown over the months.

It had started before Jamie's diagnosis, well before it.

A widening gulf…

Then the diagnosis had come, and Rohan had chalked everything up to that. Yet something as simple as a hug had sometimes gotten him a cold shoulder.

He was a tactile person. Touch was important—it was to all alphas. To lose it was devastating.

When Jamie spun and raced from the room, he knew in that moment that he couldn't go through this again. Not until he and Jamie could figure out a way through whatever this was between them. He'd thought it simple fatigue. The illness. He'd let it go, wanting to support his mate.

But now… it was something altogether worse. Being with Gray might have been the final nail in the coffin.

Jamie was sending him to another's bed to avoid him. More time wasn't going to fix things between them. They needed to reconcile… completely. No child should be brought into their home, not while it was this broken.

He couldn't do it again. There would be no baby. Not unless…

There already was one.

Rohan sat on the edge of the bed and rested his elbows on his knees. He could still scent Gray on his nose, and he hated what it had done to his body. He'd showered quickly, wanting to rid himself of the scent before he saw Jamie again, but it hadn't been enough.

He closed his eyes as he remembered the feel of Gray's hand on his body, searching… exploring and learning him. The looks of desire… the gasps of pleasure.

Too bad they'd come from the wrong man.

Chapter Sixteen

The day after Gray's return home...

Gray didn't know what to say upon opening the door and finding Tensen there at his doorstep... with a bunch of beautiful flowers in hand. His stare met Tensen's, and the man's face grew red. But Tensen didn't look away. He seemed unashamed, and there was something brave about that—it called to Gray.

"I know the last few days couldn't have been easy on you. Rohan called. He asked if I could come by and check to see how you were faring."

At Rohan's name, he tensed. "Was it really Rohan... or Jamie?"

Tensen shook his head. "No, I don't think it was Jamie's needling at all. But he didn't really have to ask me. I'd already planned to stop in and check on you."

He smiled, a glint of something to his eye.

How Gray understood what that glint was, he wasn't sure. No one had ever *glinted* for him before. He appreciated Tensen's concern, but the solicitor's attention was the last thing he needed at the moment. He'd just spent four days in another man's bed—a *mated* man. Gray didn't deserve Tensen's consideration. Yet he took the flowers as they were thrust at him... searching for the right words to say as the sweet aroma filled his nose. He brought the bouquet up and inhaled.

"You could've just called. I know how busy you are."

Tensen grinned. "I am... but I will *always* make time for you."

Gray looked away. "I'm not one you should be spending your time on."

"Oh... I think you are. I think you're selfless and amazing... and I can only wish I was more than a beta so I would be worthy of a man like you."

Gray's head whipped up. His eyes widened, his mouth dropping open. He was stunned by the solicitor's words.

His heart began to beat a little more fiercely... but it wasn't attraction. Not that Tensen wasn't handsome, because he was. He was kind and intelligent... and he was perfect in almost every way.

It was the simple fact Gray was *wanted*. That's what made his heart beat faster. Right, wrong, or in between—someone wanted him.

But this man couldn't be the one. A beta and an omega couldn't be a matched set. There were no laws to allow him to become a beta's mate. He wouldn't be free to leave the Omega Quadrant. The best he could do was become Tensen's whore.

Is it better to be alone the rest of my life or a kind man's whore?

Gray took a step back, unnerved. "I suppose I should offer you a tea or coffee since you've made a special trip here."

Tensen shook his head. "I'm not going to take any more of your time. I was just worried about you and wanted to ensure you were well."

Gray met the man's stare. "Thank you. You don't know how much I appreciate your concern."

Tensen's soft smile made him wish again that things between them could be different. The solicitor leaned forward, and Gray inhaled, worried. But it was for no reason. Tensen placed a chaste kiss to Gray's cheek before he turned to leave.

Gray watched the man's retreating form, more confused than ever.

"Who brought you those?"

Gray turned to see Lake watching him closely. "A friend. He was checking in on me."

"Does this have something to do about you being gone? Was he the one you were fucking?"

Gray slammed the door and spun to face Lake. "Excuse me?"

"It was awfully convenient that you were gone during your heat. I'm not a kid anymore… I know what men do behind closed doors."

Gray frowned and stormed closer to the teen. He pointed a finger in the middle of the boy's chest. "What I do or don't do isn't any of your business."

"Whatever," Lake spat before wandering toward the kitchen.

"No. Not whatever," Gray said, following him. "This attitude of yours has gone on long enough."

"You haven't even begun to see my attitude," Lake said from where he stared into the refrigerator.

"Oh? Really now."

Lake pulled out the juice and drank straight from the carton before Gray walked over, pulled it from his hands, and put it back into the fridge. "You are part of a family, whether you like it or not. We all share that, and I don't want your germs all over it."

The teen chuckled. "Oh? Whose germs do you have all over you, whore?"

Gray was so taken aback, all he could do was stand there, mouth open, as Lake smiled and headed back to his bedroom.

Whore.

Gray fell back onto one of the stools at the island and let that word spin around within his mind—knowing it was somewhat true. He'd demeaned himself... for money... allowed another alpha to touch him... potentially fill him with a child.

A child he would have to let go.

What have I done?

* * * *

What have I done?

Jamie looked in the mirror and didn't like what he saw looking back at him. The man he loved... who loved him in return... deserved better. Rohan deserved to be loved, in all ways. It couldn't be him, not anymore.

A tremor in his hand made him look down. When he lifted his stare back to the mirror, he could see the exhaustion in his eyes.

He'd been feeling more and more tired in the last weeks. Soon, Jamie crawled into bed in the guest room away from Rohan.

It felt so unnatural to be lying there alone.

The darkness surrounded him.

It was too quiet.

Jamie almost slid from the bed and padded down the hallway to get into the big, warm bed beside his alpha.

He needs to learn to live without me.

Heart aching, he rolled to his side and forced himself to relax... and finally drifted off, dreaming of babies and fatherhood and raising a family with Rohan.

Chapter Seventeen

Three weeks later...

After making another phone call to Avery that went unanswered, Gray drained the last of his cup, one hip resting against the counter. Worry filled him... the boy was treading thin ice.

But his emotional state wasn't great for more than one reason. The main one sat across from him. He stared at the strips on the counter, weighing his emotions. He took another sip, only absentmindedly realizing he'd already finished the cup. Turning, he put another pot on, his back to those items that had so fully captured his focus.

Once the kettle was on, he returned to look at the sticks lying on the counter. All three showed two perfect pink lines.

He was pregnant.

One heat... with one alpha in full rut... and he was knocked up. He knew he should feel elated that it happened so easily, but he wasn't.

While a good part of him hated what he'd done with Rohan, another small bit had looked forward to another heat. Shame nearly stole his breath... thinking of being in Rohan's bed again. Of course, there was a *slim* chance the pregnancy tests were wrong. He'd know for sure the following full moon. Gray was already scheduled to return to Rohan and Jamie's house for another round. If he didn't go into heat, it would be a surefire sign he was indeed pregnant.

When Avery came rushing in moments later, he still sat there staring numbly.

"Sorry I was late and incommunicado. Cell reception has been off. I just saw your ca—" Avery said as he walked in, breaking off as he came to a stop beside Gray. Silence fell between them. "Are those... are those what I think they are?"

Gray inhaled a slow breath. "They are."

More silence.

"That was quick," Avery mumbled.

The kettle whistled, and Gray moved to take it off the burner and pour himself a cup. Once he was done, he gazed at his nephew. "It was quick."

"How are you feeling?"

"Not great. You being a no-call, no-show for hours didn't help my mental state right now. You should've called and let me know what you were doing."

Gray worried the second Avery walked out the door and didn't relax until the boy stepped back inside their home.

"You're right. I should have. I turned off my phone in the library and didn't come up for air until all my homework was done. I was in a cubby, with no clear sign of any windows, so I had no idea how late it had gotten. It won't happen again, I promise." Avery turned to face him. "What's this about your mental state? You wanted to be a surrogate. Now you are. This was your choice."

"Don't," Gray murmured. "Not right now, okay?"

Avery didn't say another word.

"I know this is what I wanted, but now that the realization is sinking in, I'm... I don't know what I am. Ambivalent?" He released a sigh. "And I just can't handle your judgment right now."

"I didn't mean to sound judgmental."

"I want this," Gray whispered hoarsely. "I want to give them a child. I want to help provide for you all. I want this."

"Who are you trying to convince?" Avery asked solemnly.

Gray eyed his nephew, knowing Avery's concerns were valid. Now those concerns seemed larger than life when they'd once felt trivial.

"Have the boys eaten?" Avery asked.

"Yeah and they're off upstairs, playing video games, I'm sure. If you're hungry, there's a plate in the oven."

Avery collected his supper and placed it on the island before grabbing a drink and then taking his seat. He stared across the kitchen at Gray but said nothing.

"I always assumed my first child would've been so different," Gray said, fighting the sting coming to the backs of his eyes. "I'd always envisioned an alpha who would adore me… care for me… provide… and I'd give him a beautiful family in return."

Avery didn't say anything. The boy looked at a loss for words. It wasn't fair for him to be dumping all of this on his nephew's shoulders, not when this had been his choice—just as Avery had said.

Instead of answering, Avery slipped from his seat and walked over to Gray and hugged him tight. Gray didn't want to need that hug in that moment, but after a few seconds, he leaned into Avery's strength.

"What the hell is this shit?" Lake muttered before he walked across the room and opened the refrigerator. He stood there staring for several moments before closing it and growling. "Who ate the last of the yogurt?"

"I did," Gray answered, stepping back from Avery's embrace. "We'll get some more tomorrow."

"Doesn't help me now, asshole," Lake snapped.

"Language!" Gray roared before the boy lurched out of the room and stormed up the stairs.

"That boy really needs a *swift* kick in the ass," Gray said. "We can't let this continue."

"I'll talk to him... just let me eat my dinner first."

"No. I'm done being his punching bag." Gray marched himself upstairs and into Lake's bedroom, trying to control his anger. After taking a deep breath, he glared at Lake. "We're all getting a little tired of the attitude. Especially me."

"I don't care what you think!" Lake spat. "This isn't your house anyway. What are you even doing here?"

Gray swallowed back his rage at hearing those words. Mostly because it was true. The house *wasn't* his.

But he was family and he was doing his best to help hold them all together. "I'm here because we're all we've got now. The four of us—that's it."

A look of pain flashed over Lake's face, and then it was gone. The surly teenager was back so fast Gray wondered if he'd been mistaken. But he knew he hadn't.

"I know you're hurting. I know you miss your father and papa."

Lake said nothing. He only angrily glared at Gray.

"But *your brothers* lost them, too. I lost the brother I loved dearly, and the brother-in-law who was *so* very kind to me. I loved him, too." Gray took a step closer. "We all lost people we loved. We're *all* hurting. And you being snide and cruel doesn't help that."

"You're only sad you lost your meal ticket," Lake spat angrily.

Gray clenched his teeth. "You really think that of me?"

For just a moment, Lake looked a bit sad, but the anger came back in full force. "How would I know? You're the uncle I barely ever saw, the one leeching off the money we need to survive now. You're the reason Avery had to cut his hair... the reason he had to go get a job. Now we're stuck with you all up in our shit and ruining everything!"

Gray eyed his nephew. "You're right. You barely know me, because I can't leave this quadrant. I'm trapped here. A virtual prisoner. I could only sit back and wait for your papa to bring you here to visit. Even when you did come, you raced outside to play and barely spent more than two minutes in my company once you were old enough."

Lake didn't respond.

"But when you were a baby? You'd sit in my lap for hours. I'd hold you close and cuddle you near me," Gray sighed, his eyes shining. He'd held on to Lake... just as he had all the boys... imagining the day when he himself would be a father.

Now here he was going to be and he'd never have the chance to see the babe grow up.

"You need a scapegoat? Fine. You be as mad at me as you want to be. But you leave your brothers out of it. They lost their father and papa, too, just like you. And I won't have you treating them like shit because you think your feelings are more important than theirs, you self-entitled, selfish *brat*."

Lake frowned. "Yeah? Well... well... you're a spoiled little bitch!"

"That the best you got?" Gray roared.

"Fuck you!" the teen roared back.

"Fuck you, too, you little shit!"

Lake's eyes fill with tears. He immediately felt like an asshole for yelling.

"Get out of my room!" Lake screamed as tears streamed down his face.

Gray stood there a moment, not sure if he should stay or go as the boy asked. Going with his gut, he walked across the room and forced the boy into his arms and held tight, even as Lake tried to push him away.

After a moment, Lake's arms stopped pushing and his hands twisted in Gray's shirt. He began to cry in earnest, huge sobs coming from him as Gray held on tight. Lake was nearly as tall as he was, so he had to widen his stance to hold the boy up.

As the crying slowed, he caressed the back of Lake's head and tried to soothe his nephew. He sat them on the edge of Lake's bed and just held on—for as long as the teenager needed it.

Soon, Lake grew quiet. "Why did this all happen to us?"

Gray ran a hand down the back of Lake's head, choosing his words carefully. "Life is filled with beautiful, amazing things... but the other side of that coin is the bad. You can't have one side without the other. While we're here, we need to cherish all the good we can... and try to pick ourselves up after the bad and live on."

"They can't live on."

There was no question who *they* were. "No, but they would want you and your brothers to. They gave you life… in the hopes you'd have great adventures. You still can."

"I don't feel like I want to do anything. It feels wrong to be happy when they're not here to be happy, too."

Gray caressed the back of Lake's head. He understood how the boy felt. "Mourning those we love isn't easy. But each day it will get a little easier."

"What if I forget them?"

"I can honestly say that will never happen. Your father and papa live on in you three. They will be there every moment, looking down on you and seeing the good you do in this world. You don't want to disappoint them, do you?"

Lake lifted his head off Gray's shoulder and wiped his face with both hands. "No. I don't."

Gray missed the weight of his nephew leaning on him. He stared at the boy's profile and saw a little of Silver in the tilt to the boy's head.

"I'm sorry I said those things," Lake whispered before turning to eye Gray.

"It's okay."

Lake's eyes shone a little more, and he swallowed. "You look like papa."

Gray clenched his teeth and held on to his own emotions, not willing to lose it in front of the boy. He needed to be strong right now. It wasn't something he was good at, but he needed practice. The road ahead was going to have a lot of potholes and speed bumps, and for more than one reason.

"You look a little like him, too," Gray whispered back, lifting a hand to caress Lake's cheek.

"No. I look like father."

Gray shook his head. "You've got Silver's eyes. And the same arrogant tilt to the head. Your smile is his, though I can't remember the last time I saw it."

Lake smiled slightly, but wasn't quite yet capable of a full one, it seemed. He brushed his face and eyes again with both hands and walked over to his desk. "I've got homework I need to do."

The boy sat down, his back to Gray. Their moment over, Gray rose and crossed the room. He paused at the door and looked over at Lake—who was working away. He opened the bedroom door and exited.

Avery stood in the hallway across from him, his eyes looking a bit rimmed in red.

Gray cupped one of Avery's cheeks before heading to his bedroom before he lost it himself. Dropping to his bed once the door was closed, the floodgates opened and he mourned the brother he'd adored.

And the future he'd always imagined for himself.

Now he had a new future.

Caressing his stomach, he knew this was the good side of the coin.

It had to be.

Chapter Eighteen

Anti-climactic...

Gray stared through the window from his spot in the backseat. Outside, the heat wasn't letting up and continued on into the fall. The air conditioning was on inside the car—it was almost nippy. He rested back against the padded leather and wrapped his arms about himself to warm up.

His trip back to Jamie and Rohan's home was much different this time around.

He'd been so lost to the heat plaguing him, he'd barely seen anything he'd gazed at. Gone was the lust. He felt no overpowering desire to mate and felt quite sure his suspicions were confirmed. Once they arrived, he'd know for sure. If Rohan didn't go into rut upon seeing him, there would be no doubt left.

Until then, he enjoyed the views as they drove through the Family Quadrant. They passed landmarks he remembered from his youth, things he hadn't seen in decades. A smile came to his lips as they drove down Main Street and saw the families together.

His smile faded as he realized he would never have that.

They came to a stop at a corner just outside the park from his paintings—the ones Jamie now owned. A part of him regretted handing them over. Those had been his last links to his past life outside the O Quad. He let his stare roam over the park. Maybe he'd paint a new one.

He only wished he could paint it *in* the park.

That was a dream he'd never see come true. He'd live and die in the O Quad.

And that thought nearly made him choke. The ride to and from Jamie's home might be his last trip outside those walls.

Ever.

When they pulled into the circular drive before Rohan and Jamie's home, he sucked in a gasp. The home was beautiful… and grand. It was of the old style, with huge columns holding up a second story balcony that wrapped around the entire house. Baskets of flowers and ferns hung from the spaces between the columns, and the entire front was meticulously landscaped. Once he was outside, he could see a rose garden on one side and what looked to be a huge sunroom made entirely of glass.

He hadn't been coherent enough the last time to truly notice it… and he'd been in such a rush to leave that he hadn't looked back, either.

"You remember the rules from last time, correct?"

Gray turned to meet the beta driver's stare in the rearview mirror. It was a different man this time—apparently one who wasn't as stringent as the last. "Yes. I remember."

"Good," he murmured before turning off the car and climbing out.

Gray opened the door and saw the proffered hand before him. He took it and allowed the beta to help him from the backseat before the man went to the trunk to get Gray's bag.

"I think I might wait here," the driver said, eyeing him. He placed Gray's suitcase back inside the trunk. "I get the feeling you won't be there very long."

Gray released a breath. *If the driver can tell I'm apparently not in heat... add one more check in the 'I'm pregnant' column.*

Before he made his way up the wide front steps, he took a moment to draw in the warmth. He inhaled, catching a scent of the late blooming roses and the other flowers that filled the yard. Gray lifted his head and gazed up at the robin's egg blue sky and thought to himself that the air was cleaner here... the sky bluer.

Gray turned to see the driver staring at him and realized he must look mad. He made his way to the entrance, but before he could knock, Jamie pulled the door open. A wide smile graced his face.

"You're here!"

There was an awkward pause. Neither of them had spoken much over the last month—only in a few text messages and emails. He'd gotten the sensation that Jamie had put up a wall, and he'd been too afraid to reach out in fear of making the situation even more precarious.

"You *did* want me here, didn't you?"

A flicker crossed Jamie's face, but the smile never truly faded. "Of course. Where else would you be? Come in, come in."

Gray crossed the threshold and felt the cooler air within surround his body. The heat outside had felt good after the chill in the car. The coolness between him and Jamie only made him feel colder.

"Is the driver bringing in your bags?"

"He's waiting a moment..."

Jamie frowned before tilting his head and giving Gray an odd look. "Can I get you a drink?"

"No. I'm fine," Gray said, his voice low.

"Well, you can take a seat there and wait for Rohan." Jamie leaned down to take the handle of his overnight bag before rising to his full height. "I'll see you both in a few days."

"Don't go," Gray said. "Not yet."

"I *can't* be here… not while you two are together. I'll return like I did last time."

"Nothing may happen," Gray said.

Jamie looked confused—until Gray reached into his pocket and showed off one of the tests he'd taken.

Jamie looked up, shock and excitement visible on his face. "You're pregnant? Already?"

"I think so. I wanted to come and see my reaction to Rohan to confirm it. To make absolutely sure."

"You need to be seen by a doctor," Jamie said, looking as if he might explode with joy then and there. "Then it can be fully confirmed and we can prepare a plan for your pregnancy."

"Let's not get ahead of ourselves," Gray said.

"But you'd surely be feeling the effects of a heat by now."

Gray shrugged. "My heats in recent years have been so terrible that I don't know what a normal one feels like."

"Jamie?" Rohan called from upstairs.

"Come down, husband. We might have wonderful news," Jamie yelled up, smiling.

Rohan came down the stairs slowly, a curious look to his face.

It was then that Gray was sure. He felt no intense pangs of lust. No unflinching desire for Rohan.

Yet he did feel an attraction he had no right to feel. The intimacies they'd shared had made an indelible mark. One he'd feel for the rest of his life. He held the alpha's gaze for a moment before looking away.

Jamie captured his stare, searching Gray's face for an answer. He nodded slightly.

"He's pregnant!" Jamie cried, turning to Rohan.

Gray's stare was drawn to Rohan's.... and Rohan's to his. For a split second, they held that gaze and there was something that made him feel forever bound to the alpha. He looked down at his hands, clenched together before his flat stomach.

Jamie babbled on excitedly, talking of the months to come.

Gray could only wish to go home, away from Rohan and the terrible, tragic longing he now felt in the midst of things. He loved Jamie. He loved the man as if he were family. And he was a hateful, terrible human being for wanting what wasn't his.

"My driver didn't leave," Gray murmured. "Just in case. I should go back to the O Quad now."

"There's no need to rush," Jamie said, smiling widely. "You're free now."

Gray frowned.

"A pregnant surrogate isn't relegated to the OQ. You're in no danger of an alpha coming after you if you're with child. Once the pregnancy is confirmed, you'll be given a pass, so you can travel freely," Jamie said.

A smile came to his face. "I didn't know."

He was free.

Temporarily, but it was better than nothing, wasn't it?

It had taken an alpha's seed to free him from the shackles. In a few months, he'd be back under lock and key. Some freedom that was.

But until then... he was free.

"I've already chosen a good OBGYN," Jamie said, grinning from ear to ear. "I want to go call their office now and arrange an appointment."

Jamie scurried off, leaving him alone with Rohan. He lifted his stare to the male, unsure how the alpha felt about his current condition. From the look on his face, Gray was even more uncertain.

"You don't look pleased," Gray murmured.

"I am," Rohan said, eyeing him. "I'm glad it happened quickly so we didn't have to endure another heat."

Endure another heat.

Gray was hurt by Rohan's choice of words, but how could he expect more? Rohan's heart belonged to another... as it should be.

But it still didn't change the twisted emotions he now felt. In the span of a single heat, Gray had lost a little part of himself to the alpha. Lust and love were two very different emotions... but with his limited experience, they coalesced into one in his mind.

Even without the heat, he still wanted that which he couldn't have.

And he hated himself for it.

Without another thought, he raced out of the front door and ran down the stairs. The driver opened the door and let him inside before climbing in behind the seat.

Gray closed his eyes as the car propelled forward... away from his terrible thoughts and desires.

* * * *

The following day...

Jamie stood on Gray's doorstep, basket in hand. He pressed the doorbell again, hoping he wasn't being ignored.

When the door opened and a sleepy-looking Gray stared out at him, he sighed with a little relief. "I come bearing gifts." He lifted the basket some and smiled.

Gray's smile in return was wan. He backed away from the door some. "Come in."

Jamie entered. The house was quiet, and he remembered the boys were likely in school. He headed for the kitchen and laid the basket on the counter before reaching in and pulling out some of the fresh fruit and vegetables inside.

"I stopped by the farmer's market before I came over. I wanted to make sure you had plenty of healthy things to eat," he said, resting the apples and pears on the counter.

"Thank you," Gray murmured quietly.

Jamie made himself busy, sneaking little looks from the corners of his eyes. He wasn't sure what was upsetting Gray so much. When he was done storing the food, he showed the bottles that were still inside the basket. "Pregnancy vitamins. I bought you enough to last your entire ten months."

"I appreciate it," Gray said, still looking solemn.

"I was a little worried after you raced out of the house yesterday and didn't answer my calls."

"I was feeling a bit overwhelmed. I just wanted to be home," Gray murmured. "I've been sleeping a lot the last few days."

"Growing a baby is hard work, I hear," Jamie said with a grin. "Why don't you sit down and I'll brew us a cup of tea?"

"You don't have to do that. You're a guest here."

"No. I insist," Jamie said, hoping his tone brooked no argument.

Gray shook his head and took a seat at the island before Jamie took the kettle from the stove. He walked to the sink and began to fill it. "Oh, I got you that appointment. It's a wonderful OB in the Family Quadrant. He comes highly recommended."

"When?"

"Tomorrow. I made sure it was late enough that the boys would be in school, with plenty of time for you to get back before they come home. I've already arranged for a car to come pick you up and drive you there and back."

Gray nodded. "Thank you."

He set the kettle on the burner and turned on the heat before turning to face Gray. "I'll meet you there, of course. I want to support you through the entire thing."

"I love you, but I don't need to be micromanaged through this pregnancy."

Jamie paused. "I wasn't trying to do that. I just want to be supportive."

"Did you bother asking me if I had plans tomorrow before making the appointment?" Gray asked, lifting a brow.

Jamie's face fell. "I'm sorry. They had a cancellation—otherwise it would've been a few weeks before they could've gotten you in, and I was so excited to find out for sure—I took it." He paused. "I'll be sure to ask first before I rush off and make plans for you. I apologize." He paused, forcing a smile. "I'm just so incredibly happy with this amazing news."

"I am, too. So very happy for you both."

"And for you," Jamie said. "You're the most important person now."

"No, the baby within me is."

Jamie frowned slightly. He reached for two cups hanging from the cup tree and righted them on their bases before he turned to eye Gray. "You are important. You."

Gray's face fell, and he looked down. "I'm not. I'm a terrible person, Jamie, and you shouldn't be so nice to me."

Jamie rounded the island and took Gray's chin in one hand and rested the other on the man's shoulder. "How are you terrible?"

Gray shook his head and tried to look away.

Jamie felt the sting come to the backs of his eyes, and he fought it tooth and nail. Once he was sure he could speak without his voice breaking, he did. "You felt the bond."

Gray turned back to look at him, frowning. "The bond?"

Jamie lowered his hand, quite sure he now had Gray's full attention. "The bond. I know it's been a while since your breeding classes in school—but I'm quite sure you had the same sexual education I did."

Gray's frown only grew. "We had little to no sexual education."

"Well, I *was* a few years behind you. Maybe they changed things," Jamie said. "The bond. The alpha-omega sexual bond. It's a chemical reaction after sex. He's marked you… and it makes you want him. It aids in linking an alpha to his omega. It's what keeps other alphas at bay after the claiming."

"But I'm *not* his omega. You are."

"In some ways, you are his," Jamie said before resting his hand on Gray's stomach. "Part of him grows within you even now."

"If we'd done things in a lab… would he have marked me?"

Jamie shook his head. "No."

Gray closed his eyes.

He knew he'd asked a lot of them both… but the stakes were high. It had to be this way… for so many reasons.

"I wish now I'd put my foot down and not given in. We shouldn't have done this, Jamie."

Jamie smiled widely. He'd assumed Gray knew this part, but now felt a bit guilty for that assumption. "But look what we've been given! Already you're with child. We might've waited months… *years*… for this to happen."

Gray nodded, but didn't look mollified.

"You wanted this," Jamie whispered, feeling a sense of desperation. "To provide for your family. To ease your heats and save yourself so much torment." He brushed a hand over the top of Gray's long, thick hair. "You wanted to feel how it felt to be wanted."

"And now I know," Gray said on a sob, his stare lifting to Jamie's. His eyes glittered with tears. "And I wish I didn't know."

Jamie's heart ached for Gray. Had it been too great a thing for him to know what he was missing?

"I'm sorry," Jamie whispered, running a hand along Gray's back. "I only wanted to help you."

"No... I'm the one who's sorry. For wanting what I shouldn't." Gray met Jamie's stare. "For wanting what I can't have."

Jamie sucked in a gasp.

Gray looked down. "And now it's ripped a hole in us both. Maybe all three of us. I've lost your friendship..."

"You've lost nothing," Jamie declared, standing taller. "Nothing."

"I've barely heard from you since..." Gray paused. "Since... I was with Rohan."

Jamie swallowed past the lump in his throat. "It was hard... seeing and hearing what I did. Harder than I imagined it would be." He caressed the side of Gray's hair and smiled, tears filling his eyes. "But I don't regret it. Not one bit, especially now." Jamie caressed the side of Gray's cheek before laying a gentle kiss there. "I didn't know exactly what to say after. We all struggled in the aftermath, and I feared causing a rift between us with the wrong word."

"I was afraid of the same," Gray admitted, taking Jamie's hand in his. "And afraid I'd lost you."

Jamie shook his head before drawing Gray into his arms and holding on tight. "You haven't lost me. I'm right here. I'm not going anywhere. Do you hear me?"

Gray hugged him tight. "Promise?"

Jamie moved back some and gathered Gray's cheeks in both hands. "You and I are brothers of the heart. We are one. I adore you... and I love you."

Gray's eyes closed, and one tear slid down his cheek. Jamie hugged him again, pressing a kiss to Gray's forehead. "I knew you were the one the minute I saw you."

"So… you forgive me?"

"There is nothing for me to forgive," Jamie cried, stepping back to gaze at Gray. "You did as I asked… and you've given us this child. The world will be a better place with him in it."

"I don't know that I could be as strong as you are in your shoes," Gray said, wiping at the wetness on his cheek. "Or this unfazed given the circumstances."

"I'm not unfazed," Jamie said. "Trust me. I'm a little rattled."

"Yet here you are, comforting me," Gray said before he rose and took Jamie by the shoulders. "What can I do for you?"

Jamie rested a hand on Gray's stomach. "You already have."

* * * *

A family meeting…

Gray sat at one end of the dining room table, watching as his nephews dug into the dinner he'd made. All day, he'd felt a bit squeamish and wasn't hungry. While they all had a mouthful, it was likely the best time to have his say.

"I have some news… and it's best to tell you here and now before you have questions," Gray announced.

The boys looked his way. After a few quick chews, Avery shook his head. "Not yet."

"What time is any better than now?"

Avery sighed after a moment and placed his knife and fork down. "Go ahead."

Gray looked at both Auggie and Lake before taking a deep breath. "I'm pregnant."

Silence filled the room for a moment.

"But... you're unmated," Lake said.

"I am. I've entered an agreement with an alpha-omega couple who couldn't have a child of their own," Gray said. "They want a child. I can give them one."

Gray turned to look at Auggie, who wore a very confused look.

"But why?" Lake demanded. "Why would you do that?"

"Because they've offered to pay me for the service I'm offering them. Money we need to keep this family afloat."

"But Avery got a job," Auggie said.

Avery had. He worked the college mailroom, but told the boys he was stocking shelves at a local grocery in the O Quad. The job wasn't many hours, but it was all he'd been able to find thus far. Avery was still looking.

"And Avery said we had enough to last a few years," Lake added. "Why would you do that?"

"Because I've been a burden on this family long enough. All I've done is take... and now is the time to give. I can give this couple the baby they so desperately want, and I can help make sure our future is better." He smiled between the two boys. "I want to make sure you're both provided for."

"No!" Lake said, tears coming to his eyes. "I know I said that we couldn't buy stuff... but I don't need stuff that bad. I don't need movies and music and games... I already have enough. I don't need anything else."

Gray frowned. "It's more than games and movies... there are balls to come. Connections to be made. It all costs a lot of money, and I want to make sure all three of you get the futures you deserve."

Lake began to sob openly. Gray could barely breathe seeing the boy's emotions come.

"I didn't expect you to get upset," Gray murmured, reaching out a hand to Lake's.

The teen lifted his head. "What about you, Uncle Gray? What about you and your alpha? He won't want you now. And it'll be all our fault."

Gray rose to his feet and walked closer. He knelt beside Lake. "No... it won't be your fault. This was my decision. I don't have an alpha. I'm giving up nothing but a child... a child who will be loved so very much by two very fine men. He will have everything he could ever need or want... and so will you."

"I don't want everything," Lake whispered.

Gray reached out and hugged the boy.

When he glanced across the table, he saw Auggie with tears in his eyes. "You're not going to give us away, are you?"

"No! Of course not," Gray cried. "Come here, you."

Auggie raced to him and dove into his open arm.

"But you are just going to give the baby away when it's over?" Lake asked.

"Yes. It won't be easy, I know. But I've signed papers saying the baby is theirs and not mine."

"But it *is* yours. It's our cousin," Lake said. "You shouldn't have signed it away. How could you? We don't have much family left," the boy said, tears in his eyes. "And now you're giving away some of it."

Lake jumped from his chair and raced upstairs to his room. A resounding slam was so familiar from the teenager in recent months. Gray eyed Avery for a moment before the youngest of their clan caught his attention.

"Why couldn't they have a baby of their own?"

Gray rose to sit in Lake's abandoned chair. He turned to face Auggie and took the boy's hands in his. "You've met Jamie before, remember?"

"Yeah."

"When he first started coming here, he really didn't look well. Do you remember?"

"Yeah."

"He had cancer. And because of that, he can't have a baby anymore. I'm helping him and his alpha have a baby so they can become a family."

"That sounds nice," Auggie said. "Why's Lake so upset?"

"I'm not totally sure he even knows," Gray said. "But he's entitled to feel however he feels. I didn't think to talk this all over with you two… but maybe I should have before I made my decision."

"Will we be able to see the baby?"

Gray shook his head. "I don't think you will." Perhaps it was best if none of them saw the baby.

"Oh," Auggie said. "Uncle Gray?"

"Yes?"

"Can I go finish my dinner now?"

Gray chuckled and released the boy's hands. "Yes. Please do."

Later, once dinner was over, Gray and Avery stood shoulder to shoulder washing dishes. Silence, albeit for the sounds of water splashing and the scrub of a brush, filled in around them. He wondered what was going on in Avery's mind, but he was almost afraid to ask and find out the truth of it.

Because it was likely some of the same things swirling in his own mind.

Chapter Nineteen

Rohan's office...

Rohan stared at the mountain of work on his desk. Any other time and he'd hate seeing it, but now, suddenly, he was thankful for it. It gave him something to focus on that wasn't his home life.

Never had he ever thought he'd wish for something to prevent him from going home.

"Knock-knock."

Rohan looked up from the brief and saw Wilder leaning inside his door. "Hey."

"You're here late."

Rohan swept a hand over his desk. "Your father handed me more contracts to review. Seems he's gotten aggressive in his expansion plans."

"I'm the one at fault for that," Wilder said, smiling. "But you *could* be working on this at home. Like you normally do."

Was he really that transparent? "I can focus a little better here."

"Home a bit busy nowadays? I'm sure with the baby on the way, my brother is driving you nuts with plans for a nursery and the gods know what else," Wilder said with a grin.

Rohan lifted his stare and forced a smile to his face. "That's pretty much the gist of it."

Wilder's smile faded. "What's wrong?"

"Nothing."

Wilder frowned. "Bullshit. We've known each other long enough for me to know your poker face is *gods awful.*"

Rohan leaned back in his chair and scrubbed at his face a moment. When he moved his hands away, Wilder was already settling himself in the chair across the desk. "It's nothing, really. Don't worry about it."

"It have anything to do with Jamie?"

Rohan lifted his stare. "No."

Wilder grinned. "*Yes, it does.* Spit it out."

"I can't involve you in my marriage. It's not fair to you or my omega."

"I love my brother… and you're my best friend. If not me, who?"

Rohan stared at Wilder, knowing he couldn't share what was truly happening behind closed doors… or the wayward thoughts he was having.

"This has something to do with the baby, doesn't it?"

It had *everything* to do with the baby. Or rather— how it was made. They'd found out about the pregnancy a month before and still Jamie refused to touch him or be touched. His omega was pulling away from him more and more each day.

And spending all his days with Gray.

Rohan was becoming consumed with his surrogate omega. Wild dreams, sexual exploits, fevered memories of their four days in bed. The further Jamie pushed him away, the more Gray slipped into his mind.

Part of that was the bond. He knew the chemical reaction that locked them together was partially to blame for his errant thoughts. But he loved Jamie.

And he fought those tormenting images with everything that he had.

Maybe that was the problem.

The more he fought, the harder it became.

"I thought you had agreed to all this? I mean, I know you had some doubts, but I assumed you'd finally decided this was the right thing for you both." Wilder said. "At least, that's how it seemed."

"I couldn't say no to my omega," Rohan finally said. "He wants this baby with everything in him... but it's *all* he wants."

"All he wants... meaning?"

Rohan shook his head. "I don't know if I'm on the list of his wants anymore."

Wilder frowned. "He loves you."

"And I love him. That isn't in doubt." He surely didn't feel loved in return... "But his needs have changed since he went into remission. He's solely focused on this child and nothing more."

"I'll talk to him. See what I can ferret out."

"*Don't.* I've already told you more than I should," Rohan said. He should've kept his mouth shut, but he needed to vent to *someone*. There was no way he was creating any kind of drama between Wilder and Jamie. Period. They dealt with enough family drama as it was. "Forget I said anything. We'll figure our way through. It's just a major learning curve... after cancer and before a new baby. We just need to find our footing again. There hasn't been time yet."

"If there's anything I can do," Wilder said.

"You'll be the first person I ask," Rohan said. "I promise. Don't worry."

Wilder looked worried all the same. He rose, confusion and uneasiness on his face. "I'm going to head out. Why don't you pack up and head home? Be with your omega?"

How could he say no to that? Rohan spied the stack of papers on his desk, knowing it was likely better to stay and get work done than to go home and be ignored. "Sure. Give me a minute to clean my desk up."

Wilder leaned back, crossing his arms over his chest. Rohan saw the arrogant, alpha tilt to the man's chin and knew there was no wasting of time. He cleared up his desk quickly and followed Wilder out.

Headed home.

To what, he wasn't quite sure anymore.

And he'd continue to wonder that same question as days turned to weeks and weeks turned into months… and they were no more closer to finding a way back to one another than they had been then.

* * * *

Four months pregnant…

"How about that new place on McConnel Avenue?" Jamie asked. "I've heard their lunch menu is to die for."

Gray shifted the bags in his hands a little, his feet aching from their whirlwind shopping spree. "How far is it? I need a break. And soon."

"We can hire a car," Jamie said before lifting his hand to the rushing traffic.

Gray braced himself. He wasn't used to the hubbub of the Alpha Quad or the commerce district. He hadn't been into the city more than a handful of times as a child. The noise… the high-rises… the congestion… the traffic… the smells… it was almost unbearable.

But there was also this thrum of excitement and life in the city.

There were shops and theaters and restaurants galore. He had gone from a tiny hamlet with limited options in the O Quad to having too many choices here. It was overwhelming, to say the least.

A for-rent car and driver pulled up along the curb, the tires almost squealing. Jamie opened up the back door and turned to Gray. "Hurry! Get in!"

Gray rushed over and launched himself and his bags into the backseat before Jamie crammed in with his bags as well.

"McConnel Ave," Jamie said. "That new restaurant... I think it's called Joyous?"

"Yeah, I know the place," the beta behind the wheel said, staring at them in the rearview. "Hold on tight."

The car whipped out into traffic. Gray heard the honking of horns behind them and wondered how close they might've just come to getting hit. He'd seen the way the cars zoomed in the streets and wondered how there weren't casualties lining the pavement.

"How are you fine omegas doing today? Shopping, I see."

"We have a baby coming," Jamie said excitedly. He was beaming. "We *have* to prepare. There's so much we need to buy."

"Congratulations," the driver said. "Who's the papa?"

"He is," both Jamie and Gray said in unison.

They looked at each other and chuckled.

"So... you *both* are pregnant?"

"No," Jamie corrected. "I can't have a child." He turned and smiled warmly at Gray. "My friend here has kindly agreed to aid my alpha and I in our wish for a babe. He's giving us an amazing gift that I will never truly be able to repay."

The driver looked up into the mirror, not saying anything. Gray felt the man's stare on him—and it made him uncomfortable.

"That's a fine thing you're doing," the driver said, pinning him with a stare.

Gray nodded, not liking the attention of the stranger. Jamie felt no qualms in sharing all of their information, while Gray remained a bit more conservative with who he told. Opinions about surrogates were a mine field, it seemed. While there were many who thought his act noble—not that it was in any way—there were still some from the older generation who thought fate should be left alone and that Jamie and Rohan should be left childless.

The car came to a sudden stop at the side of the street.

"McConnel Avenue. Home of Joyous Eats. That'll be four-eighty-three."

Jamie reached through with some renos in hand. "Keep the rest."

"Thank you, kindly," the driver said. "You two enjoy your lunch."

Jamie jumped out first, carrying his bags out. He turned to offer a hand to Gray—who took it immediately. He was only four and a half months along, but the baby was almost definitely an alpha, if size said anything. He was already beginning to show a little. His back ached all the time, so any extra help up was appreciated.

They clamored out onto the street and took the few steps to the door of the restaurant. The maître d' bent over backwards to help them store their bags and find them the perfect table up front. They had a bird's eye view of the street and everyone zipping to and fro.

Menus were placed before them. Gray opened his, and his eyes widened at the prices.

As they had been doing all day long.

He'd always *tried* to live frugally. He'd often failed, but even his failures looked conservative compared to what Jamie spent.

Before long, they placed their orders and received their drinks. He took a sip from his iced tea and sighed, glad to finally have a moment of rest.

"If I haven't already said it, thank you for the clothes," Gray said.

"You've thanked me over and over again, silly," Jamie said.

"I really didn't need them."

Jamie scoffed. "I saw how tight your sweater was around your midsection and don't even get me started on the rubber band holding your pants up. Don't think I didn't see that."

"But pregnancy is only a few months out of my life. It seems extravagant to spend a lot on clothes I won't wear for long. I was making do with what I had."

"I like spoiling you a little. Where's the harm in that?"

Gray smiled a little. He wasn't going to lie. He absolutely loved the soft pants and top he was wearing now. Jamie had made him change into it after purchasing. It was incredibly comfortable.

"This baby is going to be spoiled rotten, I predict."

Jamie grinned. "Absolutely." He took a sip from his glass of wine and sighed. "Anyway... you deserve a little pampering in your condition. If it was me pregnant, I would've had an entire new wardrobe purchased, just for the hell of it. I would want the world to know I was pregnant. Those clothes help show off the baby bump." He leaned over the small table and pressed a hand to the top of the swell. "That is an alpha... it has to be."

"I think so... there's no way I'd be showing this soon if it wasn't. I'd say it's a big alpha, at that."

Jamie cringed a little. "There's only one thing bad about that."

The delivery. It was going to hurt more the bigger the babe was. "True. I will admit that I'm not looking forward to that."

"I will be there every second. Holding your hand. Helping you through the pain. I'd take it myself if I could... if it could make your suffering less."

"I know you would," Gray said.

Jamie lifted his glass—but then an odd look crossed his face and his hand dropped, clattering the edge of the glass on the table. Wine splashed, some of it cresting the edge of the glass before staining the white tablecloth.

Gray leaned forward, taking Jamie's hand and the glass. He set it down. "What's wrong?"

Jamie took a deep breath and exhaled. "Nothing." He reached for his glass again and met Gray's glare. "Nothing, I swear."

"That wasn't nothing."

Jamie took his drink and then shook his head as he sat the glass down. "I'm just tired. I haven't been sleeping well."

"Why not?"

"Well... to be honest... Rohan and I have been arguing a little lately. He thinks I'm too focused on the baby and nothing else. I keep telling him that you and the baby *need* to be the focus." Jamie chuckled. "He just misses me. I need to show him a little more attention. Don't worry."

Gray sensed there was more to it than sleeplessness, but he wasn't going to push. He hadn't seen anything else to give him doubts. But he was going to start watching the man like a hawk.

"Oh look!" Jamie said, looking through the plate glass window. "Rohan and my brothers are here."

Gray tensed. He hadn't seen Rohan since the second heat that never came. He'd been invited to meet Jamie's family, but he'd so far made excuses not to—simply to stay away from Rohan. Distance was good.

It kept his wayward thoughts to a minimum.

Jamie knocked on the window and got their attention. Moments later, the trio were inside and the maître d' was moving them to a larger table where they could share a meal. Gray did everything in his power to ignore Rohan.

"I didn't know you'd be having lunch here today!" Jamie said excitedly. He turned to Gray. "You get to meet my brothers."

He was introduced to both Wilder and Vaughn. The former looked like a bigger, beefier version of Jamie. The youngest brother—he looked completely different—with dark hair, dark eyes, and a stronger set to his chin. He'd heard a lot about them both, but particularly Wilder.

The sun seemed to rise and set on that particular brother.

Wilder offered a hand to Gray. He took it and then winced as the alpha scented him. Wilder's head whipped to the side to eye Rohan before releasing the hold. Vaughn gave him a quick nod before sitting down.

Once they were all seated, Gray felt an uncomfortable vibe surrounding them. It also didn't help that Rohan kept staring in his direction. Fortunately, the baby pressing down on his bladder helped give him an excuse to leave the table for a moment and get some alone time.

He rose. "Excuse me. I'll be right back."

Rohan pinned him with a heated glare that nearly had his knees buckling.

Gray rushed off as fast as he could, hoping like hell he could remain upright.

* * * *

Rohan watched Gray's retreating form, shocked by the swell to the omega's belly. He knew the man was pregnant, but seeing Gray ripe and growing with his child had an impact. It only made the instincts within him rise to the surface.

Bring him closer.
Protect him.
Covet him.

Rohan closed his eyes, trying to tamp down the need growing within.

Wilder sighed once Gray was out of hearing distance. "My gods, Rohan… you *marked* him? How could you do that to Jamie?"

"I demanded a natural conception," Jamie interrupted, speaking in low, firm tones. "Rohan didn't want to do it."

"That omega is drenched in your alpha's scent," Wilder said, clearly upset. "I can't believe you would want him to break his vows to you."

Wilder turned, glaring at Rohan.

"I fought your brother, tooth and nail," Rohan said, his jaw clenched. He continued to fight the protective instinct screaming for him to draw Gray closer and shelter the young growing within. Every muscle tensed, the marking scent stronger than he'd expected. Even now, he wanted to leave the table and follow the omega. "Jamie wouldn't budge."

"We can discuss this later," Jamie spat. "Now is not the time or the place."

Wilder turned to Jamie and narrowed his gaze. "You *honestly* wanted this? I can't believe that. It's insanity."

"Artificial insemination is costly and ineffective. And after all my many months in and out of hospitals and labs, I wasn't going to have this new life begin the same way," Jamie said. "Neither Gray nor Rohan wanted it. They both tried to talk me out of it. Eventually, they both gave in and saw my way was the better way."

"You sound like papa," Wilder murmured. "Selfish. I expect more from you."

Jamie looked away, disappointment on his face.

"Leave Jamie alone," Rohan said. "What's done is done. Gray is giving us the babe Jamie wants. End of story."

Wilder looked to Rohan. "End of story? What happens to this omega once all this is over? You've marked him as yours. He's your responsibility. But what about my brother?"

"We have a contract with Gray. We are paying him for this service—and handsomely at that—and when it is over, we have no more responsibility," Jamie said, matter-of-factly. Of course, he knew it was more than a simple contract, but his brothers didn't need to know all the ins and outs of his and Rohan's life, either.

Vaughn leaned in and gave his two cents. "Brother, you're an omega. You don't understand the alpha instinct. He's marked. Rohan will never let him go completely."

Rohan sighed and closed his eyes. He could feel Jamie's stare on him. When he reopened them, he saw his omega's expectant look. "What?"

"Is what he says correct? Will you always want Gray after this?"

"Time and distance will keep him out of my thoughts," Rohan said. "It's a chemical reaction—that's all. It means nothing." He turned to capture his omega's stare. "I have one mate and one mate only. I love you. Nothing will change that."

"Maybe it needs to change," Jamie whispered.

Rohan's chest clenched at Jamie's words. He frowned, opened his mouth to argue, but then stopped, realizing where they were and with who. He could barely breathe from the need to understand what his omega was thinking.

Feeling...

Or not feeling.

Had Jamie fallen out of love with him? Was he no longer wanted?

Rohan caught a scent and saw Gray returning to the table, swollen stomach and all. The instinct kicked into high gear, making him squirm in his seat.

Wilder shook his head and rose from the table, just as Gray walked nearer. "I've lost my appetite," he grated before leaving the restaurant.

Vaughn shook his head and followed Wilder out.

Jamie reached out and grabbed Rohan's hand. "Stay. Have lunch with us."

Rohan looked between him and Gray, finally drawing out the pregnant omega's seat before settling back in his own chair. Lunch was likely the most torture he'd ever endured in his life. Seated beside the man he loved more than anything in the world and the omega carrying his child and his scent.

He barely tasted the food. He barely remembered the conversation.

As soon as he'd paid for the check, he rose. "I need to get back to the office. You two stay as long as you'd like."

"Thank you for an enjoyable lunch," Gray murmured, not quite looking at him.

Rohan sensed the lunch had likely been just as uncomfortable for Gray. "You're welcome."

"Oh," Jamie cried excitedly. "We have an ultrasound appointment late tomorrow morning. Do you think you could take off and join us?"

Rohan looked between them.

Jamie looked excited. Gray looked panicked.

But the thought of seeing the baby firsthand... how could he say no? It *was* his son growing in Gray's stomach.

"I'm sure I can spare an hour or two," Rohan said. "Text me the time and location so I can plan once I get back to the office."

"Absolutely, sweetheart."

Rohan leaned into press a kiss to Jamie's forehead, only to have his omega awkwardly pull away.

He sighed inwardly and rose to his full height. His stare clashed with Gray's for a moment—until the omega looked away, embarrassed.

"I'll see you at home tonight," Rohan murmured and left before he felt any more shame.

* * * *

Jamie slid the smooth pajama top over his head before spying Rohan's broad, muscled back. Seated at the edge of his side of the bed, the alpha readied himself for bed, as well. The desire to step forward, to rest his hand and feel Rohan's warmth heat his palm… he took a tentative step forward before catching himself. All the same doubts and worries filled his mind, and he stepped back, as if singed by the thought alone.

Sadness swelled in his chest, making it hard to breathe.

For so long, they'd been lovers. Equal partners in this business of matehood. Rohan was a kind and gentle lover. A considerate and caring friend. And the man didn't deserve the hell Jamie was putting him through.

He opened his mouth. No words came. The pleading apologies wished to come to the fore and make themselves heard, but to utter them would only create another squabble as to why and why not.

Again, he'd try to explain without truly explaining, knowing his alpha would never truly understand what he was doing. If he did, Rohan would try to convince him otherwise and it would end up a circular argument, with neither of them winning, both of them losing, and leaving them both spent and exhausted.

This wasn't the way he wanted it.

So, as he had for months, he ignored the denials in his head, knowing what he was doing was right for them all.

By the gods, please let me be right.

He slid into his side of the bed, garnering a simple glance from Rohan over one shoulder. By the day, they grew more distant and that killed him, especially knowing it was by his own design. Too many nights now, they'd slipped under the covers, two strangers—never speaking the whispered words of 'I love you' and 'sleep well' that they used to.

The silence was deafening. He searched his mind for something—anything—they could talk about. "What did Wilder mean at lunch today?"

Rohan again looked over his shoulder, seeing but not seeing. "Your brother had a lot to say today."

"The part about... you marking Gray."

His alpha was silent a moment, long enough for him to wonder if an answer would come.

Rohan rose, turning, and peeled back the comforter on his side. "It happens in alpha-omega couplings. Omegas can't scent it, but alphas can. It's what keeps other alphas away from you."

"So any alpha can scent you on him?"

"Yes."

"Have I been marked?"

Rohan sighed. "Yes and no."

Jamie frowned. "Why yes and no?"

"You've been marked, but there are different kinds of marks." Rohan climbed onto the bed and pulled the covers up. "A stronger mark typically happens in pregnancy. After the babe has reached a few months. Three or four."

None of their babes had made it that far. Jamie had miscarried early each time, only a month or two along. "Oh."

Jamie was quiet a few moments. "So he's more your mate than I am."

"Are you serious?" Rohan asked, his head whipping to the side. "Not even close."

"I saw the way you looked at him over the lunch table."

"He's pregnant with our child. You know damned well an alpha's protective instinct kicks in. I tried to leave, but you begged me to stay."

Jamie turned to Rohan. "Don't be angry. I'm not jealous. I'm asking because I'm curious. I don't mean to make you upset."

"Well… maybe you should be jealous."

Jamie tilted his head.

Rohan sighed angrily. "You won't let me touch you. You won't touch me."

"I have no desire for sex, Rohan."

"I can't even get a hug without you flinching away from me!" Rohan drew in a deep breath. "I have left you alone. Other than the morning after… after Gray… I've never asked. Never assumed." Rohan tilted his head back, at a loss. "I miss the intimacy, Jamie. I miss the kisses and the hugs and you snuggling close to me in bed. Sex is only *half* of it. If you could give me those... it wouldn't be so hard to miss the rest."

"I was afraid that giving you those would make you think I wanted more," Jamie whispered. "I *can't* give you more, Rohan. The thought of sex... the thought of you touching me in those ways? I can't."

Rohan sat there, silent. But Jamie could feel a mix of emotions coming off the alpha in waves. He wanted to give his mate comfort, but he didn't know how.

"I don't understand," Rohan said. "Please, help me understand this. I thought we loved one another? What have I done?"

"You've done *nothing*. I do love you, I keep telling you that."

"And you can't even give me something as simple as a hug?"

Jamie saw the damage he was doing written in the lines of Rohan's face and couldn't keep the truth back any longer.

"They took my womb," Jamie said quietly. "And when they took it, it's as if they took my sexuality with it. The need and desire I once had? It's gone. And I hate that it's gone because I love you more than words can ever express." Jamie leaned in closer and rested his head on Rohan's shoulder. "I thought it would come back. After the treatments. After they told me I was in remission. I prayed to the gods it would come back. I wanted to be with my mate again. To have that joy and that bliss... the afterglow, lying in your arms and holding you tight. I miss it, too. I just can't be with you in that way anymore. I'm barren... and you deserve more than an empty shell of an omega."

"You're *not* an empty shell! I know you think you were born simply to hand me children, but there is more to us than that. The love we share is more than enough—I've told you time and time again. *You are enough.* You will *always* be enough. Child or no child, I love you. You... not some expectation that was force-fed to you your entire life."

Rohan leaned over slightly and pressed a kiss to Jamie's head.

Jamie froze again, unable to stop the tensing of his body. He slid away from his alpha, needing space.

Another long sigh came from Rohan. "Fine. You need space? Time? I will give them to you. I don't understand it, but if you think this is what you need to heal, I will give it to you. But I won't go far. I'm right here... I will always be right here. At your side. Where I belong."

"You would be within your rights to cast me away," Jamie said before lifting his stare to meet Rohan's. "An omega who refuses his alpha—you could be free of me if you chose it."

Rohan lifted his palm to cup the side of Jamie's face. "Never. *Never.* I love you too much for that."

"You belong with someone like Gray. You two would make a fine match."

Rohan frowned. "*No...* don't say that."

Jamie smiled. "I chose him for you."

Rohan sat up a little straighter. "What?"

Jamie's smile turned a bit melancholy. "Nothing."

"No. What do you mean you *chose him for me?*"

"I just sensed... that you would like him. That he would be a good omega for you."

Rohan stared, looking confused. "You're not going *anywhere*. There's no reason for you to find a replacement."

Jamie nodded. "Of course. You're right... forget I said anything..."

Rohan searched his face, not looking pacified. "No... I need to know what you meant by that."

Jamie shook his head. "I just..." *I cannot tell him.* "I knew I couldn't give you what you needed. I wanted to find someone who could."

Rohan stared at him, his face swirling with a myriad of emotions. After a moment, he reached for Jamie.

Jamie backed away.

He'd sacrifice his own happiness... and a little of Rohan's now... because later...

Later Rohan might need to find love again.

Without me.

Chapter Twenty

A day later…

In the late afternoon, Rohan pulled into the drive behind the long black car that had arrived moments before him. Even though it was still early, the weather and the season brought darkness early. The sky was a dark, dove-gray and looked like another snow might fall soon. Rohan watched as Jamie stepped from the backseat, oblivious he was there for a moment. Steam swirled around his mouth, the air so cold. Part of Jamie's face was cast in shadow, but even so, Rohan could see something weighed on his omega.

Would he even tell me if I asked?

Just as he pulled his long coat a bit tighter around him, Jamie lifted his stare and saw Rohan behind the wheel. A forced smile came seconds later and filled Rohan with dread. He'd seen a look similar to that once before… a dread-filled glance that had been the start down a long, dark, and winding path. A little voice screamed for him to back out and leave. Go back to the office. Anything, to avoid hearing more bad news.

Maybe I'm the bad news.

Or maybe I can be his salvation… if he'd let me.

One way or another, he wouldn't leave Jamie to shoulder whatever it was alone. Rohan shifted into park and turned off the engine as the thought he might be the one bringing pain to Jamie made it harder to breathe. Climbing from behind the wheel, he watched his omega closely. The driver of the car pulled on through the semi-circular drive and exited their property, leaving them alone.

The cold made things quieter, the hush a calm before the storm. Jamie looked as if he wanted to say something. He opened his mouth, the words appearing not to come. After a few seconds, he closed his mouth, a look of resignation on his face.

"What's wrong?"

That forced smile was unrelenting. Jamie shivered some and drew his coat tighter around him. "Nothing's wrong."

The snow that had threatened began to fall. Tiny flakes appeared in the air around them. He drew his briefcase from the car and closed the door.

"I know your looks. Something's wrong."

Jamie shook his head. "You're being paranoid." He backed up a step and pivoted. As he walked toward the house, he tossed over one shoulder. "You'd best go get ready for supper. Papa's already called, asking if we were on our way."

Rohan closed his eyes. The last thing he was in the mood for was dealing with Jamie's family. It was bad enough he had to deal with them on and off through the day in the office. He'd spent most of his afternoon avoiding Wilder's evil glares as it was. It would be harder directly across the table from them all.

And if Wynter and Warden had learned what had happened, he'd never hear the end of it.

He followed Jamie inside and lowered his briefcase as soon as he was inside. It was silent within—almost as silent as the snow falling outside. He looked around the darkened interior—only a few shafts of low light came in through the shuttered windows. The house was an empty shell. It had once held so much promise, but now... now it was a reminder of all his failures.

Once Jamie had ascended, Rohan climbed the carpeted stairs, the thick padding muffling his steps and adding to the disquiet of the place.

He entered their bedroom...

And noticed something was *off*.

Glancing around the room, he realized Jamie's belongings were... *gone*. Pain slammed into him as he searched the room. Tugging drawer after drawer... all in vain. They were all empty.

He stalked over to Jamie's closet and flung open the door.

Empty.

Rohan swallowed past the lump in his throat. His knees weakened before he leaned against the doorframe to catch his breath. Rage flew into him... and he wanted to race through the house and scream his head off.

He wanted to roar against the dying of their love.

He wanted things to be like they'd once been, long before chemo and surrogates and emptiness. Once he was sure he had better control of his emotions, he exited the room and stood in the dark hallway. He listened for sounds and then followed it toward one of the guest bedrooms. When he walked in, he saw Jamie buttoning a long tunic.

One the same shade as his eyes.

Rohan looked about the bedroom—decked out with Jamie's things.

"Don't you think we should've discussed this?" he asked, desperately attempting to control the tenor of his voice. He didn't want to argue. Nor did he want Jamie to know just how much he'd been hurt.

Jamie's head whipped up. He lifted his chin and looked completely unaffected... if not for the slight wobble of his chin. "You said you'd give me the space I need."

His hands fisted at his sides as he roared. "This *isn't* what I meant!"

Jamie's eyes widened, and he stepped back, looking afraid.

The anger leeched from him with that look. He'd never harmed his omega... *never* would. Jamie had to know that. Didn't he?

Jamie cocked his head to the side and smiled faintly. "*This* is what I need. You said you would give me what I need. Please... tell me you meant it."

Rohan stood there, unsure of what to say. He *had* promised that, but he'd never imagined his omega would resort to moving out of their bedroom.

More distance.

The ache inside was almost too much for him to bear.

"Now go get freshened up. We should already be on the way."

"Should I even bother going?" Rohan spat. A hurt look crossed Jamie's face, and he felt both joy and shame in it. He himself was in pain. He shouldn't stoop so low as to cause it, too. They both deserved better than that, but it was hard not to lash out when he felt powerless to stop the madness.

"I already told them you were coming, but I suppose I can make up some excuse as to why you're not there."

Rohan was torn in two. He didn't want to go and play the doting husband when he wasn't allowed to be one in reality. Yet the thought of forcing Jamie to face a night alone with his parents didn't sit well, either. *The farce, it is.*

"Give me a moment... I'll be ready to go shortly."

He spun and headed for his bedroom. Once inside, he hated how hollow and empty it felt. All the life had been sucked from it. Rohan sat on the edge of the bed, hands on his knees, and fought the tears that threatened to come.

He felt completely lost.

And he had no idea how to get them back to the way things were.

* * * *

A secret withheld...

Tell him.

Jamie turned his gaze from the passenger window to stare at Rohan's profile. Even in the near dark, his alpha was handsome. Square chin... firm lips... strong jaw. A smile came to his lips as he remembered the first time he'd seen Rohan. Across the huge ballroom, he'd spied his mate a good head and shoulders over the other alphas in attendance.

Rohan hadn't looked like he wanted to be there. His stare had scanned the place, as if he was searching for a way out. Jamie had gotten an image of a captive panther in his mind, pacing along the bars, back and forth. How Rohan had projected that kind of caged torment, he still wasn't sure, but he'd sensed it all the same.

When their gazes had met, Rohan had visibly relaxed.

For a few seconds.

And then there had been a ruthless look that had come to the alpha's eyes that had both scared and excited him to no end. Breathless, he'd stood frozen as his panther had stalked across the ballroom and held out his hand.

The minute they touched, Jamie had known. This was his mate. The man he'd die loving.

He looked back out the window, icy patterns spread across the glass, barely lit by the moon and stars. Sadness made him breathless again. *How can I tell him?*

Jamie had left the doctor's office that afternoon, shaken to his core. The news hadn't truly cemented in his mind—not yet. Saying it out loud... telling his alpha... would make it real. He wanted to live a little while longer in limbo. But then, if he wasn't quite dying, he wasn't quite alive, either.

He lifted his hand and carefully wiped away the tear that had spilled over his lid and drew in a shuddering breath.

No... he couldn't tell Rohan. Not yet. Not when all his plans weren't quite in place.

Soon after their silent car ride was over, they sat at Jamie's parents' table—side by side—yet miles apart.

Crystal goblets were filled with wine, the overhead chandelier giving the large dining room an amber glow. Fine silver and china graced the table. His parents' butler and manservant served dinner, as usual. The cook would likely make an appearance before the end of the night, too.

From the outside, everything looked perfect and elegant.

Elegant, perhaps, but nothing there was perfect, no matter how hard his papa tried to force flawlessness into submission.

Across the table, Jamie saw pure rage in Wilder's eyes. His brother remained silent, but Jamie worried it wouldn't last through the night. It was mostly directed at Rohan, of course. Jamie's denials at lunch had apparently been ignored.

I'm not in the mood for this fight again.

His papa seemed quite interested in what was going on, but hadn't yet been able to ferret anything out with his probing questions. Much to his chagrin. Jamie could almost feel his papa's irritation coming from one end of the table. Father was across from papa, oblivious as he always seemed at home. If it wasn't about business, sporting, or bourbon, it might as well not exist.

Vaughn was even uncharacteristically quiet. He'd barely said two words to anyone and hadn't fought with his favorite sparring partner—papa. Usually the two of them tossed barb after barb at one another, seeing who could land the best blows, but not that evening. Jamie cast a look down the table at his youngest brother, seeking something.

He wasn't sure what.

Vaughn knew their secret. Perhaps Jamie wanted one of his brothers to understand his choice—since it was apparent he wouldn't get that approval from Wilder. He cast his glance back to Wilder, only to get a narrowed glare before the alpha looked away.

Oh what he wouldn't have given to have been seated at Gray's kitchen table, sipping tea and sharing secrets. It was one of the only places he felt peace anymore. There were no expectations there. No drama. No demands.

Just friendship.

With his and Rohan's tensions and the lifelong familial drama he'd endured, nowhere else was safe for him any longer.

Especially now.

Papa lifted his wine goblet to his lips and spied Jamie over the rim. As he was placing it back on the table, he lifted his regal chin and stared down his elegant nose. "Enough with *whatever* this is… Talk!"

"There's *nothing* to talk about," Jamie answered, forcing a forkful of venison into his mouth. He chewed it, not wanting to eat at all, but it gave him time for precious silence.

Papa looked to Wilder. "What's going on between you and your brother? I can see there's something."

Wilder looked between Jamie and Rohan, anger sparking in his eyes. He then glanced down at the table at papa. "Nothing. As Jamie said."

"Lies," Papa said before taking another drink and glancing at Vaughn. "Do *you* know?"

"What's it worth to you?" Vaughn asked.

"Vaughn," Rohan growled under his breath.

Papa leaned forward, smiling. "So you *do* know. Tell me."

"You don't think I'd give it up *that* easily, do you?" Vaughn asked, smiling wickedly before winking at their papa.

Papa sighed. "I demand to know what's going on!"

"It's none of your business," Jamie spat.

Instantly, his eyes grew almost as wide as papa's. While he often disagreed with his papa, he tried to remain civil. Apparently, his desire for civility was gone.

"None... of my business?" He looked between them before eyeing Vaughn. "I'll give you a free pass on the next idiotic thing you do and not reprimand you for it—if you tell me what's going on here."

Vaughn sat back, one brow rising. "No matter how badly I behave?"

Jamie glared at Vaughn, who only shrugged. "He's going to find out eventually. I might as well get something out of it." He turned to their papa. "Rohan marked their surrogate. They apparently did things *the old-fashioned way.*"

Papa gasped.

His father looked up from his plate, finally deciding to join the gathering. "He did *what?*"

The entire table glared at Rohan.

Jamie could sense his alpha tensing beside him. It was time to help let him off the hook. *Not that it worked well the last time.* "I insisted it be done that way. It was my choice. Not his."

"Why ever for?" Papa demanded.

"For many reasons..." He was about to run down the same list he'd used on Rohan and Gray but thought better of it. He was tired of fighting to have his voice heard. *It's not like they'd listen either way.* "You know what? I don't owe anyone at this table an explanation," Jamie said before turning to glance at Rohan. His alpha sat there, eyes closed and jaw tense. "What happens between me and my alpha is no one's business. It was done. And now we have a babe on the way. Already Gray grows swollen with Rohan's baby."

"*Our* baby," Rohan murmured lowly beside him.

Jamie eyed his alpha, an ache coming to his chest.

"But it's not his, now is it?" Papa said. "It's your child with another omega. Now you'll bring this child into our home and expect us to treat it as if it was your own? It will never be a Jaymes. *Never.*"

"Can you not just be happy for me once in your life?" Jamie asked his papa.

"Is it not bad enough that you've shamed this family by being barren? Now you let your alpha have his way with another omega—marking this other man? If word gets out, do you know how the gossip mill will churn?" Papa asked. "Could you not think of the family?"

"Just *how* did he already shame this family? By getting sick? By nearly dying?" Rohan demanded, viciousness in his tone. "My gods—just how terrible of a person *are* you?"

"You don't speak to me like that, Rohan," his papa snarled.

"Shut up!" Jamie screamed, rising to his feet. "I have exhausted myself trying to win your favor and your love—but I give up. Nothing I will ever do will be good enough for you. So, I no longer care. I don't care if you don't love me or never approve of me. Nor do I care to lay eyes on you ever again."

I'm dying.

The words were on the tip of his tongue… and he wondered if they would hurt his parents at all. *Likely not.*

They would only hurt the people he least wanted to hurt—Rohan and Wilder.

His parents? Vaughn? They wouldn't care.

He was an omega. Worthless in their eyes.

Maybe a little part of him had also hoped, for once, he'd find the love and support he should've had all along.

It would never be.

Never.

He spun and headed for the door. Jamie sensed Rohan following.

But as he hit the foyer, the world went sideways. For a moment, he felt weightless. Crashing to the marbled tiles, his vision went blurry. Darkness hit him seconds after he heard Rohan's muffled, desperate cry echoing around him.

* * * *

A deadly truth…

Rohan sat beside Jamie's hospital bed, reeling. A quick trip to the ER had suddenly become an admission. No one had given him any information as to why. Nurses had come, taking vials and vials of blood. They'd set up machines, listening to his heart, his lungs… the gods knew what else. Jamie had slept through it all. Whispered voices and the slow, steady pulse of Jamie's heartbeat being monitored filtered in around him as he awaited news.

The curtain drew back, and a familiar face appeared.

Jamie's oncologist, Dr. Ford.

Rohan rose to his feet, frowning. "No offense, but I *had* hoped to never see you again."

Dr. Ford smiled wanly. "Not the first time I've heard that. Sadly, not the first time I've had to reappear, either."

A niggle of worry raced up Rohan's spine. "Why *are* you here?"

"I got a call from the attending. There are alerts on Jamie's medical file for me to be notified. I came right away."

Oh gods. No. "Why would they call you?" he demanded, knowing the answer and not truly wanting to hear the explanation.

Dr. Ford paused, his mouth opening for a moment before he closed it and appeared to rethink his words. "He hasn't told you yet, I take it?"

Rohan stared at the doctor, frowning. Panic slammed into him. His heart thundered in his chest. Tears burned at the backs of his eyes. "Told me? Told me what?"

The doctor sighed. "I told him at our appointment this afternoon that it was well past time to get you involved."

"Involved in…?"

"Against my better judgment, I didn't demand he bring you to his appointments. Jamie made me promise not to discuss things with you or anyone else in the family. Not until we were sure." The doctor paused before continuing in a lower voice. "Today we became sure."

The room began to waver back and forth a little in Rohan's vision. "What didn't you tell me?"

The doctor was silent another moment. The beeping of the machines was the only sound he heard against the rush of blood in his ears.

"Jamie's cancer has returned."

Rohan stood there for a moment, sure he hadn't heard those words. He had to be dreaming. *A nightmare.* Jamie had battled and won this fight. They had their second chance. A baby on the way...

New life...

It couldn't be real. He looked down at the bed and saw Jamie's pale skin nearly as white as the sheets. His omega looked gaunt... weak. Had he missed the signs all along?

Wake up, godsdamn it! Wake up!

His knees went weak, and he fell back into the chair he'd just abandoned. "He *just* went into remission. He's only had a few months."

Dr. Ford frowned. "Yes, but it's back... with a ferocity I've rarely seen."

Rohan glanced back to the bed, and looked at the small, sleeping form there. How fragile Jamie looked. "No."

"After his last round of chemo, we'd shrunk his tumor—to a point where we were sure he was no longer in any danger. We'd hoped for a longer lasting remission—but this type of disease—it's rarely for very long. Jamie was aware of that. He hasn't been feeling well as of late, so he came in for a visit a few weeks ago. We found his cancer had returned... and metastasized. It's spread to almost his entire body."

"So what do we do now?"

"I gave Jamie his options. More chemo. More radiation. There are even a couple of experimental treatments out there he might be able to get into—but the chances are slim any of it would work, especially as formidable as it seems to be this time around. We would likely only be prolonging the inevitable."

Rohan's head whipped to face the doctor. "So you're just giving up? Letting him die?"

Dr. Ford shook his head slowly. "Jamie has declined treatment. He says he's done fighting. I can't force him."

Rohan clenched Jamie's bed linens in his hands, as he tried to calm his raging heart. Without looking at the doctor, he spoke lowly—with a thread of violence in his tone. "And why did you not contact me sooner?"

"Jamie's my patient. Not you. I have to follow his wishes... even if my heart and mind tell me to do otherwise."

Rohan shook his head, his mind spinning. They'd been living a lie. Building for a future that would never come.

The baby...

Why had Jamie done this?

How had any of them let this happen? "You signed off on the surrogacy... you said he had a clean bill of health. It was the only reason the solicitor allowed it to happen, he said."

"In that moment, we thought he was in the clear and hoped he would have at least a few years ahead of him. We were wrong, it seems." The doctor cleared his throat. "I suggested the surrogacy might not be the best idea. But he said he wanted to give you this gift. He was so adamant he wanted this baby for you. I couldn't deflect his focus."

A gift?

Now it all felt like a nightmare. How was he supposed to raise a child alone... without Jamie?

How would he survive a world without Jamie?

"How long has he known?"

"He's known for a few weeks, though he didn't know just how bad it was until the test results we got today."

Rohan winced. How many appointments had Jamie sat through all alone? One word, and he would've been there, at his omega's side, helping to shoulder the burden.

He stared at the doctor, his mouth dropping open. Tears burned the backs of his eyes. "*No.* This is some cruel joke... tell me this is some cruel joke!" He jumped up and walked closer to the doctor, grabbing the lapels of the white lab coat and dragging the man closer. *"Tell me!"*

"I wish I could," the wide-eyed doctor said, shrinking back from Rohan.

He let out an angry roar seconds before several orderlies rushed in and dragged him—kicking and screaming—from Dr. Ford.

Rohan felt a prick of pain moments later... and the world went fuzzy around him.

They dropped him into a chair beside his sleeping omega. He lowered his head to the mattress and closed his eyes before the world went black.

* * * *

Awakening...

Jamie brushed Rohan's fine, chestnut hair, the softness of the threads like silk against his fingers. His alpha slept at his bedside, Rohan's big body overwhelming the small room. He hated the thought of Rohan awakening—of the anger and sadness that would likely come with it. Jamie wasn't sure how much his mate now knew, of course, but he sensed his secret might be out.

Until Rohan opened his eyes, Jamie could remain in that fantasy world...

A place where they were still happy. Where they still had a chance. Love. Children. Family. Tomorrows.

He wouldn't remain in that fantasy world long. Rohan began to stir under his hand and soon, those vibrant eyes awoke and pinned him with a stare. At first, the alpha looked around, as if he didn't recall where he was or what had happened. Jamie knew the split second it all came rushing back. He could see the overwhelming sadness shining in Rohan's eyes.

"How could you not tell me?" were the first words from Rohan's lips.

The look of pain on Rohan's face was almost too much for Jamie to bear.

"I did what I needed to do."

"Again you've pushed me out. You lied to me... kept me in the dark... why?"

Jamie smiled wanly and took Rohan's hand in his. "I didn't lie. I wasn't ready to tell you yet. I didn't want to hurt you."

"You didn't want to hurt me? And I'm not hurting now?"

"I know. I'm sorry," Jamie mumbled. "I just needed a little while longer... to not see the sadness I see in you now. I hate seeing you like this... I was only trying to spare you the pain, believe me."

"Is *this* the reason you've been pushing me further and further away? Because if it is... I won't have it."

Jamie looked down at his lap. It wasn't the only reason, but it was a part of it.

"Damn it, Jamie... we're mates. *Through sickness and in health.* I vowed to stand at your side for the rest of our lives, and I meant it. I love you. I deserved to know."

Jamie had once thought the old, ancient wedding vows Rohan had wanted to include sentimental and sweet. Now, he saw them as a yoke around his alpha's neck. "I won't drag you to the grave with me. You need to go on and learn to live without me."

"Because you've already given up!" Rohan blasted.

Jamie looked away.

"That's right. Dr. Ford told me you've refused treatment. How could you?"

"I don't want the last weeks of my life spent sick from the poisons they'd shoot inside my body. I just want peace. I want the pain to be over."

"Instead of standing up and fighting, you gave up. I've never known you to give up on *anything*."

"I've never given up on you," Jamie cried. "I've spent every waking moment trying to save you from this pain."

"What do you mean?"

"I needed to give you a reason to live."

Rohan's eyes widened, and his breath hitched. He sat back, silent for a moment—disbelief etched on his face. "What... what are you saying?"

"After one mate dies... the other is often not long behind. Even in mates as young as we are, I've heard of alphas lost without their omegas and dying months later of a broken heart. I needed to give you a reason to live on without me. Something to fill your heart... once I was gone."

Rohan's mouth dropped open. He was silent, his face etched in turmoil. His chin wobbled, and his eyes shone with tears.

"Now you have a child... *and an omega*... who needs you," Jamie whispered.

Rohan's gaze met his. "So this was your plan all along, hmm? To go out and find yourself a replacement? As if the love I feel for you is a switch that can be turned off and then back on with someone else." He laughed mirthlessly. "Guess what? It can't. I will go on loving you until the day I die... not the day you do."

"You have to let me go," Jamie whispered, hot tears sliding down his cheeks.

"You might be willing to give up. I'm not."

"I *didn't* give up." Jamie sighed. "The cancer is *all over*, Rohan. Further treatment might give me another few months, at the very most—but I would spend them sick and in torment. *In hell*. I've already spent so many months tortured, and I don't want to leave like that. I wanted to go out on my own terms. And I wanted to find a way to save *you* in the process."

Tears openly fell from Rohan's eyes. "By pushing the one person who loves you the most away. Pushing him into the arms of another man?"

Jamie brought Rohan's hand to his lips and laid a gentle kiss there. "I want you to find a new path... a new love... a new life... that doesn't include me. Pushing you away would make it hurt less in the end."

"You're mad," Rohan whispered.

"I'm not. I can see with a clarity I've never had in my life." He smiled. "Knowing the end is near... it puts a lot of things into perspective. I know *exactly* what I'm doing. I'm protecting the alpha I love."

"By keeping me in the dark." Rohan turned his hand to cup Jamie's cheek. "I could have lent you my strength. If only I'd known… I could've helped make these past weeks better. I love you so very much, Jamie… but I hate that you did this. I hate what you have robbed me of."

"I needed to push you away… you have another omega now. One who will need you much more than I do."

"No," Rohan said.

"I sense your bond with him."

Rohan roared in anger. "No!" He scrubbed his face with both hands before looking at Jamie. "A bond you've forced every step of the way. You *created* this situation… we are but pawns to you. Stop it. Stop it now."

"I can't. I need to know you will live on. I need you to make me a promise," Jamie cried. "After I'm gone… I want you to claim Gray as your own."

Rohan shook his head fiercely. "No."

"I did all of this… so I would know you had something to hold on to after I'm gone. I can't leave this world unless I know you'll survive. Don't make my sacrifices be all in vain," Jamie said as convincingly as he could.

"Then don't leave this world. Fight!"

"It's too late to fight," Jamie whispered. "I'm dying, Rohan. It's just a matter of weeks now."

"No! There has to be something that can be done!" Rohan jumped from the chair and stalked toward the door. "Nurse? I need to see the doctor. Now."

"He won't give you a different answer than he already gave me," Jamie said, feeling weaker by the minute.

"Then we find another doctor. One with a different point of view. We go to another province… another continent if we have to!"

"And you'll waste the last days I have searching for an answer you won't find?"

Rohan spun to face him, silent.

The quiet of the room nearly broke him. Jamie drew in a breath, his chest aching. "The doctor is looking into a care facility for me. It will have round the clock nursing staff to care for me in my final weeks. After I go… I want you to claim Gray as your mate and build the family our house was made for."

Rohan's eyes shimmered with fresh, unfallen tears. "A care facility? I'm taking you home."

"I don't want your last memories of me to be on my deathbed."

"We are forever bound in life."

"We can't be bound in death, too," Jamie whispered.

Rohan stared across the room, looking as empty and defeated as Jamie did—seconds before Wilder appeared in the door.

It was then that Jamie broke.

The tears came, and he couldn't stop crying. When he looked up, he saw Wilder's tears and it only made his come all the harder.

The two big alphas crowded on either side of his bed, held him, and let him mourn the life he'd lose… and then he barely listened as Rohan recounted what the doctor has told them.

"Your brother thinks to go to a care facility and die alone," Rohan said.

Wilder's head spun to face him. "What?"

"Rohan needs to move on with his life. He has a child coming… and an omega who needs him."

"And what are you? The trash to be thrown out?" Wilder asked. "Either you go home with your mate… or you come home with me. Your choice."

"He comes home with me," Rohan growled before catching Jamie's stare. "*Where he belongs.*"

Wilder turned to Jamie, taking his hand. "Sounds like it's all settled to me. Your alpha has put his foot down. *Finally.*"

Chapter Twenty-One

Two days later...

Gray rang Jamie's doorbell, curious why Jamie hadn't shown up at the ultrasound appointment earlier that morning. All his calls hadn't been answered or returned. A pang of worry rested low in his gut. After hitting the doorbell again, he began to wonder if anyone was even home. Gray pulled his jacket tighter around him as a cool, late winter breeze blew past.

As he spun to walk back to the rented car, the front door swung open. He turned to see an exhausted-looking Rohan glaring at him. Dark circles swept under his eyes, giving them an even more foreboding look.

Perhaps they were sick?

Gray took a step back. "Is Jamie okay? Are you guys ill?" He took another step back, just in case. He needed to protect the babe. His hand instinctively went to his swollen stomach.

Rohan's stare followed his hand as it moved down the swell. That gaze moved back up to his face after a moment of awkward silence. Their stares met, and a rush of longing filled him. Wetness seeped from him, even already pregnant. He knew it was simply the instinct, but it kept rearing its ugly head at the *worst* possible time.

The alpha's nostrils flared, and Gray's embarrassment was complete.

"Well? *Is* Jamie okay? He missed an appointment this morning."

Rohan ran a hand through his dark locks before lifting his stare again. "Jamie is... *not* well."

"Oh," Gray said. "Anything I can do to help? Although—I don't want to risk an illness with the babe. It's nothing serious, is it?"

"You can't catch what Jamie has."

A shiver raced up Gray's spine from the tone of the alpha's voice. He stared at Rohan's expressionless face, and his heart quickened a moment. A whisper raced through his mind. "What is it? What's wrong with him?"

Before Rohan even had a chance to speak, Gray felt his knees wobble and weaken. His stomach lurched, and he felt like he might vomit right there into the mums lining the stairs

"His cancer," Rohan murmured. "It's back." He winced. "With a vengeance, it seems."

Gray frowned. "*What?*"

"He's dying," Rohan whispered, a pained look hitting him. He glanced over his shoulder before looking back out. "He'll likely want to see you. Will you come in?"

For a moment, he stood there, frozen. This couldn't be. It wasn't supposed to be like this... He'd just found a friend he could confide in... a man he could love like a brother. He'd already lost his real one. Now Jamie? *No.*

Gray brushed past Rohan and stormed up the stairs.

"Wait!" Rohan said behind him, but he ignored the alpha.

He needed to see Jamie himself.

"Jamie?" he bellowed at the top of the stairs. When he heard nothing, he began working his way door by door, searching for his friend. He continued to call out to the omega.

"Gray?" he finally heard—faintly—and followed the sound.

He found Jamie lying in the middle of a large bed. He looked pale and tiny... and the bed gobbled him up. Gray rushed closer and sat on the edge before taking Jamie's hands. They were like ice, and he began warming them furiously. He felt the sting of tears burning the backs of his eyes, but he did everything in his power not to shed them.

Not yet.

He needed answers.

"Please tell me this is some sick, twisted joke. I won't even be mad at you. We can laugh and let it go... just tell me... tell me it's a joke."

Jamie shook his head slowly.

Gray bit back a sob and turned his head away. He didn't want to cry. Now was not the time for tears. They had a battle ahead of them... Jamie had won once before. He could do it again. "So what happens now? What treatments are they planning to do?"

"No treatments."

"What?"

"I don't want to endure it all again." Jamie shook his head. "I *can't*."

Gray was stunned into silence for a moment. "What about the baby? He needs a papa."

"He'll *have* a papa." Jamie smiled. "You."

Gray shook his head. "No."

"Rohan," Jamie whispered. "He needs reason to live. I need you and that babe to be his reason for going on."

Gray frowned. "*You* should be that reason. Not me."

"But I don't get that chance. Not in this life. I need you to do this for me."

"Once I have the baby, I'll have to hand it over and return to the O Quad. I won't be able to help him from there."

"Not unless he claims you."

Gray gasped. He dropped Jamie's hands and felt a wave of nausea hit him again. "No."

"It has to be this way," Jamie murmured. "That baby needs a papa. And Rohan won't be able to do this on his own."

"I can't step into your life and be... you. He loves *you*. This baby's papa is *you*."

"I've seen you and Rohan together. There *is* a bond there, made flesh within you... I've seen the attraction from you both. Don't lie and tell me it's not there."

Gray felt shame for that attraction. Even more now. "Instinct. That's *all* it is."

"What do you think drew Rohan and I together? It didn't start out as some grand love story. It was instinct. From there, we let it grow. You can have the same with him."

"He's not my mate."

"He can be," Jamie said. "In time... once memories of me fade... you two will have a chance."

"It's not that simple. You can't dictate how two people feel about one another."

"If I hadn't seen the bond with my own eyes, I'd say you were right," Jamie paused before giving a slight smile. "But I have. I knew from the moment we met that you were perfect for him. He's already marked you, Gray. You're already his... why can't you see it?"

Gray felt heat blasting his face. All the dreams of an alpha... a family... how long had he pined for that? Now Jamie was trying to hand that dream to him, but the price was too damned high. He couldn't lose Jamie.

He loved Jamie.

Jamie took Gray's hand and squeezed it tightly. "Once I'm gone, he *needs* someone. You know what happens to alphas when they lose their omega? Don't you? They fade away into nothing. I *won't* have that happen to Rohan."

Gray met Jamie's stare. Once Jamie was gone, there was a chance Rohan might follow. How a big, strong male such as that could simply wither away... it seemed inconceivable. But they'd all seen it happen, over and over again.

"Rohan needs something to live for. You need someone to free you from the Omega Quadrant. And the baby... the baby deserves a father *and* a papa."

"I won't discuss this a moment more. It's... it's *morbid*."

Jamie's head fell back against the pillows. "I just want to know you two will be okay once I'm gone. That's all I ask."

Gray couldn't help but feel manipulated. Jamie had maneuvered them into this situation from the start. But how could he be angry? Jamie's motives appeared to be coming from the right place—no matter how wrong they might be. But still—he struggled with a sensation of being forced to fit. A round peg in a square hole.

He'd been forced his whole life. When was it his choice?

He ran a hand down the swell to his stomach. The baby. That had been his choice, but it had been narrowed by his own fate and place in the world, but still, it had been his. But now? He wondered if that choice hadn't been a mistake.

"Promise me you'll look out for my Rohan and care for this babe."

Gray lifted his stare to Jamie's desperate one. "I promise to do all I can… but I *won't* promise to fill your shoes."

Jamie's face twisted in pain.

Gray grew quiet, the question circling his mind almost too terrible to ask. But he had to know. "How long?"

Jamie sighed. "Months. Maybe less."

"And there's no way you'll consider fighting?"

"I don't want to go through that pain again. I was sick *all* the time," Jamie said. "I don't want to spend my last days like that."

"How much time might it add?"

"Weeks. Maybe a few months, at best. Which is why it's not worth it."

Gray held Jamie's stare. "The baby comes in six months."

Jamie's eyes closed. Gray dug into his coat pocket to pull out the ultrasound pictures he'd brought with him. He'd seen their baby today.

Now Jamie needed to see who he needed to live for.

"You wanted this child so desperately… you've done all this planning. You've decorated his room and filled it with all kinds of clothes and toys… you planned a future with him… and you're willing to give up and leave us without welcoming this new life into the world?"

Jamie reopened his eyes and captured Gray's. Gray shoved the picture into his hands, and Jamie took it, lifting it. Tears began to fill his eyes. He ran a reverent hand over the surface, smiling as tears streaked down his face. "I forgot the appointment. I'm sorry."

"Don't be. You likely needed the rest," Gray said softly. "But that's why I came. I was worried about you."

Jamie stared at the picture and smiled widely.

"If nothing else can convince you to fight, maybe he can," Gray murmured.

Jamie was silent as he continued to stare, smiling. After a couple of minutes, he lifted his stare. "Perhaps I need to hold on… just a little longer, hmm?"

A glimmer of hope filled Gray's chest. "With treatment, you'd be more likely to. Right?"

Jamie opened his mouth to argue, but nothing came out. Tears shone in his eyes. "I *would* like to meet the little one before I go."

"And maybe there's a small chance you'd last more than months…"

"No," Jamie said. "I won't have you getting your hopes up, only to lose them later."

"What happened to that amazing attitude you had when we first met? You were *so sure* you'd beat this and win. That attitude is what saved you, Jamie. You need to believe you can make it through. You need to believe it soul deep. If you want to save Rohan… if you want to give this baby a papa… you need to fight for it, damn you! Don't give up. There's too many people who love you to leave them behind."

Jamie laughed and cried within seconds of each other, squeezing his hands. "If I fight... if I give it my everything... and I *still* lose this battle... will you take care of those people I love? Will you promise me then?"

Gray paused, fearful Jamie would back off if he said no. How could he accept those terms?

Yet how could he not?

"You're going to win this battle, so whatever I promise won't need to happen," Gray said with a smile, trying to evade a true answer.

"But if I don't... you will let Rohan claim you? You will hold our little family together?"

Gray took a deep breath. If this is what he needed to do in order to get Jamie to fight, so be it. "Yes. If you fight hard and still lose, I'll do everything I can."

Jamie met his stare. He sensed Jamie knew he'd evaded the true answer again... but he didn't say anything.

"Okay. I fight." He looked down at the picture again, smiling softly. "I'll fight for him..."

Gray caressed the side of Jamie's face and wiped the man's tears away. "So let's get started."

Jamie looked over Gray's shoulder. "Rohan? Can you call Dr. Ford?"

Gray turned, and his stare met Rohan's. *How much did he overhear?* Panic hit him... Gray hadn't even sensed the alpha there.

"I'll call him right now," Rohan said, fishing his phone from his pocket. He stepped out into the hall after dialing the number.

Gray could hear the deep rumbling tone of Rohan's voice, and it sent waves of pleasure up his spine. He closed his eyes, wishing there was a way to ignore the instinct pulsing in his veins. Gray turned back to Jamie and forced a wide smile. "I'll be there beside you. Every step of the way."

My gods, please give him strength. Save him... please.

* * * *

Rohan finished his phone call and walked back into the room, again leaning on the doorframe. He saw Jamie and Gray deep in conversation, and a little part of him was jealous of this friendship they'd formed in the matter of a few months.

After what he'd just heard, though, it made a hell of a lot more sense.

Gray had been selfless. Rohan could only assume any other omega in his position likely would've jumped at the chance to wrangle an available alpha. Freedom. Money. Privilege. Jamie was handing them all over on a silver platter.

Instead, Gray had encouraged Jamie to seek treatment—to fight for all those things— something he hadn't been able to make happen in the days since he'd learned of the cancer's resurgence. Gray had demanded Jamie not give up hope.

And given him a reason.

For the first time in a long time, Rohan felt a little of that hope himself. He also now had a glimpse of what it was Jamie saw in Gray.

Jamie's head turned toward him. "Did you get a chance to call the doctor?"

"His receptionist is fitting you in tomorrow afternoon," Rohan said.

"Great."

"How about I make us some tea?" Gray said, rising from the side of the bed.

"Actually," Jamie said. "I'm feeling a bit tired... I hate to send you away, but I'd love a nap. But, yet, I don't want you to leave... I want to know *everything* about your appointment this morning."

"How about I go rest my feet downstairs for a bit and let you sleep. I'll stay a while and maybe we can have that tea once you awaken?"

Jamie frowned. "Don't you need to get back to the boys?"

"Avery's on winter break right now. He can handle them for one night without me," Gray said before he tucked the blanket in around Jamie.

Gray headed out of the room, barely looking at Rohan as he passed.

Rohan followed him out into the hallway. "Gray?"

Gray turned, and Rohan's stare was drawn to the rounded swell of his stomach even more in profile. He lifted his gaze and met the omega's.

"Thank you... I don't even know how to repay you for convincing him to seek treatment."

Gray shook his head. "There's no reason to thank me. I did it solely for selfish reasons."

Rohan frowned. "How so?"

Gray's eyes shone with tears. "I know it doesn't make sense... we've barely known each other more than six months... but he's probably one of the best friends I've *ever* had. And I'm not ready to let him go. I love him too much."

Rohan choked back tears of his own. "That doesn't sound selfish to me."

"We both know it is. If he's really as sick as I sense he is… if it will only give him a few more months and nothing but torment… I'm a terrible person for asking him to do this." A tear slid down Gray's face. "But I want a miracle. I want him to live. I've never asked much of this world. But I think I'm owed it."

Silence hung between them as he caught Gray's stare. Rohan prayed with everything within him that Gray got his wish.

He silently added his own plea to the gods above as Gray made his way downstairs.

After going back into Jamie's room to check in and give his omega a peck on the forehead, he headed down, too. He found Gray in front of the fridge, surveying the inventory. It wasn't much, he was afraid, but he might be able to slop something together.

"Hungry?"

Gray turned to look over his shoulder and closed the fridge. "Sorry. I'm famished. I hope you don't mind."

"Of course not."

"First I'm so sick I can barely eat," he said, absently stroking his stomach. "And now all I want to do is eat."

Rohan's stare was dragged to the child growing within Gray once more. It was like a call of the wild, the instinct within driving him to reach out and caress the omega's expanding belly. But the thought of touching any man other than his own omega made him tense. He would fight the instinct as best he could. "How about I make you a sandwich and you have a seat?"

"I'm not an invalid," Gray said.

"No, but I know the way around our kitchen a little better than you," Rohan chided before pulling out a chair at the kitchen table and nodding toward it.

Gray sighed and headed over to the chair without any further argument. Rohan walked over to the refrigerator and opened it back up. "Turkey or ham?"

"*Aaaahhh*... both?"

Rohan looked over one shoulder at the omega, lifting a brow.

Gray pointed to his stomach. "Weird food cravings have already begun. Stuff I would never eat. Yesterday it was pickeltopia. I *hate* pickles. Apparently, your son does not."

Rohan tensed again at the mention of his child, his smile fading. As one life hung in the balance, another was coming and the weight of that responsibility grew by the day. Ignoring his maudlin thoughts, he pulled meats, cheeses, and other items out to make a proper sandwich. Once he cut a few slices of bread, he reached for condiments. "Mayo or mustard? Or maybe *both*?"

Gray chuckled and then shrugged. "Why not?"

Rohan continued his sandwich making, adding another for himself, as he hadn't eaten all day. And he wasn't totally sure when he'd eaten the day before, either. Food had been the last thing on his mind...

But now that there was a little glimmer of hope, he felt himself relaxing a bit.

He watched Gray from the corner of his eye, suddenly fascinated by this man he'd underestimated. Gray was like Jamie in so many ways. They were about the same height and build. Jamie's hair had been nearly the same shade before chemo had turned it mostly white. They even had similar mannerisms.

But as much as they were the same, they were different. Gray wore his hair in a plain braid down the back instead of the intricate patterns and braids Jamie had once worn. Gray's style of dress was plain, as well. He favored the loose pants and long tunics most omegas wore, but in plain, neutral colors instead of Jamie's bright ones and patterns.

Jamie was outgoing. A bright star in the night sky. Gray seemed more introverted. He had a sense of calm and peace to him. If ever they needed calm and peace, it was now.

When he was done, Rohan brought both plates to the table and went back to the fridge for a couple of sparkling water bottles. He took a seat directly across from the omega and handed Gray one of the bottles.

"Thank you," Gray said before diving into his sandwich. Two chews in, and he moaned. "*Oh my gods*, that's good." He chuckled. "Or maybe I was just that hungry."

Rohan smiled slightly as he watched Gray eat. The instinct fired up inside him again… it was hotwired in his genetic code to provide and protect the omega carrying his child. It was weird that offering a simple meal had him feeling joy.

Halfway through, Gray slowed down eating his sandwich. He looked around the kitchen, seemingly spying everything. "I haven't spent much time here at your home. It's lovely."

"Thank you," Rohan murmured.

"Avoided it, actually. I didn't want to be here near you, if I'm completely honest."

Rohan met Gray's stare and was a bit shocked by the confession at first. But he completely understood it. He hadn't wanted to be close to the omega, either—likely for the same exact reason. The instinct called for them to grow closer. The child was like a beacon. It would forever bind them. Distance was the only salvation in their case, and even then, that didn't stop the fire within completely.

It only dimmed it, at best.

"This is such a big house for just the two of you. Does it ever feel weird rattling around in here?"

Rohan finished chewing and wiped his mouth. "Well, the plan was to fill it with a family. That just hasn't work out as we'd hoped." He sat back in his chair, realizing it would never work out as they'd hoped. Surrogate, or not.

"I'm sorry, that was rude of me. I should've realized... I was just a bit shocked by the size of this place and it only being the two of you here."

Rohan smiled. "No reason to be sorry. It is a huge place for only two." He looked about the kitchen. "It had fallen into disrepair before we bought it... and so we got it for next to nothing. It took a bit to remodel and update it, but we had fun making it our own." He paused, remembering all the miscarriages that had come as they'd readied the house for a family. "I've offered to get a cook or a housekeeper more than once—just to help give Jamie a little company in this place and make it feel a little less lonely. He said there was no point until the children came and we really needed the help. Of course, we plan to get one or both once the baby comes, to lend Jamie a hand."

The words sounded odd coming from his mouth. Would Jamie even last to see the child born?

"Well, you two will soon have the family you wanted. You can hire all the help you'll need."

Rohan met Gray's gaze. "While I want to be lifted by the hope you're feeling... I've talked to his doctor. This treatment... it likely won't give us any miracles."

"Not if you think like that. You need to be positive. *Especially* around Jamie."

"I want him to die in my arms," Rohan said. Gray's eyes widened before he could finish. "When he's *a hundred and three*—after a long life filled with love and family—and I want to go with him. That's how I always saw it. Dying of old age in our bed together." He smiled wanly. How cruel the world was. "We have so much left to do. I can barely breathe just imagining him gone." Rohan fought back more tears.

"*Don't* imagine it," Gray whispered. "Don't see it in your mind. See him alive and well. See him ten years from now, twenty years on, having won this fight. We need to stay positive... so he can feed off it and be positive himself."

Rohan nodded. To see how fervent Gray was in his desire to save Jamie, it was a bit of a shock. A memory slipped through his mind, and he chuckled.

"What's so funny?" Gray asked.

"Before I met you, I told Jamie to be careful. That you were likely out for our money."

Gray frowned.

"The paintings? I assumed you'd convinced him to buy them."

"Oh no. I tried repeatedly to get him to take them. He wouldn't listen."

"I was unkind, and I'm sorry. I didn't know you, and I made assumptions I shouldn't have."

"It's okay. You were right to warn him. I'm sure there are some who are unscrupulous and would take advantage in that situation." Gray smiled, but it faded after a moment. "I almost hated to part with those paintings, but he seemed so pleased. I couldn't say no to him."

Rohan smiled. "Jamie doesn't listen very well. He likes to forge his own path."

"I've noticed. When he gets something in his mind, he has a singular focus."

"Indeed he does," Rohan replied, capturing Gray's stare.

They held it a moment before the omega looked away.

"That's why we need to convince him that there's hope," Gray said, his voice bordering on a whisper. "If he ever starts to believe it, I think he just might live forever."

Rohan smiled slightly, imagining Jamie arguing with Death itself.

And winning.

They fell into a silence, a comfortable one. That peacefulness about Gray called to him, especially now in the storm that was his life. No wonder Jamie was so drawn to the man.

The omega lifted his plate. "I can't eat another bite. Let me clean this up."

"You don't have to do that."

"You made lunch. I clean it up. Those are the rules," Gray said, grabbing Rohan's empty plate.

Rohan sat back and watched Gray move gracefully through their kitchen for a moment before he felt another pang of the instinct hitting him in the gut.

Take him.

Make him yours.

Rohan clenched his jaw, fighting the need overwhelming him. Now was not the time nor the place... not that any would be better. Yet when Gray tentatively looked over his shoulder, lust in his eyes, Rohan nearly rose from his seat and crossed the room. He could scent the omega's lust and was shocked by it. The man was already pregnant with his son...

He was almost more shocked by the need he felt in return.

The omega shut off the water, and then turned to face him, hands fisted on top of the island. "I want to be here for Jamie. He needs as much love surrounding him as he can get right now... which means we'll need to be in closer quarters than I ever anticipated when I got involved with this surrogacy."

Rohan held the omega's stare, waiting for the inevitable 'but'.

"But... we have to fight this instinct within us. The more we're around each other, the harder it might become." Gray looked away, his face darkening.

What causes his blush?

Lust?

Shame?

Both?

Rohan closed his eyes, his body quickening as his own lusts rose. The omega was right. Sharing the same spaces would be hell on both of them. He didn't need the added distraction when he had Jamie to care for. "Maybe you coming around isn't a good idea."

"No... *please*. I *need* to spend time with him. We can come up with a schedule of some kind, can't we? I can care for him during the day, so you can get some work in, perhaps... I need to be home in the afternoons for my nephews, but that would give you several hours of work each day. I can be here by ten-thirty... and leave by one or so."

That would allow him to check in at work on occasion and bring files to and from the office. There was a lot he could do from home, but he could check in here and there... but those hours didn't give him much space. "By the time I'd get to the office, I'd have only a few minutes before I'd have to turn around and come home. You couldn't get here any earlier?"

"I'm stuck to the school and trolley schedules."

"What if I sent a car?"

"Every day?" Gray asked, looking stunned. "You already send cars for my doctor's appointments. That's a lot of expense. I couldn't ask that of you."

Rohan considered that a moment. "You coming *would* be a help for me, actually." Time away, here and there, would be good for his own mental health. And it would be good for Jamie to have a change of pace... or face, so to speak. Gray had been the one to inspire hope. Jamie needed that in his life. "Two or three days a week. If you could be here by, say nine... and gone by two... I can hire a nurse, as well... to help fill in any gaps if I'm running late," Rohan said. "We can avoid each other as much as possible—and both be there for him. I hate the thought of working, but I'm in the middle of a few large projects and can't abandon them completely. If I have to leave, I'd feel better knowing someone who truly cared was here with him for the bulk of it."

Gray smiled before speaking. "That would be perfect."

The timbre of Gray's voice washed over him, and the instinct roared within him again. His stare traveled lower, to caress the swell to Gray's stomach. When he lifted it again, he saw the shock and need filling Gray's eyes.

Claim him.

Make him yours.

He closed his eyes, hating the animalistic part of him. "How much longer are you staying tonight?"

Go… before I do something I'll hate myself for.

"Just until he awakens… and then I'll get him some tea and talk a little more before I leave. If that's okay. It's become a bit of a tradition between him and I. Our afternoon teas."

"That's fine," Rohan murmured, feeling a tiny thread of jealousy that he and Jamie had grown so close when there was only distance between them. Excusing himself, he headed straight up to peek in on his mate.

And remind himself who he belonged to.

Jamie slept, his body so still it frightened Rohan. He sat on the side of the bed… wanting to see the gentle rise and fall of his omega's chest before he left. From the corner of his eye, he saw the small piece of paper on the nightstand. Rohan reached for it and drew in a shuddered breath as he stared at his child.

A pang of need swept him again. He wanted to run back down the stairs and draw Gray into his arms and celebrate this beautiful life growing within the omega. Rohan turned to see Jamie, pale and so still. They'd supposed to have that moment, celebrating a new life.

He lowered the piece of paper back to the nightstand before sliding into the bed beside his omega. Rohan drew his omega into his arms, knowing Jamie would hate him for this… but it was his turn to be selfish.

Rohan needed to hold the man he loved.

Chapter Twenty-Two

Home again…

Gray bustled into the cottage, slamming the door. He pressed his back against it once he was inside. He'd held himself together while at Jamie's.

And during the long ride home.

But once he crossed the threshold of home, he couldn't hold back any longer.

The tears came in a torrent. Sliding down the door, he fell until his butt hit the floor. Soon after, Avery appeared in the foyer, a kitchen towel over one shoulder and flour on his nose. As soon as he looked at Gray, he rushed closer and knelt.

"What's happened? Are you okay? Is it the baby?"

Gray took a moment to capture enough air to speak. "The baby… is fine. I'm fine."

"Then what is it?"

"Jamie's cancer is back." A sob rocked him. "And it's bad. The outlook is grim."

He was fresh out of hope in that moment. Gray had used every ounce of his strength trying to buoy both Jamie and Rohan. Now, he had nothing left.

"My gods," Avery said. He frowned. "What about the baby?"

"The baby is fine."

"That's not what I meant. *Who* will be there to raise the baby?" Avery murmured slowly, frowning.

Gray looked away. He didn't want to imagine a world where Jamie wasn't there to play the proud papa he'd been all set to become. He turned back to face the question. "I don't know. Jamie will soon return to treatment… and I guess we take it day by day."

"Day by day?" Avery's frown deepened. "There needs to be a plan. What if Jamie doesn't make it? Do you hand over a baby to a grieving alpha? Who will raise the child? A nurse or a manny?" Avery paused. "Or you?"

All the questions that had been circling in the back of his own mind. He'd ignored them, not willing to make the situation so dire. Avery didn't suffer the same compulsion.

"I signed over my rights," Gray admitted, not wanting to think about Jamie not making it.

"And so you'll just wash your hands of the whole thing? I know you were carrying the child for them… but the bond. There's no way you'd be able to walk away if Jamie died. I know you too well, uncle."

Gray looked away. "No. I doubt I would."

His thoughts went to Rohan. He'd nearly lost it when he'd seen the alpha's stare roaming over him. Gray knew it had been the instinct… just as it had been instinct with him.

"Are we eating tonight?" Lake called out sarcastically from the family room.

"Yeah, yeah," Avery called down the hall as he rose to his full height. "It'll come when it comes." He turned to look at Gray, offering a hand. "I hate cooking. Have I told you how much I hate cooking?"

Gray took the towel from Avery's shoulder. "You're not all that good at it, either." He started walking toward the kitchen, wiping his eyes with one hand.

Avery followed him. "I make do."

After washing his hands, Gray checked the two pots simmering, tasting them one after the other.

"Uncle Gray!" Auggie cried, a smile on his face. He raced over and wrapped his little arms around Gray. "Thank heavens. I thought we'd starve."

Gray placed a hand on Auggie's back, thankful for the little bit of joy. "Good to know I'm appreciated for *something* around here."

"We appreciate more than your cooking," Avery said as he watched Gray adding some spices to one pot.

"This isn't half bad," Gray murmured to Avery. "You're getting better."

"Better than terrible still isn't good," Avery said before he went to tackle the dishes piled in the sink. How one man could dirty so many while cooking, Gray didn't know.

"Avery'll have to marry an alpha rich enough to hire a cook," Lake said. "I know I plan on it."

"You can't plan things like that," Gray told the boy. "You get who you get."

Lake shrugged as he sat down along the island opposite where Gray was cooking. "Yeah, sure—the fated mate bit. I'm so tired of the teachers going on and on about that. Why can't we just find our own paths?"

"Good question," Avery said from the sink.

"I'm *never* getting mated," Auggie said before heading back into the family room to watch a movie.

Gray nodded his agreement before the sadness of his reality hit him hard. He wouldn't have what he wanted… yet there was Jamie, who supposedly had it all, and would never get his happy ever after, either.

It wasn't fair.

Gray fought back tears as he checked the other pot.

"Are you okay, Uncle Gray?"

Gray lifted his stare to see Lake, watching him with concern.

"I'm not," Gray answered. "Not really."

"What's wrong?"

"A friend of mine is very sick. Very sick… and he might die. And I'm sad because I don't want to lose him."

Lake's face suddenly went devoid of emotion, and Gray wondered if it was too soon to talk about something this heavy with the boy. They were all still so raw from Silver's death as it was.

"Is it Jamie?" Lake asked. "I know he didn't look well when he first started coming to visit you here."

Gray nodded. "His cancer has come back, and the prognosis isn't good."

Lake was silent a moment. "Papa once said you were his best friend," Lake said, catching Gray's stare. "That's not fair for you to lose two."

Gray felt the tears threatening to fall, but he held them somehow. He nodded. "You're right. It *isn't* fair. And I'm going to do everything I can to help Jamie live."

Lake slid out of his chair and rounded the island before wrapping his arms around Gray. Gray smiled and held on to the boy, thankful he was finally seeing a different side to the teen.

"I hope he lives," Lake whispered.

Gray felt two more sets of arms wrap around him, and he smiled. He loved his nephews so very much. "Me, too."

* * * *

Another heat…

Avery popped a *Heat Repress* pill before he slipped into his very first Ancient History class of the new Spring semester. It didn't feel like spring. Not yet. Snow still covered the ground. But there was a promise of one to come.

For most of us.

Avery frowned, thoughts of Jamie and Gray coming to his mind. He hated that his uncle was going through all this pain, but he'd also warned Gray it was a mistake in the first place.

Don't be that asshole. He was trying to do something good.

He sighed and took the first available seat in the front row. Exhaustion hit him hard. He'd gone through the whole of last semester and luckily only had to deal with two heats while in class. It had felt serendipitous. They'd either been on a break or a weekend when the moon was full. Now, here was the first day of his new semester and he was in heat.

The professor stormed in the auditorium style classroom and tossed his beleaguered briefcase onto the top of a very long black counter before the series of blackboards lining one wall. An *alpha* professor. Avery gasped inwardly and began closing the textbook he'd just been opening. He needed to put some distance between him and the alpha.

"This is Ancient Civilizations 102," the professor roared as Avery slid from his seat. The man eyed him and continued, "If you are not supposed to be in my class, I suggest you leave now and don't interrupt my lecture."

Avery made his way up the stairs, fatigue making each step seem ten times harder.

"Excuse me, sir... where might you be going?"

Avery saw a few stares coming his way. He turned to look at the professor glaring at him. "I just wanted a better seat."

"There was something wrong with being up front?"

Avery didn't know what to say. Every eye was on him, and he felt his face flame. "I see better from the back."

"Ahh," the professor said, cocking one brow. "Well, find your seat *and fast*. I don't have all day."

Avery turned and stepped at the same time, nearly missing the stair. He almost fell—but was luckily grabbed by the arm and held upright. When he lifted his stare, he saw the most gorgeous set of hazel eyes he'd ever witnessed. A rush of desire ran through him, nearly bringing a moan to his lips.

"There's a seat by me, if this is back far enough."

Avery smiled and nodded. "Yes, thanks."

The guy grabbed the notebook he'd dropped as Avery slid past and took a seat. His new friend handed it over with a sultry smile that nearly took his breath away. *The guy's a beta... I can't be attracted to a beta.*

Can I?

"Good, are we all where we need to be now?" the professor asked, pointedly looking Avery's way.

Avery nodded, feeling embarrassed as hell.

"Don't worry about old man Buckshot. I hear he's actually a big old softy."

"Buckshot?" Avery whispered, leaning in a little closer. He drew in a breath and loved the warm, spicy smell of the guy.

"He's got this huge deer's head in his office," Mr. Hazel eyes said before offering a hand. "Brett Boyd."

Avery smiled, taking the big, warm hand in his. "Av—" *Damn... I almost said my real name.* "Abraham. Abraham Norcross."

"Abraham, hmm? Good to meet you, Abe."

Avery chuckled, looking into those warm hazel eyes before turning and trying to focus on the professor. Wetness leaked a little between his cheeks, and he squirmed a little in his seat.

"If you were in my class last semester, we're picking right back up where we left off. If you didn't have me last semester for 101, I wish you well in trying to keep up."

Avery sighed inwardly. He, of course, hadn't had Professor Buckshot... *erm, Conover...* the previous semester. He took out his recorder and laid it on his desk, ready to take notes.

"We'll begin today with the Resurgence."

A student's hand shot up near the front.

"Yes?" the professor asked, lifting a brow.

"We usually just go over the syllabus and review what's expected on the first day of class."

"Oh?" the professor asked. "So I'm to lower my expectations because other professors have coddled you?"

"Well, maybe," the student joked.

And got a deadly evil eye. "I think not."

Avery looked at Brett, hoping that 'old softy' bit was true. It sure as hell didn't seem like it.

"As I was saying before I was so rudely interrupted. The Resurgence. This era began right after the Dark Period. Of course, historians argue over the exact beginning and end of either, but for our class's purposes, we will use the year 3225 as the first signs of the Resurgence Period. This was a great time for historians as we began to see some of the first true masters of painting, philosophy, and the other arts begin to emerge. After the nearly two-thousand-year period following the Great Catastrophe, and it's utter lack of recorded history, we then come into this period where almost everything is charted in one way or another. We've moved from famine to feast." The professor began to move about the room, looking into their faces as he traveled. "The early years of the Resurgence were still *very* barbaric, holding fast to stringent rules for all classes of men. Alphas continued to maintain strongholds, protecting their wealth, resources, and the harems of omegas they called mates and their children."

Harems? Avery's head bobbed up from his notetaking. He raised his hand.

"Yes?"

"Alphas had more than one omega? And called them all mate?"

"They did. Some had as many as a dozen—but of course, those were the days when omegas outnumbered alphas ten to one. Obviously, that's just an estimate—that ten to one number—as there were no true censuses then. We can only extrapolate using more recent losses to the omega number and adding data we find from written histories of the time."

"What of the fated mate? Is that a more recent occurrence?"

The professor sighed. "The idea of fated mates—in my opinion—is a construct of the alpha government."

A gasp went about the room.

Avery leaned forward in his seat. "How so?"

"What most history books won't tell you is that for thousands of years, alphas claimed as many omegas as they could. Weaker alphas had fewer omegas, if any, and their lines ended. Strong alphas had many children, increasing our number exponentially. Of course, wars, plagues, and famines occurred plentifully, claiming many of those number. Eventually, the number of omegas began to lessen. No one's completely sure why, but I credit it to a larger population and smaller family sizes as our provinces grew in size and the onset of urban living. No longer was the ratio ten to one... but five to one... then three to one... and when it went to two to one, we suddenly see the government pushing an agenda of *the fated mate*. No more harems—they were outlawed over four hundred years ago. One alpha to one omega. The government did an excellent job in convincing our people that this was the way it needed to be and in time, it became the way things were."

"But how did it work? The AO bond... how did the omegas not fight over their place with the alpha?" Avery asked.

The professor smiled, moving closer. He took a few steps up before answering. "There's believed to have been another bond, one almost lost to time. That between the omega brothers who would share their alpha."

"What kind of bond did they have?"

"From what we understand, it was much like the bond the alpha and omega shared, but less sexual and more familial. They loved one another as brothers, tied almost instantly by a chemical reaction in the brain. The same instinct to care, protect, and provide would be there, but not necessarily in a sexual manner—although some omegas did share their beds with one another."

A murmur ran through the auditorium.

"Think about it," the professor said to the room. "You're an alpha with a dozen omegas. There is no way you can focus more than a fraction of your time on each of them. No doubts there was loneliness… and from letters we have found written by omegas to their families, there are hints that speak of marital love between omegas. And in some, it even seemed to be spurred on by the alphas themselves." The professor chuckled. "I'm sure those poor alphas were exhausted all the time."

"So you're saying an alpha can have more than one mate?" Avery asked.

"Yes. An alpha can have many mates. Whereas, omegas mate with *only* one alpha, but can have the omega bonds with many."

"This sounds like heresy," another student said from across the room. "The Book states one alpha to one omega."

"The Book was written by man and ignores most of our own history," the professor stated loudly. "You can call me a heretic all you want. I don't care. I follow the facts, not some myth in a fiction you read."

Avery smiled as more chatter raced through the room.

The professor moved closer and stood beside Avery. He inhaled deeply just as Avery felt another few drips of liquid easing from beneath him. *Oh shit.*

"I will speak with you after class," the professor murmured before spinning and going down the stairs and continuing his lecture.

Avery caught a glimpse of Brett staring at him from the corner of his eye.

Fuck. I'm caught.

* * * *

Chemo, Day One…

He was back.

Jamie had spent so many hours here, being injected with poisons to kill his cancer. Rows upon rows of large recliners beside IV machines ready to be loaded with toxins. He sat back and watched as the needles were stuck into him and the first of the poison entered his body. On one side sat Gray. On the other, sat Rohan. Both of them had argued about who would be the one to accompany him there that day—until he demanded them both be there. They both hovered close now, silent as his treatment began. He could sense worry filling them both and wanted to lighten the mood.

He slid a hand through his still too-short locks. "I finally got some hair to grow and now I'll likely lose it again. I *really* hate being bald."

"Hair grows back," Gray said. "As long as you're here, that's *all* that matters."

Jamie squeezed his hand.

"I kind of like the short hair," Rohan murmured.

"Liar," Jamie spat. "You have a thing for long hair, and we both know it." Jamie turned to Gray. "Did he demand you pull it down for him? He did, didn't he? I remember seeing it was a complete mess."

Both their faces grew red, and he had his answer.

"Maybe we can get you one of those wigs," Gray said. "Give you long hair again."

"What a waste of money," Jamie replied. "I mean, it *would* be nice to have hair again, but they're *so* expensive... and for what? My vanity? I mean, I used to be much vainer than I am today, but after you go through this torture, you gain a little perspective. Now, I'd much rather waste money on better things than that. Like spoiling the people I love." He grinned at Gray. "And the baby."

Gray smiled back.

Still the tension surrounding them was thick, and he didn't quite understand it. The last couple of weeks—as they'd waited for treatments to begin—both Gray and Rohan had seemed to be avoiding one another. Rohan left for the office just before Gray arrived. Gray left moments before Rohan returned home, as if on cue. The new nurses, Jefre and Serge—who he had originally hated the idea of—were wonderful and made sure he was never alone.

And never a burden on the men he loved.

The time passed slowly with the both of them silent. He rested back into his recliner, ready to take a nap, when a familiar face appeared in his sight.

Wilder.

His brother made his way across the room. He caught a glimpse of Gray and Rohan and almost looked like he reconsidered his trek, but came nonetheless. When he stopped before them, he reached out and took Jamie's hand.

"How's it going?" Wilder asked with a slight smile.

"It's going as well as can be expected, I suppose," Jamie answered.

Wilder looked around, his stare finally falling on Gray. "I didn't expect a full house when I got here."

"I can leave and give you some time with your brother," Gray murmured.

"No," Jamie said, squeezing Gray's hand. He wouldn't let Gray be pushed aside. Not even for his favorite brother. He looked back up at Wilder. "Grab a chair. We'll have a little party."

"I don't want to be in the way," Wilder said, backing up. "I just wanted to let you know I was thinking of you today."

"You came all this way to see me," Jamie said, holding both Rohan's and Gray's hands in his tightly. "You should stay for a bit. Let us catch up."

Wilder looked uncomfortable, but ultimately didn't argue. He stole a chair from one of the empty recliners and slid in closer to Rohan's side of the chair.

"I don't think you had a proper introduction to my friend Gray," Jamie said once Wilder was seated.

Wilder's stare flickered to his and then to Gray before sliding back. "No. I didn't," he answered coolly. His jaws set some afterwards.

"You *won't* disrespect Gray," Jamie said. "I love him almost as much as I do you. So I won't have it."

"Tell me how you really feel," Wilder murmured.

"Look... I don't know how much time I have left. I won't waste one minute of it. Either you accept the choices I've made and let it all go, or you can leave."

Wilder's eyes widened some before he gave Gray a little more than a cursory glance. "It's nice to finally meet you, Gray."

"Nice to meet you, too," Gray murmured.

"We have Gray to thank for convincing your brother to go back into treatment," Rohan said to Wilder.

Wilder's stare went to Jamie. "You weren't going to go into treatment?"

"No. I wasn't. But Gray reminded me I have a baby to meet soon. And I need to last until at least then."

"Then my whole family owes you thanks," Wilder said to Gray, with only a tiniest hint of rancor in his tone.

"The whole family? I doubt it," Jamie said. "It's not as if I've seen papa since the row."

"You did tell us you didn't want to see us again," Wilder admitted.

"You had no problem ignoring me," Jamie said.

"No, but then, I knew you didn't mean me." He smiled. "You love me too much for that."

Jamie grinned. "*Maybe* I do."

Wilder leaned back in his chair. "I could ask papa if they plan to come see you."

"Don't bother," Jamie answered. "I meant it. I'm done trying to gain their approval. But their absence is also noted. It only proves my whole point."

"Don't let them bring you down," Rohan said, squeezing his hand. "The people who matter are here. And will always be here."

Wilder turned back to Jamie. "As you will be."

Jamie looked to both Gray and Rohan before giving their hands a squeeze. "I would like a moment alone with my brother."

Both Gray and Rohan rose and left them. Once they were out of earshot, Jamie faced his brother. "I know you don't want to hear the truth, but I don't have much longer."

"Don't talk like that."

Jamie lifted a hand to silence his brother. Wilder's stiff upper lip began to fade some, and fear entered his eyes.

"I need your help. You're the only one I can trust," Jamie said. "Will you help me?"

Wilder frowned. "What do you need?"

* * * *

After class…

Avery approached Dr. Conover after class was over. His heart beating madly, he stayed back, letting other students ask their own questions before he meandered closer. Add in the fact he was fighting off his heat, and he was in misery.

"Follow me to my office," the alpha said, once he'd packed up his things.

Avery watched the man take off, wondering if he was about to be turned in. A little part of him considered just running for it and heading back to the O Quad, but it wasn't like the guard wouldn't be able to find him there.

Maybe I run even farther than the O Quad.
But where?

"Are you coming?" the professor shot out as he sailed through the door and out into the hallway.

Avery raced to catch up. If he was done for, it was easier to go ahead and face the music. Luckily, they didn't have to go far. The professor's office was just up one flight of stairs. Avery followed him inside and shut the door.

The office was tiny. The building itself was old, nearly three hundred years old—if not older. There was a myth that it had been a school before the Great Catastrophe and the elders had used the bare bones of the building to rebuild again centuries ago. Now, doors didn't close well. Everything was off-balance a few inches here and there. Floorboards creaked and groaned on occasion. There was a smell, not necessarily bad, but just age.

Dr. Conover walked over to his window and opened it before drawing in a deep breath of fresh air. Avery's stare roamed over the office, stopping on the huge deer head mounted above a wall of awards and certificates.

Professor Buckshot.

His mind went back to Brett and those eyes, and he felt a bit of his cream coating him. Conover spun to face Avery and glared.

"If you *ever* come into my classroom in heat again, you and I will have issues."

Avery froze. The gig was up. *But wait. If I ever come again?* "I don't know what you're talking about."

"Don't play coy with me," Professor Conover said. "Do you *really* think you're the first omega who tried to reach above his station in life?" The man walked closer and grabbed a mechanical pencil from his desk and scribbled something on a piece of scrap paper and handed it to Avery. "See the pharmacist there. Mr. Pelham. Tell him I sent you and that you need *the good medicine*."

Avery took the slip and frowned. "What is *the good medicine?*"

Dr. Conover walked back to the window and took another deep breath, his back to Avery. After a moment, the professor turned to look at him. "*Heat Repress* is a joke. There are other medicines that will work much better and nearly stop your heats completely."

"What?" Avery asked, dumbfounded.

"They're illegal, of course, but I'm sure you've likely found the scent blockers already, so you're already breaking the law. Am I correct in my assumption?"

Avery wasn't sure if he should answer or not, but sensed he could. After a couple of seconds, he nodded.

Dr. Conover pointed at the slip. "I did not give you that, if you're caught. Do not tell anyone else what I've told you. Understood?"

"But other omegas could benefit from this."

"If too many omegas went on it, people would take notice and it could end for *everyone*. I won't have the people I care about hurt because *you* blabbed."

"But it only serves a few when it should serve us all."

"We cannot overthrow the system overnight. It comes in stages. For now, only a small few use this drug."

Avery stared at the older alpha, shocked by the man's obvious disdain for the system that benefitted… him. "Overthrow?"

"I don't mean by violence. Omegas are no match for alphas physically and there aren't enough men like me on your side. It needs to be a peaceful change. It won't happen overnight, so we're playing the long game here."

"Why are you doing this?"

"Because I'm an alpha, there's no way I could believe in omega equality? Is that what you're thinking?"

Avery was silent. He didn't want to further offend the professor.

"While I know I'm a rare breed of alpha, I *do* believe omegas have the ability to be more than what they have become. History proves we can be different. Our government has effectively imprisoned omegas, and I'm shocked more males like you don't try to escape."

The man's words were a balm to his soul. "Thank you," Avery said, wholeheartedly.

"You're welcome," the professor said. "But I have high expectations of you, Abraham Norcross." He chuckled. "If that's even your name."

Avery wasn't ready to give himself completely away. "What kind of expectations?"

"You cannot be mediocre. You have an opportunity here to prove yourself. One day, when the truth is found out, you need to be the best of whatever it is you plan to be. It's the only way to change minds."

"I'm only planning to be an accountant. I won't change the world."

"But you will. Be the best damned accountant you can be. Learn everything you can. Prove yourself not only capable, but exceptional."

"Yes, sir."

Dr. Conover smiled before growling low in his chest. "It's well past time for you to get the hell out of my office. Before I do something that will embarrass us both."

Avery rose quickly and tossed his backpack over one shoulder. "Of course." He lifted the scrap of paper. "Thanks for this as well."

The alpha nodded. "Don't come back to my class until you're on it. Understood?"

"Yes, sir."

"One last thing. That small tome on the corner of my desk before you... the dark blue one. Take it. Read it. And we'll discuss it sometime soon after class."

Avery lifted the book and looked to the man before getting a nod to ensure it was the right one. He tucked it into his backpack before offering a wave and exiting the room.

He stopped in the middle of the hallway, a smile crossing his lips. Looking down at that scrap of paper, he'd possibly found even more freedom. His uncle came to mind... the *Heat Repress* that had failed him. Had they known...?

Everything would've been different.

Before he left, he reached into his backpack and pulled out the small book. *A History of the Omega.*

Avery turned to the first page and began to read as he walked down the hallway. By the time he was on the trolley home, he was captivated.

By the following morning, he was ready for change.

Chapter Twenty-Three

A couple of weeks later…

Gray tucked Jamie into bed after the second chemo appointment with the help of the day nurse, Jefre. Once they were done, they both left the room and headed down. Gray was utterly exhausted. "Is that how it'll be with every visit?" he asked Jefre.

"Everyone is different. And every cancer is, too. There's no way of telling how bad it might get. I wasn't his nurse the last time around, so I don't have much by means of comparison." Jefre paused, clenching his stomach.

"Are you okay?"

"I think something I ate might be giving me some trouble."

Gray cast a look at the nurse as they reached the bottom stair. Jefre's color didn't look good, and sweat beaded on his brow. "Are you sick?"

Jefre sighed. "I haven't been around anyone with a bug, that I know of. But it is that time of year."

"If you're sick, you need to go home. His immune system can't take the added stress," Gray said to the nurse.

Jefre placed a hand to his forehead. "I hate to leave you alone with him right after a chemo appointment, though. It might not be an easy afternoon."

"I can handle it."

"I *am* a little warm… and I don't want to make things worse for Jamie." He walked over and grabbed his bag. "I'll call Serge on the way home and see if he can come in any earlier."

"Thanks. I'll be okay, though."

Or so he thought he'd be.

A few hours later, as he was holding Jamie for his third round of puking, he wasn't so sure he could last much longer. *Stay strong. He needs me.*

Jamie rose on unsteady legs and lunged for the bathroom counter with Gray's help. He rinsed his hands off before lifting a palmful of cold water to his lips and spitting it back out. He lifted his stare and cringed when he looked into the mirror.

"Look at me," Jamie cried staring into the mirror after wiping his mouth. "Just look at me." He reached up and ran a hand over his head. He drew a clump of his short locks away before tossing it into the sink. "I *knew* this would happen. I was finally getting hair again and now it's gone."

Gray wiped down the toilet and tossed the paper inside before flushing it. He moved to the sink and washed his hands before lifting his stare to Jamie. "Like I said before. Hair grows. It'll come back. I'd rather you lose that than we lose you."

"No… this is what I didn't want. I didn't want to be sick. I didn't want you and Rohan forced into playing my nursemaid. I didn't want this." Tears shone in his eyes. "I begged you all."

Gray felt as if he could vomit. He'd pushed for this… and now he'd gotten it. Only he wasn't the one being tortured. Jamie was.

Jamie eyed Gray's long braid. He grabbed it and ran his hand down the length. "My hair used to be like that. It was long and *so* very beautiful. Now, losing *that* was a tragedy. The first clump?" Jamie's eyes filled with tears. "I cried for three days after that first clump had come out." He looked back in the mirror. "Now it's just a joke."

Gray looked down at the thick braid still hanging over one shoulder.

Jamie raced past him and fell to his knees—just in time to vomit again. Gray rushed over and ran a hand down Jamie's back, trying to soothe him somewhat. He felt so inadequate… and hoped his presence helped in some way.

He wasn't sure it did.

Once they were cleaned up again, Gray helped Jamie back to bed. The doctors had said the first weeks of chemo were often the worst. Jamie's body would grow a little accustomed to the medicines and in time, he wouldn't get as deathly ill.

Knowing he was the reason Jamie was enduring this torment ate at him. He felt more and more selfish by the day.

He has to meet the baby… he just has to.

After getting Jamie cleaned up and back into bed, the bedroom door opened and Rohan's face appeared.

"Where's the nurse?" Rohan asked, frowning.

"Sick. So I stayed longer. Serge was supposed to be here by now."

Gray fled to the bathroom, trying to put distance between him and Rohan. He began picking up the used towels and tossing them into the already gargantuan pile of dirty clothes.

"I take it today was tough?"

Gray looked over his shoulder and nodded. "He's been sick all afternoon."

"I was afraid of that. I should've stayed. Had you called and told me Jefre was sick, I would've come home earlier."

Gray tried to act as if he wasn't breaking inside. "I've taken care of him. We've been just fine."

He lifted the heavy basket of towels, planning to start a cycle of wash. Rohan was in his way.

"You don't need to do that. I can take over now," Rohan said, moving closer.

"He's my friend. I want to be here for him," Gray murmured, the exhaustion of the day seeping into his bones.

Rohan closed the gap and took the basket from him. "I can do this."

Gray fought back tears.

"What's wrong?" Rohan asked, frowning.

"I didn't know."

"What didn't you know?"

"How bad it would be for him. He said it... he told me... but I didn't want to believe it was as bad as he made it out to be. What have I asked of him? It's *killing* him."

Rohan lowered the basket and drew Gray into his arms.

Gray leaned into the alpha's strength and warmth, surrendering in a moment of weakness. It felt so good there, safe from all the chaos in his world.

"It's killing the cancer... not him."

"Are you sure? After what I saw today, I'm not."

Rohan took a step back and gathered Gray's face in his hands. "You're the one who said we needed to stay positive... remember? He needs you and I to give him strength. You can't do that if you let this get to you."

Gray's stare met Rohan's, and the pull of the instinct nearly took his breath away. "How did you make it through the last time? After seeing what this did to him?"

"It wasn't easy. It tore me up inside to see him so sick. It's no better this time... only I know a little of what to expect now. It softens the blow some."

"I envy that," Gray murmured.

Rohan lowered his hands to Gray's shoulders, massaging. "It'll get a little worse before it gets a bit better, I'm afraid."

Rohan's hands felt good on his shoulders... his neck. When he tilted Gray's head and leaned in close, he was too exhausted to fight it.

The alpha caught himself, inches away from that kiss. He backed off, torment in his eyes. Lowering to grab the laundry, he avoided Gray's stare. "I'll go get these started. The car is outside waiting for you."

And Rohan was gone.

Gray lifted his hand to his lower lip. It ached with want. How he could want when Jamie lay in a bed next door, he didn't know.

He was a horrible, *horrible* man.

Gray turned to the mirror and eyed his reflection. His gaze went to the long, thick braid lying over his shoulder. Without telling Rohan goodbye, he raced down the stairs. Coat in hand, he strode outside and to the waiting car.

"Can you take me somewhere other than home?"

His usual driver, Sid, looked over his shoulder. "How far?"

"Not far from my home… and I can get home from there. I just need to stop in somewhere."

"Sure. Where are we going?"

Gray gave the man the directions just before they pulled out of the semi-circular drive and on toward the O Quad. When they arrived at their destination, he climbed out with a thanks to the driver.

He stepped into the hairstylist's shop and eyed the beta behind the chair. "Do you have time for a cut?"

"Yeah, I can trim you up," the beta said as he continued working on the elaborate braid for the omega in his chair.

"Not a trim. A cut. As in all of it."

Both the hairstylist and omega turned to him, dumbfounded.

"Yeah… sure… just give me a minute to finish up here."

Gray's heart beat in his chest like a tattoo. He wasn't sure he could breathe in his next lungful of air. When it was his turn to sit in the stylist's chair, he felt a cold shiver race up his spine. *What am I doing?*

"Are you sure you want to cut it all off?" the stylist asked, lifting the long braid that nearly reached Gray's knees.

Jamie's face came back to mind—crying over losing his hair. He was sacrificing a lot to endure treatment. Gray felt the need to sacrifice something of his own. "Do it. Cut it all off. But keep the braid… I want to have it made into a wig."

"If you're sure."

Gray met the beta's eyes in the mirror. "I'm sure."

The scissors sawed through his thick braid. Moments later, the rope of hair was laid into his lap, both ends tied off.

"You want me to give you a cute cut with what's left?"

Gray stared into his image in the mirror. "No... I want you to shave it all off."

"Shave? Why?"

"I have a sick friend. He's losing his hair."

The beta smiled softly in the mirror, resting a hand on Gray's shoulder. "You don't have to say another word."

The clippers came out and removed the rest of his hair. Afterwards, Gray sat there—silent—as he looked at his image in the mirror. He lifted a hand and ran it over the stubble on his head.

"I feel lighter."

The beta chuckled. "I bet."

The stylist cleaned his neck and shoulders before removing the cape he'd placed over him. Gray rose, braid in hand, and turned to the man. "How much do I owe you?"

"Are you using that to have the wig made for this friend of yours?"

Gray nodded.

"No charge."

Gray felt tears burning the backs of his eyes.

"Save those tears. You'll need them when you get the price tag on a decent wig."

"I had hoped offering up my hair would make it significantly cheaper."

"Cheaper, yes," the stylist said. "Significantly? Probably not." He reached into his station and pulled out a card. "But I know someone who will likely charge a lot less than others would. Tell him I sent you. I'll call and let him know you're calling."

"Thanks," Gray said, pocketing the card. "For everything."

"Anytime... though I doubt I'll see you back with this kind of hair for some time."

Gray laughed. "Agreed."

He left the shop, hearing the click of the lock once he was outside. The last remnants of afternoon were gone. Gray looked up at the night sky, the cold hitting him hard. His head was freezing. After pulling on his coat and wrapping it tight, he looked down at the braid in his hand and wondered if he could wrap it around his head until he got home.

The bell behind him jingled, the door opening again. "Hey!"

Gray turned.

"You'll need this more than I will tonight," the stylist said before tossing something small.

Gray caught it and looked at his hand. A small knit hat. "*Thank* you," he added, pulling it on over his bald head.

"Don't mention it," the beta said. "Be safe, okay? That hair's pretty valuable. Keep it close."

"Thanks. Have a nice night."

Gray watched as the man locked up again before he walked the short distance to the trolley station. He coiled the hair and tucked it into his coat before he arrived—just in time for the next car. After jumping up and tucking himself into the packed car, he traveled closer to home, ready for his night to end.

When he arrived, he found Avery and the boys weren't alone.

Avery and a boy were studying at their kitchen table. "Uncle Gray, this is my classmate, Brett. Brett, my uncle Gray."

Gray reached out and shook the beta's hand. He cast a look at Avery—who looked like the cat who ate the canary.

Avery avoided his stare. "We're just about done here... and I have a lasagna in the oven. We'll have dinner soon."

"I'm sure there's enough if your friend wants to stay, but then again, you might not want him to eat your cooking, hmmm?" Gray asked, smiling. He took off his coat, knocking his hat off.

"For the love of Paul," Avery spat, looking at Gray's head. "What in the hell have you done?"

Gray showed off his braid. "Need to have a wig made."

"For Jamie?" Avery asked, one brow rising.

"For Jamie," Gray said, nodding.

Avery's friend closed his book and notebook. "It looks like you two need a moment. I'm going to head out."

"No, please, stay if you'd like," Gray said. He didn't truly mean it, but he didn't want to appear rude. He wasn't in the mood for visitors and playing the game of pretending Avery was a beta after the day he'd had.

"Maybe next time," the beta said with a smile. He tossed his books into his bag before rising to his full height and casting Avery a sexy smile. He was a handsome beta... *beta* being the keyword there.

He wouldn't be able to woo Avery. When he glanced at his nephew, he was shocked to see the boy looked infatuated.

Lovely.

"Next time, it is," Gray said. "I'm already looking forward to getting to know you more, Breck."

"*Brett*," Avery corrected.

"Sorry... Brett."

Brett smiled at them both. "Thanks for the study help," he said to Avery before heading to the front door.

Once the beta was gone, Gray turned to Avery. "What was that?"

"He's cute. And interested. Why not?" Avery asked, shrugging.

"Where are the boys?" Gray asked. "And how did you convince them to not call you Avery in front of that beta?"

"They're next door. Seems we have a new omega living next door. Only fourteen."

"*Fourteen?* And he's gone into heat already?"

Avery nodded. "Apparently. I feel terrible for him. It was bad enough at seventeen. At least I was almost an adult. I couldn't imagine dealing with all these thoughts and feelings that young." He paused before heading into the kitchen to check the oven. "The kid and Lake became friends today at school. Mutual like of video games, it seems. Of course Auggie wants to be wherever Lake is, so if Lake wanted to go, he needed to take his little brother. They've been over there since school let out—while I studied with Brett."

Gray hung his coat in the hall closet before returning to the kitchen. "A beta? Is this smart? What if he learns your secret?"

"I've already been found out."

Gray spun to face Avery fully. "What?"

"My Ancient Civilizations professor. He's an alpha, and he caught me in heat."

Gray gasped. "He... he didn't hurt you... did he?"

"No. He was the perfect gentleman."

"Wait... your last heat was two weeks ago."

"Between school, work, and you at Jamie's, we're ships in the night as of late. I haven't seen you more than a few seconds in that long."

Gray considered that and realized Avery was right. "So... perfect gentleman. Did he turn you in?"

"No. He did not. He gave me the name of a pharmacist who gave me a new medicine. One that makes *Heat Repress* seem like nothing."

Gray frowned.

"I'm not supposed to tell anyone about this. No other omegas... but after your troubles, I knew I needed to tell you."

"Let me get this straight. An alpha professor caught you lying and breaking the law and instead of turning you in, he gave you the means to get medicine to help you lie better?"

"Yes."

Gray shook his head. "I don't understand."

"He's an equalist. He's given me this book, a history of the omega. It shares insights in the way things used to be and about the systemic repression of our class that has occurred over the last few hundred years. Dr. Conover believes omegas can be more than they're allowed to be and that more of us should try to escape the imprisonment we're faced with."

"An equalist?"

"Yes," Avery said with a smile. "He talks of a peaceful revolution, where omegas get more rights."

"Revolution? Avery… I need you to be very careful. All of this is treasonous. Add that on top of the laws you're already breaking and you could be in a lot of trouble if you're caught."

"You were already worried I'd be caught… I was, and it turned out alright."

"You were *lucky*. The next time, you might not be."

Avery smiled. "But… the good news is… we have a way to help you with your heats after the baby comes. If the pregnancy wasn't enough to reset your system like you hoped. That's great news."

An illegal drug. He wasn't sure if that was great news at all. "Hopefully it won't come to that."

"Uncle Gray, as soon as I started taking it, it was like I had no heat at all."

"None?"

"A barest hint of something… but easily controlled. No wetness, no readying to be taken. *None* of it."

"That's *amazing*. Why don't they allow omegas to use this?"

"Dr. Conover says it's a means of control. If omegas could choose when they got pregnant, and by who, then the birth rates might drop even more. That and the fact that alphas like power. Omegas might demand more freedoms if they weren't slaves to their sex drive. It would effectively destroy the systems in place—and the government *doesn't* want that to happen. It would be anarchy."

Anarchy. Gray sighed. While he hated the way things were, he knew there was danger in trying to create change. Avery was walking a thin line… and had two young wards to consider, too. Gray already had enough to worry about as it was. He reached for his stomach, an ache forming. "Just promise me you'll be careful and not get yourself into trouble."

"I can only promise so much," Avery said with a glittery smile.

The buzzer for the oven went off, and after Avery took the lasagna out, he walked next door to collect his brothers. Gray set the table and awaited the reaction from the youngest in his family to his new appearance.

He chuckled as they both came into the dining room and froze in place, eyes wide.

"You, too?" Lake said before sliding a hand down his own braid. A smile then formed on his face. "I want to cut mine."

"No!" both Avery and Gray said at the same moment.

"But why not? If you both did it, I should be allowed to, as well."

"You're too young to make a decision like that," Gray said. "If you still feel the same way when you're older, then you can do what you will."

"It's not fair!" Lake cried.

"Life isn't fair," Gray spat. "It's best you learn that lesson sooner versus later."

Lake scowled at him before stalking to the table and dropping into one of the chairs.

"While you're over there, you might as well help finish making the table," Avery said while checking the lasagna.

"I hate it here!" Lake spat before rising… and setting the table.

Auggie quietly went to help his brother, looking quite confused.

"I see Lake's good mood was short lived," Avery whispered when Gray neared.

"Teenaged moods are mercurial, at best. I remember some of the horror stories your papa told me about you at that age."

"I was *never* that bad," Avery whispered hotly.

Gray chuckled. "Maybe. Maybe not."

Avery looked aghast.

Of course, he hadn't been. But now he was creating new issues with his youthful optimism and progressive ideals. Gray clutched his aching stomach again.

Avery eyed him, his smile fading. "Everything alright?"

Gray nodded. "Just worry catching up to me. I'll be fine."

He sure as hell hoped he'd be fine.

The doubts began as the pains continued.

Chapter Twenty-Four

The following day...

Jamie sat in the oversized chaise in his new bedroom, curled up in a blanket. A different nurse had arrived that morning, not Jefre, and the beta wasn't as pleasant as the other man. He'd already been overly rough with Jamie while helping him dress and clean up first thing. And instead of taking him downstairs like he'd asked, the nurse had just sat him on the chaise in his bedroom.

How Jamie hated this new bedroom. He hated being away from Rohan, but it was a necessary evil. In his old room, he'd at least have had a beautiful view—plus he could watch Rohan leaving for the office and the car pulling in carrying Gray.

Jamie had recently realized the well-timed near-misses were not a coincidence, but planned. There was no way around it. It was as if Rohan knew Gray's car was nearing.

I'll have to do something about that.

Only today, the few minutes it usually was between one leaving and the other arriving stretched.

Gray's late. I hope he's okay.

His short-term nurse strode into the bedroom, hauling a tray of food. The smell nearly made him vomit then and there. A plate of greasy bacon, eggs, and buttered toast was sat before him. Jamie gagged.

Jamie reached up and covered his nose and mouth with one hand. "Please... take it away."

"I worked hard on this," the nurse said. "I was told to make sure you ate breakfast *and* lunch."

"*Had you bothered asking*, I would've told you I just had chemo the day before yesterday. I have no desire to eat *anything*."

The nurse lifted his chin and stared down his nose. "I was instructed to make you eat."

Jamie put as much power into his words as he had left. "I'm *not* hungry."

"*Eat!*" the man spat while trying to leave the tray on his lap.

"What's this?" Gray asked as he strolled into the room, scowling at the nurse.

"He won't eat," the offensive man said, looking a little less aggressive now that someone else was there.

Gray walked over and looked at the plate. "Of course he wouldn't want to eat all that. He's been sick for two days." He spun to face the man. "I assume you're Jefre's *temporary* replacement?"

"I am. Name's Saul."

"Saul... in this house, you don't force anyone to eat. You don't force *anyone* to do *anything*. Am I clear?"

Jamie smiled at Gray's forceful comment... as well as his use of *this house*... *as if it's his*.

Well... it is.

Or rather... it will be.

The nurse cocked one brow. "You aren't the omega's alpha. I *don't* take my instructions from you."

Jamie almost chuckled when he saw the anger flashing in his friend's eyes. Gray pulled a phone from his pocket and dialed. Jamie wasn't exactly sure who Gray was calling, but he had a good idea.

"Yes, sorry to bother you, but we have an issue at the house. No… no, you don't need to come back, I can handle it, but I just need you to tell this nurse he won't be force-feeding Jamie a greasy plate of bacon, eggs, and toast. Also… please tell him that he needs to listen to Jamie and I when given instructions instead of being an obstinate asshole."

Gray listened in a moment before handing the phone to the nurse. "Jamie's alpha has something to tell you."

The nurse snatched the phone before placing it to his ear. "Sir… I'm so sorry about this. I only tried to follow your instructions." He paused, and even Jamie could hear the roar of Rohan's voice on the other end. "Yes, sir. I understand. I won't make the mistake again."

The nurse handed the phone back to Gray before snatching up the tray. Gray quickly ended the call and glared at the nurse until he left the room.

"Thank you," Jamie murmured to his hero.

Gray smiled and sat down on the end of the chaise, still in his coat and hat. "So sorry I'm late. I could've prevented all this had I been here."

"Everything alright? I was growing worried."

Gray smiled warmly. "Everything is fine." He slid his coat off and laid it over one arm. "How about some hot tea? Some warm broth? You haven't eaten in a few days now."

"And the thought makes me ill," Jamie said.

"Rohan *had* asked the nurse to try and persuade you to eat a little. But he did tell the beta you were coming off a chemo treatment and weren't well."

"I'd say this man is ill-equipped for the job he now holds."

Gray chuckled. "Agreed."

Jamie looked at Gray—he looked different. He wore a beanie over his head, tight to the scalp. *Too tight. As if...* "What's with the hat?"

Gray eyed him, looking a bit reticent. "Nothing. It's cold out."

"Take it off." He narrowed his eyes, sensing something was amiss.

Gray's face reddened. He lifted a hand to his head and slowly pulled it off...

Jamie gasped when he saw Gray's bald head. *"What have you done?"*

Gray ran a hand over his scalp. "Now we're twins, hmm?"

Jamie's eyes stung with tears. "Why? Your hair was *so* lovely."

"I know how upset you were to lose your hair again. So I didn't want you to be the only one enduring baldness."

"No," Jamie said, a tear escaping. He wiped it away, stunned at what Gray had done. "I wish you hadn't. Your hair... my gods... *Gray.*"

"Since I'm the one who begged you to go into treatment, I felt it only right for me to make a sacrifice of my own. I know it's nothing in comparison to yours... but I didn't want you to feel alone in this." Gray took his hand and squeezed.

Jamie bit back a sob. Seeing the heights of Gray's love for him nearly broke him. This omega he'd known for a few short months was becoming another piece of his heart. Another who he'd have to leave behind before he was ready. And he almost couldn't bear it.

"At least my head isn't misshapen," Gray joked, breaking the intensity of the moment with levity. "Or this would've been a *real* bad idea."

Levity Jamie desperately needed. He chuckled. "I do hope you kept it. Good hair like that could make you a bundle."

Gray nodded. "I kept it."

Jamie tilted his head, a thought occurring to him. "Did you do this because you needed the money?"

"No!" Gray answered. "We're doing fine. Avery is a budgeting master… and the boys are learning to be more creative with less. We're actually doing better than fine."

"You do know… that if you ever needed anything, I would help you."

"You've already been more than kind… and there's no reason to be concerned. We're fine, as I said."

"I think of you as my brother," Jamie said. "And by extension… your nephews are family. Family takes care of one another."

Gray brought Jamie's hand to his lips and pressed a gentle kiss on his knuckles. "The sentiment is appreciated. We are *fine*."

Jamie relaxed into the chaise.

"How about that tea and broth?"

Jamie sighed. "Tea, yes. Anything more, I'll try, but I make no promises."

Gray rose. "I'll fix you a tray." He grabbed his coat and hat and headed for the door. "I'll be back in just a moment. Rest up."

Jamie couldn't stop staring at Gray's bald head as he left, thunderstruck.

Twins.

Brothers of the heart.
Indeed.

* * * *

Later that afternoon…

Rohan sped into the drive an hour early. Jamie had texted him, demanding he come home immediately. After parking and climbing from his vehicle, he stormed in through the front door and raced up the swirling staircase, taking two treads at a time. Once he was inside Jamie's bedroom, he rushed to the bed where his omega lay.

Asleep.

He reached out and caressed the side of his omega's face.

"What are you doing back home so early?"

Rohan looked over his shoulder… and did a double take. He rose from the bed and turned, staring at Gray—his mouth dropping open.

Gray looked embarrassed. He ran a hand over his bald head, his gaze down to the floor.

"What happened?" Rohan asked.

"I just decided… I don't know," Gray said lifting his stare. "I didn't want Jamie going through this alone. I can't take his pain… but I can suffer an indignity with him."

Rohan's heart twisted in his chest. He wanted to go to the omega, draw him close…

He closed his eyes and forced the thoughts away. When he reopened them, he met Gray's lonely stare, and the need once again roared within.

"What did Jamie say when he saw it?"

Gray chuckled. "He was a bit shocked, to say the least. Told me I shouldn't have. But I think there was something within him that was pleased."

"I bet." Rohan turned to look at his still sleeping omega. "He sent me a message, begging me to come home early. Is there something wrong?"

Gray frowned. "We've had a lovely day. He hasn't been all that sick. I was able to get a little broth into him, which was a small miracle, I think."

Jamie was once again meddling, more than likely. "And the new nurse?"

"I already sent him home," Gray said. "He's terrible. I hope Jefre will be returning soon."

"I've already called the service. They'll send another tomorrow. Hopefully one better than this one. Jefre should be ready to return later in the week or the beginning of next."

"Good," Gray said. "I wasn't supposed to come tomorrow, but perhaps I should? In case the nurse isn't any better?"

"I'm working from home tomorrow. We should have it all in hand."

Gray nodded, looking away. "Alright then… I suppose I'll go ahead and head home."

"The car won't be here for a while," Rohan said.

"It's fine. I can catch the trolley. If you can call and cancel the car?"

"You'd still be home sooner if you waited for the car," Rohan said. "There's no reason to rush on my account."

Gray hand slid down his swollen stomach, drawing Rohan's stare along with it. He bit back a groan, his inner beast loving the look of the omega growing large with his child.

"There's every reason to rush on your account," Gray whispered. He spun and headed down.

Rohan followed Gray and caught the omega at the bottom of the stairs. He drew Gray into his arms and hugged the man close. When he pulled back, he lifted the omega's chin up with one finger.

"I never understood this connection you and Jamie had... and almost thought my omega daft for his romanticized comments about his love for you."

Gray met his stare, his eyes shining with a mixture of want and need.

"Now I understand. I can see you for the man you are... and a tiny part of me wishes things were different for you and I. Because I could see myself falling quite in love with you, too."

Gray remained silent, but there was a look to his face that spoke volumes. "But things *can't* be different for us. No matter how much either of us wishes... and I'm glad for it. Because I wouldn't have Jamie in my life if it had been any different."

"I love my Jamie with all my heart. I didn't mean for it to sound as if I wanted him any less. He's *everything* to me."

Gray lifted a hand and cupped the side of Rohan's cheek. "As he should be."

Rohan didn't want to let go when Gray swept out of his arms, but he did, still feeling the bare caress at the side of his face. He watched as the omega slipped out of the house, leaving him in silence.

"And when I'm not here anymore?"

Rohan lifted his stare to see Jamie watching from the gallery, gripping the bannister tightly. He righted himself and turned to face his omega, shame making it hard to speak. "What are you doing out of bed?"

"Go after him."

Pain slammed into Rohan. Jamie's constant pushing was rubbing him raw. He shook his head. "No. I won't."

"I won't be here much longer."

"I won't imagine a time or place when you aren't at my side where you belong."

Jamie scoffed. "My love... we *both* know our time is at an end."

Rohan closed his eyes for a brief moment, trying to erase that thought from his mind.

"When I'm gone... you'll be free to love him. *With my blessing.*"

Rohan shook his head. "I won't hear any more of it."

Jamie wobbled a bit and gripped the railing. Rohan rushed up to be at his mate's side. Lifting the slight man into his arms, he looked down at the man who held his heart. "Come back to our room... *please*. If our time is so short, I want to make the most of it. Can you give me that?"

Jamie lifted a hand to caress the same spot Gray just had.

"I will."

Rohan smiled.

"Only... if you promise me you'll go on and live your life after I'm gone. That you will love again."

Rohan's smile faded. "I will go on. More than that, I can't say."

Jamie smiled. "You just admitted you already loved him. I suppose that will have to be good enough for me. For now."

Ignoring those words, Rohan carried his omega into their bedroom and laid him to one side. "I'll pack up your belongings and bring them back in here."

After returning Jamie's things to the closets and the drawers, he felt somewhat better. Later... when he drew his mate into his arms without protest, he sighed with pleasure.

And pain.

Fearful of what came next.

But he wasn't going to let fear win that night. He'd already gotten one victory... he needed to hold tight to that and celebrate the small victories. Enough little ones and maybe he'd get that miracle after all.

* * * *

A new head of hair...

A few weeks later, Gray got the call that the wig he'd made was done. He gathered the very tiny bit of money he had in savings and headed across town to pick it up. As soon as he stepped off the trolley, he walked the three blocks to the shop.

Waddled was more like it.

He'd passed the six-month milestone some days before. Even though he still had four more to go, he was already extremely swollen. There was little doubt now that he carried an alpha child. He'd be more surprised if it wasn't.

Traveling was becoming much more difficult, but he was happy to make the trip to see how things had turned out. As soon as he entered the shop, the bell over the door tinkled.

"Hello!" a voice called from the back. "I'll be out in just a moment."

"Hello," Gray answered as he slipped inside and shut the door, garnering him another ring of the bell.

Like the last time he'd been there—to drop off his hair—his stare searched the room. It was filled with mannequin heads in all manner of wigs. From short to long, with all kinds of shades, they gave plenty of ideas. But these out front were made of artificial hair, and therefore less expensive and less desired. Gray had been assured the wig made of real hair would look more like the real thing once worn.

"Hello again," the wig stylist said as he exited the rear of the shop. "Sorry to keep you waiting."

"No problem," Gray said with a smiled.

"Oh, Mr. Tomlinson, so nice to see you. I've got your wig ready in the back. Just give me two seconds to grab it."

The beta went back to fetch it and returned in an instant, carrying the long, flowing wig on a mannequin head. Gray gasped at how lovely it looked. It was even styled, pulled away from the face and the temples swept into an intricate braided weave—though most of it still hung straight toward the floor.

"I hope you don't mind. I went ahead and put it into style I thought your friend might like. It'll make it a little easier to put on and keep neat."

Gray smiled, running a hand over the silky strands. "It's perfect." He pulled out his wallet and turned to the man. "How much do I owe you?"

The stylist hedged. "I know we discussed a certain amount..."

Gray tensed. He wasn't prepared to pay any more than what was quoted.

"...but after thinking it over and talking to you... I'm only going to charge you for the supplies it cost to make."

Gray relaxed a bit. "Why?"

The beta smiled. "I see men coming in almost every day to sell their hair. Never have I met anyone who cut theirs off in order to honor an ill friend and gift them with it. It made me feel as if charging you would be unfair of me."

"You put many hours into making it. You deserve to be paid for that."

The beta shook his head. "No. I won't have it. I was very touched by what you did for someone you love. It helped to remind me to appreciate the ones *I* love." He chuckled. "And it helped end a quarrel I was having with someone I care about. So consider it my thanks to you."

Gray smiled. "I'm glad it helped you, then."

The shopkeeper rung up the sale, and Gray very much appreciated the lower cost. He paid for the wig and watched as the beta wrapped it up and explained how to care for it. Once he'd given his thanks, Gray raced out, more than ready to deliver it.

The following morning, the brown paper package rested over his lap. Gray nearly bounced in his seat with excitement, and the car seemed to be moving much slower than normal. "Can we speed it up a little?"

The driver was one they'd had before several times and liked. He looked through the rearview mirror at Gray. "Does Mr. Jamie have an appointment today?"

Gray smiled. "No. Not today. I just have something I'm very excited to give him."

"Ah," the driver said before hitting the gas a bit more. "Then we can't keep him waiting."

* * * *

Visions of the past...

Rohan helped settle Jamie on the chaise in the sunroom before rising to his full height. "Would you like something to eat or drink?"

"No. I'm not quite ready yet," Jamie admitted.

He chuckled. "Do I not make your tea and toast right? Or is that a job better left for Gray?"

Jamie smiled. "He *is* a bit better of a cook."

Rohan looked at his watch. "Well, you won't wait too much longer. He should be here any moment... which means it's time for me to go."

"I really wish you wouldn't," Jamie murmured.

"Wouldn't what?"

"Go."

Rohan eyed Jamie.

"As if I couldn't tell you both avoid each other whenever possible," Jamie added.

"It's best this way. He and I agree."

"Best for who? Me?" Jamie asked.

Rohan sat down on the edge of the chaise. "I wish you would stop. I love you. *You*. Not him." They'd finally gotten back into one room... with Jamie allowing him a few hugs and caresses again. After the famine he'd been through, he felt rich.

But he hated the constant badgering about what came next. It seemed to come more often now.

Jamie sighed. "You have room for us both in your heart."

"Perhaps. But the more you push, the more I want to fight against it. And I haven't given up on *us* yet."

Jamie growled as Rohan placed a chaste kiss on his forehead.

"Growl all you want," he said. "I refuse to let you continue pushing me away."

Rohan heard the door open and shut, and realized he was late leaving. "Damn."

Jamie reached a hand out and grabbed Rohan's arm. "There's no rush. You can at least say hello. Ask him how he's doing. See how big his belly is getting."

Rohan hadn't laid eyes on Gray since they'd had their moment at the base of the stairs, when he'd nearly stepped across the line. He wasn't ready to face the omega yet.

But he'd have no choice, it seemed. Gray came rushing into the room, looking excited.

"Good morning!"

"Morning," Rohan murmured, rising from the chaise. His stare went straight to Gray's full belly and a rush of lust hit him. How he wanted to move closer… stroke the swell… lay kisses along Gray's stomach.

"I have something for you," Gray said, brushing past Rohan to lay a brown paper package in Jamie's lap.

Jamie grinned and opened it.

Rohan frowned when he saw Jamie's scrunched up face, lit with horror. Worry hit him when he saw a shine of tears in Jamie's eyes.

"Well. Let's put it on," Gray said before lifting a wig from the wrapping and sliding it onto Jamie's head.

Once it was settled, Rohan stared. It was almost like he was looking at the mate he recalled from so long ago—a past he scarcely remembered anymore. Before the cancer. Before the division Jamie thought would save him. Before, when things were wonderful and there was no fear in their lives.

"This is your hair," Jamie murmured to Gray. "Isn't it?"

Gray smiled as he sat on the side of the chaise to look at Gray. "It is. I remember you saying my shade was close to what yours was before chemo."

"You shouldn't have," Jamie replied, but even as he said it, one hand swept down the smooth locks, a true smile growing on his face.

It had been a few weeks since Rohan had seen that smile. And he was damned grateful that Gray had put it there.

"But you could've sold this hair... you should have. I didn't need it."

Gray brushed a few errant strands back, a loving smile on his face. "No. Maybe you didn't *need* it. But sometimes the best things in life are those that exist just to make us happy. Seeing this smile on your face now... makes it more than worth it."

Jamie blinked back tears... and Rohan had to admit to fighting his own.

Gray rose to his feet. "Ready for some breakfast?" He grimaced and placed a hand to his expanded belly and took a step back.

Rohan leapt forward, concerned. "What's wrong?"

"He's got a hell of a kick is all," Gray said before grimacing again. The omega then grabbed one of Rohan's hands and pressed the palm to his belly.

Rohan felt the next kick, and a smile spread across his lips. Gray reached for Jamie's hand, too, and placed it near Rohan's.

"He's strong," Jamie whispered before lifting his stare to Gray's. A smile illuminated his face. "I knew he would be."

Rohan turned his attention to Gray, who wore a smile of his own. *My gods he's glowing.* Rohan's heart skipped a beat, and he felt the instinct rising.

Gray met Rohan's stare and backed away a step, his smile fading. He looked to Jamie. "I'll go grab us our breakfast."

Rohan hated that he seemed to cause that reaction in Gray. He watched the omega leaving, wishing there was a way they could exist in the same world without him feeling shame every damned time.

He turned to look at Jamie—who seemed to have been watching him intently. Ignoring the question in his mate's eyes, he focused on the shimmer of hair tumbling down his back. He reached out and touched it, his hand sliding down the silky strands. "It looks good on you."

"I can't believe he did this. I wish he hadn't… his hair was beautiful. And now it's gone."

"It'll grow back," Rohan said. "As yours will soon."

Jamie smiled wanly. "You know… I'd had a thought before he gave me this gift… and now I really want to do something for him. I can't do it all on my own… and I hate asking the nurses to do more than they already do for me."

"What do you need?"

Jamie looked about the room. "This would be a lovely art studio for Gray."

Rohan frowned. "Already trying to move him in?"

"No," Jamie said. "But I asked him a few days ago if he'd been painting and it seems he hasn't in months. With all the long hours he's here with me, he could possibly spend some of it doing something he loves. And I think I'd be fascinated just watching him create." Jamie paused. "Really… I just want him to know how much we appreciate him coming and making sure I'm not alone. His friendship… it means so very much to me."

"Then how can I say no?" Rohan looked around the large room. At one point, Jamie had tried his hand at growing things. The last remnants of the dried-up plants left in the room reminded him how that had fared. It might as well find use one way or another. "I haven't the foggiest what he'd need."

"I'm sure the art supply store could help us get started. And then, I can ask him later if there's anything we might've missed."

Rohan nodded. "I'll call an art shop once I get to the office. Maybe they can gather it all and deliver, as well."

Jamie squeezed his hand. "Thank you."

Rohan looked down to their linked hands and hated how skeletal his omega's was. Every day Jamie was slipping further away. He lifted his stare to the gaunt face inside the wig and forced a wide smile. "You're welcome, my love." He leaned down to kiss Jamie's hand. "I better get going. Enjoy your breakfast."

As he reached the bottom of the stairs, he saw Gray exiting the kitchen with a tray. A tea pot, two cups. Fresh cut fruit. Toast with marmalade on the side. And there was a dark pink tulip sprouting from a small vase. Spring was coming, but he hadn't seen many flowers yet.

"Where did you get the tulip?" Rohan said as he pulled on his jacket.

"From my garden at home. Jamie leaves the house so infrequently... I thought I'd bring a little outside to him."

Rohan lifted his briefcase and eyed Gray. "You're good to him. I can't tell you how much it means to me. I'll never be able to repay your kindness."

"I love him," Gray murmured with a slight smile. "So *nothing* needs to be repaid."

Rohan held Gray's stare, his heart aching.

"Have a good day at work," Gray said before passing him and heading up the stairs.

Rohan watched him, wanting nothing more to stay and be with them both. When Gray was out of sight, he headed for his car and slid inside. He gripped the wheel, knuckles white, and roared in rage. He wanted to put his fist through something... someone... anything to take away the fury he felt.

At himself.

The feelings he had were wrong.

He could see Gray in his mind whispering, *I love him*, and wishing it had been about him.

Because somewhere along the way, he'd fallen in love with Gray.

And hated himself for it.

Chapter Twenty-Five

Eight months pregnant…

Gray waddled to the cottage's front door, not sure who would be visiting. All three boys were at school, and he wasn't expecting guests, not until later when the car arrived to take him to his monthly doctor's visit. When he finally opened it, he saw Tensen standing there, all smiles.

With another bouquet of flowers.

"Well, this is a surprise. What do I owe the pleasure?"

Tensen smiled. "I've just been thinking about you."

Gray smiled wanly. "Oh… well, why don't you come in?"

Tensen handed over the flowers before crossing the threshold and removing his hat. He looked about the house. "Very cozy."

Gray smiled. "It's more than enough for us." He ushered Tensen into the small formal living room at the front of the house that was rarely used. "Have a seat. Can I get you something to drink?"

Tensen grinned. "Just point me to the kitchen and I'll get us both something to drink." He took the flowers. "And get these in some water. You look like you're ready to pop any minute now."

Gray sighed and pointed. "Thank you."

Tensen wandered off as Gray rested in one of the large armchairs in the room. He heard some noises—the opening of cabinets and such—before the solicitor returned with two glasses of lemonade. "I hope this is okay?"

"Perfect," Gray said, taking one of the glasses.

Tensen took a seat in the armchair beside him. "When are you due?"

"I have another two months still," he answered before taking a sip. "I don't know how I'll bear it much longer."

"Soon... it'll all be over," Tensen said. "And your life will get back to normal, I hope."

Gray seriously doubted he'd ever again feel normal. "Perhaps."

"I came today... because I have a question of you."

"Oh?"

"After the babe is born... and you've had a little time to recover, of course..."

Gray tensed, hoping the solicitor wasn't about to ask if he'd consider another surrogacy.

"I wish to call on you. As a suitor." Tensen smiled slightly, his face darkening a little. "If you'll have me."

Gray froze, shocked.

"I know you already told me I wasn't for you... and I know there are things I cannot do for you as an alpha could... but I find myself unable to stop thinking about you. You are an incredible man, Gray."

An alpha would offer him freedom. Children. A future. What could he possibly have with a beta?

Love?

His heart clenched as he realized he'd already fallen in love with someone else.

He closed his eyes, knowing it was never to be. Even if they lost Jamie, he wasn't sure either he or Rohan could love again. Tensen was kind. He was considerate. And he'd likely treat Gray with respect.

I want more. I want love.

"I don't know," Gray murmured. "My life is in such a state of chaos right now, it's hard to make any kind of decisions now."

Tensen smiled wanly. "It's not a no. Perhaps we can discuss it again—after you've had the baby and some time to readjust to your life."

"Perhaps," Gray said.

Tensen took a sip from his glass. "How are Jamie and Rohan, by the way? I've reached out to Jamie a few times in the last couple of weeks, but we keep playing phone tag, it seems."

"He's doing as good as can be expected, all things considered," Gray said. "The new round of chemo hasn't been easy on him."

From the look on Tensen's face, Gray realized he might've said too much.

"His cancer is back?"

"Ah, yes. I assumed you knew. But then… if you haven't been in contact in a few weeks, maybe not. I'm sorry, that was their news to share."

"It was news they *should've* shared with me." Tensen rose quickly. "I'm afraid I have to cut our visit short. I'll try to stop in again and see you very soon."

Gray rose unsteadily and followed the beta to the door. Before he left, Tensen leaned in and placed a chaste kiss to Gray's cheek.

"Just don't forget about me," Tensen murmured before he left.

Gray shut the door and lifted a hand to the place where the man had kissed him. And then he remembered the almost kiss he'd gotten from Rohan. He'd felt more thrill... more delight from a near miss than he did one to his cheek.

But could beggars really be so choosy?

A kind, attentive companion had to be better than nothing.

Gray wandered into the kitchen and saw the flowers in a too small vase. After pulling more appropriately sized one from the pantry, he readjusted them, adding his own flair to the arrangement. Once he was done there, he waddled his way out to his studio—which he hadn't used in weeks.

Months, really.

Since the onset of Jamie's illness, he just hadn't had the time. Nor the desire. It also didn't help that he hadn't been sleeping well. His girth made it hard to remain comfortable—and lifting Jamie so often was killing his back even more.

Gray sat in front of a page of blank newsprint with a charcoal in hand, searching his mind for some inspiration. Nothing came.

He dropped the charcoal onto the table beside his easel and inhaled slowly.

Gray felt lost.

He wasn't the same person anymore... and it impacted everything in his life. His body was so swollen and changed, that he simply didn't feel like him anymore. Gray spread a hand over his growing stomach and rose, his back aching from sitting on the stool.

By the time the car came to pick him up for his monthly exam by his obstetrician, Dr. Forsythe, he had tried reading, a crossword puzzle, and yoga to keep his body and mind focused—all ending in massive frustration. He slid into the backseat and saw Jamie and Jefre were already there.

Gray cozied up to Jamie... and suddenly that frustration and angst he felt all day evaporated. A sense of peace came over him, and he smiled. "I'm so happy to see you're feeling well enough to come today."

Jamie leaned over and rested a hand on Gray's belly. "I'd be here even if I felt like hell. I'm always excited to get more news on this little guy."

"Little, he is not," Gray said.

"Agreed. I'm almost getting nervous for your delivery."

Gray didn't want to think about the pain to come. He pushed it from his mind and chatted with both Jamie and the nurse about their day.

"I tried to get Rohan to come with us, but he's busy catching up on some project at home."

"You need to stop trying to force us together," Gray mumbled under his breath.

"This is his child, too. He should be here," Jamie said, lifting a brow. "It's not me pushing. I just want him to take on a more active role."

Gray knew why Rohan wasn't coming to the appointments, and a part of him was glad for it. Their situation was hard enough as it was without having to be in the same room with one another for more than a few minutes.

Once the car drew up before the obstetrician's office, the driver and Jefre helped get Jamie into his new wheelchair. They entered the office and were soon called back into one of the exam rooms. Jefre accompanied them, so he could be there to help Jamie.

A nurse took his vitals, and Dr. Forsythe came in shortly after.

"Well, hello there! The gang's all here," the man said with a grin before he walked over to the small basin and washed his hands. They all said their hellos as he washed. When he was done, he turned and scanned the room, stopping at Gray. "How are we doing today?"

"Good," Gray said with as much enthusiasm as he could.

"That didn't sound like a good," the doctor said as he looked down at the chart the nurse had left for him.

"I'm just exhausted. It's hard to get comfortable, and I haven't been sleeping so well because of it. And I'm huge. Huge."

The doctor nodded and lowered the chart to the counter. "You are just above normal in weight gain for this stage of your pregnancy—and by eye, I can say you're more than likely above average in growth. Let's check you over and see if everything appears normal."

The doctor instructed him to lie back. Dr. Forsythe pressed around his stomach and then lifted his stare to Jamie. "Mind if your helper rolls you out for a moment so Gray can have some privacy?"

"Is something wrong?" Jamie asked, blanching.

"No... but I need to do an intimate check. I can call you back in shortly."

Jamie squeezed his hand before Jefre rolled him out. As soon as they were alone, the doctor helped him get onto his knees. The doctor checked the mouth of his womb and then had him lie back again.

"I think I want to do another ultrasound," the doctor said.

"Is something wrong with the baby?" Gray asked, panicked. The baby had to be okay… it was the only thing holding Jamie to them.

Dr. Forsythe smiled. "There's no reason to get upset. I'm just going to take another look."

Usually when someone said not to get upset, there was a reason to get upset. He fisted his hands into the material covering his waist and just tried to breathe.

"I'll be back in a moment. A nurse will come in and get everything ready for us," the doctor said, patting Gray's knee. "No worries, we'll have you up and out of here in no time. Just relax."

Just relax. How could he?

Jefre wheeled Jamie back in. Jamie's face was tense. "Did he say something was wrong?"

Gray shook his head. *Stay calm. Stay calm.* "He just wants to take a look, he says."

Time slowed. Jamie held his hand as a nurse came in and set up the ultrasound machine and got him ready for the exam. It felt like an hour had passed, but he knew it likely wasn't. By the time the doctor returned, his heart was pounding in his chest and his mind was full of all the tragic scenarios he'd read about in pregnancy books.

The first thing he heard was the heartbeat. This time, there was a weird echo to it. "Why does it sound off?"

"Just relax… and let me look around here," the doctor murmured, never taking his eyes from the screen. The light from the machine washed over his face in the darkened room.

Dr. Forsythe rolled the paddle all the way over to his side—almost his back—and pushed and prodded. "Just relax and breathe for me, Gray."

"What are you looking for?"

The doctor didn't answer, just frowned and looked harder at the screen. Gray turned and looked himself... he saw the baby's profile... two arms... two legs.

Wait...

There was another arm or leg. It was thinner than the others. "What is that?"

"I think I know," the doctor said before pushing a little harder with the paddle. "If I can just get him to turn a little in the womb."

The baby did a moment later... and there it was. *Another baby.*

Both Jamie and Gray gasped in unison and turned to one another, their stares meeting before they both looked back to the small screen.

He was tiny in comparison to his brother. He was maybe half the size.

"*Twins?*" Gray asked, shocked.

The doctor smiled. "Twins." He continued working, taking measurements on the screen and entering them into his charts.

"But how did we not know until now?" Jamie asked.

"My best guess is... you've got a very rare alpha and omega set of twins. The omega is so small that the alpha child hid him from view during the earlier ultrasounds and tests." The doctor took a few pictures and then moved the paddle. "He's tiny. *Really* tiny. In these scenarios, there's always a fear that the larger babe might be using up more of the resources and putting the smaller babe at risk. That little guy is likely underweight and small for his gestational age, but in most cases, they catch up once they're born and return to average ranges within the first few years."

"Is he in any danger?" Gray asked.

"His heartbeat sounded good just now. The nurse took some blood when you got here, and we'll get it tested to see if there are any abnormalities. But going from the test results we've already done these past months, it's been consistently good, so I'm not worried right now. If I see anything in this new draw, I'll bring you in and we'll talk decisions then."

"What happens next?" Gray asks, worried.

"I'm going to strongly suggest bedrest," the doctor advised. "And we may need to take the babes sooner than your due date if we see he's struggling. The real estate in there is getting real tight, but I want them to remain where they are as long as possible. For now, he's small, but not severely undersized. And as long as those test results don't show any signs of an issue, we'll play things week by week now."

"Bedrest?" Gray cried, worriedly looking at Jamie. "I have too many things to do. I can't spend the next two months in bed." He had his nephews… Jamie… it was all too much for him to give in and lie about.

"You come live in our home," Jamie said. "We can hire a cook… a manservant…. Whatever else we need. We'll take care of you."

"I appreciate your kind offer, but… I can't abandon my nephews."

"Auggie and Lake can come live with us as well," Jamie said. "That will allow Avery to focus on his studies."

"I can't ask you to do that. It's too much of a burden. Plus… you can't speak for Rohan." The alpha wouldn't want him under the same roof. They couldn't be so close.

"I'll speak to Rohan, but I'm sure it's what he'll want to do," Jamie said. "Protecting you is his instinct. He'll do what's best for the babies." Jamie grinned. "Two… two precious little ones. We need to prepare!"

Gray opened his mouth to argue, but when he saw the light of hope that shone in Jamie's eyes, the one that had been slowly fading, he couldn't speak for a few seconds. "We'll see what Rohan says and then decide."

"Are we settled now?" the doctor asked, crooking one brow.

"Yes, sorry," Gray said.

"For now, I'll schedule your home birth nurses to visit you once a week and I want you in the office every week. Unless you have any issues. If you see any bleeding, have any pain—anything—I want you to go to a public hospital immediately. Call us on the way, if possible."

"Yes, of course," Gray said.

The doctor smiled. "That said, while your situation is rare, it is not unheard of. We know how to handle an AO twin pregnancy, and I'm sure everything will end up just fine."

Gray damned well hoped so.

* * * *

Three's a crowd...

Rohan heard Jamie and Jefre returning from the doctor's visit. He rose from his desk and wandered out to see how the appointment had gone—only to see Gray was with them. Their eyes met. Gray gave him an odd look before looking down at the floor.

"What's going on?"

"Gray has come to live with us," Jamie announced, a broad smile on his face.

Rohan frowned. He tried to search Gray's face again, but the man wouldn't look at him. "Shouldn't we have... discussed this?"

"We had an appointment today... remember? The one I asked you to go to?"

Rohan sighed. "Yes, I remember."

"Well, we have huge news," Jamie said. He looked to Gray and grinned. "You want to tell him?"

"No... this is your news, not mine."

Jamie looked like he could bounce out of his wheelchair. Even Rohan had a hard time not smiling, given how animated his omega looked.

"Twins!"

Rohan's eyes widened. "What?"

"There's a little twin hiding under the bigger twin," Jamie said, his eyes shining with excitement. His smiled faded some. "There is a little concern because he is so small. The doctor is going to start monitoring the situation very closely from here on in. We have to go see him every week now, not every month. And Gray needs to go on bedrest."

Two babies? Rohan took a moment to mentally chew through all that information before he looked to Gray.

"Jamie suggested I should stay here. I told him it wasn't a good idea, but he wouldn't listen to me."

"Rohan... he'll be confined to a bed for two months. We were already going to hire a cook and a manservant to help around the house once the baby came. We'd *just* be doing it a little sooner than later," Jamie cooed.

Rohan felt his omega trying to manipulate the situation. "What about his nephews? He can't leave them alone in the O Quad."

"They can come here, too," Jamie said. "You're going to love Lake and little Auggie. He is just the sweetest. Auggie. Not Lake. Lake is a teenager, and you know how teenagers are... but they can stay here, right?"

Rohan opened his mouth to argue and saw the look in Jamie's eyes.

There would be no arguing. His omega had already made up his mind.

"Right. Of course. I'll go ahead and call the service about the cook and manservant in the morning."

"Perfect," Jamie said, clapping his hands together. "We'll be one big, happy family."

Rohan shook his head. He scrubbed his face with both hands. When he lifted his stare, he looked at Gray—who still stood in the middle of the foyer.

"If he's on bedrest, shouldn't he be in bed?" Rohan asked.

Gray met his stare.

"Can you show him to a room?" Jamie asked, leaning back in his chair. "I'm just exhausted and want Jefre to take me up."

"Of course," Rohan mumbled. He glanced at Gray. "Follow me."

Rohan waited until Gray was at the steps and helped usher him up. He noticed just how large the omega had become. Gray waddled up the stairs, taking one at a time.

"Are you okay?"

Gray cast a glance his way. "I'm a whale... trying to mount a ridiculous number of steps."

Rohan shook his head before lifting Gray into his arms and carrying the pregnant omega to the second floor. He tried to ignore the purring within, the satisfaction he felt in having the papa of his children in his arms. Rohan carried Gray to the bedroom Jamie had abandoned and lowered him to the side of the bed.

Gray kicked off his shoes and took off his sweater before Rohan helped him into bed. Rohan sat on the edge of the bed, eyeing the swell again. Without thinking, he reached out and caressed Gray's stomach. He leaned over and pressed his lips to the belly before resting his forehead there.

Two babes...

Twins were rare, and the birth would be just that much harder on Gray. Birth was already dangerous, and many omegas didn't make it through. Adding more danger scared him.

What if Gray didn't make it through?

His heart stopped at that thought.

Rohan lifted his stare. Gray watched him, a mixture of concern and want in his eyes.

"I need you to take care of yourself," he whispered.

"I plan on it," Gray responded.

"Two babies... that makes this a high-risk pregnancy. I need to know you're going to make it through this." *Because I can't lose you, too.*

"I can only follow the doctor's instructions. Other than that, it's up to fate."

Rohan rushed from the room and grabbed an item in the hall. He returned and set the bell at the bedside. "I'm going to get an intercom system put in. Until then, you use this if you need anything. You're not to get up. At all."

"What if I need to pee?"

"You ring the bell. And we'll be here to help you," Rohan said.

"Speaking of peeing," Gray said. "I should've asked you before you brought me in here."

Rohan offered a hand. Once Gray was out of the bed, he scooped the omega up and carried him to the adjoining bathroom. It was a little awkward, but Rohan refused to leave. He wouldn't give things up to chance.

Now he had two omegas to watch like a hawk.

Trying to make it a little less awkward, Rohan asked a question as Gray tried to pee. "We need to get your things and the boys. I can send a car."

"Already done," Gray said after he'd finally gone and wiped up. "Jamie had me call on the car ride over. Avery is packing my bag, and the boys are collecting whatever they need for now. And the car was going to pick them up tomorrow."

"I can hire the manny early, if possible. See if he can start now to help with your nephews."

"You're already going to a lot of trouble and expense for me. It makes me feel horrible."

Rohan lifted the omega into his arms and looked down into the man's face.

"This is probably the most awkward thing that has ever happened to me."

"My job is to protect you… which I will do in whatever way I need to. You're carrying our children," he murmured. "I'm your alpha…"

Gray held his gaze, his cheeks darkening. "For now. In a couple of months, you'll be free of me and we'll never have to see one another again."

That thought nearly made Rohan's heart break. Two months. That's all they had left together.

He couldn't speak… only stare down at the handsome omega.

"Can you take me back to bed?" Gray asked, averting his stare.

After carrying his pregnant omega back to the bed, Rohan lowered Gray and got him covered. "I'll order us some dinner for tonight. I didn't know we'd have company. Are you hungry for anything in particular?"

"Chicken soup sounds good."

"Okay."

"But a steak sounds yummy, too," Gray added suddenly. He frowned and looked at Rohan. "Do you have any walnut maple ice cream, by chance?"

Rohan chuckled. "Sounds like I need to go run to the grocery."

"I don't want to be any trouble," Gray said. "Unless you were already going to go?"

"I was," Rohan fibbed. "Is there anything else I can get you while I'm there?"

"Pickles? The sliced dill kind." Gray nodded. "Oh, and some plums. Toffee popcorn? Maybe some caramel sauce for the ice cream."

Rohan eyed him. "Do you have your phone?"

Gray reached into his pocket and lifted it out. "Yep."

"Text me a list. You have until I get to the store to add items."

Gray smiled. "Thank you."

Rohan returned the smile. As much as he hated the thought of Gray being there, a part of him had wanted it from the start. His pregnant omega was under his roof.

And he was pleased.

* * * *

Greetings from home…

Avery knocked on the mansion's front door. In the dark, it was hard to truly get the size and scope of the place, but apparently Jamie's alpha did alright for himself. The door whipped open, and a harried looking alpha filled the doorframe. Avery tensed… he was still getting used to being in tight quarters with alphas, and he'd yet to relax completely in their presence.

"Can I help you?"

He lifted the two bags in his hands. "I'm Gray's nephew, Avery. I brought his things."

"Wonderful," the alpha said. "Come in."

Avery passed the huge man before turning to face him.

The alpha looked outside and then back at him. "Your brothers aren't here?"

"No, I left them at home. I'm not so sure it's the greatest idea to send them here for the next two months. I was hoping I could talk to my uncle?"

"Sure," the man said. "If you don't mind, I'm trying to get some groceries put away. Can I give you some directions?"

"Absolutely."

"Top of the stairs, hang a left. Second to last door on the left."

Avery nodded. "Thanks."

The alpha headed off to wherever he'd come from, and Avery took the curving staircase. Nosy, he checked the place out as he walked up. The foyer was huge… and there was a second-floor gallery hallway that traveled three sides. A railing wrapped the hallway, giving a perfect view down. Huge paintings graced the walls of the foyer—which was more great hall than foyer—and more graced the walls of the second floor halls.

Avery turned left and then paused. One of the paintings looked familiar, and he was almost sure that it was one of his uncles. He smiled and continued on.

"Knock, knock," Avery said at the door Rohan had directed him to.

"Avery?" Gray asked from behind.

He entered and showed his uncle the bags. "I got your message and brought your things." He lowered them at the foot of the bed and looked around the huge bedroom. "So bedrest? For how long?"

"Until the babies come."

"*Babies?*"

"Apparently there are two. A smaller omega twin was being hidden by his larger alpha brother."

"My gods," Avery said. He sighed. "How in the hell are we going to manage for two months?"

"Well, like I said in the message, Jamie and Rohan want me to stay here—"

"And take care of the boys, I heard."

"Where are the boys? Are they getting settled?"

"I didn't bring them," Avery replied.

"How in the world are you going to work, go to school, and raise two boys on your own? They've offered to let Auggie and Lake stay here, so it doesn't impact your studies."

Avery sat straighter. "Does Rohan know?"

"Know what?"

"About me? I feel quite sure Jamie probably does."

Gray smiled wanly. "Yes. Jamie knows, and he won't say a word. Rohan does not. Nor will he."

"I wish you hadn't told Jamie."

"It slipped... an accident. And he'd just about guessed. But trust me... Jamie and I are very close. *Very*. He's almost like a brother."

Avery's head whipped up, the comment striking him. "You know... I learned something interesting in my history class a couple of months back. It rang a bell for me then, and I couldn't understand why... now maybe I do."

"What was it?"

"Did you know that an alpha can have more than one mate?"

Gray looked at his nephew and shook his head. "No... there is one fated pair. One alpha to one omega."

"The government created the idea of the fated mate when omega numbers began to decline. During the Resurgence, and before actually, alphas had as many as a dozen omegas who were mated to them."

"A dozen? There's no way one alpha could handle a dozen omegas and their needs."

"I've read up on the subject. It was real. Alphas can have more than one mate... while omegas only have one, they have this other kind of bond that's similar. It's not sexual... but it was called 'the brotherhood' by one author. Omegas mated to the same alpha would claim they felt this brotherly bond of love, and sometimes it actually did go farther."

Gray eyed his nephew. "I've never heard anything like this before in my entire life."

"Of course not. Because they don't want us to know there are options out there."

"The birthrates are too low... if alphas could claim more than one mate, why wouldn't they want them to? More babies is a good thing for our society."

"A theory I read said this. The omega numbers declined... and there were large numbers of alphas without an omega. Fighting and chaos erupted. That's when the harems were outlawed and the one-to-one ratio was made law. One scientist claims our chemistry changed some after that... that we somehow acclimated to this new world order after a few generations." Avery tilted his head and looked at Gray. "Maybe you're a throwback to that older system... a quirk to the new chemistry."

"A quirk. Sounds about right. Everything in my life has been strange."

"But doesn't that sound like you and Jamie—you said you loved him like a brother. And you've said Jamie seems to feel the same for you."

The idea stunned Gray. Did they *both* truly belong to Rohan?

"I can bring you one of the books sometime soon. Let you read it for yourself."

Gray nodded. "It'll give me something to do while I'm stuck in this bed for two months." He smiled. "You can bring it when you bring the boys."

"I don't know how I feel about Lake and Auggie coming here. They're my responsibility... and with you being down and Jamie sick... there's too much going on here. I don't want to add to the chaos."

"But if they remain home... there's no way you could work and go to school. No way. I won't have you quit because of me. I did this to help pay your tuition. We can't lose it now."

Avery wasn't convinced it was the right thing for his brothers. "If you're on bedrest, who will care for them? No... we can't do this."

"Jamie and Rohan already have round the clock nurses who can help watch over me, as well. They now plan to hire a cook and a manservant, which they already planned to do once the babies were here. The boys can come home every afternoon and do their homework right in here—at that table there. The schools are better in the Family Quad, and they can visit some of their friends while they're here. They'll have someone to ensure they're fed. I already suspect Jamie will spoil them... he spoils everyone. I've told him not to, but he got that twinkle to his eye. Your brothers will be in heaven."

"And in two months, after the babies are here, they'll be sent right back home to reality. Do we really want that upheaval in their lives?"

"It's a necessary evil," Gray said. "You *need* to focus on your studies. They'll be safe and cared for here—being told repeatedly that this is a temporary situation and not to get too attached."

Avery was still unsure. "I'd like to think it over." He smiled. "I'd miss them tremendously."

"It's not like you couldn't visit, *Mr. Norcross.*"

Avery rolled his eyes. "I already hate that name with a passion."

Gray chuckled. "Three more years. More, if you have to quit a semester."

"You don't have to push," Avery said, rising. "I should get home and get the boys something for dinner."

"There's an emergency casserole in the freezer. The blue dish."

"When did you become so responsible?"

"I'm trying," Gray said with a smile.

Avery paused. "Should I stop in to see Jamie? I don't want to bother him… yet I don't want to appear rude, either?"

Gray pressed a button at the side of the bed. "Hold on."

A moment later, a beta walked into the room in nurse's apparel.

"Serge, is Jamie awake?"

"He just got up a little while ago. Would you like me to bring him in?"

"Yes… if he'd like to visit a moment with Avery before my nephew leaves. If not, tell him we understand if he's not up to having a visitor."

"Give me a moment to ask him."

A few minutes later, Serge rolled a very weak looking Jamie into the room. Avery tried not to look surprised, but the change in the omega was staggering. He was gaunt and extremely pale... almost skeletal. He turned his head, catching Gray's stare before looking back at Jamie.

He walked over, forcing a smile. "How wonderful it is to see you, Jamie."

Jamie grinned widely. "It's been too long since I've had the pleasure." He reached out a hand and gripped Avery's weakly. "I expect your uncle has been telling you of our plans. I hope you'll agree. We'd love to host your brothers."

Avery didn't quite know what to say. He'd known Jamie was ill, but seeing it before him almost made him want to break down and cry for the man. "I fear having a pre-teen and a teenager in the house might be too much for you."

"Nonsense," Jamie cried. "It'll liven up the place. We need that around here right now."

Avery turned to meet Gray's stare again before looking at Jamie. He forced another smile. "I'll go home and discuss it with my brothers and see what they say. It's a lot of upheaval for them—but I truly appreciate your kind offer."

"Upheaval?"

"Well, they'll come home in a couple of months."

"I very much doubt that," Jamie said with a chuckle.

Avery frowned, not understanding. "Excuse me?"

Jamie just smiled and waved a hand. "Never mind... you'll see."

Avery looked at Gray—who looked as if he knew something more, but from his expression, wasn't telling. He turned back to Jamie. "I'll see?"

"In time," Jamie said with a wink.

"I should be going," Avery said. "The boys are already home... we'll discuss things once I get them some dinner."

He gave Gray a hug before taking Jamie's tiny hand and squeezing it. "I'll see you both soon."

"Wonderful!" Jamie said with a smile.

Avery left, casting one more glance at Gray before he left.

It was all a terrible idea, and he knew it... but he also knew Gray had a point. Without their help, he'd likely have to quit the semester.

And he wasn't ready to do that, either.

He'd worked too hard to reach for something supposedly unreachable for him. To let go now?

It just didn't seem right.

Chapter Twenty-Six

Home sweet home…

Rohan and Jamie welcomed their two new residents to the house—although Rohan immediately second-guessed the decision as soon as he laid eyes on the two. Both of them resembled Gray in some way… and that's all he needed. Two little reminders of the man he did his damnedest to ignore.

But then, he'd have his own two little reminders in two months' time.

After Avery had finally agreed, they'd sent a car to pick up the boys and their belongings and awaited them on an abnormally warm spring morning. Rohan didn't quite understand why he felt so nervous about meeting the two boys Jamie and Gray had already told him so much about, but he was.

As soon as the car pulled into the drive, he opened the front doors and waited at the top of the outer stairs. The boys were wide-eyed as they climbed from the car and even more wide-eyed when they saw Jamie. Rohan could sense their shock at seeing Jamie… and that made his gut twist all the more.

The driver began to unload the boys' bags and their new manservant, Tole, trotted down the stairs to gather them. Both boys climbed the stairs and stared at the exterior of the house.

"Hello, Jamie," Lake said solemnly as he stood just outside the door. The boy turned his gaze to Rohan. "Thanks for letting us stay here."

Auggie, the younger of the two, hid behind his brother some and peeked at Rohan.

"You're welcome," Rohan said as he realized he was looking into a set of eyes almost identical to Gray's. He'd already noticed the familial resemblance in Avery when the young man had come to visit a few days before. He'd hold out hope his own children looked more like him.

"Come on in," Jamie called, waving them inside.

The pair crossed the threshold and stopped just before Jamie's chair.

"How do you like the house?" Jamie asked, all smiles.

"It's even bigger than the one we *used* to live in!" Auggie said with glee as he looked around.

"We put you both into a bedroom beside Gray's. He's upstairs now if—"

Lake scowled. "One bedroom? Really?"

Rohan's brow shot up. "There was only one more left on that floor, and we *thought* you'd want to be close to your uncle."

Lake adjusted the strap in his backpack. The teenager eyed Rohan as if the boy was sizing him up. "I guess that's fine."

"*So glad* you agree," Rohan murmured. "Why don't I take you up to see your room?"

He took the boys up, leaving Jamie in Jefre's care. The youngest omega asked a ton of questions as they made their way up.

"Who else lives here?"

"Just me and my omega."

Auggie looked up at him, surprised, before looking back to the stairs. "Just you and him? This house is *so* big."

"Well now we have a little help filling it up for a while," Rohan said.

"Are you the father of Gray's babies?"

Rohan stopped at the top of the stairs and looked down at the earnest boy. "Why don't we go find your uncle?"

"Well, that's why he's here, right?" Auggie asked. "And why Jamie came to visit us all the time."

Rohan didn't know how much Gray had shared with his nephews before and didn't know if he should be the one answering the questions. "Let's just find your uncle."

"We're not idiots," the teenager said just behind them. "We know you're probably the father."

Rohan eyed the boy again and sighed. "It's not my place to answer those kinds of questions... so I'll leave it for your uncle."

"In other words... yeah, you are," Lake said before pushing past them. "Left or right?"

"Left," Rohan said on a sigh.

Lake led the way to the last bedroom on the second floor. It was even bigger than the one Gray was in, but hadn't been properly prepared when the omega had arrived. He showed them to the bedroom... one with two double beds and double dressers. It still had enough space for two small desks and a nook with a small couch and a TV.

"I assume you boys like video games?" Rohan asked.

"Oh yes," Auggie said, wide-eyed. "Do you play?"

"I haven't in many years," Rohan answered.

"He'd probably suck at it now," Lake said, wandering over to the TV. But his eyes got even wider. "You've got the new Playkit 5? It's not even for sale yet."

"A friend of mine works for the company and gave me a system for you to try. There are a few games included, too. Not sure exactly what he put in there."

Lake shrugged off his backpack, without another word, and started the game. Auggie tugged on Rohan's arm.

Rohan looked down.

"Thank you."

He smiled. "You're welcome."

"Lake would say thank you, too, if he wasn't such a butthead."

Rohan chuckled, and the boy smiled up at him.

"Would you like to see your uncle?"

"Sure," Auggie said excitedly.

They walked next door, and he watched as Auggie rushed in and jumped onto the bed. He wrapped his arms around his uncle and squeezed tight. "Uncle Gray!"

Gray smiled and hugged the boy back…

And Rohan had to take a step away. The sight of his omega, filled with child and holding another…

Not my omega. He's not mine.

Nevertheless, the instinct roared in his chest.

Gray's stare slid to his, as if he sensed the bond tightening.

"I'll leave you two alone," Rohan murmured.

"Where's Lake?"

"Playing the new Playkit Rohan got for us," Auggie said.

"Did you thank Rohan for that?"

"He already did," Rohan said, forcing a smile. He took another step back. "I'll call the boys down for dinner later."

Gray's stare went to his, and he felt the pull wrapping around him again. "Thank you."

"No problem," Rohan murmured, looking away.

"No... I mean for *all* this. It was too much to ask of you. Two boys and a pregnant omega invading your home."

You belong here.

Rohan drew in a breath, shocked by the thought—but that didn't help when Gray's scent filled his nose. Before he could stop his mouth, it spoke the words he'd thought. "This is your home, too."

Gray's eyes widened.

"For as long as you need it to be," Rohan added, trying to save them both the discomfort.

Gray nodded, wide-eyed, and looked away. "So have you any homework?" he asked Auggie.

"I just had to read, and I did it in the car on the way."

Rohan escaped the room and rested back against the closed door, breathing heavily.

"Are the boys settled for now?"

Rohan turned his head to see Serge seating Jamie in the wheelchair at the top of the stairs. Jamie had a knowing look on his face...

"Lake is attacking the video games, and little Auggie is inside with Gray."

Jamie smiled softly. "Good. I'm going to take a nap until dinner. Serge will bring up my broth and tea, so why don't you have dinner with the boys."

"Okay. My love."

"Maybe you can have it in Gray's bedroom. There's a small table and chairs in there, so it could work. And it would keep him company."

"I don't think that's a good idea. Who's going to keep you company?"

"Oh, I will," Serge said with a smile.

"I've already instructed our new manservant to set everything up," Jamie said with a smile.

Serge rolled the chair toward their bedroom, leaving Rohan there to wallow in self-loathing.

* * * *

Together, at last…

"Hello again."

Gray lifted his stare from the book Avery had sent over in Auggie's backpack, reeling from the little he'd read. He opened his mouth to say hello and suddenly realized he couldn't remember the man's name. Shame hit him as he searched his mind.

"I apologize, but I think the pregnancy hormones are destroying my brain. What was your name again?"

"Tole," the manservant said as he dragged the small table from the corner of the bedroom closer to the bed.

"That's right. Tole. How are you?"

"Wonderful," the man said before slipping from the room. He walked back in an instant later with a large crate in his hands. After placing it on the floor near the bed, he pulled out a tablecloth and covered the table.

"Might I ask what you're doing?" Gray asked, frowning.

"Mr. Jamie asked that I set up dinner here—so you didn't feel so lonely," the manservant said as he began to take china from the crate and place it on the table. "I'll still bring you a tray so you can stay in bed, but the others can eat at the table alongside you."

"You shouldn't have to go to so much trouble. They can come up and visit with me *after* dinner," Gray said.

"It's no trouble," the manservant said with a smile. "I think it's rather sweet of Mr. Jamie. To think of someone else when he's got *so* much to be worried about himself."

Gray clenched his hand at the sound of pity in the manservant's voice. "Soon, he'll be well and I'll be out of this bed, and we won't have those same worries."

The manservant lifted his head from where he was placing silverware, looking somewhat confused.

He will get better... don't count him out yet.

The beta's expression faded, and he went back to work, setting the table.

For three.

"Is Jamie joining us?"

"No. He'll be having his supper in his room. He's feeling a bit tired tonight, he said."

Gray eyed the third place at the table. "Who's our other guest?"

The manservant gazed at the table, frowning. "Other guest?" He stepped back and looked. "Lake and August... and Mr. Rohan." He lifted his stare to Gray. "There's only the three of them. Have I made a mistake?"

"Oh, no, I suppose not," Gray murmured. "My mistake."

The manservant smiled. "I'll head down and bring the food up. Be right back."

A few moments after the manservant left, the door opened and Rohan strode in. "Knock, knock."

Gray drew in a slow breath. Being this close to the man who'd claimed his body was getting harder by the day. The house was filled with Rohan's scent. It lingered in every room. "Hello."

Rohan smiled slightly. "I understand we're having dinner in here tonight."

"You don't have to... if you don't want," Gray said, looking away. If he stared into Rohan's eyes too long, he felt the need to babble. If he opened his mouth, all the wrong things would come out. "I know we probably shouldn't."

"Since my muleheaded omega set this up, I don't think we can get out of it now."

Gray lowered his head, shaking it. "I suppose not."

The things Avery had told him slipped into his mind. Gray looked at the book in his lap, wondering if he should show it to Rohan. He felt such a strong tug toward the alpha... and sensed the man felt the same. Were they truly mates? But if the laws had changed... did that really matter anymore? And with Rohan's deep and abiding love for Jamie, how could he even bring up the possibility?

Gray's affection for his friend also kept his mouth shut. There was no way he was going to try to legitimize the feelings he had. "How's Jamie? I heard he wasn't feeling well."

Rohan lifted his stare and met Gray's. "Tired, he says. I just checked in on him before I came here."

The manservant slipped into the room, without dinner. "Sorry, gentlemen. Seems like you've lost a couple of your eating companions." He began taking up two of the plates and the silverware.

"Lost them?" gray asked.

"Mr. Jamie was feeling a bit better, so Lake and August are teaching him how to play a video game in their bedroom. They've asked to eat in there this evening."

Gray's stare went to Rohan's and vice versa.

Tole went to the door, plates and silverware in hand. He paused and smiled. "I'll have dinner up momentarily."

Once they were alone, Gray opened his mouth, but Rohan cut him off.

"It's one meal. It won't kill us," Rohan said before taking a seat at the table beside Gray's bed. "Jamie and the boys are being taken care of, so there's nothing to worry about."

"Isn't there?"

Rohan eyed him. "Instinct or not, I don't think we're in much danger of crossing any lines as big as you are at the moment."

Gray chuckled some, trying to relax. "Thanks for reminding me I'm as big as a whale."

Rohan tilted his head to the side. "That's not what I meant, and you know it."

"Isn't it though? I'm *huge*." He ran both hands over his very swollen stomach. "I'm so big I'm not allowed to stand up for more than a few minutes now."

"I think you're beautiful," Rohan whispered, leaning closer. He placed his own hand on Gray's stomach and caressed the swell. "Seeing you big and full with my children?" He paused, smiling, his eyes all aglow. "It's likely one of the most stunning things I've ever seen in my life."

Gray closed his eyes and felt his womb spasm. He cried out in pain and reached for his stomach.

"What is it?" Rohan was immediately at his side, sitting on the edge of the bed. Worry was painted on his face.

"I don't... I don't know," Gray said between trying to breathe. The pain increased by the second, until he was crying out.

Rohan fished out a phone. Gray could barely pay attention to anything the alpha said... or even who he was talking to. He could only focus on the pain wracking his body.

Just breathe.

Just breathe.

Another pain slammed into him, bowing his back and bringing a scream from his lips. He felt movement in his stomach, like the babes were moving within him.

But something was wrong.

He didn't know how he knew, but he did.

Gray opened his eyes and saw a wall of faces observing him. Everyone in the house was there, watching in his moment of agony.

"We're taking you to the hospital," Gray heard Rohan saying at his side. "There's an ambulance on the way."

"Get him on his knees," Serge said, pushing through. "It will put less pressure on his back."

Another pain hit and took Gray's breath away. He felt the covers pulled back and a cry of anguish. Looking down, he saw nothing but blood soaking the sheets.

"Dear gods."

He was rolled to his side... the pain letting up just a little, but not enough to make much difference.

A hand took his from the other side of the bed. He looked up and saw Jamie's concerned face.

Don't let our babies die... don't let them die...

* * * *

As the EMTs were readying to wheel Gray out, Rohan turned to everyone. "Serge, can you stay with Jamie... Tole, can you keep an eye on the boys?"

"I want to go," Jamie said. "I can't sit here and worry."

"Me, too. I want to be with Uncle Gray," Auggie said, concern etched on his face.

"Same here," Lake said. "We deserve to know he's going to be okay."

"And I will call you as soon as I know anything," Rohan said.

"We go," Jamie said, turning to Serge. "Can you go with me and help?"

"Absolutely," the nurse answered.

The last thing Rohan needed was to worry about the three of them, but he knew Jamie wouldn't take no for an answer. "Fine," Rohan said, urging the ambulance on. "I'll drive us."

"No," Jamie said. "Go be with your children. Serge can drive the rest of us."

"*Our* children." Rohan paused a minute... until he heard Gray's scream of pain and the instinct took him again. He turned and raced for the ambulance before they shut it up and slipped into the back.

He took Gray's hand in his as he sat alongside the omega, doing his best to calm the man down. "It's going to be okay," Rohan murmured, not sure who he was trying to convince.

* * * *

Gray knew the minute the drugs kicked in. He was still in pain, but there was a dullness to it… and the world around him seemed a little fuzzy. Shiny. *Beautiful.* He smiled. "I feel *better.*"

Rohan eyed him before smiling slightly. "Better than the screaming pain you were in while we drove here."

"It still hurts," Gray mumbled, laying back on the bed. "Just… not as bad."

"Good," Dr. Forsythe said as he pulled back the curtain and moved into the small room. "Because I need to go inside and move the babies."

"What?" Gray slurred.

"Do you remember what I said earlier?" Dr. Forsythe asked him.

"Not really," Gray murmured. He had been in a lot of pain. He remembered something about the babies had turned, but everything else was a blur.

"The babies turned. They got into birth position, but they're crowding one another and both trying to go first," the doctor said. "I need to move them and then you're going to give birth."

"It's early," Gray muttered. "I have almost two more months."

"It's okay," Rohan said, suddenly appearing through the fog around him. "The doctor said they're far enough along."

"I'm so glad you're here," Gray mumbled, watching as Rohan's hand took his. He felt the warmth there, and it filled him. "I needed you here with me."

Rohan wiped a cool cloth at Gray's forehead and smiled down at him. "There's nowhere else I'd be right now."

"Our babies are coming," Gray said, smiling. "*Two* babies." He chuckled, the world suddenly very funny. "I can't believe I'm having *two*."

"That's right," Rohan said with a smile. His face was really rather handsome and even more so when he did that.

"You should smile more. You're definitely sexier when you do."

Rohan's mouth opened, but he said nothing.

"Since we have two, maybe I can keep one. You and Jamie have one… and I get to go home with a souvenir. A little piece of you."

Rohan still didn't say anything. He looked to the doctor. "Just how much drugs did you give him?"

"He'll need them in a few more minutes, trust me," the doctor said.

"I really do feel kind of funny," Gray mumbled over his shoulder. He began to laugh. "Funny's a funny word, isn't it?" He wiggled his lips. "*Funnnnnnneeeeee.*"

"We can laugh about funny once your babies are here. Let's get you up on your knees," the doctor said.

He, Rohan, and a nurse helped Gray to his knees before he felt a hand behind him.

"This isn't going to be comfortable," the doctor said. "Just try to breathe through it."

Already semi-forgetting what was happening, Gray looked over one shoulder. "What?"

Rohan and the nurse held one each of his hands as he knelt on the delivery bed. Behind him, the doctor reached within. At first, the pain wasn't too terrible, but when the doctor began pushing, he felt as if he was being ripped apart. Gray bit back a cry of pain. The humor immediately evaporated as he felt clamps stretching his inside open.

"Breathe," Rohan murmured. "You've got to breathe."

"Almost there," the doctor yelled.

Gray drew in a shuddered breath before crying out as a pain slammed into him. Sweat broke out heavily on his brow, his whole body trembling from the discomfort.

And then it was simply... *gone*. He took a deep breath... and then felt a contraction hit.

"Got it," the doctor said. "They're ready to deliver. Let's get us the omega first, hmm?"

Gray heard the doctor murmuring quietly to the other nurses behind him. He looked to Rohan.

"What're they saying?"

Rohan's frown made him sense it wasn't good. "Nothing... nothing at all," Rohan answered.

Gray was about to argue, but another pain hit him—not as bad as the ones he'd had before, but still strong.

The doctor said something behind him, but his own cry covered most of it.

"Push, my darling," Rohan said. "Push!"

Gray bore down, just as he'd been taught by the birth nurses in Dr. Forsythe's office—or at least the best he could remember to. The pain was intense… the more he pushed, the more the pain became.

"Perfect," the doctor called. "Let's take a few second break and then I want you to do it again."

"You're amazing," Rohan said at his side before wiping his brow of sweat. "You're doing *so* well."

Gray didn't feel as if he was doing anything well. He hurt all over, his body one giant spasm. "I just want them *out*! Get them out of me!"

"Let's push again," the doctor called.

Gray squeezed the hands in his and bore down with all his strength.

"I can see a head," the doctor yelled. "One more good push and we'll get those shoulders!"

Gray paused a second and drew in a breath before bearing down again. He felt as if he was being ripped apart… and then moments later, he felt a let up and something sliding from him.

"Baby number one is here!" the nurse at his side said.

"I want to see him," Gray said, trying to turn around.

"In a moment," the doctor said. "We still have one more baby to deliver."

Gray looked up at Rohan—and could see concern on his face as he looked to the other side of the room. "Is he okay?"

Rohan forced a smile to his face. "Perfect."

He sensed there was something wrong. "*Liar*," he spat seconds before another pain hit. He was already exhausted. There was nothing left in him to birth the bigger boy. "Gods… can't you just take him out?"

"I'll do what I can," the doctor said. "But I need your help."

"Come on, Gray... you can do it," Rohan said before pressing a kiss to his temple.

"I can't," Gray cried, his body shaking.

"Yes, you can," Rohan said. "You have to... don't you want Jamie to see these beautiful babies you've made?"

Gray lifted his stare to Rohan. "Yes."

"Then let's go." Rohan smiled.

"Gimme a push!" the doctor said behind him.

Gray summoned everything he had in him and bore down. Again, he felt ripped open. The second babe was bigger than his twin... and would tear Gray all the more. The pain was excruciating... and he didn't know where the strength came from to push the huge boy from his body.

But he did.

Later, when Gray heard the child wailing, he collapsed to the bed and cried himself—a mixture of pain, joy, love, and sadness welling within him unchecked.

He barely felt the doctor finishing things up and closing his womb. He'd learned all about the many stiches he'd have and how careful he would need to be for many weeks after the birth, but it was a distant thought in his mind.

A tiny tot all wrapped up in a blanket was laid beside him and nestled into his arms. Gray smiled down at the babe, more tears coming. When he looked up, he saw Rohan had a fresh shine to his eyes, as well.

He checked the boy over, counted the toes and fingers, and then looked about.

"Where's the other baby?"

Rohan's face tightened. "They're still working on him."

Gray lifted his head and saw the tiny omega in an incubator, several doctors working over the still child.

No.

Oh dear gods, no.

Gray sat up, holding one babe.

"We'll get you two up to a room now," one of the nurses said as he tried to take the alpha babe from Gray's arms.

"No," Gray said, moving his arm out of the way. "We won't leave until we know he's okay."

"It's best if the doctors have the space they need to take care of him," the nurse said.

"He said we're not leaving," Rohan said, placing a hand on Gray's shoulder. "And we're not leaving until we know."

Not once had Gray heard the smaller baby cry. "Is he breathing? Why isn't he crying?"

"He is breathing… but his lungs are weak."

Gray's doctor walked over and interrupted the nurse. "Your omega was gripping the cord when he was born… and because of that he wasn't getting enough air. Adding to our concern is the embryonic sac was torn *before* he came out…he's opened up to infections without that protection. But he's in the best place right now… our pediatric doctors are *excellent*. Let's get you upstairs so you can get cleaned up and rest some. You just went through hell."

"I won't leave until—"

A cry came from the tiny omega. A loud wail, in fact. And after that, he kept on wailing.

Gray sagged against Rohan in relief. He looked up and saw Rohan's smile. "Thank the gods."

When he looked back over, he saw relief in the doctors attending the omega and knew they were likely in a better place now.

"We need to get both babes cleaned up. Weighed and measured. Check all their vitals and make sure they're both in tip top health," Dr. Forsythe said. "So can you hand over your second boy so they can do all that?"

Gray lifted the babe to the nurse, even though he didn't want to hand the child over. He'd be doing that soon enough.

For good.

A sob rose up his chest as he felt the child-bond wrapping around him. Just handing the infant over for a moment had him close to whimpering.

"We'll get you wheeled up to your room. The nurses will take good care of you... and by the time they're done, we'll get these little guys up to visit with you before you get some rest."

The nurses and Rohan helped him move onto a stretcher that was rolled into the birthing room. Lying on his side, felt his body growing more and more liquid. The world was fuzzier by the second, too.

Rohan's hand slid into his after the stretcher was wheeled out of the room.

"We did it," he slurred... and then giggled. "They really must'a given me good drugs."

"Starting to kick in, hmm?"

"They usually come on a little stronger once the babies are born. Which is a *very* good thing," one of the nurses said. "As bad as he'd been ripped up, he needs it."

Gray sighed. "Ripped up? I don't feel ripped up."

"You will later," the nurse said with a grin.

Rohan took Gray's hand and brought it to his lips. He pressed a gentle kiss there. "You were amazing in there."

"Yeah?" He looked up at Rohan and smiled. "I love you."

* * * *

I love you.

Rohan froze a little inside. A piece of him wanted to revel in those words and repeat them—pronounce his love for this omega who'd just given him children.

And another part of him shamed him for wanting it. How could he be in love with two men?

I can't.

I love Jamie… I love my omega.

"That's just the drugs talking," he murmured, trying to explain it away. Because if it was true… if Gray was in love with him… then their situation was even more pathetic.

Luckily for him, Gray soon drifted off to sleep, or so it seemed. They rolled the omega up to the paternity ward and Rohan followed, his heart in his throat.

I love you, too.

Chapter Twenty-Seven

Two ends of the spectrum…

Gray awoke, feeling groggy and hurting *all* over. He lifted his head slightly—and saw Jamie lying in his hospital bed, too. Jamie wasn't the only one. Two tiny babes lay between them, swaddled in soft blankets, and sleeping away.

"They're beautiful," Jamie whispered, tears in his eyes. "You made beautiful babies, Gray. I knew you would."

Gray caressed one soft cheek and then the other, adoring these little ones. He cringed at the thought he would have to hand them over and walk away. Tears burned the backs of his eyes at the thought.

"What's wrong?" Jamie whispered, frowning.

"I have to let them go." His face twisted in pain, the instinct to hold on to them screaming in his veins.

"No, you don't."

Gray ignored Jamie. "I knew it would be hard… and I was sure I could do it…" He closed his eyes tight before letting one tear go. Gray reopened them and smiled at Jamie. "I'll figure out a way. Because you deserve this family."

Jamie took one of Gray's hands and squeezed it. "No… you don't have to let them go."

"I *do*. We have a contract… and now that they're here… they belong to you."

Jamie smiled and began to cry. "I love you so very much."

"I love you, too."

"I love you… because you still have hope… even when you can see that there's not much more time."

Gray stiffened. "Stop."

"I promised I would try to hold on until they were born," Jamie whispered. "And I did as I promised. I see they're beautiful and perfect in every way, just as I knew they would be. But I see what comes next, too." Jamie's face twisted in anguish. "It's time."

Gray fought back the tears, begging himself not to sob. His face screwed up, and he shook as he tried not to cry. "Don't leave me. I can't lose you, Jamie. I love you too much."

Jamie pressed a kiss to each of the baby's foreheads before leaning over and pressing his lips to Gray's. "And I love you, my brother. I leave this world knowing you and Rohan will take great care of these sweet blessings."

"No," he whispered.

Jamie laid his head down and smiled… and closed his eyes.

For the last time.

Gray sucked in a breath, his lungs burning.

No… no…

A sob wracked his body as he sensed the stillness coming from Jamie's body. He leaned closer, lifting a hand to search for a pulse… a breath… any sign of life.

"No, damn you, no!"

Gray lifted his head and looked behind him. Rohan slept, all sprawled out on a recliner. "Rohan!"

Rohan's lids fluttered, and he opened his eyes. After he scrubbed at them, he looked at Gray, confused. "What's wrong?"

"Jamie."

Rohan slowly rose to his feet and rounded the bed. He saw Jamie lying there and reached over to check his mate. His hands stilled... just before he dragged Jamie's body into his arms, tears sliding down his face.

An anguished roar rose from his lungs as the pair of them slowly slid to the floor together, Jamie wrapped in Rohan's strong arms. Gray wanted nothing more than to slide down there and hold his friend, too.

The babes awakened, and Gray did all he could to quiet the pair, his vision blurred by tears.

Serge came rushing in moments later with Lake and Auggie behind him. He spun and called for a nurse to come help before the chaos truly erupted.

All Gray could do was lie there in shock, holding the babies, and sobbing. Later, once Jamie's body had been removed and Serge had taken Lake and Auggie home, Gray looked at Rohan.

He was shell-shocked.

The alpha looked completely lost and empty... his expression numb and his eyes glazed over.

They should've all been celebrating the two new lives... instead they mourned the one taken too soon.

When a nurse rolled the babies back to him a little while later, all Gray could do was burst into tears again, remembering Jamie wouldn't be there to see them grow.

I needed him, damn it. Gods be damned... because I needed him...

* * * *

An ending in the middle...

Gray hated funerals.

And this one was hitting him harder than any of the others he'd endured during his life. Of course, that could be because he was still coming down on his pregnancy hormones, healing from being ripped apart, and lacking sleep as he'd been kept up the last few nights trying to take care of barely week-old twins.

Rohan was doing his best, but the alpha had been hit even harder than Gray. Jamie and Rohan had been together over fifteen years. His year of loving Jamie paled in comparison to what the two of them shared. Between the nurses, who'd stayed on to help with everything, and even help from Lake, Auggie, and Avery, they'd managed to survive a few days post hospital.

Much more past that, and Gray wasn't sure.

Soon, his free pass would expire and he'd be forced back to his old life, imprisoned in the O Quad. His stare went to the front of the room and realized it could be *much* worse.

Jamie's casket sat on a dais at the front of the living room. Flowers crowded the space. Rows of chairs lined the room, now empty and awaiting well-wishers. Jamie's brothers, Wilder and Vaughn, had arrived early to help make sure everything was in place. Wilder looked almost as rough as Rohan, his eyes rimmed in red with dark circles under them.

Wilder walked over before the service began and knelt beside the large basket carrier where both babies lay swaddled side by side. He reached in and caressed each one's cheek with his forefinger before lifting a tear-filled stare to Gray.

"Rohan tells me the last thing he saw was these two."

Gray held back his tears as he nodded.

Wilder eyed him a moment, silent. "I know I wasn't as kind to you as I should've been. I'm sorry for that."

"You saw me as a rival to your brother. I wasn't."

"I know." Wilder smiled. "All he could talk about was you, Rohan, and these babies." Wilder looked down at the babies again before lifting his tear-filled stare. "You brought him a lot of joy before he was gone. And for that, I can't thank you enough."

Gray couldn't help but let a tear slide, too. "Thank you... for saying that."

"What happens with the babies now?"

"I... I don't really know. Rohan and I haven't discussed things."

"My brother told me his wild plan for the two of you."

Gray met Wilder's stare. "Your brother was a bit delusional when it came to that."

"Was he?" Wilder asked before rising to his full height.

Gray's gaze sought Rohan's... who stood off to the side, watching him. Rohan broke off the stare and turned to the casket, his back to Gray.

Two men swept in, an alpha and omega pair. Almost instantly, he recognized the familial resemblance and assumed it was Jamie's father and papa. Gray lifted his chin, trying not to instantly hate the pair. In all the months of being at Jamie's side, he'd not once seen either man. Of course, the two might've come on the days he wasn't there—but near the end, he'd been there every day.

Jamie's papa looked about the room with scorn on his face before glancing at Jamie's father. "Lilies? Could they have been any more *common*?"

Gray clenched his jaw and repeated to himself to not hate them.

Jamie's papa turned a bit more and saw him there. He lifted his chin and stared down at Gray before walking over. He waved his hand toward the sleeping infants. "Are these Rohan's children?"

"Yes," Gray said, his voice low.

"And I assume you're the manny?"

"Well, n—"

"A funeral is no place for infants, especially ones born to *another* omega. So let's get them upstairs, hmm?"

"I'm not going anywhere," Gray said. "And neither are Jamie's children."

Jamie's papa eyed him, looking stunned. "I hope you didn't like this job, because it's the last one you'll have."

Rohan stepped in seconds later. "What's going on here?"

"Your manny refuses to take these children upstairs."

"He's no manny," Rohan said. "And the children were everything to Jamie. Why would we not have them here?"

"Not the manny?" Jamie's papa's eyes went wide before he spun to face Rohan. "You brought *him* here? Your whore?"

"What did you call him?" Rohan growled.

"You marked this omega and made him yours... and then while your own omega lay dying in this house and you brought this one to live here, too? You're despicable."

"At least he was here," Gray spat.

Jamie's papa glared at him. "What?"

"He was *here*. And so was I. In all that time..." He paused, hating to repeat the words, "while Jamie lay dying... I never saw you here once. Not *once*."

"How dare you?"

"He's right," Rohan said. "You stopped in for a matter of, what... ten minutes? If that. And that was once. Weeks ago." He spun to face Jamie's father. "And you never came here once in all that time." Rohan shook his head. "You stand there trying to make us feel bad? When neither of you gave a damn about your own son. Had it not been for us, he'd have died alone."

Jamie's papa looked like he could shoot fire through his eyes. "At least I didn't parade my pregnant whore in front of my dying mate."

"Stop it," Wilder spat from the side.

Everyone spun to face Jamie's brother.

"I *did* visit Jamie. Often. And we talked for hours... he loved Gray like a brother. He loved Rohan more than life itself. He also told me why he'd concocted this whole surrogacy plan." Wilder looked at Rohan. "He wanted to give his alpha something to live for. Children... and an omega to be there when things went wrong. Because he said he knew from the start that his years were few. Those babies were everything to my brother, and I won't stand here letting you make them both feel like hell for giving in to Jamie and giving him what he desperately wanted."

"So who now raises these babies your brother so desperately wanted?" Jamie's father asked. "You, Rohan? Or was the plan for you to claim another omega on the heels of the first one dying so you could have a live-in babysitter?"

Gray gasped.

"No one's claiming anyone," Rohan spat, tears in his eyes. "Today, I bury my mate—the man I loved more than life itself. Leave it to you two to make a mockery of that and ruin this day. Why don't you both just leave?"

"You want me to leave my own son's funeral?" Jamie's papa asked.

"You didn't care about him when he was alive!" Rohan roared. "You're only here to put on a show and make people think you actually have hearts."

"Fuck you, Rohan," Jamie's papa said. "There are reasons my relationship was not good with your mate… most I doubt you truly know."

"I can't imagine any reasons bad enough to keep a papa away from his son's deathbed," Rohan murmured.

Tears formed in Jamie's papa's eyes. Real tears, from the looks of them. He opened his mouth to speak, but Jamie's father interrupted.

"Leave it, Wynter. Just let it go."

Gray eyed the pair, wondering what Jamie ever could have done to cause the rift between him and his parents. Or how he'd become so amazing after being raised by *them*.

"I will *stay*," Wynter said, eyeing Rohan and then Gray. "I won't be forced from this funeral."

The first of the guests began to arrive, murmuring in the foyer. Rohan eyed them before staring at Wynter. "Stay. But keep your opinions to your own damned self. And stay away from Gray and our children."

Our children? Gray wasn't sure who was included in that 'our'. His instinct roared within... *his* children...

Wynter eyed him before taking his alpha's arm and heading up toward the casket. Gray hadn't had a chance to say his goodbyes yet. Jefre had sat him in the chair before helping with set up... and it was still hard for him to walk without help.

"Hey there."

Gray looked up and felt relief when he saw Avery's face. Both Lake and Auggie had gone home with him to get their suits... the same ones they'd worn at their parents' funeral. "Hey guys. I'm glad to see you."

They all took seats on either side of him before more guests came in and filled the room. He was glad to have some support there, especially as Jamie's papa kept sending him ugly looks from across the room.

"Can you help me to the front?" Gray asked Lake. Lake nodded and rose.

Gray turned to Avery. "Keep an eye on the babies, please."

Avery agreed and helped Gray to his feet. Lake took his arm and walked the narrow aisle through the chairs toward the casket. Each step was painful. The stitches felt as if he was being ripped open again.

Before they could reach the front, Rohan strode up the aisle and scooped Gray into his arms. His gaze was drawn to Jamie's papa—who of course scowled at the spectacle.

"You shouldn't," Gray mumbled under his breath as Rohan led them to the front.

"I'll do as I damned please in my own home," Rohan shot back. "I should've helped you sooner. I forgot. I'm sorry."

"You're preoccupied. I wouldn't expect you to think of me."

Rohan met his stare before lowering him before the casket. He got his first look at Jamie, and the tears came immediately after. Draped over his head and flowing on both sides was the wig Gray had had made. He reached in and brushed some of the strands away from Jamie's face before leaning in to press a kiss to his friend's cheek.

He took Jamie's hand, but it was cold against his. Tears streamed down his face, and his knees weakened. Had it not been for Rohan, he'd have fallen. The alpha scooped him up again and began to carry him to the back. Rohan paused. "Why are you sitting so far back?"

"Jefre sat me in one of the only seats already placed and I don't walk so well right now."

"You should be up front with me," Rohan spun to face that direction.

"No. I've got the boys and the babies… we can't all move."

"You belong at the front," Rohan repeated.

After getting Gray situated in a seat between him and Wilder, Rohan went to collect the basket with the babies. When he got back, he placed it at Gray's feet. Both boys still slept, fortunately. By the time the funeral was ready to begin, the room was overfilled. The seats were packed, and other mourners stood along the walls. There was an abundance of love for

Jamie, and it made Gray's heart full to see there were so many there to mark his passing.

The preacher stepped up to the podium to begin his sermon. "You'll have to bear with me some here. Jamie and I wrote this eulogy together before he passed."

Gray turned to meet Rohan's gaze. Of course Jamie had planned everything, down to his own eulogy.

The preacher smiled. "Something I learned very quickly about Jaymes Parker was that when he got an idea in his mind, there was no way anyone would sway his course."

Gray smiled, tears forming in his eyes. Everyone had learned that lesson. Jamie had been a force of nature. You might as well have tried to scream down a hurricane than to change Jamie's mind.

"He had very strong ideas for his eulogy, you can imagine. So, most of these are his words, not mine. And given how much thought he'd put into them, I felt it insincere to add too many of my own." The preacher unfolded a few pieces of paper he had stored in his book and placed his reading glasses on his face before clearing his throat. "Jaymes Parker died as he lived. With love. Love for his mate. Love for his brothers. Love for his best friend, Gray, and love for the babies that Gray was bringing into their world."

Rohan reached over and took Gray's hand, squeezing it.

The preacher stopped and smiled to himself before continuing. "I once asked him about those babies, and I'm sure there are many of you here now who are very curious about them, too. I asked him if it would be harder to leave knowing he'd have to say goodbye to them. 'Of course', he answered me, a small, sad smile on his face. And then he said something that amazed me. He said, 'who would want to live a life that was easy to part with?'"

Gray clenched his jaw, his eyes stinging.

"And that's the rule I think Jamie lived by. He made dying harder by living his fullest. He fought for his happiness and for that of the ones he loved." The preacher turned to Rohan. "And he spoke of so much love and the joy you brought into his life, Rohan. The smiles on his face when he talked about you made me smile. But then, Jamie's joy always seemed to be contagious." The preacher laughed. "I'd say that's one virus we should all catch. Isn't it? We could all use more of that in our lives. Joy."

The man paused, smiling at the crowd.

"One of his greatest joys, after his mate and his brother Wilder, were his children who grew within his best friend, Gray. He called Gray a brother of his heart, and his face lit up when he spoke of that relationship, as well."

Gray couldn't hold back any longer. The tears came again, and he let them flow.

"I hear from Rohan that Jamie passed this world holding those babies close. He already loved them so much and will continue to from above. He will watch over his mate, his family, and his friends and hopefully ensure they find their own joy now that he's gone. I know it will be hard, after losing such a precious light, but after the darkness, there *will* be joy again."

The preacher led them in a prayer. Everyone in attendance murmured it together, in concert. After, the preacher tucked away his papers and closed his book. "If there's anyone else who would like to come up and speak about Jamie, please do."

One by one, men went to the podium. An old omega friend from school. Another who'd gone to many balls with Jamie. An old friend of the family. Jefre and Serge took their own turns. Wilder. Vaughn. Jamie's father.

Finally Rohan came up to speak. A tear-filled gaze lined with red searched the crowd until it landed on Gray for a moment. He looked down at the podium and cleared his throat before lifting his stare. "I don't have much to say that hasn't already been said about my mate. He was a shining light... gone too soon." Rohan paused, collecting himself. "I loved him. With everything I am." He looked down. Silence filled the room. Hushed murmurs came next. Rohan finally lifted his stare and met Gray's eyes. "That's a lie. I didn't love him with *everything* I am."

Tears filled the alpha's eyes.

"I should've given him everything I was... and for years, I did that. He was the only one for me." Rohan met Gray's stare again before he closed his eyes, a pained look on his face. "I didn't deserve him. I wasn't good enough. He should've had a better man than me."

Wilder leapt to his feet. He went to the podium and tried to calm Rohan down. Gray wanted to rise and go to the alpha, but he dared not. Not just because of the pain, but he sensed he was part of the reason for it.

The two mumbled between them, unheard.

"No!" Rohan suddenly roared. "I was *weak!*"

Wilder dragged Rohan away from the podium and out of the room. Gray sat there, the instinct screaming for him to help calm a raging alpha was a call in his blood. But just as he was about to rise, one of the babes began to cry. He reached down and lifted the alpha babe into his arms and calmed the child.

An omega in the row behind leaned forward and smiled. "How old?"

"A few days," Gray whispered.

"Oh! They're newborns... oh wait..." he frowned. "Are these Jamie's? The ones the preacher was talking about?"

Yes. Not mine. Jamie's. Remember that. "They are."

"Oh, that's so incredibly sad... that he won't be here for them." The omega smiled wanly. "And you are?"

"Gray."

"The surrogate," the omega said.

"The best friend," Gray corrected. He was more than just a surrogate. Wasn't he? He stiffened at the thought of being less... but he knew ultimately, that's all he truly was.

"Of course," the omega whispered. He turned and reached into his pocket before pulling out a small piece of paper. "Here's my card."

Gray took it, not sure why the stranger was handing it over. "Okay."

"My alpha and I have been looking for a good surrogate. And it appears you've done a wonderful job bringing babies into this world. Twins are so rare."

Gray shoved the card back. "No thanks."

The omega looked bewildered. "Sorry… I just assumed you might be interested in another job."

Gray laid the alpha babe back into the basket before forcing himself to rise. "This wasn't a job. It was an act of love. I loved Jamie. Please don't belittle that by calling it a job." He grabbed the basket and forced himself to go in search of Rohan.

Chapter Twenty-Eight

Broken...

Rohan paced his home office, shoving a hand through his hair. Dust motes danced in the morning light flooding the large picture window. As he paced in one direction, he saw the wall of books. The other, he saw outside, the drive was packed with cars of every color. Sunlight glinted off their shiny paint and chrome.

He glanced out as he paced and considering jumping in one and just driving. As far as he could go. *To the ends of the earth.*

Anywhere to get away from the pain he now felt. *Nowhere I can go. Nowhere I can hide.*

"Come on, Rohan, you need to calm down." Wilder murmured. "You've got a hundred guests out there, and we don't need to make a scene."

"Do you think I give two shits about the people out there?" Wilder sounded like Wynter talking. He didn't want to hear that voice in his head. Not now.

Wilder pressed his lips into a firm line and remained quiet.

Rohan went back to his pacing. "I should've been stronger. I should've told Jamie no."

"About what?"

"The babies," Rohan spat as he spun to face Wilder. "What else would this be about? If I'd told him no, we wouldn't be in this... mess."

Wilder was quiet a moment. He sat in the corner where the light didn't quite reach. Half his face was in shadow until he lifted it. "Rohan... it's what he *wanted*."

Rohan shook his head. He didn't want understanding. He wanted anger. "Your father warned me of this. He told me that Jamie had me wrapped around his little finger and one day it would get me in trouble when I couldn't say no. Did I believe him? No. I didn't."

"Loving your mate and wanting to make him happy isn't a crime," Wilder said.

"It is when I ended up falling for a man who wasn't my mate," Rohan said, his voice low.

Wilder met his stare, eyes wide. Rohan could see the disappointment in his best friend's stare... he'd just told the man he'd been untrue to Jamie. Of course he was disappointed. Rohan was more than disappointed in himself.

"I love him."

"I *heard* you." Wilder looked away, his jaw tight. He remained silent when all Rohan wanted was for Wilder to lash out. Scream. Roar.

He wanted Wilder to *hit* him. Make him feel as bad on the outside as he felt on the inside.

"I just told you that I fell in love with another man and you're just going to *sit there*?"

Wilder lifted his stare, but didn't fully look at Rohan. He didn't speak a word, but Rohan could see the tick in the man's jaw.

"I thought you loved Jamie? You're not going to stand up for him?" Rohan asked, his voice rasping in his own ears. "Maybe you didn't love him after all."

Wilder's eyes flashed with anger when his head whipped up. He rose from the chair where he sat and advanced on Rohan... but stopped inches away, clenching his fists at his sides. Rohan rushed forward and pushed the alpha's chest.

"That's all the anger you can muster? *Pathetic.*"

Wilder grabbed the front of his shirt and glared. "*What're* you doing?"

"You should be furious with me!"

"I am!" Wilder roared. He pushed Rohan's shoulders back, eyes lit with rage.

"Then *hit* me!"

The light faded from Wilder's eyes. His mouth parted, a frown creasing his brow. Wilder took a step back, looking confused.

"No! Godsdamn it...*Hit me!*" Rohan said, shoving Wilder again. "Fucking hit me!"

Wilder spun them and slammed Rohan to the wall. "Stop this! Stop it now!"

Tears burned the backs of Rohan's eyes. "I *should've* been a better man, Wilder. I should've loved him more. I should've been *faithful* to him."

Wilder took a step back, tears shimmering in his eyes, too. "You did as he asked. He told me so... and he told me how broken you'd been after. He told me it nearly killed you. You *were* faithful to him and his wants. You gave him *exactly* what he wanted. And knowing your children were coming gave him *joy.*"

Rohan hit the wall with the back of his head, needing to feel the bite of pain Wilder refused to give him.

"I'll admit that I don't completely understand all his choices. And I was angry as hell that you went along with it. At first." He paused, wiping at the bottom of his eye. "But I have to honor Jamie's wishes. Now more than ever. He wanted a life for you after he was gone." Wilder sat on the edge of the desk, looking as defeated as Rohan felt. "He made me promise to help him. After."

Rohan cringed. "He pulled my strings enough in life. I can't... I can't do what he wanted me to do."

"You just admitted you have feelings for Gray."

Rohan winced. "And that's exactly why I can't. I'm weak... when I need to be strong. I need to honor Jamie's memory. I need to honor his life and the love I had for him."

Just then, Gray limped into the room, the babies' basket clutched in his hand. He looked to be in pain—and shouldn't have been walking. Instinct flared within Rohan.

Protect him.
Claim him.
Make him yours.

He cringed as the thoughts came into his mind...

Now... as one mate was about to go into the ground? All he could think about was claiming another? Anger swelled within... It only proved how terrible a man he was. Going against his instinct, he glared at Gray. "What're you doing here? Couldn't you tell I needed time alone?"

Gray visibly blanched. "I... I was worried about you."

Get him off his feet. He's still healing. Don't let him be hurt. "I don't need you running after me, making sure I'm okay. I don't need you at all."

Gray gasped.

"He didn't mean that," Wilder murmured.

"I meant every word," Rohan spat. He looked to Wilder. "Can you give us a moment?"

Wilder looked between them cautiously before nodding. He left in silence, closing the office door behind him.

Rohan turned to eye Gray again. "Soon we'll be free of one another and we can go our separate ways."

Gray frowned. "We haven't discussed the babies."

Rohan turned his head away. "I'll raise my boys. As is my responsibility." He paused. "Per our contract."

Gray winced. "I thought we were well past contracts and agreements now."

"Meaning?"

Gray lifted his face. "I thought…"

"Thought what?"

Gray's stare met his, the omega's eyes filling with tears. "I thought you'd let me be a part of the boys' life in some way… especially now that Jamie can't be."

Rohan swallowed the bile rising in his throat. He hated himself for the words in his head, but he needed to sever the bond between them if he was going to honor his mate. "We had a contract. You agreed to the terms. Now they're here and our time together is soon over."

"Really?" Gray asked, tears shining in his eyes. "You can stand there and be so cold? I thought I meant *something* to you?"

"You meant *nothing* to me."

As soon as the words were out of his mouth, Rohan regretted them.

Gray sagged against the wall for a moment. One of the babes began to howl… spurring on the other one. Gray gave Rohan one last look… before he silently turned and left the room.

Go after him.
Protect him.
Protect them.
They're your family now.

Rohan stood frozen, his heart wanting to move forward, his mind telling him he had no rights to.

He could hear Jamie's voice in his head.

You stupid fool.

* * * *

Running away…

Each step was agony. Not just because Gray was healing, but the pain in his heart was almost worse than that of his body. Tears streamed down his face, his heart breaking. He struggled to get air into his lungs. The babies were feeding off his pain, he knew it. Their howls filled the room. He paused by the dining table, catching his breath, when he felt a firm hand on his shoulder.

He lifted his stare, only to see Wilder at his side.

"Let me help you," Wilder murmured.

Gray stood there a moment, trying to pull himself together.

"Come on," Wilder said before taking the basket from Gray's hand.

Wilder rested the babes on the table before he ran his hands over the babes and murmured soothing words over them, gentle rocking the basket. After a moment, the infants calmed and drifted back to sleep.

Wilder seemed to have the magic touch. He felt a little flash of jealousy and wished he had the same.

Rohan turned to look at him. "How about you sit for a moment—I'll go grab someone to help grab the babies and I'll get you all upstairs and in bed."

"I want to go home," Gray whispered as the alpha helped him sit.

Wilder knelt before him. "You can't let the words he said in anguish send you running."

"I think he was the most honest he's ever been with me. He wants me gone... so I should go."

"No. He absolutely wasn't honest in there. I have no idea what he said but if it was enough to send you racing away..." Wilder sighed. "I can attest to that, especially seeing your face now," Wilder said. "He's angry with himself... and we always take out our pain on those... those we love."

Gray met Wilder's stare, confused. "That *wasn't* love."

Wilder tilted his head, cocking a brow. "I think I know Rohan well enough to know."

Gray wanted to hope Wilder was right, but Rohan's vile words still rung in his ears. "Jamie's your brother. Why would you try to help me?"

Wilder looked away. "I love Jamie. I'm not exactly happy with this plan of his..." Wilder looked back. "But it's what he wanted. And I made promises. Promises I intend to keep."

"Perhaps Jamie pushed too hard. He can't force us together."

Wilder nodded. "Maybe he did push too hard. But I think we both know Jamie had good reasons to push. You love him... don't you?"

Gray looked away.

"Let me go get that help. I'll be right back."

The swinging door into the dining room reopened moments later... but it wasn't Wilder. It was Wynter Jaymes, Jamie's papa.

The omega wandered closer to the table and stopped at the basket, smiling down at the sleeping babes. He reached down and caressed their faces and cooed. Gray tensed, wanting to drag the basket out of the man's reach, but he held back the desire.

"You have such a tight hold on these children. By law, those babies belong to Jamie and Rohan." Wynter smiled down at the sleeping twins. "Rohan's *obviously* not in any shape to care for them, so that leaves them to me and Jamie's father."

Gray's heart nearly stopped beating.

"You can't just come in and take my—" He stopped.

They weren't his. Never were.

Jamie's papa smiled. "That's right. They're *not* yours. You apparently signed away your rights. And I believe Jamie would want family caring for these children."

I'm his family. "You mean the same parents who couldn't be bothered to come see their dying son? *That* family?"

Wynter scowled. "Because you played nursemaid to him for a few months, you seem to think you have some right to these children. Let me remind you that you gave your rights up the minute you signed their lives away. *For cash*. You sold your children."

Gray gasped inwardly. Wasn't there some truth to that? He'd effectively sold the lives of his children... and sent them on a path right into this man's hands. *No. There has to be another way.* "I might not have rights, but Rohan *does*."

"He's a mess," Wynter said, lifting his chin. "No judge in his right mind would leave two newborns with a grieving alpha. Especially after his explosion in front of a hundred witnesses." He smiled wickedly. "Enjoy what little time you have left with them, dear. We'll have them in our home soon enough."

Wynter stalked over to the swinging door, and he left.

Gray looked down at the babies, fear in his heart. Jamie's dreadful parents couldn't take his children away.

They were his… no matter what anyone said. Jamie would want this, he knew it. He would want Gray to protect the twins.

Wilder came back with Jefre a few moments later.

"Did I see my papa in here?" Wilder asked, frowning.

He nodded.

"What did he have to say?" the alpha asked

Gray looked at Wilder and knew he needed to make a gamble. "Do you think Jamie would've wanted your parents raising these children?"

Wilder cocked a brow and frowned. "Hell no."

"Well… your papa just said he's going to try and get custody," Gray told him.

Wilder's eyes widened. And then his jaw clenched tight.

"Rohan's not in any shape to raise these babes. Not yet. I need to protect them until he is." *If he ever is but I'll cross that bridge when it comes.* Gray sucked in a slow breath. "*If* you truly loved Jamie, you'll take me home. With them."

Wilder lifted his stare, looking conflicted.

"Wilder?"

Wilder dragged his gaze away for a moment. But then he nodded. "Okay."

Gray sighed in relief. He turned to Jefre. "Can you go pack my bags?"

Jefre looked between them for a moment before nodding. "Yeah. Just gimme a few minutes."

Gray turned back to Wilder. "Can you get my nephews? We can go back in the car that picked them up if it's still out there waiting."

Wilder nodded. "I can go check on the car after I send your nephews in." Wilder rose and got an odd look on his face.

"Please tell me you're not having second thoughts?"

Wilder eyed him before shaking his head. "It's not that… it's…" He shrugged. "Never mind. I'll get everything situated."

The alpha left the room, leaving him alone with the twins. Gray reached into the basket and softly ran his hand down their bellies. "We're going home, boys."

* * * *

Regret…

After just about everyone finally left his house, Rohan sat in the front row before the casket. Later, the mortuary would come to collect it and then in the morning, a small gathering of family would be there to watch the body interned. Now, the caterers, servants, and extra hired staff moved about the house, quietly cleaning up behind the last of the mourners.

He leaned his elbows on his knees and drank his fifth pour of scotch, hoping the alcohol would make him stop hurting and knowing deep down it would only make things worse.

I just want to forget.

The look on Gray's face was burned into his mind. He hated himself even more for what he'd just done to the omega.

What choice did I have?

Wilder appeared at his side and took the unoccupied seat to his left.

"Where have you been?"

Wilder was silent a moment. "Taking care of shit you should've been taking care of."

Rohan glanced to the side and saw Wilder and his clenched jaw. Anger sparked within him... the alcohol was starting to cloud his reason. Not that he felt all that reasonable in that moment. "Meaning?"

Wilder turned slightly, an eyebrow rising. "I don't know what you said to Gray, but whatever it was... you're an asshole."

Rohan narrowed his eyes. And then he realized he hadn't seen the omega or the children since their confrontation earlier. "You already had your chance for a fight earlier." He took another drink from his glass. "Too late now."

Wilder didn't say a word.

"Where *is* Gray?" Rohan asked.

"I don't know." Wilder turned to him and smiled.

"Where are the babies?"

"With Gray."

Rohan glared at Wilder. "But you don't know where he is."

"He's nowhere you can get to him right now."

Panic hit him. Rohan rose on wobbly legs. He raced up the stairs and went to Gray's bedroom. As soon as he opened the door, the omega's scent filled his nose. Inhaling deep, he filled his lungs.

But the room was empty. He crossed to the bassinet. *Empty.*

He ran to the gallery and looked down from the second floor. Wilder stood in the middle of the foyer, eyeing him.

"Where are they?" he roared.

"You all needed a little space apart. I think it would be good for all of you."

"*Where?*" Rohan demanded.

"*Godsdamn* it, man... you're a fucking wreck! Let the omega care for the babies so you can get your damned head on straight."

Rohan leaned against the balustrade, wanting to demand Wilder tell him. Instead, he sucked back the last of the scotch in his glass before wandering down the stairs. As soon as he got back into the living room, he poured himself another drink and lifted a glass to Jamie before he sucked half of that down, too.

"Is that a good idea?" Wilder asked behind him.

"Can't you let me have one day to be a wreck? I think I'm owed at least that much."

"One day? I suppose you're allowed that," Wilder said. "But I'm staying with you."

Rohan shook his head. "Whatever." He drained the last of his glass.

Wilder came over and poured himself a scotch before refilling Rohan's. He clinked glasses with the one in Rohan's hand.

"To Jamie."

Rohan looked to the casket, sadness swamping him. It still didn't feel real. No matter how sick Jamie had been, none of what had happened so far felt real. He just wanted to close his eyes and wake up from the nightmare that was his life.

By the time they'd finished the bottle of scotch off, Wilder was passed out on the leather couch in his office. Rohan was wide awake. He hadn't slept in almost a week and wasn't sure he could sleep again. Sitting at his desk, he looked at Jamie's cell phone. On the screen—a selfie of a very pregnant Gray hugging a weak, but exuberant looking Jamie.

His stare washed over the surface. Rohan searched Jamie's face before his gaze moved to look at Gray's.

What have I done?

He pulled out his phone and queued up Gray's number. Before he lost his drunken nerve, he hit Call and lifted the phone to his ear.

It rang once... twice... by the fourth ring, he wasn't sure if the omega would answer.

A sleepy *"Hello?"* came just before he was about to give up.

"Did I wake you?" Rohan slurred.

"It is... three A.M."

"Sorry," Rohan mumbled, not sorry.

"Are you drunk?"

"I am," Rohan said with a smile. "I am very, *very* drunk."

Silence filled the other end. Pain slammed into his heart, knowing he'd done wrong. Tears burned the backs of his eyes. *I'm sorry.* The words were on the tip of his tongue. He wanted to say them and he wanted Gray back under his roof with their children.

But, to say those words would tarnish him all the more.

I love you... and it's eating me alive.

"Is there a reason for the call?"

Rohan closed his eyes. "Are the babies okay?"

"Of course they are."

"Are you?" Rohan asked.

"Does it really matter?"

Of course it matters. I love you. He remained silent.

"I'm going back to bed. Please don't call again unless it's a decent hour and you're not drunk," Gray said before hanging up the phone.

Rohan let his hand slide down. He hung up the call before dropping the phone on the surface of the desk. He wandered up the stairs and stopped at the top. Two bedrooms... two scents... one gone forever. One he was pushing away. He slid into his bedroom and climbed into the bed he'd shared with Jamie.

Tears came to his eyes...

He brought a pillow to his face and inhaled.

Jamie's scent was already fading from the room.

* * * *

The following morning...

Gray's first stop that morning was the only card he had to play.

He stared across the desk at Tensen.

After explaining his situation in full, he finally asked the man, "What rights do I have?"

Tensen smiled as he leaned back in his high-backed leather chair. "*All* of them."

Gray tensed. "What?"

"Because of his illness, I purposefully wrote in a line about revision of parental rights if anything were to happen to Jamie in the first three years of the child's life… Jamie was fully aware and agreed with it. Thanks to that clause, your rights were reinstated the moment Jamie passed. Both Rohan and Jamie signed the document, so it's legally binding. The children are yours and Rohan's."

"Does Rohan know this?"

Tensen smiled. "He *is* an attorney, as well. I assume he read over the contract before he signed it."

"In other words, you and Jamie didn't point it out."

Tensen only smiled wider.

Gray relaxed some, but he knew he was nowhere near out of the fire. "But Jamie's parents could still fight?"

"They could."

"And they have money. Power. Influence. What do I have?" He sighed. "Nothing."

"You have me," Tensen said.

"Tensen… you're an amazing man. You're kind and caring and… I wish I could be what you want me to be."

"You have me… as your attorney," Tensen said, sitting up a little straighter. Gray thought he saw a hint of disappointment in Tensen's eyes, but if it was there, it was gone in an instant. "It's been blatantly obvious I had no chance for some time now. Wishful thinking on my part."

"I'm sorry."

"Don't be," Tensen said. "But can I ask a question?"

"Sure."

"If I'd been an alpha?"

Gray sighed, knowing the truth might sting all the harder. *Of course* he would've considered Tensen's proposition more if the man had been an alpha. "Things might've been quite different, I'm sure."

Tensen closed his eyes and sighed before reopening them. "Too bad."

Gray smiled faintly. "You're a *very* special man who I hope finds happiness someday. Your kindness and consideration…" Gray smiled. "I honestly considered your offer for that alone."

"But I couldn't offer you freedom."

Gray's face grew red. "It wasn't just that, Tensen. You *deserve* someone who loves you. Not a lonely man craving your kindness. If you'd been with me, maybe you would've missed meeting the right man for you."

Tensen's smile turned faint. "Maybe… but let's talk about the business at hand. Like I said… we have the contract on our side. Plus there's Jamie's will… which will need to be reviewed before the case goes to trial."

"His will?"

Tensen nodded. "He asked me to draft it up for him at the same time we discussed the surrogacy. After his first scare with cancer, he knew he wanted to be prepared for the future."

"And I assume there's something in it about the children?"

"I can't share that now. All those named in the will need to be present before it can be opened." Tensen flipped a page in his calendar. "Since you are named—I hope to get the reading over before your temporary freedom ends. That's this Friday, is it not?"

Gray nodded, an invisible hand feeling as if it wrapped around him, ready to squeeze. His taste of freedom had been too short. He craved more.

"Will or not, there's still Rohan. He has rights… I wouldn't be able to keep the boys away from him."

"Would you want to?"

"No! He's given no cause… but if he takes them, Jamie's parents could potentially get ahold of the twins through him. They could take the boys away… and then where would I be?"

"I can work on a temporary custody order, so the law would be on your side."

"Perfect," Gray replied.

"I think we need to bring Rohan into this fight."

Gray didn't want to include Rohan in anything. Not after the things he'd said.

One of Tensen's eyebrows rose. "Is there a problem?"

Gray swallowed back the lump in his throat. "Rohan's grieving his mate. He's not in a good mental space right now."

"That only adds to your case and makes it stronger."

"I don't want to use him as ammunition." Gray was only trying to be a caretaker for the children until Rohan was ready to take responsibility. *If* the alpha *wanted* to take responsibility. Gray gazed down at the sleeping babes in the basket, his heart filled with love for them. He didn't want to part with them, but they were Rohan's children, too. While he'd always see them as part Jamie's, legally it couldn't be that way. Not when the omega's parents were a threat. Gray needed the law to protect them.

He had no alpha to do it.

Tensen cocked his head to the side. "We have to tell the judge Rohan's not capable now."

"He's hurting enough as it is."

The beta leaned his arms on his desk. "You have feelings for Rohan?"

"That has *nothing* to do with custody."

"That's not a denial... and I'd say it has *everything* to do with what's about to happen."

Gray looked away. "I don't want Rohan hurt. No more than he already is."

"Fine. I'll take care of filing everything with the court. I can go ahead and make a motion to restore your rights and give you full legal custody while at the courthouse, too."

"*Temporary* full custody... reverting to shared once Rohan has had time to grieve his loss and can make a decision on what happens next. And we need to ensure Jamie's parents are blocked from being with the boys unsupervised."

"I don't know that we have enough reason to do that. Just because they want to care for the children isn't means for revoking any and all rights they might have. Unless you can prove them dangerous?"

"I don't know that I could. I have visions of Wynter Jaymes taking them and refusing to give them back," Gray said. "Just please make sure that doesn't happen."

"I'll do everything I can. You know I will."

Gray released a slow breath. "Thank you."

Tensen made some notes at his desk before looking up. "You really should consider talking to Rohan before I submit the papers. He won't like getting a summons handed to him out of the blue." He lifted his head. "Isn't the burial this morning? You can tell him there."

"I wasn't planning on going. I'm not in great shape physically at the moment." He hated the thought of missing it, but he needed to protect himself and the children. And he'd said his goodbyes the day before.

To more than just Jamie.

"Probably for the best," Tensen said. "Wynter and Warden might be there." The solicitor lifted his head. "But make sure you contact him. I don't need a rage-filled alpha calling me."

"I will," Gray said before changing the subject. "I really need those papers submitted as soon as possible."

"I'm on it," Tensen said. "It'll be there by the end of the day."

"Thank you." Gray uneasily skirted the desk and hugged Tensen before he grabbed the basket and the baby bag and headed out of the office. Limping to the trolley stop, he pushed on, trying not to feel the pain. He should've been on bedrest a good two weeks after the babes came, but such was life. You had to push on. As soon as he was seated in the vehicle and on the way home, he gazed down at the sleeping children and smiled. He reached for his phone and pulled up Rohan's number.

You're nothing to me.

Gray shoved the phone back into his pocket and tried to not let those words torture him any more than they already had. When he was home… alone… and better prepared for that conversation, he'd call.

Later, after he'd fed, changed, and gotten both babies to sleep, he reached for his phone again. After a few minutes of willing himself to make the call, he finally got enough courage.

No time like the present.

He dialed the number and held his breath.

"This is Rohan Parker. I'm unavailable at the moment…"

Gray sighed inwardly, almost glad the alpha hadn't picked up. Yet there was a little part of him disappointed his call hadn't been taken. He tried not to let the deep rumble of Rohan's voice wash through him and waited for the beep to come.

"Rohan. It's Gray. I need to speak to you. Please call me."

Chapter Twenty-Nine

The day after the burial...

"Rohan. It's Gray. I need to speak to you. Please call me."

Rohan played the message again... for the fifth time. He hated how cold and distant Gray sounded, but it was his own damned fault. He'd done that... made Gray hate him. He'd pushed so hard that the omega hadn't even come to the burial. Rohan had endured Wynter and Warden—and their questions.

Why the pair were suddenly so interested in Gray and the children, he wasn't sure. They couldn't have been bothered when Jamie was alive.

He played the message for a sixth time, closing his eyes and letting the omega's voice burn into his ears. Rohan had called back and left a message for Gray to call him—and all he could do was sit and wait.

Breathless with anticipation.

A knock came to the door. He clumsily climbed from the couch in his office; still wearing the same clothes he'd worn the day before. Still wearing the stink of the new bottle of scotch from the day before, too. He dug his fingers through his hair as he stumbled to the door and tried to make himself somewhat presentable. Rohan opened the door, narrowing his eyes to the shine of the sun.

"Rohan Parker?"

"Yes."

A letter was placed in his hands.

"You've been served."

Rohan looked down at the envelope. Before he could say a word, the man was gone. He closed the door and stumbled to the nearest chair before he ripped open the envelope.

Custody papers?

Gray Tomlinson... full custody...?

A growl rose up his throat, and he crumbled the papers in his fist. Tossing it away, he let out a roar. After he collapsed back in the seat, he reached for the phone. He called for a car, knowing he was still a little drunk from the night before. As soon as he got off the phone, he jumped into a shower and tried to wake himself up a little.

Once dressed, he went to his safe in his office. He opened it up and took out a few stacks of cash, pocketing them. He turned toward the knock at the door and closed his safe. Rohan snatched the crumpled papers from the floor before he reached the front.

Exiting, he eyed the driver. "I need to go to the Omega Quadrant."

"Sir," the beta said, his eyes growing wide. "You're an alpha. I *can't* take you there."

"Just drive me to the gate. I'll handle the rest."

An hour and a few thousand *renos* later, he'd bribed his way through the gate with half the cash in his pocket—with the promise of the other half on his way out. Not long after, the car came to rest before a small, handsome cottage not far away. He looked at the house. It was comfortable and serene, kind of like Gray.

Of course this is where he lives.

"I need you to knock on the door for me," he said to the driver. "I need Gray Tomlinson to come to the car."

The driver smiled. "I know Gray." The beta turned to Rohan. "He should be getting ready to pop right about now, huh?"

"I assume you've driven for us before then?"

The driver smiled. "Oh yes. I've taken Gray and Jamie to a few appointments."

Rohan eyed the back of the man's head. "Gray's had the babies." He drew in a shuddering breath. "And Jamie... died."

That statement had tasted like vinegar. He cringed having said it.

The driver's head whipped around, a look of grief on the man's face. "I'm so, *so* very sorry. I didn't know. He was a kind man. I liked driving for him... for them both, really. They were such good friends. Always laughing and smiling." The driver looked forlornly toward the house. "I suppose that means I won't be driving for Gray anymore, either."

Rohan's jaw tensed. He was in no mood to be nice. He wanted Gray in the car now, not an hour from now. "No. I suppose not. Maybe you could say goodbye... once you go talk to him like I asked."

The driver's head whipped around again. "Of course. I'm sorry." The beta jumped out of the car and walked up the path through the well-tended lawn. Rohan watched impatiently from the car as the driver knocked on the door.

It opened, and he saw Gray in the doorway.

His heart beat a little faster in his chest at that first sight, and he needed to remind himself he was angry. *Custody... he thinks to take the children from me.*

Gray looked his way, but couldn't see him through the darkened glass of the car.

Claim him.

Make him yours.

Rohan clenched his jaw. The instinct should've lessened now that Gray had had the babies. If anything, it felt stronger. His whole body came alive as Gray made his way to the car, following the driver. His cock began to thicken, the need to reclaim his omega pounding in his veins.

Just after Rohan hit the button to raise the partition between the front and back of the car, the beta opened the back door and Gray climbed in. Rohan did everything in his power to hold back the urge to take what was his—but then Gray's scent filled his nose, and he lost his mind. Rohan grabbed Gray's wrist and pulled the omega onto his lap.

Right on top of his hard cock, pulsing with need.

"What in the hell do you think you're doing?" Rohan asked him.

Gray's hands rested on his shoulders and pushed away. "I'm not the one *manhandling* me in the back of a car."

Fire raced through his body. The animal part of him craved Gray's submission. He held tight to his control… but he was slipping fast. "Custody?"

Gray's eyes flashed with anger. "Saving our children."

Our children. "Saving them from me?"

"*No*, from Jamie's parents," Gray spat, pushing again.

Rohan released his hold, and Gray slid off his lap and onto the seat beside him. Some cold water was tossed on the instinctual need he'd felt. He scrubbed a hand over his face, reminding himself why he was there.

Gray righted his clothes before scowling at Rohan. "After you blew up at me at the funeral, Jamie's papa came up and said he was going to get custody of the children—that you weren't in any frame of mind to care for them. I went to Tensen and found out that my rights were restored if Jamie passed within the first three years of the child's life. Tensen put that into the contract because of Jamie's illness."

Rohan suddenly recalled reading the clause. He'd thought it morbid, but hadn't expected it to be enforced. "That doesn't explain why you're taking them from *me*."

"*Temporary* full custody… reverting to shared once you had some time to grieve and were back on your feet." Gray eyed him. "Did you even *read* the papers? You are an attorney, are you not?"

Rohan reached for the crumbled papers on the seat and looked them over. He read over it again, realizing his mistake. "I saw custody… and I lost my mind." He scrubbed his stubbled face, knowing he likely looked a sight. "I'm sorry. I thought you were trying to take our children away from me."

Gray relaxed a little, but still kept his distance. "After seeing how revolting Jamie's parents were… I couldn't let the twins go there. And I wasn't sure I would get any help from you. That's all I was doing. Protecting our children. From them. Not you." Gray paused. "I knew you needed time to mourn."

Rohan lifted his stare and met Gray's. "I'm glad one of us is thinking clearly enough to protect the twins." He scrubbed a hand over his face. "Because I sure as hell am not in a position to do that right now."

Silence fell between them.

"I should get back inside. The boys should be waking up from their naps soon."

"Can I come inside and see them?"

"An alpha? In the middle of the O Quad? I think not."

Rohan's face fell. He wanted to see his babies. Desperately. Especially if it gave him a few more minutes to spend with Gray.

"I can bring them out to the car. How's that?"

"I want them home, where they belong," Rohan said. He held onto Gray's stare. *Where you all belong.*

Gray looked away. "We'll cross that bridge when we get there."

The instinct roared again in his blood.

Take them all home. Now. Apologize. Beg his forgiveness.

He couldn't get the words to come, no matter how much the need within demanded it.

Gray opened the door and turned to look at him. "I'll be right back."

A few minutes passed before Gray came back out of the house, the basket in one hand. He slid into the backseat and set the basket on Rohan's lap. Both twins were asleep, cuddled together as they always seemed to be.

He gently brushed his hand over their soft heads, smiling. "They already look bigger. It's only been a couple of days."

"They can grow a few ounces a day. Especially our big boy. He likes to eat."

Rohan smiled. "I noticed they were listed as Baby A and Baby O in the court documents."

"Well, they *haven't* been given names yet."

"We've been preoccupied." Rohan looked at Gray. "What did Jamie want to name them?"

Gray looked away, and it hurt his heart that the omega was keeping his distance, even though he was to blame.

"Jamie never said. He kept saying it would be a surprise," Gray answered.

"Of course he did," Rohan said. "What do *you* think they should be named?"

Gray smiled forlornly. "The big guy should be Jaymes. In honor of Jamie. And our little man… I know it would be a lot to ask. But I'd be honored if he was named after the brother I lost not long ago. Silver."

"Silver. I like it. But Jamie?" Rohan winced. "That would be too hard. I'd think of my mate every time I looked at him."

"*Exactly*. We'd look at him and think of Jamie. Every. Single. Day. At first, it will hurt. But eventually we'd have new joys associated with that name. First giggles. First steps. First words. First day of school. First loves. They'd all be pinned to that beautiful man we lost and maybe it would make the hurt a little less." Gray reached into the basket and caressed one of the baby's heads. "And I'd have the same for my brother, one of the best friends I ever had. Both of them really. My brothers… one by flesh, one by heart. I lost my best friends one after another…"

Rohan turned to look at Gray, tears in his eyes. "It's perfect then. Jamie and Silver."

Gray broke down, the tears coming. Rohan slid the basket to the seat beside him and drew the omega into his arms. He held Gray and somehow found quiet and relief in allowing another to grieve. He could ignore his own hurt and focus on the beautiful man in his arms.

There was no way he could be sure of how long they sat there, holding on to one another. He was more than prepared to sit there forever in that moment.

Where he could find a little peace.

That was, until Gray looked up and seemed to remember all the ugly things he'd said. The omega pushed him away.

And it stung. Soul deep, it burned.

"I should go back in. My nephews will wonder where I am, and we don't need to broadcast that there's an alpha in the quadrant." Gray cocked a brow. "How *did* you get in?"

"Bribe," Rohan said with a grin. "Hopefully it works on the way out, too."

Gray sighed, shaking his head.

"I wanted to see my babies. I'd do anything to get here." *For you.*

Gray met his stare before he looked down at the twins. "I'm amazed the boys haven't woken up yet." He reached for them.

Rohan passed the basket back over before he leaned in and pressed a gentle kiss to both their heads. He lifted his stare and wanted one more kiss.

Gray seemed to sense it and reared back, eyes wide. He reached for the door and scrambled out before Rohan touched him again.

Once the omega was safe inside with their children, Rohan lowered the raised partition between him and the driver.

"Home, sir?"

"Yes," Rohan said, even though all he wanted was to stay. He gave the cottage one last glance before they sped away.

* * * *

Needing to inhale…

Gray could barely breathe through the want pulsing within him. He leaned against the door, drawing in air, his body shaking with need. The looks Rohan had given him had burned him through and through—and were the complete opposite of the words the man had spoken days before.

There had been *want* in Rohan's eyes.

His cock had been hard and throbbing under Gray's ass.

Gray closed his eyes and demanded his traitorous body calm. He lowered the basket, and the alpha began to howl. He smiled. Jamie. The boys finally had names, and he was happy for it.

Gray lifted Jamie into his arms and soothed the boy before Silver awoke and began to bawl, too. Although, it would likely happen any minute, as any time the two were apart, they weren't happy.

A knock came to the door as he cradled Jamie in his arms. He frowned. Had Rohan come back? Before he could open the door, Silver began to cry, making Jamie begin to cry again.

Gray whipped open the door, exasperated.

A stranger stood outside, not Rohan's driver.

"Gray Tomlinson?"

"Yes?"

A pack of papers was thrust at him. He took them.

"You've been served."

Gray sighed and watched the beta wander away from his door.

Lovely. While trying to cradle the babe, he ripped open the packet and looked inside.

Wynter and Warden Jaymes... suing for full custody of his children.

Gray looked down at the papers while both twins howled crying and felt completely defeated in that moment. *Oh gods, give me strength.*

"Need some help?"

Gray looked over his shoulder at Lake and Auggie. The boys stood at the base of the stairs.

"I would *love* some help," Gray said, shutting the door the rest of the way. He turned to his nephews and smiled, thankful.

Lake came over and took Jamie from his arms while Auggie grabbed the basket. "I'll go warm some bottles for them," he said as he watched the boys carry the twins into the family room. After one last glance at the summons, he wandered into the kitchen to warm two bottles.

Once they were ready, he handed one to Lake and helped get Jamie started. Then he turned his attention to Auggie and Silver. After nestling the baby into Auggie's arms, he helped his nephew hold the bottle at the right angle.

He smiled watching his brother's children caring for his own. Tears came into his eyes as he watched them. "The boys have names now."

"What are they?" Auggie asked.

Gray nodded to the alpha child. "Jaymes… and we'll call him Jamie." He looked to the littlest. "And Silver."

"Like papa?" Auggie asked.

Gray nodded, trying to hold back his tears.

"I like it," Auggie whispered, looking delighted to be holding his papa's namesake. Gray turned to look at Lake and saw the teen's eyes were full and shining.

"What's wrong?"

Lake shook his head. "Nothing. It's a good name. A really good name."

Gray placed a hand on Lake's knee. "I'm glad you approve."

Lake wiped a tear and looked away. When he turned his gaze on baby Jamie, he smiled. "We got our family with us after all."

Gray nodded. "And I'm going to do everything in my power to keep it together."

"Good," Lake replied. "Although, I'd like to vote for less crying in the middle of the night so I can sleep."

"Oh, this is just the start of things," Gray said, grinning. "Just wait until they're three or four and following you two around like little shadows."

Lake eyed Auggie. "As if I don't have enough of that already."

Auggie gave Lake some side-eye. "I'm a big brother now," the boy said. "So I don't need you anymore."

"Technically, you're a cousin," Lake shot back. "Do you not know how family works?"

"Well, I'm a big *cousin*. I've got responsibilities now."

"There's no such thing as a big cousin."

"Yes there is!" Auggie looked at Gray. "I'm a big cousin, aren't I?"

Gray smiled, brushing a hand over Auggie's head. "A big cousin?" He cocked a brow at Lake before looking at Auggie. "Indeed you are."

* * * *

A few days later…

Gray paced Tensen's office. Avery sat in one corner, watching over Silver as Gray carried Jamie in his arms. Rohan's voice boomed over the speaker on Tensen's desk.

"I'm looking over the original contract now, and it's airtight. Jamie's rights were revoked—so Wynter and Wilder technically can't use their claim as his parents to gain access to the children." He sighed. "But they do know people in the right places. They likely won't give in. Knowing Wynter Jaymes, he definitely *won't* back down. He and Jamie are too alike in some ways."

"Dog with a bone?" Tensen asked.

"Exactly," Rohan's voice rang out.

"Well then, it looks like we'll have to go to court," Tensen said.

"But they have no case, right?" Gray asked.

Tensen shrugged. "In our opinion, yes. But I know too well that it depends on the judge and his interpretation of the law. Surrogacy laws have too many gray areas. I try to write contracts to protect everyone as best as I can, but this is an odd case."

"Plus it depends on how much cash Warden's willing to use to grease a palm or two," Rohan added. "He can gain favor with enough."

"We still have Jamie's will to read. There's something there that will help our case."

"And you can't tell us until it's read," Rohan said. "Are the Jaymeses still dragging their feet in agreeing to a meeting?"

"They are. My guess is they might know there's something there to help your case. They'll push to have the case heard before the reading."

"You representing us and handling the will could be called a conflict of interest and bring Jamie's will up for dissection," Rohan said.

"You have a point." He looked at Gray. "Perhaps you two would be better in finding another solicitor."

"I can handle the case," Rohan said. "Perhaps use you as a sounding board until we go in to see the judge—since you are the one who wrote the surrogacy agreement."

Tensen nodded. "Of course." He eyed Gray a moment before eyeing the speaker. "There's one suggestion I would be remiss if I didn't make."

"And that is?" Rohan asked.

"If you claimed Gray as your omega, it would strengthen your case. Judges like to see happy families raising babies. They likely wouldn't take a child from an AO pair."

Gray stopped mid-step and glared at Tensen. The other end of the speaker went silent.

"I didn't ask him to say that," Gray spat. "And I don't think it's a good idea, either."

"But you have to see how it would benefit?" Tensen asked.

"To help win custody, sure. But then what?" Gray asked.

"You'd be free," Tensen murmured. "And you could raise your children instead of sharing custody. They wouldn't have to be shuffled back and forth, like little nomads."

"I'd be a glorified babysitter. No thank you," Gray said.

Still, nothing came from Rohan's side.

"Don't worry," Gray called out. "We're moving on."

"Actually… Tensen has a point," Rohan's voice rang out over the speaker.

Gray turned to look at the little box, aghast. "No."

"Wynter and Warden will likely use the fact we're not together as weapon to fight against us. We would take away their ammunition. And like Tensen said. Judges *do* like babies with a mated pair. Wynter and Warden have that. They've been together for nearly forty years."

Gray walked closer to the desk, shaking his head as if Rohan could see him. "It might save us now. But later… we'll resent one another and it'll turn into a nightmare. I won't be with a man who wants nothing more than to be as far away from me as possible just to win this case. And I won't subject the children to the fallout of that failure of a relationship."

More silence at the other end.

"Of course. You're right," Rohan finally said. "It would be a mistake."

Gray did everything in his power to not let those words crush him. He held little Jamie closer to him and closed his eyes.

"We need to push for the reading, Tensen. Do you think we could get an injunction to stop any court proceedings without the reading of Jamie's will?"

"You could try," Tensen said. "But they might claim you were dragging things out. Might make the judge more sympathetic to them."

"All they'd have to do was attend the reading and it would proceed," Gray said. "That makes no sense. This game of chess played out in a courtroom simply makes no sense to me."

"If they can drag things out and make it appear that it is your fault, it could get them a visitation. And then there's a chance they might not return the children… and then they drag things out even longer, so they could hold on to your children."

Gray shook his head. He didn't want Wynter Jaymes around the twins.

"If there's something there to help us in that will, we need to push. Set the date for next week. If they don't show up, set it for the week after. And again for the week after that. If they're no-shows three times, by law the will can be read without them on the fourth," Rohan said.

"That's true," Tensen said, scribbling down a note. "Good plan. Consider yourselves both notified the reading of the will will take place next Thursday at three."

"Understood," Rohan replied.

"Same," Gray murmured.

Tensen lifted his stare. "So you're aware, Gray's pass expires today. I had hoped to have it read by now, but that's just not been the case. We'll have to set up a conference room on the border."

"Oh," Rohan said.

"For the first three, Gray won't be allowed into the room unless all are in attendance, so you won't be able to see one another for a month," Tensen said. "He'll be allowed into the fourth and final, with or without the Jaymeses in attendance, as it will be read one way or another."

Gray cringed. A month without Rohan? But then, he needed to get used to *a life* without Rohan.

"I've hired a manny," Rohan said. "I can send him to help at your house… and he can bring the boys to visit me on the weekends, perhaps?"

"I think we have a full enough house as it is without a manny floating around. But he can come pick up the boys each Friday and take them to you on the weekends," Gray said.

"Thank you," Rohan said.

Tensen interrupted. "I'll leave the rest in your capable hands, Rohan. I'll see you both over the next few weeks."

"I'll call with more details about the boys, Gray. Until then, be safe. Take care of my boys."

"Of course," Gray said before Rohan clicked off.

Gray breathed a sigh once the line went dead. Tensen eyed him, but said nothing. He turned to look at Avery.

"Idiot," Avery murmured.

"Agreed," Tensen added behind him.

"How was I an idiot?"

"You should've said yes," Avery said, rising and lifting the basket with Silver in it.

"He doesn't want me."

"Of course he does," Tensen said.

"I didn't ask for your input," Gray tossed over one shoulder.

"Ah, yes you did," Tensen said. "I'm your solicitor."

"*Were*," Gray added, but then felt bad about it. He turned to look at Tensen. "You've done an amazing job helping me. *Thank you.*"

Tensen smiled. "No worries. Rohan's going to get my bill."

Gray chuckled, shaking his head.

And wondering if he hadn't just made a huge mistake, just as they said.

* * * *

Over in the Family Quadrant...

Rohan hung up the phone and stared at it a moment, aching inside. He'd opened the door, hoping to see that Gray wanted to take the chance.

Instead, the omega had effectively slammed it shut.

"You, my friend, are too smart to be this stupid," Wilder said.

"What did I do?"

"Instead of telling Gray you love him and want him and the babies in your life, you toss him a bone. One without any meat, I might add. No wonder he told you to go fuck yourself."

"You can leave any time you want," Rohan spat, dragging the files Wilder had brought closer. "Is there much point in me reviewing these? I figured I was out of a job, all things considered."

"I told father that it would look bad for his case if he fired you and was the cause of your loss of income." Wilder smiled. "When he said he didn't care, I told him I'd resign if he fired you."

Rohan sat up straighter. "What? You wouldn't."

"Wouldn't I? I can start at the bottom if I have to. And I know a damned good attorney who'd be at my side in a minute when I started my own company."

The thought of working for Wilder and not Warden had him excited. "I don't want you destroying your chances to take over the family business on my account."

Wilder smiled wanly. "I promised Jamie I'd look out for you and Gray. A promise is a promise." He rose to his feet. "And just so we're clear, I'm still Uncle Wild to the babies. Just because my parents lose out, I shouldn't have to."

Rohan smiled. "Of course, Uncle Wild."

Wilder grinned. "Now... back to the wooing of your new omega."

"I'm really *not* discussing this with you."

"Go to him. Beg him for forgiveness. And then beg him to marry you."

Rohan sighed. "And he'd always wonder if I did it for the babies. No, I think his mind is set. After the things I said, who could blame him?"

Wilder gave him an exasperated look. "Idiot."

Rohan glared at his brother-in-law. Wilder waved before leaving the office and shut the door behind him. Soon after, he grabbed Jamie's phone from the drawer and turned it on before gazing at the picture on the screen for the millionth time. Wondering if there were any others, he unlocked the phone and began to scroll through, looking for more pictures.

He found the gallery and began sorting through, smiling at some of the antics Gray and Jamie had gotten up to. How happy they'd been… it nearly broke him to see it.

Then he came to a video. Jamie's smiling face was frozen with the play symbol over his face. Rohan stared at it for a moment before he got the courage to hit play.

Jamie's lean face lit up the screen.

"Hi Rohan. How are you?"

Rohan sat up a little straighter.

"If you're watching this, then I'm likely gone." He paused, looking away from the screen for a moment before turning back, his smile wide. "The thought of leaving you, Gray, and the babies breaks my heart, but the one thing that keeps me going is knowing that you'll have each other to lean on. I know I pushed you both hard in the direction I wanted you to go, but in my mind, I was planting a seed." He smiled again, and it nearly took Rohan's breath away. "But, in all truth, I didn't need to plant anything. There's a bond between Gray and you that has been there from the start. You think I didn't see how you both reacted to one another during your first meeting? It reminded me of the reaction you and I had so long ago. In that moment, there was no doubt in my mind that he was yours, too."

Rohan gasped.

"I don't know how or why or what brought him into our lives other than it was fate for me to meet him and bring him to you. He is your mate, as much as I am. Can you imagine a world where we'd never met? Never loved? Never slept side by side in the same bed? Never dreamed of a forever together?" He paused. "I can't imagine that world. And I doubt you can, either. Gray is just as much yours as I was… and if you refuse him, it would be like refusing me. Refusing to have that love you both deserve in your lives." Jamie paused and wiped a tear from his eye. "I don't know how much time has passed since I died and you watching this. Too soon and I can imagine you trying to be gallant and refusing him out of love for me. Too long and I worry the light inside you will have died. Not only will you have lost me, but him, too. And if that happens, you won't be long for this world, either. I hope you've seen this in time. In time to know that you *need* him to get through this pain. You're not being honorable to him at all. You're making the both of you suffer for no good damned reason, and I won't have it." Jamie smiled. "He's the brother of my heart, and I *want* you both to be happy." Jamie smiled, reaching for the phone. "I love you, Rohan. *To the moon and back*. I always will. And I love Gray. I'll be watching you both from above." Jamie blew a kiss at the screen before the video ended.

Rohan sat there for a long time, staring at the screen. He played it again, wanting to memorize the words and the curves of Jamie's face. After, he turned the phone off and lifted it to his lips. "I love you, baby."

Shoving the phone back in the drawer for safekeeping, he rose and headed upstairs. This time, he turned toward the room Gray had stayed in. He opened the door, and the omega's scent filled his nose. Weak, but it was there.

He strolled through the room, looking to see if there was anything the man had left behind. Seeking to be closer to Gray somehow. The drawers were empty, as was the closet. Rohan sat on the edge of the bed and stretched his neck. That's when a book on the nightstand caught his attention.

A History of the Omega.

Rohan lifted the book and breezed through it, getting another whiff of Gray's scent. He scanned one of the pages and read a few paragraphs.

And frowned.

Before reading on…

Chapter Thirty

A month later...

Rohan fidgeted in the small chair in Armond Terizano's office. The lawyer was one of Tensen's partners and was ready and prepared to read the will. Wilder and Vaughn sat opposite him, quiet as they waited for the fourth and final meeting. The will would be read today. But there was no sign of Wynter, Warden, *or* Gray and the boys. Rohan could care less about the two former, he was more worried about the latter. If *both* the Jaymeses *and* Gray didn't show that day, they would have to start the cycle again and wait several weeks to read the will.

He didn't expect Jamie's parents to come. Today was all about seeing his omega and his babies, and getting Jamie's will read. When the door finally opened and Gray bustled in, looking exhausted, Rohan released a sigh of relief. He jumped to his feet and took the basket and bag from Gray's hands.

"Sorry I'm late," Gray said, looking exhausted and frazzled. "It's a lot harder to get around with babies than I ever realized."

"You need some help," Rohan said before looking down at the boys. Both were awake and bright eyed. He grinned down at them, and Silver cooed up at him. "I'm ready to help all you need."

Rohan sat down and lifted Jaymes from the basket, cradling the infant in one arm. "Help me with Silver," he murmured to Wilder.

His brother-in-law lifted the tiny omega from the basket and nestled him into Rohan's arm. Rohan relaxed once they were both in his grasp. He leaned back in the chair and just looked at them, memorizing their faces.

And realized they both had Gray's eyes.

He lifted his gaze and caught his omega staring at him. Jamie's words repeated in his head, coupled with his own instinct. This was his male, the papa of his children. Rohan wanted them all home where they belonged.

He'd made the offer, albeit a terrible one but denied all the same. Now it was time to make a better one. Now that he knew the truth. Gray was his omega, too. And his omega deserved to be honored.

Jaymes rubbed his face against Rohan's chest. Soon after, he bellowed and Silver followed. Gray began to frantically search through the baby's bag, but didn't seem to find what he was looking for. "Damnit," he whispered before standing up straight. He looked to the babies. "I left their bottles on the counter, it seems."

"So what? Do I need to send a car for them?" Rohan asked.

"That would take an hour at least," Gray said. "I'll have to take them home."

"No," Rohan said. "If you're not here either, and Wynter and Warden show up—we start again. Another month."

Gray stared at the babes a moment. "Then I have no other choice. I can't make them wait an hour to be fed." Gray blew out a breath before shaking his head. He sat down beside Rohan and began to unbutton his tunic. Rohan sat up straighter, suddenly realizing what was about to happen.

"Out," he spat at Wilder and Vaughn.

"I'm just feeding the babies. There's nothing wrong with them being here."

Rohan didn't exactly agree. His protective instinct wouldn't have two other alphas in the room while his omega nursed their babes. "Out," he repeated.

Vaughn and Wilder rose, as did the solicitor, and they wandered out just before Gray lifted Silver out of his grip and toward one nipple. Rohan watched in amazement as the babe latched on and began to nurse hungrily.

"Hand me Jamie, please."

Rohan carefully place the larger alpha babe in Gray's arms and watched as their second child latched on to Gray's nipple. Both were swollen with his milk, but still small. Gray leaned back into the chair as the babes nursed. Rohan could only watch in admiration.

"This isn't good," Gray said. "I've been pumping for them and bottle feeding."

"Not good how?"

"I'm not exactly used to them nursing. And if they prefer this to the bottle, we'll have problems."

Rohan caressed his sons' heads as they drank greedily. "Does that happen?"

Gray looked down. "Some babies refuse a bottle once they've had the real thing. If that happens, we could have issues on future visits to your house."

"Meaning they couldn't come without you."

Gray shrugged slightly. "Let's hope all the bottle feeding I've already done has got them accustomed to that."

"Would it really be so terrible if you had to come with them?" Rohan asked as he brushed a hand over Jaymes' head.

Gray looked at him. Rohan lifted his stare and saw the question in his omega's eyes. He knew it was past time for him to beg for that forgiveness he didn't deserve.

"The things I said..." He paused, searching for the right words. He had no decent excuse for what he'd done.

"Don't," Gray whispered, looking away. "I can't do this right now. I've had the worst day today. I haven't slept in over a month. I'm stretched too thin and ready to break. I'm just holding on by a thread, Rohan. I *can't* today."

Rohan knew he only had a small chance here. He wasn't going to stop things. "I was wrong."

"You only said what you truly felt," his omega said, stiffening.

"No," Rohan said.

"What's done is done," Gray said, ignoring him. "And it's for the best, really. Now we can raise our children. Separately, but together, the truth laid out between us. No expectations. We just need to get through this case."

"What I said wasn't the truth."

Gray's lower lip wobbled.

"It wasn't anywhere *near* the truth." Rohan reached over and cupped Gray's cheek. He drew Gray's face to the side, until their eyes met. "I *love* you, Gray. And I've missed you so much these weeks apart... and I don't want to be apart another moment."

Gray met his stare. His gaze searched Rohan's face for a moment. Then he looked away. "I thought I meant *nothing* to you?"

"I said a lot of awful things in anger that day... that anger was at me, not you. I'm sorry I hurt you. I was trying to push you away..." Rohan leaned in closer. "Because I thought what I felt for you was wrong. That it diminished Jamie somehow. Now I know that's not what it is, this love I feel for you."

Gray looked at him. "What changed your mind?"

Rohan smiled. "Jamie and I had a conversation. And you also left a book at my house that confirmed a lot of the things we've all felt."

Gray eyed him, confused. And then a realization seemed to dawn on him. "The history book."

Rohan nodded. "And I read it... have you?"

Gray looked away. "I have. We can't know that's what's going on here. It's a theory, at best."

"Theory or not, I think we both know the attraction we feel isn't something either of us can ignore." Rohan cupped the side of Gray's face.

"Instinct because of the babies."

"It's more, and you know it. I feel it even now. Do you?"

Gray lifted his stare, and it was apparent without words that he did.

"Add in our children... add in the fact I'm in love with you... add in the fact you and Jamie loved one another as brothers and he *wanted* this for us... I want you at home, where you belong. With our babies."

Gray held Rohan's stare. "Not a glorified babysitter?"

"No," Rohan said. "As my mate... as my *omega*. The honored papa of our children." He leaned in and kissed Gray's lips. "I love you. And I *think* you love me, too."

Gray smiled, one eyebrow cocking. "Oh?"

"You *did* tell me once."

His omega smiled, looking perplexed. "I did?"

"After you gave birth. You were *so* drugged, so I didn't truly believe it. Of course I wanted to, but I couldn't let myself." He paused and saw Gray's slight smile. "If you don't... if it was the drugs and not what you feel in your heart... maybe you can learn to love me, too."

Gray's lip trembled as he opened his mouth. "I already do."

Rohan rested his forehead on Gray's, holding the back of his omega's head. He released a shuddering breath, his whole body shaking. He captured Gray's lips, starving for the kiss he'd waited over a year to taste again.

Gray kissed him back, just as hungrily.

Rohan lifted a hand and suddenly remembered they weren't alone. He backed away and chuckled as he looked down on his twins. Both were half asleep, still nursing away. He leaned in and watched his boys.

"They're beautiful," Rohan whispered before looking up at Gray. "We make beautiful babies."

Gray smiled.

Rohan looked back to their children and smiled. He wanted more... he wanted to have another time when he could love and cuddle his swollen mate and love the man as he deserved. He would dote the next time around... and let the instinct rule him.

Instead of fighting it every step of the way.

Silver was the first to release his hold on a nipple.

"Grab a towel from the bag and get to burping, daddy," Gray said.

"Glad to," Rohan said. He'd gotten a little practice during his weekends with the boys. Now he'd get to be there every night, as well. He grabbed the towel and their omega before resting the babe on his shoulder. Rohan patted softly, watching as Jaymes finally finished his meal.

"Well, isn't this lovely?"

Rohan looked up and saw Wynter and Warden watching them. Part of him hated that the pair had witnessed any of their private moments together. But another part was thrilled they'd actually shown up, late or not.

Wilder peeked in and eyed Rohan. "I couldn't stop them."

"Might as well get back in here and let's get this thing over with," Rohan said as Gray righted his tunic.

Everyone slipped back into the room quietly. Terizano went to his desk and pulled out the will. "If everyone is in agreement and ready for the reading, I'll begin."

No refusals were made, so the man began.

Most of it was basic legal formalities. Jamie had little that he'd owned coming into the marriage, but technically, he did have some claim on part of the marriage properties. "As for the share of the shared assets via marriage, Jaymes Parker has assigned those to Mr. Gray Tomlinson, Mr. Rohan Parker, and any living children between the pair, including any liquid assets, home, and belongings, other than those assigned to Mr. Wilder Jaymes."

The attorney continued. "To Mr. Wilder Jaymes, Jaymes Parker assigns his photo albums from their youth and a small jewelry box containing a ring, given to him by his grandpapa. A note is left here, that Wilder should give it to his mate, as it was their grandpapa's wedding ring."

Rohan eyed his brother-in-law. Wilder lifted a brow, but said nothing.

Terizano turned the page. "As for Mr. Vaughn Jaymes, Mr. Wynter Jaymes, and Mr. Warden Jaymes, they are to receive nothing but Jaymes' wishes they can find happiness once he is gone."

"Of course," Wynter said. "I wonder why we bothered coming. He had nothing to give."

"He had love," Gray spat. "And you're all poorer for never realizing it. Now you'll never have the chance again, and I hope it haunts you for the rest of your lives."

Wynter eyed him scathingly before looking to Warden. "It's time to leave."

"Wait," Terizano said. "There's one more part here you need to hear."

Wynter sat back and crossed his arms.

"In regards to the children born of the surrogate, Mr. Gray Tomlinson, I, Jaymes Parker, hereby release any and all legal claims to the children. The rights revert to Mr. Tomlinson and my alpha, Rohan Parker. I do not want my parents, Wynter and Warden Jaymes, to play any role in their lives for they've never given me one ounce of love or affection, and I refuse for them to harm the children in the same way."

Rohan smiled. *Good job, Jamie.* He looked at Jamie's parents and saw them both tight-lipped. "I'd say any judge that heard that would have to be insane to give you two custody."

"Maybe they could just do the right thing and give up. Instead of causing more pain," Wilder said, giving his parents a glare.

"Fine," Wynter said to Wilder.

"We gave you boys *everything*," Warden said. "And this is the thanks we get?"

"I've always wondered how you and Jamie managed to be halfway decent people with *them* as parents," Rohan said.

"They did give us everything," Wilder said. "Including a *really* good manny, Alberto." Wilder looked at Vaughn. "Too bad papa fired him when you were a baby. Maybe you wouldn't be such a shitshow."

Vaughn laughed sarcastically before he rose and eyed the attorney. "Can I go now?"

Terizano nodded.

"Good," Vaughn said before leaving.

Warden eyed Rohan. "Remember that warning I gave you a while back?"

He shook his head. "You were wrong. I gained *everything* by being weak for my omega."

"Well, you lost something. Your job," Warden said.

Wilder coughed.

"Go ahead and quit. See if I care!" Warden railed at Wilder.

"What?" Wynter said, looking between them.

"I told father I'd quit if he fired Rohan," Wilder said.

"You *wouldn't*," Wynter said.

Wilder smiled. "Oh, I believe I just did."

Wynter turned to Warden. "There goes your retirement. And our travel plans. No... I won't have this!"

Warden pushed Wynter out. "We'll discuss this in the car."

Once they were both out, Wilder laughed. "I'll get a call before I get home demanding I stay. And I'll demand your job back when he calls."

"To be honest, I don't think I want to work with your father any longer. I waited as long as I could, hoping you were in line for his chair, but it's been too long."

Wilder grinned. "What you don't know is... my father wants to retire. Papa has travel plans and wants to tour the world before he grows too old to enjoy it. If I leave, my papa doesn't get what he wants... and we both know my papa always gets what he wants." His smile grew. "Stay? I promise to protect you until I'm running the show."

Rohan sighed. "You're already nearly running the show."

"In theory, yes." Wilder tilted his head. "Stay?"

"I will. For you," Rohan said.

"Wait... they were planning to travel? Wouldn't two infants have gotten in the way?" Gray asked.

"Mannies raised my brothers and I. My parents either would've left the twins in the care of mannies or dragged the whole show along with them on parade through Eurasia and the Golden Isles, I'm sure."

"But what would've been the point?" Gray asked. "If they didn't *want* the children?"

"Who knows?" Wilder said. "My best guess? Appearances. My papa would've made himself out to be some kind of martyr to his friends and acquaintances more than likely. Everything is about what people think of them... hell, even the fact they attempted to fight will be a long story Papa tells over drinks. I can almost hear him now. How the legal system destroyed his chances at raising Jamie's poor, papaless children."

"Your parents are a piece of work," Gray said to Wilder.

Wilder nodded. "They are."

"Our children won't be papaless." Rohan turned to Gray, offering a hand. "You ready to make this thing official?"

Gray laced his fingers through Rohan's and nodded.

Wilder looked between them. "Official?"

Rohan turned to the lawyer. "Anyone in your office able to broker a claiming?"

Wilder slapped his hands together. "Wooo! Perfect timing." He grinned. "I can be the witness."

Terizano smiled. "I'm happy to do it... but I think perhaps someone else might want to play a role in this union."

Rohan frowned and looked down at Gray, who shrugged.

Who else is there?

* * * *

A beginning at the end...

Gray's heart beat a mile a minute. He'd called Avery and begged his nephew to leave work early and pick up the boys—and the bottles he'd neglected to

His Surrogate Omega

bring. He wanted his family there when he was bound to Rohan. And they arrived just in time.

All three stood behind them. Avery watched over the babies so Gray could focus on his alpha. Wilder stood to Rohan's left, seeming a bit anxious himself.

"We're gathered here to witness the claiming of Gray Calais Tomlinson by Rohan Williamson Parker," Tensen said, a broad smile on his face. He looked down on the scrap of paper Rohan had dug up on the internet, an ancient set of vows. "Rohan, do you promise to protect, comfort, love, and honor Gray, in sickness and in health, from this day forth… until the day of your death?"

Rohan turned to Gray and smiled. "I do."

"Do you, Gray, promise to protect, comfort, love, and honor Rohan, in sickness and in health, from this day forth until the day of your death?"

Gray smiled up at him. "I do."

"Rohan, place the ring on Gray's finger." Tensen paused and lifted his head from the printed piece of paper. "Sorry, do you have a ring? I'm not familiar with this old ceremony."

Rohan reached into his pocket, smiling. He'd apparently come prepared. "I do."

Gray gasped, wide-eyed.

"Place the ring on Gray's finger, a circle, the symbol of your everlasting love."

Rohan took Gray's hand and slipped the circle of gold down Gray's ring finger before he handed another gold band to his omega. "Your turn."

"Gray, place the ring on Rohan's hand, a circle, the symbol of your everlasting love."

Gray's eyes teared up as he slipped the ring onto Rohan's finger. He loved Rohan, and never imagined they'd end up where they were. It almost felt like a dream. One he feared he'd awaken from too soon.

"If there's no one here with any reason for these two not to be wed—"

Jaymes let out a howl, making them all laugh.

"I'll assume that's hunger, gas, or a full diaper," Tensen continued. "If there's no one here with any objection, then it is my *honor* and privilege to pronounce these two husband and wife." Tensen looked at the paper again. "Wife? What's a wife?" He shook his head and looked up. "Husband *and husband.*" Tensen looked down at the paper. "Kiss your bride? Whatever a bride is."

Rohan chuckled and drew Gray closer. "I think I'll kiss my *husband.*"

He captured Gray's lips. Gray melted against his alpha. His body quickened, ready for the rest of the claiming...

Only he wasn't ready for that. He was almost healed from the birth, but the doctor hadn't yet given him the green light. And he'd yet to have a heat, which wasn't uncommon right after a birth, but it again said his body wasn't ready for more.

He wanted it... and could sense Rohan did, too.

"Okay, you two. Get a room. We have underage eyes in here," Avery said.

Gray parted from Rohan. He turned to look at their new little family and smiled.

"We have Jamie to thank for all this," Gray said, reaching over to Wilder. "And knowing you were here, standing up for us in his place means the world."

Wilder took Gray's hand and kissed his knuckles before his stare seemed to drift to Avery. "Trust me," he murmured. "I'm glad to have you as a part of the family."

Gray glanced at Avery, who appeared to be working very hard to avoid Wilder's stare.

"Why don't we go out to celebrate?" Gray said, turning to Rohan. "Dinner with everyone before we go home."

Rohan looked a little disappointed for a split second, but he nodded. "Of course. Wherever you wish to go, mate."

Gray smiled up at him. *Mate*. He liked the sound of that.

"I don't know. I have an early class in the morning," Avery said, his stare flitting to Wilder.

"Your uncle only gets married once in his life," Rohan said. "Come. Celebrate with us."

Gray saw Avery's discomfort and sensed something between his nephew and Wilder. "It won't be too long. I need to get the babies to bed at a decent hour."

Avery nodded. "Okay then."

Auggie rushed forward and wrapped his arm around Gray's waist. "Does this mean we can live in the big house again?"

"Oh?" Lake said. "Can we?"

"You'd seriously just *abandon* me?" Avery asked.

"Well… yeah," Lake said. "Have you seen their house? And I could be back with my friends. Better school. Better community. Better *everything*."

"Don't get ahead of yourself," Gray said. "Rohan, Avery, and I will have to discuss the arrangement."

"If it would help Avery focus on school," Rohan said. "I don't mind. Actually, if Avery would be closer to school and work, we have room for him, as well."

Gray knew the alpha was supposed to care for the omega and his family responsibilities, but he couldn't ask too much of Rohan. They'd barely found their own footing, as it was.

"See. Rohan doesn't mind," Lake said, smiling at Avery.

"We'll talk about it," Avery said, shoving Lake and Auggie out of the office.

Rohan walked over and collected the basket with the babies and their bag. Wilder stepped closer to Gray.

"Your nephew's in college," Wilder asked.

"Yes," Gray answered.

"He's a beta?"

Gray tensed, hating to lie. "Yes."

Wilder frowned.

"Why?"

Wilder shook his head. "I got this weird… *vibe*. At the funeral and now here, too. It's only when he's around."

"A vibe?" Gray asked.

"Almost like…" Wilder frowned even more. "If he's a beta…" Wilder shook his head. "Never mind. I'm apparently imagining things."

Gray sucked in a breath. Was Wilder sensing Avery was an omega…? If so, he needed to let his nephew know to be more careful.

"Imagining things?"

Wilder smiled before he shoved a hand through his head. "I work too much. And now, after losing my brother..." He smiled again, a little sadness seeping into it. "I just need to get some rest and refocus."

Rohan offered Gray an arm, which he took, and the three of them headed for the door.

"I wish you luck," Gray murmured. "You've been more than kind to me. I hope you find some peace."

Wilder smiled down at him. "Maybe now that this is all settled and I've completed my promise to Jamie—maybe now I can find some peace."

Gray smiled up at him. "I hope you can."

"Peace? With a fight with your parents coming, I hate to say I doubt you'll find much peace."

Wilder sighed. "You're likely right."

Gray smiled up at him. "Well, let's forget about fights for one night. Tonight's a *celebration*."

* * * *

One more hurdle...

After dinner and the twins were down in their crib, Rohan joined Gray in their bedroom. For tonight, they were alone. Avery had taken his brothers home, and Rohan had sent the staff away. For his first night with his mate, he only wanted Gray and their children under the roof.

The bedroom they'd share was not the same one he'd shared with Jamie, but the one Gray had spent time in before. He approached Gray from behind and spread his hands on his omega's shoulders.

Gray immediately stiffened, and Rohan got flashes of the past—of being pushed away. He released his hold and stepped back.

His omega spun to face him. "Sorry... don't stop."

Gray turned again, waiting. Rohan released a breath and took a step, closing the gap. He lifted his hands to Gray's shoulders and massaged them again.

But Gray tensed again.

"What is it?" Rohan asked.

His omega sighed. "Two things, actually."

"Tell me."

Gray turned to face him. "One... I'm not fully healed from the birth yet. We can't have a full claiming," he said, his voice low.

"And the other?"

"I want to be with you... but..." he lifted his stare and looked around. "This is Jamie's house. The one you and he built together in hopes of a family. I suddenly feel out of place."

Rohan smiled. "I have something to show you. Come with me."

He led Gray down the twisting staircase and toward the back of the house. Once they were inside the sunroom, he flipped on the lights.

Gray gasped.

"This was Jamie's idea. He asked me to get everything ready, but then before he could show you, the babes came early and then, he passed." Rohan's stare washed over the art equipment, and then he turned to a wide-eyed Gray. "Jamie wanted you to feel at home here. He even suggested you come live here much earlier than you did. He saw this as your home, with us."

Gray met his stare.

Rohan turned to him. "If you truly *want* to move, we can. I'll sell this old place and buy you a home just as huge, with rooms we can one day fill with children." He looked around. "But a part of me loves that he haunts these walls. I don't want to forget him. He lives and breathes here still."

Gray nodded, tears in his eyes. "He does." He turned back to the studio they'd made for Gray. "I don't want to leave him behind, either."

Rohan cupped Gray's cheek and pressed a gentle kiss to his omega's lips. Gray kissed him back, hunger in the clench of his hands at Rohan's shirt.

"Can we go back up? I want to hold you in my arms tonight," Rohan said.

Gray nodded. He led Gray back up and spun to face him, stealing another kiss.

"I don't want to wait. I want you to know how much I want your touch. How much I wish I was ready for your full claiming," Gray murmured.

Rohan smiled and held the back of Gray's head so he could claim a kiss. He drank from his omega's mouth, greedy for those and nothing more.

"You're not mad, are you?" Gray asked.

Rohan leaned in and kissed his omega again. "You gave me two beautiful children. Your body endured pain and trauma from that... how could I be mad?"

Gray sighed a little in what looked like relief.

"Just let me hold you in my arms tonight. We have forever for the rest of it," Rohan whispered before kissing Gray again.

He wouldn't make demands of his omega. He was a patient man, and could wait. Rohan wanted it right... wanted Gray to find ecstasy in their pairing, not pain. But he *did* want to see Gray's naked body again, even if it would torture him until they could be together. Thoughts of his omega's nakedness had tormented his dreams, and he had to learn the curves again and compare them to the memories he had.

Slowly, he began to undo the ties on Gray's tunic, revealing an inch or so of skin with each one. Between each button, he stole another kiss until they were both breathless and shaking. He urged Gray toward the bed, dropping the tunic to the floor. His omega kicked off his shoes before Rohan lowered to his knees to peel Gray's pants off.

Once naked, Rohan looked his fill. He urged Gray to turn so he could see it all. Slick coated Gray's ass and inner thighs—and made it harder for Rohan to hold back. He leaned forward and trailed his tongue over it, tasting Gray's juices.

His omega trembled in his hands. Gray's knees nearly gave out, so Rohan urged him into the bed. He climbed in after his husband and laid himself between Gray's thighs, licking more of the slick away before he crawled closer and licked the length of Gray's hard cock.

A moan escaped his love before he took the head inside his mouth. More moans followed as he began to feast, swallowing Gray's hard staff to the back of his throat and out again for his lips to graze over the plump head. Gray's fingers slid through his hair, twisting in the strands, as he cried out with need.

Gray's body tensed more with each lick, each caress, until finally, he came in a rush. Rohan swallowed Gray's orgasm, loving the taste of his mate. When he'd licked Gray clean, his omega fell to the bed, boneless and writhing. Rohan smiled, pleased he'd helped his omega find release. He crawled up

Gray's body and wrapped his arms around his mate, loving he way their bodies fit together.

Gray brushed a hand through Rohan's hair before cupping his chin. "That was... amazing. But then, I didn't expect any less."

Rohan kissed his lips, letting Gray taste some of his release. "Nor did I."

"My turn," Gray said before trailing kisses down Rohan's neck.

Rohan smiled and lay back on the mattress as Gray went to work. He traveled down Rohan's neck and chest before pausing at one nipple. His omega sucked the tip inside his mouth, circling it with his tongue before moving on to the second. Rohan sighed, liking the attention and wondering if Gray's nipples were more sensitive now.

He reached down to squeeze one. Milk flowed over his fingers, and Gray moaned against him.

Definitely sensitive. Take note.

Rohan smiled, bringing his fingers to his lips and tasting the milk that flowed from Gray. His omega traveled farther down, crossing his abdomen and coming to the throbbing heat of him. He tensed as Gray's tongue circled the tip of his cock. When his omega sucked him in, he cried out, the sensation of it almost too much.

Gray's unpracticed licks and caresses proved overpowering. He fisted the sheets beside him, trying to hold on to the vestiges of his control. It had been a year since he'd been with Gray, the last time he'd had sex. Other than a few tugs from his own hand between, he'd been abstinent all those months between. And he'd been without for two years before that, too.

He felt like a schoolboy, ready to come in an instant. But he couldn't hold back. Gray's eager mouth, tongue, and fingers drew him to the edge quickly and his omega's lust-filled stare as he sucked was enough to toss him over the edge and into the abyss. Rohan came. Hard. He cried out Gray's name as his seed shot out.

And when he was empty, he crashed back to the bed, dazed. Gray crawled up and into his arms. Rohan dragged in closer, pressing his face into his omega's neck.

"I love you so very much," Rohan whispered against Gray's ear.

"And I love you," Gray whispered back, squeezing him even tighter.

* * * *

Near the next full moon…

Rohan lowered his briefcase in the foyer, hearing noises coming from the family room. As he approached the doorway, an exhausted looking Gray came out to greet him.

"What's wrong, my love?" he asked, lifting his omega's chin.

Gray smiled. "Nothing's wrong. I have *wonderful* news."

"Oh?"

"I've been to see the doctor today."

Rohan cringed. News from doctors, in his experience, was rarely good. "And?"

"I'm fully healed."

Rohan smiled wickedly. "Oh, are you now?" He kissed his omega, but noticed Gray seemed distracted. "Something's not quite right, though."

Gray sighed. "The full moon arrives tomorrow."

Rohan nodded.

"I'm likely going to go into heat."

Rohan grew quiet, the instinct within him growing.

"The doctor doesn't want me taking *Heat Repress* while the babies are still nursing, so I'll go into a full heat." He looked up at Rohan. "Are you ready for that?"

Rohan cupped Gray's face with one hand, excited by the prospect. A growl rose from his throat. "*Very* ready."

Gray moaned lowly. He turned to look toward the family room. "I'm struggling already," he whispered. "I can feel it coming. Felt it all day."

Rohan knew that omegas began to feel some of the early effects of their heat a day or two before the full moon. He could feel himself reacting to Gray's need. His cock thickened and he could scent the slick coating his omega. They needed to escape upstairs… but he hated to abandon the children to a manny… even if their manny was *wonderful*.

"You think we can sneak up early tonight and let the manny watch the boys?"

Gray met his stare. "*Yessss.*"

"Good," he whispered, cupping the back of Gray's head. "I want to care for you through your heat."

"Tonight's just the pre-game," Gray said with a smile.

"Which is likely better. We won't be controlled as much by the instinct," Rohan said. "And I can be gentler with you and get you well prepared before tomorrow comes."

Gray shuddered against him.

Rohan growled. He could scent Gray's slick coming even stronger, and it made him harder. When his omega rolled his hips, he feared he'd come right there in his pants.

"Let me kiss my babies," Rohan said, taking a step back. He pressed a kiss to Gray's lips. "And then I'll meet you upstairs in our bed."

Gray nodded before heading up. Rohan struggled to let his omega go, but he couldn't rush up without making sure the boys were safe and sound—and that their manny would tend to the children for the rest of the night.

After taking some long, deep breaths to gather his control and calm his raging body, he forced himself toward the family room. Once he got there, he gathered Silver into his arms from one of the rockers and kissed the happy gurgling child before the manny brought Jaymes over for another kiss.

"Hi, Uncle Rohan," Auggie said from where he sat beside Lake watching television.

Rohan walked over and eyed the boys. "Homework done?"

"Yes," they said in unison.

"Chores?"

Again, a dual "yes."

"Good. Your uncle and I are going to bed early tonight, so I want you to listen to Alberto."

Alberto smiled. "The full moon is upon us, hmm?"

Rohan blushed a little.

The older beta, the same manny who'd raised Jamie and Wilder, just smiled wider. "Good. Keep me in babies to raise. *Please.*"

Rohan knew they weren't ready for more children. Not yet. He'd wear protection to help prevent putting too much stress on his omega's body. But in time, he couldn't wait to fill Gray with another child or two. Or five. They had a big house to fill. "Let's give him a *little* break between, hmm?"

Alberto chuckled as he laid Jaymes into one of the rockers. "If you must." He came over to take Silver from him.

Rohan kissed his son, and moved over to the rocker to kiss Jaymes. He then stopped beside the couch. "Be good. I'll see you in the morning to check in."

"Check in?" Auggie asked.

"It's the moon time," Lake whispered hotly. "They'll be gone for days, remember?"

"Oh yeah," Auggie said. "Are we gonna have more cousins?"

"Someday, but not quite yet," Rohan answered.

"Okay," Auggie said with a grin.

Rohan ruffled Auggie's hair before he headed up to find his omega lying naked in the middle of their bed.

"Hi there, handsome," Gray whispered. "How about you get naked with me?"

Rohan released his tie with a grin. "You don't have to ask me twice."

* * * *

Pre-heat and more...

Gray trembled as he lay on the bed. He could feel his slick easing out, coating him. Watching Rohan's strip-show only added to the lust he felt. He did everything in his power to appear cool and collected—when all he wanted to do was crawl to the end of the bed and drag a half-naked Rohan into their bed.

It didn't take long for his alpha to climb in, smiling a sultry, come-hither smile.

Rohan slid a hand to the back of his head and captured his lips with a hungry kiss. Gray sighed against his alpha's mouth, opening for the tongue that speared inside and tasted him. Their tongues warred with one another, both eager to tempt the other higher.

When Rohan pinned Gray to the bed, his back arched under his alpha. Gray writhed against Rohan, the coming moon's effect on him taking a toll. But even without that, he wanted this claiming to happen. They'd been together for nearly a month now, unable to seal the pact begun in Tensen's office.

"Take me," Gray whispered, too far gone for niceties now. They'd had weeks of learning one another's body. Tasting... sampling... without having the whole treat. He was done playing games. He needed to feel Rohan deep inside him.

"I thought we were going to be gentle... careful?" Rohan asked between gentle kisses.

"Not too gentle," Gray said. "I need."

Rohan let out a growl before tugging on Gray's chin to lift his gaze. "A little rougher, hmm?"

Gray moaned. "*Yesss.*"

Rohan slid his hand over Gray's still short locks and tugged his omega's head back. And then he leaned in for a kiss... pausing less than an inch away. Gray moaned, writhing for that kiss.

"I shouldn't give in too easy," Rohan whispered. "Where's the fun in that?"

Gray trembled even harder, needful. "*Damn you.*"

"Oh... you don't mean that," Rohan said before giving him a barely there kiss. He lowered one of his hands and rested it on Gray's belly. "Do you want my seed to fill you here? And give you my baby?"

Gray shook with need. He wasn't ready for another child, not yet, but the instinct fired within. It was too strong for him to deny Rohan's words. He *did* want another child. He wanted to be big and round and tended to by his alpha.

His womb clenched within, and he moaned in pleasure.

"Oh... you do want my baby." Rohan slowly turned him over, their bodies sliding over one another. "I can't wait to fill you again... and watch you grow swollen with my babe. And this time... I can love you the way you deserve to be loved. Held close and protected. All while my seed grows within you."

Gray shook, his ass coated in slick. He could barely breathe... he trembled so hard, he worried he'd never stop. He could feel the head of Rohan's hard cock pressing against his slickened hole and pushed back against it.

"Wait," Rohan mumbled, pulling back.

Gods no. Gray looked over his shoulder as Rohan rose on his knees, shaking almost uncontrollably. The alpha reached into the nightstand drawer... and pulled out a condom package. Gray sighed in relief as he watched Rohan roll the condom on—protecting him so soon after the birth.

The words had been the instinct talking... building his need. His body would *always* wish to be pregnant by his alpha... and he'd been too far gone to say no. He was thankful Rohan was shielding him from harm.

And then he was there again, ready and hard behind Gray. Gray pushed back as he felt Rohan enter him. His slick was heavy, coating Rohan and allowing the huge cock to enter him without more than a slight pinch of pain. When Rohan was planted fully, he paused, trailing kisses along Gray's shoulder and giving them both time to adjust.

When Gray felt his body ease, he leaned forward a bit and then slid back down on Rohan's cock. It was all the alpha needed to know he was ready. Rohan took over, drawing out and back in again.

It was too slow at first. Gray urged Rohan faster, but his alpha refused him. His body remained in a pleasure-filled limbo... too good, yet not enough to push him over the edge. But when Rohan pressed him to the bed harder, gripping his hips even tighter, he knew his alpha had passed the point of return.

Rohan drove into him harder, faster. Gray sensed the rising need within Rohan, and he pushed back, meeting thrust for thrust. He turned his head and pressed his lips to Rohan's. "I love you, my alpha."

The man tensed, and he pushed the head of his cock against Gray's womb. Gray shuddered... his womb opening and accepting the head of the shaft within.

Rohan's cock knotted at the base, locking them together—and he came with a roar. His arms wrapped tight, just as the first wave of orgasm slammed into Gray. Gray's cock erupted, coating the sheet with his satisfaction. Rohan cradled him close, their bodies bound. Gray shook against Rohan as he felt the heat of the seed filling the end of the condom.

They fell to the bed together, Rohan's arms holding him close. Still locked together, they lay there, catching their breath, until the knot faded.

Rohan's hands massaged him all over. Gray had never felt so loved and cared for as he did then. He looked over his shoulder. "Thank you for wearing the condom. I hadn't even thought to buy any, and I should have."

His alpha smiled down at him. "Of course you're not ready for more now. You just healed from the last two." He carefully pulled out, gripping the base of the condom. "But you *do* want more someday, don't you?"

Once the condom was discarded, Gray turned to face Rohan. "I do… just not quite yet. The instinct was *so* strong. I wanted to tell you no babies, but I couldn't say the words." He felt heat filling his face. "And the things you said… they were driving me crazy."

Rohan pressed a soft kiss to his lips. "An omega in heat can only think about becoming pregnant. I was trying to get you excited. The problem is an alpha can only think about making you pregnant. I almost got lost in those words. I'm thankful I was able to stop long enough to put the condom on."

"Do we have enough for the next few days?"

Rohan nodded before nuzzling Gray's nose. "I'm ready and prepared, my love. No babies… not this time."

"But soon," Gray whispered, smiling.
Rohan smiled, too. "Soon."

Epilogue

Three years later...

"Don't forget, we need to be at the school at nine on Friday." Gray paused, smiling. He looked down at their year-old babe, Jasyn, nursing before lifting his stare again. "I can't believe Avery's graduating." Gray ran a hand down his expanding stomach as he watched Rohan bathing their three-year-old twins. Or more like they were bathing *him*. Both loved the water and made sure to splash everything in a ten-mile radius as best they could once inside it. Rohan was drenched... as was Gray and Jasyn all the way over at the counter.

"I can't believe he didn't get himself caught," Rohan said. Along the way, Rohan had figured out that Avery wasn't a beta and even if he hadn't, Gray didn't like lying to his alpha. He had been on the edge of spilling the beans for weeks before Rohan asked. "He's lucky he made it this far."

"Well, once he gets to work with you, you can help protect him," Gray said, checking Jasyn again.

"Do you really think him being in an office with Wilder is a good idea? I think he suspects something as it is."

Gray smiled. "I suspect something, too."

Rohan looked over his shoulder, looking completely clueless. "What?"

"Come on!"

Rohan shrugged. "What?"

"In four years, only two alphas figured out something was amiss with Avery. The first was when he was in heat and only on *Heat Repress*, so that one makes sense. The only other was your brother-in-law."

"So? Wilder's attention to detail is staggering. He must've noticed something. Which makes me even more nervous to have Avery there."

"What if Wilder noticed because he's Avery's alpha?"

Rohan's eyes got even wider. "Then this is a really, *really* bad idea, Gray. If Wilder's switch gets blown, he'll blow Avery's cover and then what?"

"Who better to protect Avery out in the world than his alpha?"

Rohan opened his mouth to argue, but got a mouthful of water. "Will you two stop it," Rohan cried, trying to sound like the authoritarian and alpha father was supposed to be, but that was hard to do with a wide smile on his face. "I'll have to replace the floors before you guys make it to eight."

"Sooner with how much you let them get away with," Gray murmured.

Their manny, Alberto, entered the bathroom just as Gray was finishing up with Jasyn. He took the sleeping babe. "It's amazing he can sleep through all this racket."

"Can you get him to bed? I'll help Rohan with the twins," Gray said to Alberto.

"Of course." The manny exited with Jasyn.

Rohan looked over his shoulder at Gray. "Are you ready for a naked butt? I think they're as clean as they're going to get."

Gray grabbed a towel. "Bring it on."

Rohan lifted Silver from the tub first, sending the little omega on his way to his papa. Gray wrapped the warm towel around the tyke before lifting him up and drying the wriggling child. His alpha lifted Jamie from the tub and did quite the same.

"Why are we doing this again?" Rohan said later, after they'd put both boys to bed and could hear them giggling from their bedroom.

"Because Jamie, Silver, and Jasyn bring joy to our lives… and we need an abundance of that. You said you wanted a tribe."

When the padding of little bare feet was heard, Rohan sighed and rose from the bed. "Exasperation, yes. Joy?" He grinned. "Yeah, I suppose they do."

A few minutes later, Rohan came storming into the bedroom, one twin under each arm. "Look who I found wandering in the hallway, papa!"

He tossed both boys onto the bed and then climbed in after them. Jamie and Silver curled up between them, smiling and giggling.

"You caught us, daddy!" Jamie said.

"I did!"

Alberto knocked on the door. "Do you need my help?"

"No, I think we can manage," Rohan said before he tickled both boys. Gray joined in. Soon Rohan was tickling Gray, which was even funnier to Jamie and Silver. They laughed in fits before finally crashing. One by one, Rohan carried the boys back to their bedroom and tucked them in. After he was done, he crawled back into his own bed and drew Gray into his arms.

"You ready to make a baby tonight?"

Gray frowned at his alpha. "We already have a baby coming, you dolt."

"Well, just because you have one coming doesn't mean I can't continue to enjoy the making part, right?" He rolled, pinning Gray to the bed. He smiled down and trailed a finger over Gray's lower lip. "That is... if you're interested."

"Hmmm? *Am* I interested?"

Rohan smiled. "We don't have much longer before you're too big and then after that, it's all about diapers and midnight feedings. We better enjoy the quiet before the storm."

"Well, when you put it that way, how could I refuse?" Gray said sarcastically.

Rohan smiled all the more. "You know what I mean..." He cocked a brow. "At least, I hope you do."

Gray lifted his head. "Of course I do."

And he kissed his mate.

Rohan wrapped an arm around his back and rolled them until Gray was on top.

"Oh? My alpha's going to let me lead, hmm?"

Rohan smiled and ran a hand down Gray's stomach. "I just noticed tonight how much you're showing. I don't want to hurt you *or* the baby. So... you lead. I'll follow."

Gray smiled, knowing just how lucky he was to have an alpha like Rohan. "I love you."

Rohan brought both of Gray's hands to his lips and kissed them, one after the other. "And I love you. To the moon and back."

Coming in 2019

An Omegaverse Book, Two

Omega Avery Stephens refuses to be the compliant, submissive mate he was raised to be. He's tired of being told he's less than and will have to wait for an alpha to come and 'save' him.

After his fathers die in a tragic accident, he must stand up and be responsible for his younger omega brothers. Knowing their savings will only go so far, he looks to the future. Avery will need an income and not the pittance an omega makes. He shears his long locks, purchases illegal scent blockers, and lies his way into college under the pseudonym Abraham Norcross, a beta.

Avery does everything in his power to prove an omega can be more than 'a womb with legs' but when he comes across his alpha, he struggles not to be the stereotypical weak and needy omega. Yet all he wants to do is go to his knees and beg the man to fill him with a child.

Can he find a path somewhere between heaven and hell—and still hold on to his self-respect?

Kelex

Find Kelex at Twisted E-Publishing

Omegaverse

The Omega Quadrant
His Surrogate Omega
Unexpected Heat – Short
Suddenly His Alpha – Short
His Reluctant Omega – COMING SOON

Alphas of the Western Provinces
One Wild Heat
One Wild Omega

*

Bear Mountain
Bound to Two Bears
Theirs by Bond, Book 1.5
Claimed by Two Bears
An Omega for Two Bears
Promised to Two Bears
A Second Chance with Two Bears
A Stag for Two Bears
Redemption for Two Bears
Surrendering to Two Bears
A Beta for Two Bears
A Sheriff for Two Bears
Finding His Two Bears
Cherished by Two Bears
Mated to Two Bears
A Marine for Two Bears
A Wolf for One Bear
A Bear for Two Big Cats
A Rhino for Two Bears

Kelex

A Homecoming for Two Bears
A Panther Comes Between Two Bears
A Decision for One Bear
A Monster for Two Bears

Project Zed
Beast
Savage
Devil,
Monster
Fire & Ice
Predator
Cyborg

Midnight Mississippi
Bearly Midnight
QuarterTil Midnight
Dead Til Midnight
Theirs by Midnight

*

Sacrificed
Sacrificed to the Harvest God
Sacrificed to the Sun God
Sacrificed to the Ice God
Sacrificed to the Gods of Spring
Sacrificed to the Mountain Gods

*

Hitman
Hitman
The Hitman's Weakness

His Surrogate Omega

Bloodlines
The Last Dire Wolf
Crying Wolf
His Wolven Warrior
Hungry for His Wolf

*

Novus Prime
Captured
Rescued

*

The Fire Dragon Trilogy
Rhaege, Fire Dragons, 1
Phrenzy, Fire Dragons, 2
Khaos, Fire Dragons, 3

Earth Dragons
Carreg
Graig

*

The Slave World Series
~Banned from Amazon!~
Book One: The Auction
Book Two: The Initiation
Book Three: The Training
Book Four: The Return

*

The Duke's Plaything
Part I & II

Kelex

Part III & IV
Part V & VI
Part VII & IX

*

The Master's New Toy
Part I & II
Part III & IV
Part V & VI

*

Bears in Bondage
Part I & II
Part III & IV

*

Wolves of Mt Alexis
Remy's Wolf
Rafe's Wolf
Theo's Wolf
Tristan's Wolf

*

Quads of Alpha S Series
Crash Landing
Tripp's Claiming
Wynne's Surrender
Adrian's Submission

*

Shifter Rebellion
Best Little Whorehouse on Planet X

His Surrogate Omega

The Whorehouse Oracle
The Forgotten Prince

*

Le Cachot
The Dungeon, Level One
The Dungeon, Level Two
The Dungeon, Level Three
The Dungeon, Level Four
The Dungeon, Level Five

*

Tales of Aurelia
The Barbarian, Book One
The Barbarian, Book Two
The Barbarian, Book Three

*

JLC Construction Stories
Golden and the Three Bears
Linc's Little Piggy
Plumbing His Depths
Six Men and a Wedding
His Skittish Sub
Nailing the Foreman

*

Men's League
Huddle
Tackle
Receive

Kelex

Bound BDSM Club
Bound By Him
Bound to Them
Bound by Three
Bound by Lust

*

Alaxian Heirs
Claiming Callum
Taking Kye
Mating Jasek

*

Tales from Triple M Ranch
Rode Hard
Hell Fired
Wild Ride
Pony Ride
Bronc Buster

*

Daddies
My Girlfriend's Daddy
My Best Friend's Father
My College Professor

*

Standalone Titles
Chained to the Tiger's Bed
Flesh for Fantasy
Betting on His Demon
Falling Overboard
Sleeping Beauty

In Bed
Best Friends
Next Door Neighbor
Past Lovers

Writing as Alex Bowman

Kent Street Tales
Exposed
(FREE on the TEP Website!)
Simmered
Nailing the Foreman (Nailed)

The Soul Collector Series
Losing His Religion
Laying Down the Lawman

ABOUT THE AUTHOR

International bestselling gay erotica/erotic romance author Kelex lives in Hampton Roads with her twenty-something slacker kidult and two semi-loveable masses of fur who are often found snarling at the mailman or UPS driver—or pooping on the brand new carpet.

When not being a pain in her daughter's ass, a gardening goddess, the baker of bread, the master of cake disaster, or the drinker of *allllll* the coffee, she writes under various pen names all over the erotica and erotic romance genre map.

Twisted E-Publishing, LLC
www.twistedepublishing.com

Printed in Great Britain
by Amazon